Storm of Passion

"Don't make me hold you down, Faithe," Luke said as he held her fists tight while she struggled beneath him.

Thunder reverberated as he whispered her name. She opened her eyes and met his gaze as quavering flashes of lightning played over her. For one long, heartstopping moment she lay still, gripping his hands as tightly as he gripped hers.

"I love you, Faithe," he said shakily. "I do, I swear it to God."

A crack of thunder made them both flinch. He released her hands and she wrapped her arms around him, holding him close, her damp face pressed into the crook of his neck, as rain sizzled onto the thatch roof of the hut.

"Would you tell me again?" she asked, very quietly, lying there joined with him, as nature's fury mounted outside—and within. . . .

Secret Thunder

Patricia Ryan

A TOPAZ BOOK

TOPAZ
Published by the Penguin Group
Penguin Books USA Inc., 375 Hudson Street,
New York, New York 10014, U.S.A.
Penguin Books Ltd, 27 Wrights Lane,
London W8 5TZ, England
Penguin Books Australia Ltd, Ringwood,
Victoria, Australia
Penguin Books Canada Ltd, 10 Alcorn Avenue,
Toronto, Ontario, Canada M4V 3B2
Penguin Books (N.Z.) Ltd, 182–190 Wairau Road,
Auckland 10, New Zealand

Penguin Books Ltd, Registered Offices:
Harmondsworth, Middlesex, England

First published by Topaz, an imprint of Dutton Signet,
a division of Penguin Books USA Inc.

First Printing, May, 1997
10 9 8 7 6 5 4 3 2 1

Printed in the United States of America

Dedicated with love
to my uncle,
Dr. Thomas Guy Burford.
My sisters and I still have
those Wives of Henry VIII
dolls you gave us so long ago.
See what you started?

Chapter 1

March 1067
The village of Cottwyk
in Cambridgeshire, England

"It's not much of a whorehouse." Luke de Périgueux tugged on the reins, halting his mount next to his brother's at the edge of the clearing. He could barely make out the humble cottage against the darksome woods that surrounded it; English forests were black as hell at night.

"At least it's shelter," Alexandre said through a yawn. " 'Twill rain soon, and I'd rather be in there than out here when it does."

A shudder coursed through Luke. He rubbed his arms beneath his mantle.

Alex grinned and punched him on the shoulder. "So, my fearsome big brother feels the cold just like us ordinary men."

Luke nodded, though it wasn't the damp night air making him shiver, but a cursed weakness of the body and soul—a weakness too shameful to reveal, even to Alex. His hands fisted involuntarily, and he gritted his teeth. *Ride it out,* he commanded himself. *'Twill ease up. It always does.* A good, hard tupping should help. Flicking his reins, he approached the cottage.

Alex followed, eyeing the crude wattle-and-daub hovel, a doubtful expression on his face. Yellowish light shone through the skins tacked over the windows, and wood smoke scented the air, but not a sound came from within. "Perhaps we've got the wrong place," Alex said.

"Nay, this should be it." One of Luke's fellow crossbowmen had directed him here: *There's just the one wench, and she's not much, but she'll spread her legs for anyone with tuppence and a hard cock—even a hard* Norman *cock. Most of these Saxon bitches run and hide when they see us coming.*

Little wonder. Every inhabitant of this miserable, rain-choked island feared and despised the Norman conquerors, and why shouldn't they? Five months had passed since Luke and Alex crossed the Channel to help William, Duke of Normandy—and now King of England—seize this godforsaken country in a single, bloody battle. Hastings should have been the end of it, and it would have been, if only these English barbarians would cease their pointless uprisings and accept Norman rule. All winter, William's army—including many landless knights, like Luke and Alex, hungry for English holdings—had confiscated estates and subdued the locals with a pitiless zeal calculated to crush rebellious tendencies. Yet, still the people of England defied them, holding on with pathetic tenacity to lands forever lost to them on the fourteenth of October, 1066.

The deerskin covering the doorway parted, and a figure emerged—the figure of a woman carrying a lantern. She was plump, her bosom and hips stretching the wool of her coarse brown kirtle, and her hair was a mop of flaming curls. Holding the lantern high, she sized up the two strangers on horseback with a whore's practiced eye.

Alex chuckled. "Seems we've got the right place, after all."

"Do you speak any French?" Luke asked her as another bout of trembling overtook him. *Hold on . . . 'twill pass.*

"Quite a bit," she answered in a guttural accent. "My husband, God rest him, hailed from Beauvais."

A stroke of luck. Most of these Saxons didn't understand a word of their new ruler's language. Luke had picked up a little English—he had a facility for languages—but he had no desire to struggle with it tonight.

She smiled coyly. "I don't imagine you came here to talk, though." Her doughy cheeks were sprinkled with pockmarks, and her teeth were crooked, but Luke wasn't feeling very particular at the moment.

King William had issued regulations forbidding his knights and men-at-arms from molesting women or frequenting brothels. Unlike some of his colleagues, Luke had no trouble obeying the mandate against rape. Brutalizing innocents held little appeal for him; he was brutal enough on the battlefield. Unfortunately, the only practical alternative was to patronize whatever local brothels would serve the Normans, and he felt no compunction about doing so.

"My name is Helig," the red-haired woman said. Luke couldn't remember having asked. *Helig,* for God's sake. Why the devil did these Saxons give their women such grotesque names?

" 'Twill be sixpence for the both of you together," Helig said. "Tuppence apiece if you want me separately. More if you'll be wanting something out of the ordinary."

"Tuppence apiece, then," Luke said. Alex might not want her at all, given his fussiness about the women he bedded. Handsome and congenial, the young swordsman was remarkably adept at coaxing wenches out of their kirtles. Luke, on the other hand, lacked his brother's agreeable nature, and his fierce reputation made women uneasy. He couldn't remember the last time a woman had given herself to him for free.

Helig directed them to an attached byre around back, where they stabled their horses, and through that to the cottage proper. Luke squatted on the earthen floor by the central fire pit to warm his jittery hands while his brother went about the pointless business of flirting with this homely Saxon whore.

"Your hair looks like new copper," Alex told her.

She snorted. "You don't seem in no hurry to get on with things. Care for a pint, then?"

"Aye, and one for my brother."

"Ah, I figured you and him was kin." Helig filled two tankards from a pitcher of ale. "I must say, I never seen such black hair on a Norman as you two have."

"That's because we're from Aquitaine, not Normandy. Folks are darker in the south." Alex unpinned his mantle and tossed it onto one of the two roughhewn benches facing the table. Luke wrapped his own more closely around himself, hoping his brother wouldn't notice his tremors. He felt like a cocked crossbow, quivering and ready to fire; his jaw ached from clenching it.

Helig set a tankard on the table with a *thunk* that made Luke bolt to his feet. *Easy.* As she reached across it to place the other on the opposite side, Alex came up behind her and lifted her skirt. She had thick legs and a generous white rump, which he fondled freely.

She smirked at Alex over her shoulder as he moved against her. "Seems you're in something of a hurry after all."

"Your charms are intoxicating."

"There's straw up in the loft, and blankets." She tilted her head toward a ladder leading to a niche between the byre and the ceiling beams. "We'll be more comfortable up there."

Lowering her skirt, Alex raised a tankard and drank from it. "Truth be told, I'm more tired than I am randy. We've been fighting since yesterday morning, with no sleep. It only ended at sundown."

"I know." Of course. She would have heard the sounds of battle as they wrested nearby Cottwyk Castle from her countrymen. Her expression sobered only momentarily. Nodding toward Luke, she said, "What about you, then? Are *you* too weary to take what you came here for?"

"Nay." He craved sleep as desperately as Alex did, but even more pressing was the need to release some of the savage energy thrumming in his veins.

Alex set down his half-emptied tankard, grabbed his mantle, and lay down on the floor next to the fire pit, arranging the woolen cloak over him like a blanket. "Wake me when you're done," he told Luke, "and I'll take my turn." He shifted to get comfortable in the packed dirt, let out a great yawn, and closed his eyes. Within moments, his breathing grew steady and one hand fell open limply. Knowing his brother, Luke very much doubted he'd be able to awaken him for his turn with Helig, but then he suspected Alex was a good deal less keen on the wench than he'd let on. He'd just thrown her skirt up that way to show a little polite interest. If he'd really wanted her, he would have taken her right then and there. Alex wasn't shy.

"Nice fellow, your brother," Helig said.

Luke grunted in affirmation and accepted the tankard she offered him, draining it in one tilt. It wasn't half bad. One thing these Saxons could do was brew ale.

"You were thirsty." The whore took the empty tankard from him and reached up to unfasten his mantle pin. She held it close to her face, her eyes widening as she examined the little onyx dragon imbedded in the golden brooch. Looking up, she said, "You're him."

Luke took the pin from her and clumsily refastened it to the cloak. It had been a parting gift from his father when they left to join William. Alex had received one also, inset with tiny pearls in the shape of a wolf's head, which he was forever misplacing. Luke treasured his pin and had always taken care not to lose it, especially after receiving word of his sire's death at Christmastide. Both pins bore the same hopeful inscription on the reverse side: *Be strong and of good courage.*

"You *are* him, aren't you?" Helig said. "You're the Black Dragon."

"I'm Luke de Périgueux."

Helig's gaze lingered on his hair, which he wore long and braided in back, in the style of his father, rather than closely cropped in the Norman fashion. It was the feature that distinguished him from the rest of the occupying soldiers, including his brother. "Aye, you're him," she said, nodding. "You're the one they talk about."

Luke knew what they said about him, the words they used to describe him: bloodthirsty, ruthless, brutal. Now she'd be wary, perhaps even refuse him, tuppence or no. He waited for the fascination in her eyes to turn to apprehension.

But it didn't. If anything, she seemed more enthralled by him now that she knew who he was. Her eyes lit with an interest he knew could not be feigned. Some women had a weakness for monsters in the guise of men, and Luke suspected this Helig was one of them. As she undraped the mantle from his shoulders and hung it on a peg, Luke reassessed her attractiveness as a bed partner. If her heart was in it, as it seemed to be, she might give him quite the lively ride. God knew he could use one.

She approached him with a sway in her hips and a look of frank desire. There was something crudely seductive about her, an unwashed sexuality that stirred his loins. He backed her against the table and ground his hips against hers as he gathered up her kirtle with trembling hands. Arousal merged with the bloodlust still surging through him to rob him of all reason or self-control. He needed this woman, this release, and he was going to take what he needed now.

Unbuckling his belt, she said, "Let's get you out of these things first." Luke yanked the heavy, calf-length tunic over his head and tossed it onto the bench, leaving himself in his shirt and chausses. Helig untied the shirt, exposing his chest, and combed her fingers through the dark curls there. "What have we got here?" She pulled out the first of two leather cords looped around his neck and ran her thumb over the crudely carved wooden cross. "My word. You're full of surprises, aren't you?"

He whipped up her skirt and lifted her onto the table as she pulled out the second cord. "What's this, then?" She fingered the little leather pouch, causing the dried herbs within to crackle. "Yarrow?" A reasonable assumption. Many of Luke's fellow knights carried a pouch of the all-purpose medicinal herb.

"Aye," he lied as he reached beneath his shirt and fumbled for the drawstring of his chausses. His madness had become a carnal drive, hot and urgent.

She brought the pouch to her nose and sniffed, then frowned. "That's not yarrow. What's in there? Catnip?"

Luke stilled in the act of untying the woolen hose.

"I recognize the smell," she said. "My brother, Ham, uses it. Perhaps you know of him. You're under Lord Alberic's command, are you not? Ham is the hangman at Foxhyrst."

Luke and Alex were quartered at Foxhyrst Castle, under the rather inept command of Lord Alberic, one of King William's most ambitious lapdogs. Alberic's devotion to his liege—combined with a certain amount of sly manipulation—had recently earned him the coveted title of sheriff. Most of the soldiers who'd served under him since Hastings—including Luke and his brother—remained with him as men-at-arms charged with suppressing rebellion. As Luke recalled, Alberic's hangman had more or less come with Foxhyrst Castle; Ham was a bearish, bald-headed Saxon who brought a great deal of savage enthusiasm to his work and cared little that his countrymen counted him a Judas.

"Ham says he can't work up the stomach to torture and kill folks lest he chews some catnip first," Helig explained. "That's what this is, isn't it? Catnip?"

Among other things. Luke took the pouch from her and tucked it back into his shirt.

"Ham says it makes him half mad. Makes him evil as the Devil himself, so he don't care about nothing but killing. Takes a day or more for it to wear off." She looked at him knowingly. "You chew it before you go into battle, don't you? That's what makes you such a ferocious—"

Luke closed one hand over her mouth and clamped the other around the back of her neck, hard. Bringing his face very close to hers, he stared fixedly into her wide green eyes. "You talk too much," he said quietly. "I don't want to talk to you. I just want to fuck you."

She nodded. He eased his hands away, and she licked her lips nervously. "Let's go upstairs to the—"

He covered her mouth with his hand again. It was shaking. "Right here is fine." With his other hand, he parted her stout thighs and positioned himself between them.

She looked over his shoulder at Alex, unconscious on the floor.

"My brother can sleep through anything." He jerked on the drawstring again, but his palsied hands seemed unequal to the task of freeing himself from his chausses.

Luke felt a gust of cold air at his back. Helig sucked in a breath and pushed him away, her eyes on something behind him. Wheeling around, Luke saw a man standing in the doorway, holding the deerskin aside.

The intruder was big and unmistakably Saxon, with long red hair and an unkempt beard. His skin was pale as parchment, and dark circles rimmed his eyes. Even from across the room, Luke could smell him. He smelled like sickness and sour ale.

The Saxon growled something at Helig while gesturing to Luke and the sleeping Alex, his expression one of outrage. From what Luke understood of the local tongue, the whore was being berated for consorting with Normans.

Luke took a step in the other man's direction, the quivering bowstring inside him humming with murderous fury. His fists shook with the unreasoning need to punish this creature, to smash his face in, pummel the life out of him.

Jumping down from the table, Helig grabbed Luke's arm and said something to the other man in an appeasing tone. The Saxon barked something back at her, then reached beneath his tattered cape and produced two pennies. He pressed these into Helig's hand, then began pulling her toward the ladder that led to the loft.

Luke seized the Saxon bastard and spun him around, hauling back with his fist.

Helig closed both hands over his wrist. "Please, no!"

He could have easily wrested himself from her grip, but a small, still-sane voice added its soothing whisper to the cacophony inside his head: *It's the herbs . . . hold back . . . ride this out.*

"Please," the whore begged in a tremulous voice. "I don't want any trouble here. This fellow, he's a bit touched. Don't know what he's doing, really."

That's two of us, Luke thought. *Two madmen, fighting over a poxy whore.*

"He comes to me regular," Helig continued. "All he wants is what he came for, and then he'll leave. Just let me do him first, and then I'll do you for free. You can have me all night. I'll do anything you want."

Luke yanked his hand out of her grasp. He could

kill this man, the state he was in. Christ, he almost did. *Let it go . . . ride it out.*

With a heavy sigh, Luke snatched his mantle off the peg and wrapped it around himself. "Wake me when he's gone."

From the unsteady way the Saxon climbed the squeaky ladder, Luke could only conclude that he was drunk. It could be a long wait before Luke's turn came around.

He knew he'd never get to sleep with the battle madness still upon him. He searched the cottage for something stronger than ale, something to take the edge off, and came up with a jug of brandy. Half filling his tankard, he drank the brandy in one long, scorching swallow, then reclined on the other side of the fire pit from his brother and stared into the flames. They danced and swayed, like a field of wheat beneath a rippling breeze—a golden field, ignited by a setting sun.

The image brought to mind the Abbey at Aurillac, where he'd spent an untroubled youth avoiding his lessons in favor of tending to the monastic wheat fields and vineyards and sheep pastures. Luke fingered the rough wooden cross beneath his shirt, remembering those years—happy years, the only truly happy years of his life. Often lately he found himself wondering if he'd still be happy—or at least content—if he'd taken Holy Orders as his father had intended, rather than rejecting cloistered life for soldiering.

Luke ached to exchange the tools of warfare for those of the farm. He would surely have been granted a conquered holding already—either outright or by marriage to an English heiress—as had most of the others who'd fought at Hastings, but his skill with the crossbow made him too valuable an asset for subduing the locals. It was said that William had his siege towers, his battering rams, his stone-throwing machines . . . and Luke de Périgueux. His fellow soldiers had long ago dubbed him the Black Dragon, in honor not just of his dark Aquitaine coloring, but of the fiery beast within him, the image of which adorned his battle pennon.

A light rain began to patter against the thatch. From the loft came whispers and the crackling of straw. Envious of Alex's blessed oblivion, Luke reached for the brandy jug and drank directly from it.

If only he could embrace warfare as Alex did. The White Wolf, they called Alex, a tribute to the stealth that made him such an effective swordsman. The enemy never knew he was there until they felt his steel sliding through them. In another man, such lethal skill might earn him a measure of envy from his colleagues, but the amiable twenty-year-old was the most popular soldier at Foxhyrst.

Luke kept his dependence on the potent herbs a secret from Alex out of shame. What kind of weakling was he that he must resort to such measures before he could aim his crossbow at the enemy?

At one time he had truly felt the dragon's fire in his breast, and would enter each engagement screaming war cries and eager for blood. But his blood-thirst had come to sicken him, and now he must chew that loathsome herbal concoction before battle to reproduce it. If only it didn't affect his senses so. Often he could recall little of a battle until weeks, even months, later. In fact, he had no clear memory of having taken Cottwyk Castle today—just fractured, nightmarish images, and the vague sense that he'd done something particularly irredeemable. Were it not for his blood-spattered chainmail, he might think it had all been a dreadful, half-remembered dream.

The voices in the loft grew belligerent as the rain intensified, dribbling through a hole in the thatch to form a muddy puddle near Luke's head. Seething with anger at the whore, the Saxon, and himself, he brought the jug to his mouth again and gulped. Every time he moved his head, things spun sickeningly, so he tried to lie still. He stared in the fire, squinting to make out the form twitching and writhing in the flames. Moving closer, he saw that it was a young man, little more than a boy. He was saying something in English. Luke strained and heard the word "Please."

Nay! He reached out to sweep the specter away, but it just leapt back up, writhing in torment in its hellish inferno, its eyes trained on Luke, its mouth working silently . . . "Please."

Something flickered on Luke's arm, and he struggled to focus on it. "Jesu!" His shirtsleeve was on fire. Sitting up, he slapped at the burning linen, but the flames spread swiftly, consuming the thin fabric and searing his arm. Grimacing at the pain, he pulled his mantle tight around himself to smother the flames.

"Christ." A sudden bout of shivering racked him. He wrapped his arms around his updrawn legs and squeezed his eyes shut. *Ride it out, ride it out . . .*

The brandy, the lack of sleep, and those damned herbs had joined forces to drive him even further into madness than he'd already sunk. "Ride it out," he whispered, lowering his head to his knees. "Ride it out, ride it out, ride it out . . ."

When he opened his eyes, Luke found himself crouching on the floor of a strange cottage, rocking back and forth, back and forth. He blinked at the dreary, unfamiliar surroundings, at the flames crackling in the clay-lined pit, at the dark form of a man on the other side of the fire, asleep.

"Alex?" The man didn't move. Luke shifted to get a better view of his face. It *was* Alex.

Over the sound of heavy rain came a man's voice, from above. A woman spoke then, and Luke had a mental picture of a fleshy wench with curly red hair.

The whore.

The place began to look familiar. He remembered coming here. He'd come here for a woman, and Alex had tagged along to be companionable. But someone had stolen the woman from him and was upstairs with her now.

He had a senseless urge to climb that ladder and take what he'd come here for. His hands curled into fists, and his mind's eye saw him slamming them into the Saxon's head until he didn't move anymore.

Luke rubbed his fists on his forehead and forced deep breaths into his lungs. *Ride it out.*

Lying down, he tucked his mantle around himself. Sleep. That was what he needed. To sleep it off.

Luke snapped the bunch of small, purplish grapes off the vine, imagining the velvety wine the brothers would make from it. Holding the fruit over his open mouth, he crushed it in his hand so that he could drink its juice. The grapes burst open with a moan, spilling thick red blood over his fingers and into his mouth.

No! He gagged and choked, thrashing against his confining mantle. Another moan echoed through the tiny cottage, and another, accompanied by the rhythmic crackling of straw overhead.

A woman's breathless voice: the whore.

His whore. Not the Saxon's. His.

Luke leapt to his feet, fury blooming red hot within him. He crossed to the ladder in a single stride and climbed it three rungs at a time. The Saxon, rutting away between the whore's pale legs, turned with an expression of outrage. Luke grabbed him and jerked him off her, then smashed his fist into the bastard's face. The Saxon groaned. Luke hit him again, and again, and again, until he lay limp and bloodied in the straw.

The whore was trying to crawl away. Luke seized her from behind, whipped her skirt up, and mounted her.

She cried out.

Luke came abruptly awake. *What . . . ?*

He sat up, trembling and sweating and struggling against the mantle that enclosed him like a cocoon. Next to him, coals glowed in a fire pit, on the other side of which his brother slept soundly. From the loft came the sounds of enthusiastic coupling.

Was that a dream? It had felt so real, so . . .

Tremors racked him. He was a menace, the condition he was in—a mindless beast, capable of anything. He must leave this place. Now.

Gaining his feet awkwardly, he circled the fire pit and knelt down next to his brother.

"Alex." Luke grabbed the sleeping man by his shoulder and shook him. "Alex, wake up." He slapped his brother on the face. "Come on, Alex. Let's get out of here. Let's go."

Alex didn't so much as alter his breathing. He wouldn't wake up till he was good and ready. What was Luke to do? He couldn't leave Alex here alone; it was dangerous. A lone Norman soldier asleep in an English brothel with a lunatic Saxon upstairs who hated their kind? No, Luke couldn't just ride away, much as he would have liked to.

Luke returned to his spot on the other side of the dying fire and lifted the brandy jug to his mouth again. He'd drink himself insensible, that's what he'd do. He'd drink himself into a deep and harmless stupor.

A crack of thunder jolted Luke. He raised his head and looked around, disoriented to find himself lying facedown in straw. He'd been on the packed earth by the fire pit the last he remembered.

He tried to rise, but his head hit something hard—a ceiling beam—and he sank into the straw again. *Christ, where am I? What's happening?*

Another discharge of thunder made him flinch. Lightning flickered through a tiny window, briefly illuminating a cramped space between a straw-strewn floor and a thatched roof: the loft. Dread shivered through him.

Luke crawled backward toward the ladder, but his feet met something heavy and unyielding. He turned as another flash of lightning revealed the obstruction: the Saxon, on his back in the straw, his eyes half open, blood trickling from his slack mouth.

No. Luke shook him; he was entirely limp. His chest didn't move; no breath came from his mouth.

God, no. Luke suddenly felt all too sober. *No.*

An anguished cry from outside drew him to the little window. Thunder crashed as the sky lit up. He saw the whore running away in the rain with her skirts gathered up, her white legs flashing, her kirtle unlaced down the back.

Before the wavering light died away, he saw something else as well—blood on his hand. He flexed his fingers; his knuckles stung.

Luke closed his eyes and remembered his fist impacting the Saxon's face with savage force. It wasn't just a fanciful imagining this time, but a real and vivid memory—the memory of something he'd done just moments ago. He'd pulled the Saxon off the whore and punched him as hard as he could, killing him with a single blow to the head.

He tried to remember more, but it was all a red blur, just as in the aftermath of battle.

What have I done?

"Luke?"

Alex! Even he couldn't sleep through this violent thunder. Luke clambered over the Saxon's body and peered down into the main room of the cottage. His brother stood at the table, lighting the lantern, his tunic rumpled and his cropped hair sticking out at all angles.

"Bring that up here!" Luke called out. "Hurry!"

Alex joined him in the loft, bending over nearly

double as he held the lantern over the dead Saxon. "Who's this, then?"

"He came in after you went to sleep."

Alex nudged the corpse with the toe of his boot. "Did he smell like this when he was alive?"

Luke kneaded his forehead with his sore knuckles.

"What happened?" Alex asked in a tone of mild curiosity.

"I killed him."

Alex yawned as he squatted down. "Why'd you do that?"

"I . . . I can't remember much."

Alex smiled crookedly. "I'm not surprised, considering that empty brandy jug I tripped over."

"How can you find this amusing?" Luke demanded. "I killed this man. This isn't like taking a life on the battlefield. This is unconscionable."

His brother shrugged. "You must have had a reason."

"Aye. I murdered him over that woman! I took a man's life over a two-penny whore."

Alex waved his hand dismissively. "Nay—I meant you must have a *good* reason, even if you're too drunk to remember it."

"I think I'm mad," Luke said hoarsely. "Is that reason enough?"

"You're drunk, but you're not mad." Alex glanced around. "Where's the wench?"

Luke nodded toward the little window. "I saw her running away."

"In this storm?"

"She seemed upset."

Alex frowned and held the lantern toward his brother. "What happened to your arm?"

Luke looked down to find his right shirtsleeve hanging raggedly, the edges scorched. His forearm was reddened and blistered, the hair singed off. "I don't know. I must have burned myself." He stood, cursing when his head collided with the ceiling.

Alex chuckled. "I think you're more a threat to your own safety than anyone else's."

"This dead man might not agree." Luke stepped over the Saxon's body and started down the ladder. "I'm going to find her."

Alex followed him downstairs. "Why bother?"

"She was here. She saw it all. She can tell me what happened. I've got to find out."

Alex sighed. "I suppose 'twill set your mind at ease. We should wait for dawn, though. And perhaps by then the storm will have let up."

"Aye, and perhaps by then she'll be miles away."

"She's on foot," Alex reminded him. "She won't get far."

She didn't, but it took them a while to find her on the obscure trail she'd taken. They spotted her around midmorning, sprawled faceup at the top of a hill, unmoving in the cold, gray drizzle.

"Mother of God," Luke muttered as they rode toward her.

Even the normally implacable Alex blanched when they were close enough to get a good look at her. "What do you suppose—?"

"Lightning." Luke slid off his horse and knelt to close the woman's eyes and murmur a prayer over her burnt remains.

Alex dismounted as well, but walked a few yards in the other direction to vomit at the side of the trail. "Let's go," he called out as he remounted his horse.

"We can't just leave her here," Luke said.

"Someone will find her."

"Nay!" Luke rose to his feet. "This is my doing. I'm not going to just ride away as if nothing—"

"Shh!" Alex grew still, and Luke followed suit, knowing how uncanny his brother's hearing was.

"Men." Alex pointed down the dirt track. "From that direction. On foot, so they're probably English. I suggest we continue this conversation from a more private location."

Luke grudgingly mounted up, and the brothers secreted themselves in a nearby copse of trees as a cluster of dark shapes materialized in the rain. When the Englishmen got close, Luke could see that one of them led a mule dragging the Saxon's body on a stretcher. They gathered around Helig's corpse with expressions of rage and horror. One began to sob into his hands. A burly fellow squatted down and inspected the body with open curiosity, poking at the charred feet and peering closely at the strange, fernlike pattern burned onto her face and arms. Two men fled into the bushes, their hands covering their mouths.

The burly fellow stood and withdrew a small, shiny object from his tunic. Luke squinted to make it out, groaning when he recognized it. "Alex," he whispered, "that's your—"

"Damn!" Alex clutched at the collar of his open mantle, where his pin should have been.

Luke shook his head in dismay as the Englishmen passed Alex's mantle pin among themselves, examining the little pearl-encrusted wolf's head, turning it to puzzle over the Frankish inscription. Several of them raised pickaxes, reaping hooks, and pitchforks into the air. From their outraged exchange, it was clear that they intended to find and punish the Norman bastard who murdered one of their brethren over a whore.

They tied Helig's body over the back of the mule and returned the way they had come, brandishing their weapons.

"They probably won't connect that pin to me," Alex said. "Only our own men know me as the White Wolf. Still, I think it's time we put some distance between ourselves and Cottwyk, don't you?"

He flicked his reins, but Luke grabbed them, halting

his progress. "I'm going to surrender myself to Alberic."

"What?"

"He's the sheriff now. He'll see I get tried in the king's court for—"

"Are you mad?" Alex exclaimed.

"Very possibly," Luke said softly.

"Do you have any idea what these Saxon savages will do to you if you admit having killed one of their own?"

"I'll be in the custody of the Normans."

"They'll get to you somehow. Why invite trouble when we can just ride away and no one will be the wiser?" Alex closed a hand over his brother's shoulder, looking as grave as Luke had ever seen him. "I can't let you do this. You're exhausted, and you've got a head full of brandy. You're not thinking straight."

"What if they do find out that's your pin? I can't let you be implicated in a crime you didn't commit."

"And I can't let you go on stepping into harm's way for me."

"I don't know what you're—"

"You're always looking out for me," Alex said. "Even in battle. I see you keeping an eye on me. And when something goes wrong, you're always there. You've saved my life more than once, at risk of your own. I owe you."

"You don't owe me anything. And you can't stop me from giving myself up."

Alex grinned smugly. "If you do, I'll tell them you're lying to protect me. I'll say I did it. They'll believe me, too. They've got the evidence right in their hands—that pin."

"I'll just tell them you're lying to protect *me,*" Luke said.

Alex shrugged. "Then they'll probably just hang us both. 'Tis a far better course of action to simply return to Foxhyrst and pretend this never happened."

Luke rubbed his eyes while he pondered the trap that had snared him. Alex kept quiet for as long as he apparently could before saying, "Well? Can we leave here?"

Luke nodded slowly, and the brothers set out through the woods, away from Cottwyk. "I'm not going back to Foxhyrst, though."

Alex gaped at him. "You're not—"

"There's a monastery at St. Albans. I'm going there."

Chapter 2

Two months later
The Cambridgeshire manor of Hauekleah

"Milady! Milady!"

Faithe looked up from the daisies she was tying together to see young Edyth burst through the open doorway of Hauekleah Hall, red-faced and breathless. Ewes' milk spilled from her two full buckets, soaking into the fresh rushes.

"Edyth!" Faithe scolded. "Slow down. You're getting the new rushes all—"

"There's two Normans headin' up the road," the dairymaid gasped. "One of 'em must be him—the Black Dragon."

Silence fell over the great hall as the house servants turned apprehensive gazes on their young mistress. Faithe's fingers grew cold, and she realized she had stopped breathing. She set down the daisy garland and rose from her bench, summoning all the composure at her disposal.

"His name," Faithe said quietly, "is Luke de Périgueux."

Edyth blinked. "But Master Orrik, he says they call him the Black—"

"His name is Luke de Périgueux," Faithe repeated, her gaze sweeping every member of her raptly attentive audience, "and as he's to be your new master"—she drew in a steadying breath—"and my lord husband, you are to address him with respect or suffer the consequences. Am I understood?"

Faithe's *famuli,* unused to such threats or admonishments—for Faithe rarely found them necessary—exchanged uneasy glances.

"Am I understood?" Her words were softly spoken, but clear.

There came a chorus of murmured assents, accompanied by the occasional pitying look. They viewed her as a martyr, she realized—first widowed by the Normans, then forced to choose between marriage to one of their own or the loss of her ancestral home.

Faithe tucked her hair behind her ears and smoothed her kirtle, hearing the crackle of parchment in the pocket of her skirt. The letter from Lord Alberic, the Norman sheriff to whom she now owed allegiance, had been treacherously courteous in that manner the Normans seemed to have perfected. He'd told her little about the husband he'd chosen for her, only that he was a knight named Luke de Périgueux and that he was famous for his soldiering skills. Skills used against her people . . . her husband.

Know, my lady, his lordship—or, more likely, his lordship's clerk—had written, *that you would be fully within your rights to refuse this marriage. In such an event, I will endeavor to dispose of the estate by other means.* In other words, she could marry the notorious Luke de Périgueux and remain at Hauekleah, or refuse to marry him and let the Normans seize it—in which case she'd no doubt spend the rest of her days languishing in some convent somewhere. Worse, the sprawling farmstead that had been her family's for over eight hundred years would fall into the hands of strangers, *enemy* strangers.

Better to give myself to some Norman devil and keep Hauekleah, she'd decided. Her grandmother, Hlynn, had done much the same, entering into a loveless marriage to a Danish warrior chief rather than relinquish

Hauekleah to the Northmen. Finding farm life tiresome, Thorgeirr had stayed but a single summer—long enough to build a new manor house and plant the seed of Faithe's father in Hlynn's belly—and then moved on. Although it was rumored that he lived for many more years, Hlynn never saw him again, and counted herself lucky.

Perhaps, Faithe told herself as she stepped out into the warm spring afternoon, she would be as fortunate. Her new husband, used to the ways of the sword and the crossbow, might be so bored here that he'd leave her in peace and she'd have Hauekleah all to herself again.

All eyes were upon her as she walked slowly through the entry gate that provided passage through the stone wall surrounding Hauekleah Hall—a wall that had stood since Roman times. Shielding her eyes against the sun, she squinted down the dirt path that connected her manor and the village it encompassed to Foxhyrst and the other great market towns to the west.

Two men on horseback rode toward her on that path, one tall in the saddle, the other slumped over. Faithe's mouth felt chalky. She wiped her damp palms on her plain wool kirtle. Field-workers abandoned their plows and livestock and ran to join her house staff in what felt like a defensive phalanx around her. As always, their loyalty and affection moved her immeasurably. If for their sakes only, she could never abandon Hauekleah to the Normans.

As the riders drew closer, she saw that the upright man gripped a sword in one hand and the reins of both mounts in the other. The insensible one swayed in his saddle. The fellow with the sword dropped the reins and grasped the other man's tunic to keep him from falling. Leaning over, he whispered something into his companion's ear and gently patted his shoulder.

"He's hurt." Faithe stepped forward.

Her young reeve, his eyes full of worry, grabbed her arm. "Nay, milady . . ."

"That man's hurt." Faithe shook Dunstan off and approached the two men, wondering which one was Luke de Périgueux. They were sizable men, both of them, with hair as black as ink. The injured man—she saw the blood on his tunic now, and a raw gash on his forehead—had his hair shorn in the Norman style, while the other wore his unusually long and bound in back.

Faithe's servants followed her, Dunstan and some of the burlier men flanking her protectively. The man with the sword pointed it at them as they approached. Faithe hesitated, along with the others. It wasn't the weapon that gave her pause, for although he was armed, he was but one man and they were many; it was the way he looked at them.

Some of his hair had come loose and hung over his broad forehead, enhancing his feral image. His eyes were deep-set and fierce against oddly swarthy skin. Black stubble darkened his grimly set jaw. He didn't look like any Norman soldier Faithe had ever seen. He looked untamed . . . as menacing as a beast with its fangs bared.

Faithe's gaze traveled to the ornate pin holding his mantle closed—a golden disk inset with black stone in the shape of . . .

A dragon. A black dragon.

Merciful God.

"That's him," someone whispered.

Faithe stifled a sudden urge to cross herself. So this was the man to whom she would be wed within a matter of days, this dark, savage creature with murder in his eyes and a quivering broadsword in his hand.

Forcing her fear beneath the surface, Faithe stepped forward, her escorts at her sides.

"Stop right there," de Périgueux ordered in French-accented English as he thrust the weapon toward them. "I'll have none of your Saxon tricks." His voice rumbled like thunder; his tone was that of a man accustomed to being obeyed. That he spoke English came as something of a shock. She'd never known a Norman to utter a word of her native tongue.

Faithe clutched her skirt in both fists. "We mean you no harm."

"Tell that to my brother. We were ambushed in the woods not a mile back."

"Ambushed!"

He scanned the faces behind her. "Where's your mistress? My brother needs help. He's badly wounded."

Faithe lifted her chin, consciously ignoring his sword, which was aimed directly at her. "I'm Faithe of Hauekleah. I'll tend to your brother."

Those intense eyes of his pinned her with a look of astonishment, his gaze lighting on the handful of brass keys hanging from a long golden chain around her neck, which he evidently hadn't noticed before. He surveyed her from head to toe, taking in the unbound hair that hung loose over her breasts, the humble kirtle she'd shortened for field work, and the patched slippers soiled from that morning's gardening. As usual, she'd gotten too caught up in the day's chores to bother overmuch with grooming, and as a result looked more like an untidy adolescent than a chatelaine.

Even when she did bother to dress in her finest silks and adorn herself with jewels, Faithe looked far younger than her four-and-twenty years. She'd learned to counteract her youthful appearance with displays of unflinching confidence, even when they had to be feigned. Therefore, when Luke de Périgueux's attention returned to her face, she met his eyes steadfastly.

He held her gaze. She saw his throat move as he swallowed; his penetrating eyes darkened from brown to black. So . . . it unnerved even the infamous Black Dragon to come face-to-face with his betrothed.

Faithe nodded toward his sword, still aimed at her throat, and said quietly, "If you'll lower that, my lord, I shall see to your brother."

"Gently, now . . . gently," Lady Faithe urged as six of her men, gripping the edges of Alex's mantle, carried him through a gate in an old stone wall and over the threshold of the enormous timber manor house it surrounded. Alex was unconscious, his face drained of color. Luke muttered a quick prayer as he followed his brother into a vast whitewashed hall flooded with sunlight, its lofty roof supported by two rows of thick oak posts. Each post, he noticed, had a garland of flowers wound around it from top to bottom, and floral swags hung from the ceiling beams. The green rushes that crackled underfoot were likewise strewn with sweet blossoms whose scent perfumed the air.

Lady Faithe gave orders for a pallet to be placed next to the central hearth, a stone slab on which a low fire crackled beneath a brass kettle. "Lay him down carefully," she said, and her men obeyed, handling Alex as if he were a newborn pup. "Bring me some soap and my medicine box," she told two maidservants as she ladled warm water from the kettle into a bowl. "And clean strips of linen and blankets." Her soft, girlish voice seemed unsuited to command, yet her servants jumped to do her bidding.

Odd, Luke thought as he divested himself of his mantle, for such authority to be invested in a girl of such unassuming appearance. Not that she was plain. Indeed, she was slender and fair, as Lord Alberic had promised in the letter in which he'd offered Luke her hand in marriage—and therefore her estate. Her light brown hair, fine as silk, framed a face as appealing as any he'd ever seen. She had those soft hazel eyes he'd only ever seen in England.

Luke was grateful for his bride's comeliness, although he'd expected someone more . . . polished. Saxon or no, she was a high-born lady, yet she wore no veil or fur or jewels, and her face was as sunburnished as that of a common field laborer. The chatelaine's keys hanging around her neck were the only indication of her rank.

Kneeling beside Alex's pallet, she unbuckled his swordbelt—empty, since Luke still held his brother's sword in a fierce grip. Luke took the belt before she could hand it to the woman helping her, buckled it over his own tunic, and sheathed the sword. That he chose to keep the weapon close at hand was clearly not lost on Lady Faithe, who glanced warily in his direction, then proceeded to unlace Alex's boots.

Luke wished he didn't feel the need to defend himself and his brother from these people. After all, he was their new lord. Yet they regarded him as the enemy. No doubt Lady Faithe found his presence here particularly loathsome. He was a victorious invader, she his war prize. Who knew what depths of bitterness might simmer beneath her seemingly harmless exterior. Saxons *were* tricky. It was in the nature of defeated people to use cunning to resist their conquerors—to put on a show of cooperation while fighting back in whatever sly way they could. He'd have to keep a close watch on her and those whom she commanded with such subtle skill. Hence the sword, although in truth Luke felt ill at ease bearing arms. In fact, this was the first he'd done so since entering the monastery after the incident in Cottwyk.

Two months of prayer and seclusion had lulled the fury within him into an uneasy hibernation, yet it would be naive to think he was free of it forever—or to blame it on a handful of dried leaves. Those herbs had merely awakened a beast that lay curled up within him, waiting for the chance to kill and maim—a beast that was part and parcel of who he was, that had always been with him and would never leave him in peace.

Squatting down, Luke lowered his head and rubbed his left arm below the painful knot near his shoulder, thankfully his only souvenir of the ambush. When he looked up, he saw Lady Faithe's hand slip into the pouch of her girdle. Steel flashed as she withdrew a knife and brought it to Alex's throat.

Luke whipped out an arm and seized her wrist, jerking her hand—and the knife—away from Alex. She cried out and tried vainly to pull away from him. He grabbed her other hand and yanked her to her feet, clenching his teeth at the searing pain in his upper arm. The knife fell into the rushes.

"None of your Saxon tricks," he growled. "I told you." She struggled. He tightened his grip on her wrists.

She winced, but met his eyes squarely. "Let go of me," she rasped, "or they'll kill you." He followed her gaze to see every man and woman in the huge room closing in on them, many wielding crude weapons—hatchets, shears, cleavers—that they'd produced with remarkable speed.

Leaning down, Luke stared directly into her eyes. "If you harm my brother," he said quietly, "I'll kill *you*." He squeezed her wrists to underscore the threat. She hitched in her breath.

A young, fair-haired man advanced menacingly on Luke, but Lady Faithe shook her head. "Nay, Dunstan. It's all right." Dunstan stopped in his tracks, glowering at Luke, a dagger at the ready.

"You'd kill your own wife?" she asked unsteadily.

"We're not married yet."

She was trembling, he realized, but to her credit she raised her chin and said, "You Normans think you're so civilized, but I've never yet heard an Englishman threaten to kill a woman."

"I've never yet seen a woman—Norman or English—try to slit the throat of a wounded man entrusted to her care."

"You think so little of me?"

"I don't know you," he said. "And I'm beginning to think I don't want to. Much less be wed to you."

Her soft eyes frosted over. " 'Twould suit me well if you were to ride away from here and leave me in peace."

Luke allowed himself a grim smile. "And 'twould suit *me* if this estate were simply appropriated and given to me outright . . . Sister Faithe."

Her golden face paled, and Luke knew he'd threatened her where it mattered this time. Hauekleah must be very dear to her heart. Indeed, why else would she have agreed to marry a strange Norman knight rather than lose it? That her stake in this union was as great as his was useful to know.

"You're hurting me," she said tightly, glancing at her immobilized hands. "Let me go."

Luke released her. She let out a ragged breath and rubbed her wrists, now marred by livid marks where his fingers had dug into her. He bit back an apology, reminding himself that, just moments ago, this woman had been aiming a knife at his brother's throat.

"Go about your business," she told her staff. They slowly dispersed, except for young Dunstan, who stayed close in an apparent effort to keep watch over his mistress. A plump, older woman brought her a wooden box with brass fittings and a bar of yellowish soap, which she set on a nearby bench. "Thank you, Moira."

"We could simply take Hauekleah from you," Luke told Lady Faithe, only to see her face lose even more of its color, highlighting a constellation of pale freckles across her nose and cheeks. "But t'would be a brutal business. Regardless of what you may think, your new rulers *are* a civilized people. Why settle with the sword what we can settle with a marriage?"

In point of fact, Lord Alberic would undoubtedly have seized Hauekleah by force, as was his inclination—provided he could observe the fighting from a safe distance, as usual—had not the alternative of granting it to Luke amused him more.

Alberic was a petty and pampered creature, his one great weakness a paralyzing fear of battle—a rather inconvenient attribute in a military commander, which was what he'd been before he'd maneuvered William into naming him sheriff. He'd managed to hide this flaw from everyone but Luke, who'd seen him hunker down in a ditch at Hastings, blubbering and shrieking as the battle raged around him. The other witnesses to this shameful display had perished at the hands of the English, and no doubt Alberic wished Luke had succumbed to the same fate. From his lordship's attitude toward Luke since then, it was clear that he despised his most celebrated knight for being privy to his cowardice. Not that he was outwardly hostile; fancying himself a diplomat, Alberic couched his maliciousness in a facade of remote disdain. For his part, Luke had never revealed what he'd seen to a living soul, except for Alex; it would be his word against that of Alberic, still very much a favorite of King William's.

For months, Lord Alberic had resisted the idea of granting a conquered estate to Luke. Finally, under pressure from William—who'd interpreted Luke's seclusion at St. Albans as a form of protest for his lack of reward, and didn't want to alienate one of his most renowned military heroes—the sheriff gave him Hauekleah by means of marriage to Lady Faithe. It was meant as a sort of mean-spirited jest, of course. Hauekleah was a humble farmstead, nothing like the grand estates he'd bestowed on his other knights. Little did Alberic know that the holding he'd intended as a subtle insult suited Luke perfectly. His fondest boyhood memories were of farm life. He could live contentedly at Hauekleah—provided he managed to keep his Saxon bride and her villeins under control.

Another serving wench laid a pile of blankets and linen on the bench. Lady Faithe started to turn toward them, but Luke grabbed her shoulder and forced her to face him. "Hauekleah is mine now, my lady, with or without you. Rest assured I'll be keeping a close watch on you. If you even think about causing harm to my brother—if I but see it in your eyes—then I'll refuse this marriage and let Lord Alberic take Hauekleah by force."

Lady Faithe twisted out of his grip. "You can't honestly think I meant to cut your brother's throat."

"I saw you with my own—"

"I was trying to cut his tunic off."

Luke studied her seemingly guileless eyes, then looked at his brother, lying on his pallet in his blood-soaked clothes.

"Do you think," she said, "if I'd intended to murder him, that I'd do it right in front of you?"

A good point, Luke had to admit. She knelt and retrieved her knife from the rushes. Crouching, Luke snatched it from her. "I'll do it." Most likely she was telling the truth. If not, she was a consummate liar. Regardless, he'd best reserve judgment on her character—and withhold from her the right to wield knives around his brother—until he'd gotten to know her a bit better.

Anger flashed in her eyes, but she backed away, giving him room to maneuver. As he cut through the heavy wool of his brother's tunic, she pulled the pieces off and handed them to the plump maid, Moira. Alex's undershirt sliced easily. She peeled the crimson-stained linen from his injured side with great care.

Her hands were those of a woman who spent her days working. They looked strong and capable, and even slightly work-roughened, but well-shaped. She wore no rings and kept her nails blunt.

"What weapon did that?" she asked as she examined the ghastly wound.

" 'Twas some type of mallet, with a spike on top."

She nodded. "That's a farm tool. We use it for driving stakes and breaking up the earth. How many men were there?"

"Just two, but they surprised us. They popped out of the woods a mile down the road. One had that mallet, and he went straight for Alex. The other had a sling." He touched his left arm high up, where it had been hit, sucking in his breath as the hardened lump throbbed with pain.

"Are you hurt?"

He gritted his teeth. " 'Tis of no concern. If you Saxons could aim, 'twould have been my skull that stopped that rock, and then I wouldn't be here to tell the tale. No doubt they meant to knock us out and then finish the job with that mallet, but they weren't up to the task."

"I take it they got away."

Luke grimaced at the memory. "I would have gone after them, but Alex needed me. The one with the mallet may not get far—I took Alex's sword and stabbed him in the gut before he ran off." He paused for a heartbeat. "Did you send them to ambush us?"

Seeming unsurprised by the question, she tossed her head in a partially successful attempt to flip her hair over her shoulder. "My men have standing orders to give all Normans a wide berth. I care far too much about Hauekleah to jeopardize it by encouraging my people to attack yours." She stripped away the last of Alex's shirt. "The bleeding has stopped." She began untying Alex's bloodstained chausses. "Here, help me get these off him."

Luke hesitated, discomfited by the sight of her loosening his brother's hose and untying the drawers beneath them. "Isn't there some manservant who could do this?" he asked. "Someplace else?"

She cast him a wry look. "If it's your brother's modesty you're protecting, I assure you he's quite unaware of what's happening, and my servants have all seen—"

"Nay, I meant . . ." Why was he fumbling for words? "Surely it's not considered proper for a lady of rank . . ." He shook his head in exasperation.

She laughed, and he was torn between pleasure at her luminous smile and humiliation at being the cause of her mirth. "You're serious," she said.

"No Frankish lady would expose herself to a naked man, much less take his chausses off herself."

Lady Faithe chuckled as she carefully worked the chausses and drawers down over Alex's wounded hip. "I can't think that makes the Frankish husbands very happy."

Luke almost smiled. He tried to imagine his stepmother or sisters saying such a thing, but they'd rather die than let even the most mildly bawdy remark pass their rouged lips. Just as they'd rather die than undress a man with their soft white hands; no wonder their husbands always looked so unhappy. "Here." He used his knife to cut the remaining garments from his brother's body, leaving him entirely naked. Alex certainly wouldn't mind. One thing he'd never been was shy.

Lady Faithe tucked her hair behind her ears and folded back her sleeves. Taking the soap, she washed her hands, then lathered up one of the linen cloths and gently blotted the gash on Alex's hip.

"Would you like me to do that?" Luke asked.

"Nay, it takes a light touch." She smiled lopsidedly, which Luke found oddly engaging. "You really needn't trouble yourself over my delicate sensibilities, my lord. I'm a widow, not a blushing maid."

This reminder of Lady Faithe's widowhood took Luke aback. According to Lord Alberic's letter, her husband had left for Hastings last summer and never returned. Luke thought back to all the Saxons he'd dispatched with his crossbow at Hastings—and since—and felt an uneasiness in his stomach. For the first time since Alberic's letter had arrived at the monastery last week, he contemplated this union from Lady Faithe's perspective: Having killed her husband but seven months ago, the Norman conquerors now expected her to enter meekly into a marriage to one of their most ruthless soldiers. That she could accept this with such seeming composure was really quite remarkable. Either she did have some treachery hidden up her sleeve, or she was one of a singular breed—those true survivors who prevail against adversity by virtue of adaptation and sharp wits. At any rate, she did not strike him as being deep in mourning over her late husband, which was all for the best.

She wrung out the cloth, ordered a fresh bowl of water, and went to work on the ragged laceration along Alex's side. Tendrils of hair fell across her eyes, and she blew them out of the way. "They're ugly wounds," she said, "but now that they're cleaned off, I'm encouraged. The one of his hip is deep, and I daresay 'twill take him a while to get back on his feet, but no bones are broken. If we can keep the wounds from festering, he should be fine."

"Thank God." Luke crossed himself. She spoke with such confidence that he accepted her assessment unquestioningly. He felt weak with relief.

She cleaned the swollen cut on Alex's forehead. "This doesn't look like the other wounds."

"That's from a stone. The sling found its mark that time."

"Can you identify the men who attacked you?" she asked.

"They were dark-haired, both of them. Around my age."

"Mid-thirties?"

"I'm six-and-twenty."

Her gaze flickered over him. "You strike me as older than that."

He felt older than that. "The man I stabbed," Luke said, "the one with the mallet who'd attacked Alex, was missing an eye. The other one had a big red birthmark on one cheek."

She exchanged a knowing look with the watchful young man, Dunstan, as she twisted the cloth over the bowl of water.

"Do you know these men?" Luke asked.

She tossed her hair out of the way, which made her keys rattle softly. "They're incorrigibles, both of them. Hengist and Vance—cousins. They prowl the woods around here, robbing travelers—Saxon or Norman, it makes no difference to them."

"Only they don't usually attack this close to Hauekleah," said Dunstan, taking a step forward. "In fact, they never do. Orrik and I make it our business to keep those woods clean of bandits."

"Orrik?" Luke said.

"My bailiff." Lady Faithe opened the padlock on her medicine box with one of her many keys and sorted through the contents. "He manages the farm for me. Yesterday he went to Foxhyrst to buy a cart and some supplies. He should be back tomorrow. Dunstan is his reeve. He looks after things for me when Orrik is gone."

"Another thing about Hengist and Vance," Dunstan interjected. "Those two are robbers, not murderers. I never knew them to attack to kill."

Luke absently rubbed his arm. "They did today."

"Aye." Dunstan regarded Alex's mauled body with a thoughtful expression.

Luke gritted his teeth in frustration. His instinct was to chase after these bandits, but he didn't dare leave Alex's side.

"I want those curs found," Lady Faithe told her reeve. Luke stared at her; young Dunstan merely nodded. "They had no business venturing this close to Hauekleah, not to mention trying to kill our new lord. I won't have such misdeeds tolerated."

Her quiet leadership both impressed and disturbed Luke. He admired how well this young woman in her dirty slippers and rough kirtle controlled her men. And, of course, he was eager for the bastards who'd done this to Alex to be apprehended. But what if this was all a trick? What if she *had* arranged for the ambush, and was now merely pretending to send a party of men after knaves who'd, in fact, done her bidding? Even if it wasn't a trick, the authority she wielded so effectively was authority that Luke himself should be exercising. He'd crossed the Channel and soaked the earth with blood to acquire this farmstead. Hauekleah was his now. He could lay down his crossbow and live in peace—but first he'd have to prove to these people that he was their master.

He considered the notion of wresting control of this situation from Lady Faithe and giving the orders himself, but in the end he kept quiet. For one thing, Hauekleah wasn't officially his until after the wedding. For another, the men who'd ambushed them were even now in flight. For Luke to delay their pursuit while he tussled with Lady Faithe over command of her villeins would be ill-advised in the extreme.

"Take some good men," the young widow told Dunstan, "and see if you can pick up their trail in the woods. It shouldn't be too difficult. From Sir Luke's account, Hengist is badly hurt, and possibly dying. Look for blood."

"Aye, milady." Dunstan left. Luke had but a few moments to be surprised that the earnest young reeve had left his mistress unprotected against the Black Dragon. As Dunstan exited the great hall, he called out, "Firdolf!" to a fair-haired, brawny young man who was hauling in firewood. After dumping the wood next to the fire pit, this fellow stood in the spot Dunstan had vacated, arms crossed, and glared at Luke.

Retrieving two parchment packets from the box, Lady Faithe ordered some honey and salt brought to her. Two voluptuous young flaxen-haired wenches—twins, from the look of them—sprinted through a door at the far end of the hall and returned with the requested items.

"Thank you, girls," said Lady Faithe in obvious dismissal. They backed up a step, but couldn't seem to wrest their gazes from Alex. Luke's little brother had the face of an angel and the well-muscled body of a soldier. His many old scars—mementos not of the battlefield but of the savage beating he'd taken at seventeen after a liaison with the wrong woman—only served to add an intriguing edge to his beauty. It was little wonder women were drawn to him, but they usually didn't get quite this much of an eyeful on a first meeting. The young man standing guard, Firdolf, scowled at Alex, then at the girls.

"Bonnie, Blossom . . ." their mistress said, "that will be all."

"Can we help, milady?" one of them asked plaintively.

"Nay!" Firdolf snapped.

Lady Faithe raised an eyebrow at him, and he muttered an apology; it appeared to Luke that she was trying to keep from smiling. "Nay," she echoed softly as she poured some salt and honey into a bowl. "Go out back to the cookhouse and see if Ardith needs anything."

"But . . ."

Lady Faithe smiled. "When he wakes up, I'll let you feed him."

The girls brightened instantly and left amid giggles and whispers.

"Your brother won't mind, will he?" her ladyship

asked as she unfolded the first packet, revealing a number of narrow, dried leaves.

"I should hardly think so." The twins were pretty and, from all appearances, already ripe for Alex's persuasive charms.

Lady Faithe crumbled several leaves into the bowl and then opened the second packet, which held smaller leaves. When she crushed those between her hands, they released a familiar aroma.

"Mint?" Luke asked.

"Pennyroyal. The other was hyssop. They're excellent for wounds like this." She stirred the herbs with her fingers into the honey and salt, spread the mixture onto a strip of linen, and laid it over the wound on Alex's hip.

Alex moaned as she gently pressed the poultice into place. "Easy," Luke said, patting his brother's shoulder.

As Lady Faithe worked on smoothing the poultice down, that disorderly hair of hers kept getting in the way; each toss of her head only seemed to make it worse. She lifted a hand to tuck it behind her ears, but her fingers were coated with the greenish herbal mixture. "Moira," she said without looking up from her work, "would you braid my hair?" Receiving no response, for the stout maid who'd been hovering so closely was now nowhere to be seen, she let out a little growl of exasperation.

Reaching behind him, Luke unwrapped the long leather thong from his own braid. Lady Faithe watched him out of the corner of her eye as he knelt behind her, slipped the thong between his teeth, and began gathering up her hair.

It was perfectly straight and slippery-smooth; no wonder it was so unruly. He divided it into three sections, combing his fingers through the slick strands to coax out the little tangles, and then began weaving them together.

His knuckles brushed her long neck, as soft as the skin of a peach, and warm. He could have avoided the contact, but instead he let the back of his hand caress her, again and again, as he slowly braided her hair. It felt oddly comforting to touch her this way, like stroking a kitten.

The skin on her upper back was especially smooth, a film of warm satin over the delicate bones of her spine. Tiny goose bumps rose on that skin as he worked his way down, and her breathing quickened to keep time with his. He felt disappointed at the first rough touch of her wool kirtle.

Soon she'll be your wife, he thought, *and then you may do more to her than braid her hair.*

Luke tried to concentrate on keeping his hands steady and his work neat—on resisting the urge to pull the ribbon that laced up the back of her kirtle and watch it come undone. He imagined doing just that, imagined reaching inside to glide his hands around her narrow back and close them over her breasts. He imagined how they'd feel, warm and heavy, their nipples stiff against his palms.

When he took the leather thong from between his teeth, he found that he had bitten it in half.

Chapter 3

Faithe's chest hurt from the thudding of her heart. She felt a gentle tugging as de Périgueux tied off the braid, and then she felt his large, callused hand resting on the curve where her neck met her shoulder.

The heat of his palm permeated her, easing the ache in her chest and filling her with a shivery warmth. His hand shifted as he gained his feet, grazing her throat like the delicious scrape of a cat's tongue.

He stood behind her. She looked over her shoulder and found him staring down at her, his loose hair falling about his face, his expression guarded but alert.

"Thank you," she managed, and quickly returned her attention to his brother. She made a show of patting the poultice, which she'd long since forgotten, then dipped her fingers into the bowl and spread the mixture on another strip of linen.

He cleared his throat. "Is there any ale to be had?" She turned toward him, but he looked away from her—pointedly, it seemed—and rubbed the back of his neck.

"Of course. Willa?"

The kitchen wench filled a horn for him, and he sat on a bench to drink it while Faithe applied the second poultice to his brother's side.

"Why the flowers?" he asked presently.

She looked up. He avoided her gaze, indicating with a sweep of his arm the garlands and swags with which they'd adorned the great hall that morning.

"It's May Day." She covered her patient with a blanket.

"Ah." He still looked confused.

She smiled. "On the first of May we decorate our homes with flowers. 'Tis a celebration of spring." And fertility, but she hesitated to tell him how her villeins would observe the holiday that night. With any luck, he'd be too wrapped up in caring for his brother to venture outside.

"I see."

Faithe glanced up to gauge his expression. Many of the Normans viewed their ancient customs as ungodly. Would he attempt to ban them now that he was master of Hauekleah?

She saw a muscle tense in his jaw. Lifting his horn, he drained it. He didn't like to be read, this one, to be examined and interpreted. From all appearances, he was a man very much sealed within himself, like a soldier buckled into his armor. She wondered if he ever took it off.

As she pressed a small poultice to the wound on Sir Alex's forehead, he began to stir, muttering things in blurry French. She washed her hands, then tied a bandage around his head to hold the herbal compress in place as de Périgueux came and knelt next to her in the rushes. "Open your eyes, Alex," he said softly, in his own tongue. "Wake up." His gentleness struck her as touchingly at odds with his fierce demeanor.

Faithe listened to de Périgueux coax his brother into wakefulness as she repacked her medicine box and tidied up the area.

"That's it," Luke said as Alex opened his eyes and squinted at his surroundings. "Welcome back, little brother."

The young man turned toward the voice and winced. "What in the name of God . . ."

"We were ambushed in the woods."

Sir Alex's large brown eyes narrowed in concentration. His coloring was as dark as his brother's, and he looked to be nearly as tall, but with a somewhat leaner build. The men bore a strong family resemblance, and were both very striking, but in different ways. Despite the scars, both new and old, young Alex's clean-shaven face had an open, almost innocent beauty, whereas there was nothing innocent about Luke de Périgueux. He had the savage eyes and firmly set jaw of a flesh-eater. Faithe had the sense that if she pushed him too far, he might leap upon her and sink his teeth in her throat.

"Ambushed," Alex murmured. "That's right. Two of them, weren't there? Saxons?"

"Aye. Ugly bastards they were, and out for blood."

Alex shrugged. "Can't blame them. If I were one of them, I'd be trying to kill us, too."

Faithe thought this a rather singular sentiment, coming as it did from a Norman soldier.

Sir Luke quirked his mouth in a way that conveyed bemused forbearance. "They tell me those two are ordinary bandits, not insurgents hungry for Norman blood. They got away, worse luck. Supposedly a party of men is looking for them now."

"Supposedly?" Frowning, Alex reached up to gingerly finger the bandage wrapped around his head.

Sir Luke cast a furtive look in Faithe's direction; his brother seemed unaware of her presence. "I don't know what to believe from these people. They could be lying just to keep me from going after them myself, so they have time to get away. We can't trust the English, Alex. They despise us."

He has no idea I can understand him, Faithe realized. And why should he? The notion of her knowing French was as unlikely as his knowing English. She eavesdropped shamelessly as she gathered her things.

"Of course they despise us," Alex said. "How could they not?" He groped around for something beneath his blanket. "Where's my sword?"

"Here." His brother unbuckled the swordbelt and handed it over.

Alex hugged the sheathed weapon to his chest. "Where are we?"

"Hauekleah Hall."

"Oh, yes? Have you met your bride?"

"Aye."

The young man grinned. "Is she pretty?"

Faithe stilled, listening intently.

"She looks like a goose girl," Sir Luke finally said.

Alex chuckled. "But is she pretty?"

Sir Luke glanced uneasily toward Faithe, who pretended to be absorbed in refolding a pile of linen strips. She noticed Sir Alex follow his brother's line of vision.

"Is that her?" the young man asked delightedly.

Sir Luke rubbed his forehead. "Aye. Don't stare."

Alex did stare, openly. "She *is* pretty! You lucky dog! Aren't you going to introduce us?" He tried to sit up, but groaned in pain and sank back down onto the pallet.

"Lie still!" Luke shook his head in vexation, then turned to Faithe and said, in English, "My lady, I'd like you to meet my brother, Alexandre de Périgueux." To his brother he said merely, "Lady Faithe of Hauekleah."

"I'm very pleased to meet you, Sir Alex," Faithe said in her nearly perfect convent French. Both men looked as if they'd just been smacked in the head with a war hammer. "Now, if you'll excuse me, I believe I'll go out and tend to the geese."

Rising, she turned and walked away to the delighted laughter of young Alex. As she passed beyond the front door, she glanced back and saw Luke de Périgueux with his eyes closed, rubbing the bridge of his nose.

* * *

That night, Faithe awoke to the sound of distant laughter.

Arising from bed, she crossed to a window and swung open the shutters. The light of a full moon washed into her bedchamber, and a mild breeze fluttered her thin night shift. She rubbed her bare arms as she gazed out over the thatched roofs of the village, where revelers still danced around a bonfire in the middle of the green, and beyond it to the vast woodlands and rolling meadows that surrounded her manor.

Somewhere, a woman shrieked. Faithe tensed, but presently the same voice erupted in giggles, and she relaxed. A movement near the sheep fold caught her eye. Squinting, she made out a couple racing hand in hand into the woods. The woman's white-blond hair whipped behind her like a flag. Faithe recognized her as Willa, one of her kitchen wenches. The man must be Nyle Plowman. Some of the couples who celebrated this night in the forest were longtime sweethearts, like Nyle and Willa. Some were married—usually, but not always, to each other. Others, transported by the festive atmosphere, or the ale, or the simple lure of the flesh, came together for this night only.

A splash made her turn toward the river that cut through her demesne like a horseshoe. Two faraway figures—a man and a woman, naked in the moonlight—emerged from the water and ran into the tall grass on the opposite shore. Faithe thought the woman might be Edyth, the young dairymaid. At first she took the man for Firdolf, the bondman who did odd jobs for her, but then she realized it couldn't be him. Firdolf had been mooning after one of the twins for some time now—Blossom, that was the one—to the exclusion of all other women. If he hadn't been able to talk Blossom into celebrating this night with him, Faithe doubted he would do any celebrating at all. The fellow with Edyth must be one of Firdolf's many look-alike cousins.

The dairymaid's companion fell upon her, and soon they were a tangle of arms and legs, writhing together in an age-old rhythm.

Faithe closed the shutter and rested her forehead against the slatted wood, but the image of the couple on the shore refused to fade. It had been so long since she'd experienced the pleasures of the flesh that she couldn't remember clearly what it felt like to take a man inside her—to take Caedmon inside her, for her husband had been the only man she'd ever given herself to.

Faithe didn't think what she'd felt for Caedmon could rightly be called "love." She'd liked him well enough, though. He'd treated her with respect and been a good husband in many ways, despite his lack of interest in Hauekleah—or perhaps even because of it, for his unwillingness to involve himself in farm life had meant that Faithe could govern Hauekleah as she pleased. When she'd learned of his death, she had grieved, but her dark melancholy had quickly vanished in the light of all her duties as mistress of Hauekleah.

She and Caedmon had shared few interests, and in truth had rarely even conversed—except in bed. Sex had been the highlight of their marriage, and certainly the only pastime they had in common. For close to a year now, Faithe had lived chastely, but not by preference. Many times she had ached for a man's touch. Since Caedmon's death, she had oftentimes thought of marrying again—a husband of her own choice this time, a union of the heart.

The breezes carried another voice from the woods: a man calling, "Elga . . . Elga!" and then crying out in surprise. He must have found her—or she him. Elga Brewer and her husband were the happiest couple Faithe knew. Their mingled laughter made her smile.

A union of the heart . . .

Her smile faded. There would be no such union for her, it seemed. Instead, there would be Luke de Périgueux. The Black Dragon. A creature with a taste for blood.

Saxon blood. And yet . . .

Closing her eyes again, she recalled the mesmerizing caress of his knuckles as they'd brushed her neck, again and again, while he braided her hair. The thoughtful gesture had stunned her; it had also ignited a longing in her, a desperate ache born of long months alone in a cold bed.

She could still feel the ticklish warmth of his touch on the back of her neck.

She could also still feel the imprint of his fingers on her wrists. Opening her eyes, she held her hands up and inspected the red-hot marks that would be bruises by this time tomorrow.

Fool. Luke de Périgueux was a monster, the last man in the world she should want in her bed; yet he'd be there soon enough. Shivering, she donned a wrapper over her shift, whispering, "Please, God, let him tire of me quickly. Let him leave here, like Thorgeirr, and never return." Grimly, she crossed herself.

Thinking to check on Sir Alex, she quietly opened the door of her chamber, situated over the service rooms—the buttery, pantry, and dairy—at the north end of Hauekleah Hall. Looking down into the main hall, dimly lit by a single oil lamp, she saw the figure of a man wrapped in a blanket, standing with his back to her at a window—Alex. His brother, who'd been keeping watch over him, was nowhere to be seen. The servants had all either retired to their own cottages nearby, or were out celebrating tonight; only hirelings slept in the hall, usually at harvest time.

The young man turned toward her as she descended the narrow staircase; he must have had good hearing, for she was silent as the night in her bare feet. "My lady."

"Sir Alex."

He made a rueful face. "We're being a bit formal for brother and sister, don't you think?"

"Ah. Yes, I suppose so." Soon he'd be her brother by marriage. Faithe tugged her wrapper more snugly around herself.

"Call me Alex."

"Then you must call me Faithe."

"I'm sorry I can't speak to you in your own language," he said. "I haven't my brother's gift with foreign tongues. I can understand English passably well, but as far as carrying on a conversation in it . . ."

"That's perfectly all right." England was now ruled by those who spoke the Frankish tongue; she'd best get used to it. "You must return to bed," she said, noting his pale complexion and glassy eyes. "You have no business being on your feet." That he could stand here like this, chatting casually, in his condition, was a testament both to his youthful fortitude and lack of sense.

Far-off laughter made Alex turn back to the window. "What's going on out there?"

Faithe looked down and tightened the sash of her wrapper. " 'Tis a holiday. The people are celebrating."

He scratched his smooth chest thoughtfully. "Those two girls who fed me supper, the twins . . ." His smile was so lewdly wistful that Faithe couldn't help but chuckle. He cleared his throat, but the smile remained. "Charming girls."

"Aye."

"They wanted me to come into the woods with them tonight, but of course I'm not up to the walk. When I tried to find out why, they both turned the most beguiling shade of red and refused to answer. It made me wonder."

The only thing Faithe wondered at was that Bonnie and Blossom, the most merrily wanton creatures she'd ever known, had the capacity to blush. She shrugged and attempted to change the subject. "Where is your brother?"

"Luke went out to investigate, after we started hearing all the laughter and such. I think he headed for the woods."

Dear God. Faithe cleared her throat. "Yes, well, then it's up to me to get you back to bed. Come." Guiding him by the arm, she led him to his pallet. It was slow going; he grimaced with every halting step. When they got there, she helped him to lie down.

He unwrapped the blanket, murmuring an apology for his state of undress, although it clearly troubled him little, and rearranged it on top of him.

"You really ought not to have gotten up," Faithe scolded. "Let me check those poultices." They all needed changing. She lifted the perforated clay firecover off the hearth, added a log to the glowing coals, and put a small pot of water on the trivet to warm. Alex watched her quietly as she mixed up a new batch of the herbal compound and spread it on the linen.

"My brother's lucky to have gotten himself betrothed to you," he said.

Faithe's cheeks grew warm. "I suppose it's handy to have a wife who knows how to fix cuts and scrapes."

"That's not what I meant," he responded with a smile. "You're very beautiful."

The warmth became a scalding burn that encompassed her entire face. "This one's ready," she said without looking up. "If you'll just fold back the—"

"I didn't mean that the way it sounded." He rose onto an elbow, letting out a little grunt of pain. "That is, I don't want you to think . . . well, that *I* fancy you. Perhaps under other circumstances, but as it is—"

"I understand. Would you just fold back—"

"You're betrothed to my brother, and I would never—"

"Yes, I understand. Now, please—"

"I was just stating a fact, that's all. That Luke is a lucky man to have such a beautiful bride."

"Lie down." Faithe turned back the blanket herself to expose his hip, keeping the rest of him modestly covered, and peeled off the old poultice. His skin felt hot to the touch; she'd have to do something about that fever. "Your brother doesn't seem very impressed. He said I look like a goose girl."

Alex laughed. "I've never known a goose girl who wasn't pretty." He shrugged. "But then, almost all women are pretty if you just look at them from the right angle."

"The right angle?" She couldn't resist a smile as she ran a damp cloth over his wound, which was blessedly free of swelling or redness. "I assume you mean looking down on them as they lie on their backs beneath you."

A pause, and then he burst out laughing. "By God's eyes, you'll be good for Luke. He needs a woman like you to shed some light on that dark soul of his."

Faithe's smile subsided. She prepared another poultice as he studied her unself-consciously. "You're very different, you and your brother," she said.

Alex gazed thoughtfully at the ceiling for some time while she substituted the second poultice for the one on his side. "Not as different as you might think."

"He's got a darker temperament." She covered him back up and unwrapped the bandage from around his head. "You said so yourself."

"Aye . . ."

"And there's his reputation." She cleaned his head wound and spread the last of the hyssop and pennyroyal mixture on a small square of linen.

"The Black Dragon," Alex said, "is *what* Luke is, not *who* he is."

She washed off her hands and wrapped a bandage around his head. "I don't understand."

"People see the beast with the crossbow, and they

think that's all there is to Luke de Périgueux. But inside"—he tapped his chest—"in here, he has the heart of a man. A good man."

"Yes, well . . ." She tied off the bandage. "Is that too tight?"

Alex struggled up onto his elbow again, although it was clearly painful for him. "He's saved my life five times."

"Yes?" She rose to fill a jug with boiling water from the pot.

"The fifth time was this afternoon, when those two men attacked us." His dark eyes glittered with fever and sincerity.

Faithe added sprigs of lemon balm and wood sorrel to the jug and stoppered it, then set about straightening up the mess she'd made.

"They came out of nowhere," he said, lying back down with a grunt and folding an arm over his face. "We were riding along, looking for Hauekleah, and suddenly there was a man next to me, swinging that mallet. He got me in the side first, with the spike, and I ended up on my back in the dirt. I went for my sword, and he aimed for my hand, but got my hip instead."

Faithe sucked in a breath.

"Better my hip than my hand," he assured her, peeking out from beneath his arm with a smile. "A swordsman's not worth much without his sword hand."

"I suppose not," she muttered.

"I managed to get my sword drawn, but I couldn't get up to use it, and I knew one swipe of the mallet would send it flying. I reckoned there was a good chance I was going to get my skull bashed in. The other son of a . . . the other bandit hung back and aimed his sling at Luke, but I gather he wasn't a very good shot." Alex squinted, as if to focus his memory. "Luke dismounted and came right up to the fellow with the mallet, which took some nerve, since he was completely unarmed."

"A soldier traveling without a weapon?"

"They weren't permitted in the monastery."

"Monastery?"

"The abbey at St. Albans. Luke spent the past two months there. I thought you knew."

"Nay. Why did he . . . was he doing penance?"

Alex hesitated, then finally said, " 'Tis best you ask him yourself."

"I can't ask him. I hardly know him."

He grinned. "You hardly know me."

"Aye, but you're so easy to talk to, and he's . . ."

"The Black Dragon," Alex finished.

Faithe nodded.

"Not in here," he said softly, touching his chest. "He came right up to the Saxon with the mallet—right up to him—with his arms held wide, shouting, 'Over here! Take *me* on, you bastard!' " Alex smiled a little sheepishly. "Pardon the language, my lady."

"It's 'Faithe,' " she reminded him, returning his smile. "Did Hengist—the fellow with the mallet—did he attack your brother?"

"Of course. He turned and swung that godforsaken thing, but Luke ducked and rolled beneath it, then grabbed my sword out of my hand and ran the whoreson—sorry—ran the gentleman through."

Faithe let out her breath in a gust.

"I don't remember anything after that," he said.

"That must be when you got hit in the head with that rock. Vance gave it one last shot, and then they both fled. Your brother stayed behind to help you rather than go after them."

"You see?" Alex grinned smugly. "He's a good man."

"He's a good man to you. He's been a bad man to many others."

Alex scowled. "He's a soldier. He's supposed to do bad things. That's his vocation."

Having no answer for that, she unstoppered the jug and poured some of the dark, fragrant infusion into a cup. "This will ease your fever. Can you sit up?"

He did so, making a face. "I hate the taste of tonics."

"You'll like this one." She stirred a generous dollop of honey into the cup and brought it to her nose to inhale its tart-sweet aroma, then handed it to him.

He sniffed it suspiciously, then blew on it and took a small sip. His expression lightened, and he drank some more. "It's good! What is it?"

"Balm tea, of a sort." She poured a cup for herself, simply to enjoy its lemony warmth, and settled down in the rushes next to him. " 'Twill cool you down and help you to sleep, so you can heal. You should be on your feet in a few days, assuming you stay on that pallet and stop wandering around."

He shrugged as he sipped the hot brew. "It's hard just to lie there and do nothing. I get bored."

"Would you like me to read to you?"

He blinked. "You have a book?"

"I have four," she proudly stated, setting aside her cup and rising to cross to the locked chest in the corner. "A book of the gospels, a herbal, Aesop's *Fables,* and a book of Frankish poetry."

"I'd like to hear some of the fables, I think."

She pulled her key chain from beneath her nightgown and unlocked the chest. "*Fables* it is."

Luke eased open the front door of Hauekleah Hall as quietly as he could, to avoid disturbing Alex. He was sleeping, Luke saw, and sitting at his side, cross-legged in the rushes, was Lady Faithe.

She had her back to Luke and didn't appear to hear him come in. Slipping inside, he silently closed the door, but made no move to walk farther into the hall;

the rushes would crackle underfoot, announcing his presence, and he wanted to watch her unobserved for a few moments.

Watch her and listen to her, for she was speaking, quietly, despite that his brother, the only other person there, was oblivious to her. Her voice, soft and high, drifted across the huge hall to him like a breeze across a meadow, and within a few moments he recognized her words; she was telling the story of "The Fox and the Grapes"—in Latin! A movement of her hand caught his eye. He heard the muted crackle of parchment and noticed the book in her lap for the first time.

He rubbed his beard-roughened jaw. So. His little English goose girl not only spoke French and Latin, but could read as well—and better than he could, from the sound of it. She must have had lessons, and taken them more seriously than Luke had taken his.

Lady Faithe still wore her hair in the braid he'd plainted for her, although it sprouted numerous wispy strands that had come loose. She wore white linen night clothes, through which the fire from the hearth glowed, giving her a radiant, otherworldly aura.

He stood by the door and listened to her as she read. At one point she yawned, raising a graceful hand to her mouth and lowering it, without interrupting the hypnotic cadence of her reading. All her movements were like that, Luke reflected, without artifice but elegant nonetheless, a refinement born of economy.

She *was* refined, he realized with a shock. Despite her humble attire and earthy nature, she was a person of breeding, civilized and educated. He'd envisioned something quite different before he'd met her. True, he'd mistakenly anticipated jewels and furs—she was, after all, a chatelaine, and even the Saxon nobility dressed the part—but he hadn't expected much of the person who wore them. Indeed, he'd formed a mental image of a coarse, uncultured creature done up in a lady's finery. What he'd gotten was quite the opposite, and he found himself pleased by the turnaround.

She was quite a contrast to the general run of Saxons—a decidedly uncivilized people. That assessment had been confirmed by what he'd seen in the woods tonight. If they celebrated May Day by fornicating out of doors, what other pagan rituals did they cling to? His mind conjured up blue-painted savages howling at the moon, then offering some hapless Norman to one of their forest gods in a human sacrifice.

Luke shook his head to dispel the absurd image. The English were Christians. They worshiped the same God he did, obeyed the same Roman pope. But why, then, did they persist in bringing in spring with this barbaric practice? There was much he needed to learn about these people—his people now—and who better to teach him than his bride, who seemed to have one foot in civilization and one in the primitive world of her ancestors.

Lady Faithe concluded her story and closed her book. She chuckled softly, apparently having discovered that the man she was reading to had fallen asleep. Setting the thin volume on a bench, she rose onto her knees to lay her hand on Alex's chest. The pose allowed the firelight to silhouette her body through her gauzy linen garments. Her waist was surprisingly narrow, a fact not evident from the baggy kirtle she'd worn earlier. The contrast of that slender waist with the feminine roundness of her hips incited an innate masculine urge—the instinct to possess, to penetrate.

Luke took a step forward, but she was shifting position, so she didn't hear him. Leaning over Alex, she touched his cheek, then his forehead. One breast, full and round and clearly outlined by the flames, swayed slightly as she moved. He could just make out the delicate peak of a nipple, and felt a hot spark of lust at the sight.

He'd been fighting a low hum of arousal all the

way back from the woods. What he'd seen there had astounded him, yet he'd also felt an element of lurid fascination that heated his blood. As he watched the Lady Faithe tending to his brother, unaware of Luke's probing gaze, that heat took shape and chose a target, like a crossbow bolt aimed at its quarry.

She was his—their overlord had promised her to him—but he'd best wait until their wedding night to claim her. Not that she'd necessarily reject him if he pressed the issue now—but she might. She might be outraged by his presumption—after all, she was a lady, and presumably a lady of virtue—or she might simply lie down and spread her legs for him. He couldn't begin to imagine her response. She was an enigma to him, this delicate young widow with her Aesop and her herbs and her bawdy sense of humor.

As Luke watched, Lady Faithe braced her hands on either side of Alex's head, leaned down, and kissed him on the forehead.

Shock vanquished Luke's ardor, reheating his blood to a furious boil. She'd kissed his brother—kissed him! He'd seen it with his own eyes.

He stalked toward her like a beast after its prey, crushing rushes and sweet blossoms underfoot, his hands curled in soldierly readiness at his sides. Heat pulsed behind his eyes. She'd kissed his brother. She'd kissed Alex!

She looked up as he approached, startled at first, and then wary. His face must have reflected his simmering rage. He saw a flash of fear in her eyes, and then the light of realization as she glanced first at Alex and then back at Luke.

Schooling her features, she stood, chin valiantly raised, hands clutching her linen wrapper. Its sash had come loose, exposing the shift beneath. Between the cushions of her breasts hung the long golden chain with its cluster of keys, a symbol of her authority, which she evidently never took off.

He stopped inches from her, glowering down; she had to crane her neck to look at him. Before he could speak, she said, quietly, in her own tongue, "I was gauging his fever with my lips."

Luke narrowed his gaze, seeking the truth in her eyes. She accepted this scrutiny with unblinking equanimity.

Turning away from her, he squatted down and laid the back of his hand on his brother's forehead, finding it cool. "He has no fever." He spoke in French, a deliberate reminder of his dominion over her and her estate. For years he'd longed to settle down to a life of farming, a good life, a life without bloodshed. Now he had his chance. Hauekleah was his, or soon would be. She was his. Her world was his. Her body was his. Her land and villeins and livestock all belonged to him. They would live by his rules, now and forever. And as a mark of their fealty, they would speak his language, at least in his presence.

She squared her shoulders, but answered him calmly, in her remarkably good French. "He did have a fever. I gave him some balm tea to lower it." She handed Luke a cup. "We'd best not discuss this here. Your brother will wake up."

"Nothing wakes up Alex." Luke sniffed the dark liquid cooling in the bottom of the cup, as if that might allay his suspicions. He smelled lemon balm and honey and something else he couldn't identify.

He stood with his back to her, staring into the cup. "I never heard of measuring a fever that way."

Rushes rustled as she took a step toward him. " 'Tis a trick I learned in the convent where I grew up."

"You were raised in a convent?" That would account for her learning.

"My mother died giving birth to me, my father when I was six. Orrik convinced my overlord that it was best for the nuns to raise me. There was one, Sister Beatrix. She used to nurse me in the infirmary when I was ill. If I felt hot, she'd press her lips to my forehead to determine how bad the fever was."

She came around to face him, lifting the cup from his hand. Her fingers brushed his, sending hot chills up his arm and into his chest. "And then she'd give me balm tea." Burying her nose in the cup, she closed her eyes and inhaled. A smile of pure, transfixed delight spread across her face. "How I loved it. It always brought my fever down, and then I'd sleep. And sometimes, in the middle of the night, I'd feel a kind of soft tickle on my forehead, and I'd half awaken and know Sister Beatrix was checking up on me. And then I'd fall back asleep again, content that I was being cared for and all was well with the world."

Luke wondered what she'd looked like as a child. His mind formed a picture of a delicate girl with flushed cheeks, asleep in bed. Unexpectedly, he felt a wild, nearly overpowering urge to gather her up and hold her close. Instead, he took a step back. God knew what he'd do once he had her in his arms.

He felt very much the fool for having assumed the worst. His reaction had been automatic, unthinking, fueled by what he'd seen in the woods and possibly by jealousy over watching her minister so tenderly to his brother. Absurdly, he wished he could be in Alex's place. He'd gladly trade those hideous wounds for the chance to feel her solicitous hands on his body, her lips on his brow.

You'll feel those things and more, soon enough. Patience.

She smiled up at him, a mischievous light dancing in her eyes. "This afternoon you accused me of trying to kill your brother. Just now you thought I wanted to kiss him. Is it so hard to believe that I merely want to help him?"

"Why would you want to help a Norman soldier?"

Her smiled faded. "He's to be my brother by marriage." She examined the cup in her hand with a thoughtful expression, and then looked up guardedly. "And you're to be my husband. I've little affection for your kind. How could it be otherwise, after—" She bit her lip, cutting off what undoubtedly would have been a litany of Norman sins against her and her people. "But I've no illusions about soldiering. You and Alex have merely served your sovereign as my husband served his. My quarrel is with William of Normandy, not the brothers de Périgueux."

"Graciously spoken. Yet I'm sure it won't be easy for you and your people, accommodating yourselves to a Norman master."

That devilish little smile of hers returned. " 'Twill be harder by far for you, my lord, getting used to our Saxon ways."

The scenes Luke had encountered in the woods bombarded his mind's eye—a mosaic of carnal images. "After what I saw out there tonight, I can't help but agree with you."

Spots of pink bloomed on her cheeks. "I should have explained that to you earlier."

"How could one explain such a thing?" One image took focus in Luke's mind—the first couple he'd come upon, clearly visible in the light of the full moon. The man had the woman against a tree, her legs around his waist, his braies at his ankles, groaning as he pounding into her. She wore white night clothes, such as the Lady Faithe had on, and clawed at her lover's shirt, gasping in the time to his thrusts, her head thrown back.

The memory—and Lady Faithe's closeness, her warmth and sweetly mysterious scent—stirred his loins. He quickly backed away from her, turning and raking his hands through his unbound hair, which made the knot on his upper arm pulse with pain. "This is a savage country," he said, "with savage customs."

Again he heard her approach from behind. Folks normally kept their distance from him, but Faithe of

Hauekleah appeared to be the exception. "We're not savage," she said, "just different from what you're used to."

"We?" He spun around. "Have you ever . . ." His imagination substituted her face for that of the woman in the white nightgown, getting tupped against that tree, and he felt a rush of desire mingled with revulsion.

"Nay. I spent my youth in a convent and was married at sixteen. Caedmon thought it unseemly for us to—"

"Caedmon?"

"My husband. He'd been brought up in Worcester, and the custom struck him as . . ."

"Barbaric?"

She stiffened her back. "These are people of the land, celebrating a time of rebirth. Their lives revolve around the seasons. They've survived another winter, and they want to celebrate it with an act of release—an act of procreation."

A thoughtful rationale, he had to concede. Every culture had its customs, and all people harbored an animal side that strained for release; who knew this better than he? And he couldn't deny the primitive appeal of a night of unleashed passions. Still . . . "Where I come from, such acts are conducted in private."

"We're a rustic people, my lord," she said gravely, "a simple people. But we share the same values as the rest of Christendom. We know right from wrong, and we try to be good. I hope, in time, you can come to accept us for what we are."

She spoke with such heartfelt sincerity that Luke was disposed to reassure her, at least to some extent. "I did not come here thinking to transform your people into something they're not," he said. "All I ask is their fidelity, and in return I'll make every attempt to tolerate their ways."

Her entire being seemed to light up from within. "I'm gratified to hear that, my lord."

"I do demand their allegiance, though," he felt compelled to add. "I want that understood. They don't have to like me, and undoubtedly many will despise me, but I won't tolerate disloyalty."

"They won't despise you," she said, "unless you do despicable things. My people hate Normans in general because they've stolen our kingdom from us, but it's difficult to hate a person who treats you well and fairly. Be good to them. Spend the days between now and the wedding showing them what a just and fair master you'll be, and by the time you're lord of Hauekleah—"

"We're to be married tomorrow," he said.

She stared at him.

"I'd assumed you knew. Didn't Lord Alberic tell you—"

"Lord Alberic has told me very little," she said flatly.

Luke rejected the notion of offering to postpone the wedding, anxious as he was to claim Hauekleah, and its mistress, as his own. "His lordship wants an expedient wedding, since I'm already living under your roof. Frankly, so do I. He'll arrive tomorrow morning, along with his wife, the Lady Bertrada, and his personal chaplain, who will solemnize the union. The preliminaries are being dispensed with."

"I have my own priest. I don't see why—"

"His lordship," Luke said carefully, "is a man who likes things done his way. I understand that you have preferences, but I wouldn't waste my time quarreling with him over the details if I were you."

"Quarreling with him," she said tightly, "or with you, is that correct?"

Luke sighed, wishing she could accept matters with a bit more grace. He didn't relish having to limit her power, for she exercised it uncommonly well, but it was imperative that he take some of it for himself. "You will need to learn to acquiesce to me, yes."

She yanked at the sash of her wrapper, tying it into a tight knot. "Thank you for the advice, my lord. I'm sure it's presumptuous of me to want to have any say in the particulars of my marriage—or my life."

"My lady—"

"You and Lord Alberic are in a much better position, I daresay, to attend to the details and make the decisions. I'll refrain from involving myself in them any further."

She set the cup on a bench, stalked to the open corner stairway, and climbed it. Opening the door to her private chamber, she looked down at him and said, "Might I inquire when and where the nuptials are to take place?"

"Nones, at the chapel door, followed by a Mass. My lady—"

"I'll be there," she said and closed the door behind her.

Chapter 4

Faithe twisted her wedding ring around and around on her finger as she glanced surreptitiously at her new husband, sitting next to her at dinner. He'd been subdued during the ceremony and Mass, and quiet all through the afternoon meal. Blossom came up behind him with a jug of spiced wine, but he waved her away.

"More for you, my lady?"

"Aye." Faithe intended to be as relaxed as possible when she retired to her marriage bed that night.

While Blossom refilled the large goblet, Faithe watched her sister, Bonnie, working her way down the opposite side of the table with a bowl of hazelnut crumble. The only way she could tell the twins apart was that Bonnie wore her hair in two braids, Blossom in one. When Bonnie got to Alex, propped up with pillows directly across from Faithe in Hauekleah Hall's most comfortable chair, his head still bandaged, she leaned in close and purred, "Something sweet, Sir Alex?"

Alex caught Bonnie's gaze and held it, smiling. "I'll have whatever you've got." To Blossom he said, "I wouldn't mind some of yours, too, just for balance."

The twins graced him with slyly sweet smiles and continued down the table.

Dinner had been a relatively modest affair. If Lord Alberic and his wife had expected a lavish bride-ale under the circumstances, they'd been sorely mistaken. Faithe had resolved, after her testy exchange with Sir

Luke the night before, to leave all the day's arrangements to her betrothed and his overlord. Let them prepare a proper wedding feast, if they were so determined to manage all the details and make all the decisions. Of course, they hadn't, and so it was dinner as usual, shared with her demesne staff and those villeins doing week work for her, at a row of trestle tables in the great hall.

Alberic had sputtered quietly upon entering the hall after the nuptial Mass and discovering no formal celebration—no musicians, no decorations, no high table. Sir Luke, on the other hand, hadn't seemed to mind. In fact, given the glint in his eye as he led her by the arm to her seat, he might even have been amused—just one hint among many that he and his overlord were not on the best of terms.

In truth, the house staff, in honor of the wedding, had prepared a more extravagant meal than usual—several courses, including her favorite carp in nettle broth—but it had undoubtedly been meager by Lord Alberic's standards. He sat through the meal with a pinched expression, picking uninterestedly at his food. By contrast, his wife, the pink and fleshy Lady Bertrada, had talked nonstop during the entire meal, and eaten multiple servings of everything with gusto. Several times she had begged Faithe to visit her at Foxhyrst Castle, claiming to be starved for feminine companionship. It must be lonely, Faithe realized, to be the wife of an invader—particularly one as cold and foul-tempered as Lord Alberic.

Bored by the humble fare and lack of entertainment, the sheriff had insisted on departing early, to his wife's disappointment and Faithe's immense relief. She could tolerate Bertrada fairly well—mostly she felt sorry for her—but she couldn't bear the lady's husband; with any luck, he'd found her hospitality so lacking that he would avoid further visits.

Faithe sipped her wine, careful not to let any drip

on her lap. Her one concession to the occasion had been to bathe and dress in her best kirtle, an elegantly simple gown of plum-colored silk ornamented by a golden sash draped low over her hips. A veil, secured by a floral chaplet, drifted over her two long braids, and garnets dangled from her earlobes.

She smiled inwardly, remembering her bridegroom's expression—surprise followed by appreciation—when she had joined him at the chapel door at nones. Sometimes when she glanced his way, she found him looking at her with those dark, penetrating eyes. He always quickly looked away, which she found most interesting.

I'm doing it again . . . twisting and twisting that ring. Flattening her hand on her lap, she ran her thumb over the emeralds embedded in the thick gold band. It was an extraordinary piece of jewelry, the finest thing she'd ever worn. Where had he come by a ring like this on such short notice, she wondered.

" 'Twas my mother's."

She started at the sound of Sir Luke's voice, deep but soft, like distant thunder. He leaned toward her slightly, his gaze on the ring. She breathed in his scent, warm and clean. Moira told her he'd been seen bathing in the river early that morning; he'd even washed his hair.

"How come you to have your mother's ring?" she asked.

"They gave it to me when she died."

"And . . . you've been carrying it with you?"

His response was a half shrug, half nod. He reached toward her lap, lightly rubbing the encrusted stones, as if trying to polish them with his fingertips. The gesture struck her as unexpectedly tender, and strangely sensual.

"It's beautiful," she said.

"You should wear beautiful things. You're . . ." Clearly discomfited, he withdrew his hand and lifted his goblet, frowning to find it empty. "You're the mistress of a great farmstead. You should wear silks and jewels every day."

You're a beautiful woman. That's what she'd thought he was going to say. She wondered whether he'd intended to say that and changed his mind. Soothing her nerves with a sip from her own goblet, she said, "I need to wear clothes I can work in."

"Why must you work so hard?" he asked. "You have villeins for that."

She chuckled. "And what, pray, would you propose I do to keep busy?"

"My stepmother and sisters do needlework."

A huff of laughter escaped from her before she could stop it. "I'm sorry." She pressed on her lips in a futile attempt to dampen her smile. "I mean no disrespect to your stepmother and sisters. It's just that I'd go mad passing a needle in and out of cloth all day. I couldn't bear it."

She thought he'd be miffed with her, for in essence she was belittling what seemed to be the primary occupation of the de Périgueux women. Instead, that half-amused little glint ignited in his eyes again. "So be it." He lapsed into taciturn silence again.

Faithe stole another look at her husband as he gazed in an unfocused way across the great hall. He'd shaved for the occasion and pulled his hair back into a neat queue, making him look much less savage than he had the day before. His pitch black ceremonial tunic, snug across his broad shoulders, hung nearly to the floor, giving him an ascetic air. He might almost have passed for a man of God, were it not for his bearing—remote, guarded, and tightly coiled. Luke de Périgueux carried himself like a creature bred to shed blood.

Faithe made a little sound of disgust with herself when she realized she was twisting the ring again. With an uneven sigh, she picked up her goblet and took a generous swallow of wine. Tonight she would take the Black Dragon to her bed, and then she supposed she would find out how savage a beast he really was.

She drained the goblet in one tilt and gestured for more, but before Blossom could pour it, the front door opened. Dunstan walked into the hall, spotted her, and opened his mouth to speak, but paused. His nonplussed gaze took in her luxurious dress, then shifted to Sir Luke and back again.

Faithe addressed him in their own language. "I'm sorry you had to miss my wedding, Dunstan."

The young reeve's mouth formed a solemn line. "All for a good cause, my lady," he said tonelessly. "We've caught Vance. He was hiding out in a cotter's shack in Upwood."

Dunstan nodded to someone outside, and two men—Nyle Plowman and Firdolf—escorted Vance, his hands bound in back of him, into the hall. A collective murmur rose from the assembled villeins as the men half dragged the ragged bandit toward her table. His eyes darted wildly around the great hall, and for a moment Faithe almost felt sorry for him.

She was about to ask him about Hengist, but Sir Luke rose slowly to his feet, stilling her tongue. The murmuring tapered off as Hauekleah's new lord regarded Vance in grim silence.

The bandit blinked nervously at the man he'd attempted to slay the day before.

"Where is your companion?" Sir Luke demanded in English.

Vance's throat bobbed. "Dead."

Dunstan nodded in concurrence. "Hengist bled to death in the woods, milord. We found the body."

De Périgueux nodded. "Why did you attack us?"

Vance shrugged elaborately without meeting his accuser's eyes. "Just out for a bit of silver, milord. Sorry for the inconvenience." He stretched his lips into a nearly toothless grin, which dissolved in the face of Sir Luke's unwavering glare.

Circling the table, Luke rested a hand on the back of the chair in which Alex sat surrounded by pillows, quietly observing this interrogation as he sipped his wine.

"My brother," Luke said with quiet menace, "was somewhat more than inconvenienced."

"Aye, well . . ." Vance licked his lips, his gaze leaping everywhere. "Hengist, he got carried away."

"I seem to recall you wielding that sling with enthusiasm."

The bandit nodded jerkily. "Heat of the moment, sire. 'Twill never happen again."

"I intend to ensure that it doesn't."

Faithe cleared her throat; her husband turned to look at her. "I can call a . . . that is, *you* can call a hallmoot."

"Hallmoot?"

"A manorial court. Orrik normally presides over them."

"Or I could hand this dog over to Lord Alberic for a taste of Norman justice."

Alex's expression suddenly sobered, and he aimed a pointed glance at his brother. Norman justice, Faithe knew, would involve a fair measure of torture before execution. Not that her own people wouldn't punish Vance, perhaps even hang him—he and his cousin had preyed on them for years—but it wasn't their custom to engage in the cruel preliminaries the Franks seemed to relish. She wished Orrik were here, instead of dawdling in Foxhyrst. Or perhaps he'd combined the marketing trip with one of those mysterious errands of his—if they *were* errands, and not simply visits to the Widow Aefentid. Orrik could gather a dozen men together and try Vance this very evening, which might satisfy Sir Luke enough that he wouldn't bother getting Lord Alberic involved.

Panic widened Vance's eyes. "Nay, milord, you can't give me over to his lordship."

Sir Luke folded his arms. "The sheriff is better equipped than I to deal with this matter. He's got a cell beneath his castle, and a hangman on staff—a hangman who's got ways of coaxing the truth out of lying mongrels like you before sending you to the Devil. I mean to find out why you attacked us, and if that's what it takes, so be it."

Faithe had heard about the things Norman executioners did to men to get them to talk. Visions of bubbling oil and red-hot irons and gruesome instruments made her shiver. She drew in a breath to beg mercy of her husband, but Alex caught her eye and shook his head fractionally, so she bit her lip and waited. Vance deserved to die, of that there was no question, but it made her ill to think about what would happen to him first.

"Where's Master Orrik?" Vance asked, his gaze skipping frantically over every face in the hall until it lit on Nyle's brother, Baldric, a compact but sturdy fellow with wiry black hair and a nose misshapen from a badly healed break.

"What's it to you?" Baldric snarled. "And how the devil should I know, anyways?" He didn't—Faithe had already questioned him herself about her bailiff's whereabouts—but it was reasonable to think he might. Baldric, as everyone knew—even, it seemed, this sorry bandit—was Orrik's most trusted underling. Dunstan, as reeve, assisted the bailiff in managing Hauekleah, and did a fine job of it, but it was Baldric who acted as Orrik's devoted right hand. When Faithe had questioned Orrik's wisdom in relying so on the foul-tempered and secretive Baldric, he'd pointed out that such men, if they were truly loyal, had their uses.

"My bailiff in elsewhere," Faithe told Vance, "attending to estate business. Why?"

"He'll see things are done right," Vance said, his

gaze shifting. "He'll make sure I get tried in the hallmoot."

"I wouldn't rely on that if I were you," Baldric muttered menacingly.

Sir Luke unfolded his arms and took a step toward Vance, his hands curled at his sides. "I'm master of Hauekleah now. I could have your eyes gouged out this very instant if it suited me. I could have your hands and feet crushed between rocks. I could have your arms and legs pulled until they—"

"Sire, no!" Vance wailed. "I beg of you! Hang me quick, but don't—"

"Silence!" Luke barked.

"Please, sire. I'll tell you everything."

"You heard him," Baldric snarled. "Shut up!"

"I'll tell you why we done what we done, but don't—"

"Save it for the hallmoot," Luke said.

A rush of silence enveloped the great hall, followed by gasps and whispers.

"You'll be tried tomorrow afternoon at compline," he added. "If you cooperate with the questioning, I may be disposed toward mercy—a flogging, perhaps. If not, you can expect a swift hanging."

Vance broke down in tears, blubbering his thanks and promising to tell everything. Alex smiled and winked at Faithe.

"My lady," said Sir Luke, "is there some secure place where this knave could spend the night?"

Faithe nodded. "We have two storehouses out back, near the cookhouse and granary. The smaller one is nearly empty, and it locks. Dunstan knows where Orrik keeps the key."

"Put him there," Sir Luke told the reeve. "Give him bread and ale and some straw to sleep on, but don't let him out for any reason."

"Yes, milord."

Yes, milord. It came so easily from Dunstan's lips,

and sounded so respectful, free of any underlying rancor. Her husband had earned that respect this afternoon. He'd chosen Saxon justice over Norman brutality, and she doubted her people would soon forget it.

"Let us pray," intoned Father Paul, Hauekleah's elderly parish chaplain, as he concluded the blessing of the candlelit marriage chamber. "The Father, and the Son, and the Holy Ghost bless you"—he crossed himself with a quavering hand—"triune in number, and one in name."

"Amen," muttered Luke, flinching under an abrupt spattering of holy water—the final blessing of the bridal couple. At last the old priest bid them good night and shuffled away through the herb-strewn rushes. The witnesses followed him down the stairs into the main hall, except for her ladyship's personal maid, who lingered uncertainly.

"You may go, Moira," said Lady Faithe. "I can get ready for bed by myself."

"Yes, milady." Looking relieved, Moira closed the door behind her.

Luke and his bride stood in pensive silence for a few moments, listening to Moira's heavy footsteps on the stairs. He watched her discreetly as she twisted his mother's emerald ring around and around on her finger. She'd buffed her nails for the occasion, he noticed. That purplish gown turned her hazel eyes cat green and heated up the pink in her cheeks—or perhaps she was blushing.

" 'Tis a handsome chamber," Luke said—in French, mindful that he needed to reinforce his authority even here, in the privacy of his bedchamber. She stiffened slightly, but murmured her thanks in the same language.

He'd said it just for something to say, but it was true. His bride's bedchamber—and now his—was surprisingly spacious and airy, with enormous windows on the back wall. The side walls, being part of the roof of Hauekleah Hall, slanted up to the raftered ceiling, and embroidered tapestries were affixed to these. The furniture, heavy pieces carved of dark woods, included a bed draped with a blanket of silvery wolfskins.

Apparently noticing the direction of his gaze, Lady Faithe turned awkwardly away, plucking out her earrings and storing them in a cabinet that she opened and closed with one of her keys. Reaching up, she lifted off her chaplet of wildflowers and unpinned her veil. She placed both in a big carved chest at the foot of the bed, removing from it a folded linen garment. When she shook it out, he saw that it was a night shift.

She looked down at the dainty gown for a long moment, then reached behind her to fumble for the golden cord that laced up the back of her kirtle. No doubt Moira normally did this for her; it looked to be a challenging maneuver.

"Here," he said, a bit too gruffly. Coming around behind her, he untied the cord and slid it through the first set of eyelets, and then the next and the next, gradually loosening the kirtle—just as he'd imagined doing yesterday. To his disappointment, the gaping silk revealed, not the bare skin of her back, but a white undershift.

Luke wasn't used to finding underclothes on the women he undressed. For the most part his bed partners had been whores; the few who didn't charge outright for their services generally bartered them for gifts of some sort. Such women rarely wore anything beneath their kirtles.

Never in the twelve years he'd been wenching had a woman of rank granted him her favors. Now that one was presumably ready to, he wasn't quite sure what was expected of him—or what to expect from her. There was an unaffected sensuality to her, it was true, yet she was convent-bred, and from all accounts a lady of virtue.

Gently bred women, Luke's father had taught him, were repelled by matters of the flesh. When bedding one's lady wife, the considerate husband should endeavor to spare her tender feelings in every respect. He should be gentle and quick, raising her night clothes only far enough to do what was needed and not touching her more than strictly necessary. Moreover, the act should be performed in darkness, to avoid exposing her eyes to the instrument of her ravishment. Ladies had been known to swoon from the sight.

Lady Faithe hadn't swooned when pulling Alex's chausses off, Luke reminded himself. As he recalled, she had laughed at his concern for her modesty. But, but of course, the situation had been a far cry from the marriage bed, and the instrument in question as quiescent as its owner.

He'd best aim for gentleness, but he wasn't sure he knew how to tup a woman gently. With whores he could do as he wanted, and most often what he wanted after the fury of battle was a hard, mindless rutting that would make him forget, for one long, screaming moment, the creature he'd become. He shouldn't use Lady Faithe that way—didn't want to use her that way—yet it was the only way he knew.

"Thank you," she said when he'd gotten her unlaced all the way. She laid the night shift across the foot of the bed, hesitated, then began gathering up the kirtle to take it off.

Her hands were trembling.

Luke hated being the cause of a woman's trepidation. What would his father do? Yes . . .

He turned his back in a deliberate way and unbuckled his belt. From behind, he heard the rattle of her keys and the whispery rustle of silk.

"May I ask you something, my lord?" she said.

My lord. How he hated to hear the formal address from her lips—especially in the bedchamber. He felt certain she hadn't called her first husband "my lord."

"Aye."

"Why did you choose to have Vance tried in the hallmoot? Why not let Lord Alberic's hangman extract the information you wanted?"

Luke pulled his tunic and undershirt over his head and hung them on a hook with his belt, then untied his hair and combed his fingers through it. "I was merely taking your advice, my lady."

"*My* advice?"

He squatted to remove his boots. "You told me your people would not despise me unless I did despicable things. I have no desire to be despised, only obeyed."

"But you threatened to do those things. You recited a list of tortures, as if you meant to . . . I mean I thought . . ."

"You thought I was monster enough to order those things done to that sorry wretch."

She made no answer. He tossed his boots into a corner a little too forcefully, then rubbed his arm below its throbbing injury. "Often a prisoner will confess his crimes on merely viewing the instruments of torture. The threat of punishment can be as effective as the punishment itself, and far less trouble for all concerned."

"I see," she said quietly.

By the time he was down to his linen drawers—he'd leave those on for the time being, he decided—he heard the squeak of the ropes supporting the mattress. Taking a deep breath, he turned and saw her sitting in her nightgown on the edge of the bed with her back to him, brushing out her hair. The braids had molded it into ripples that reflected the candlelight in shimmering waves. The sight captivated him, and for a moment he merely stood and watched her, admiring the uncomplicated grace of her movements.

Her arms, revealed to the shoulders by her sleeveless nightgown, were slender but solid, shaped by underlying muscle that flexed as she drew the brush through the wavy satin tresses. They were the arms of a woman unafraid of hard work. Luke's stepmother and sisters felt bonelessly soft when he embraced them, and little wonder, given their pampered lives. Lady Faithe wasn't pampered, a fact reflected in her laborer's hands and sun-gilded complexion and supple arms. He wondered how the rest of her would look, when he got that gown off her.

That thought spurred a quickening in his loins. He turned down the wolfskin blanket and linen sheet and sat in bed with them tucked around his waist. The mattress felt deliciously soft beneath him. He'd expected straw; the feathers came as a pleasant surprise.

Setting down her brush, Lady Faithe got under the covers and cast a quick, self-conscious glance in his direction. No sooner had she turned away, however, than she looked back . . . and reached out to him!

Luke's heart hammered in his chest as she touched him, her fingertips gliding lightly up his arm. But when they reached the knot just below his shoulder, they ignited a current of pain that sucked the breath from his lungs.

"I'm sorry," she gasped, recoiling. "I didn't mean to hurt you. It's just that I had no idea your wound was so . . . why didn't you tell me?"

Luke followed her horrified gaze to find his arm from elbow to shoulder stained with angry streaks of purple and red. A spider web of broken capillaries surrounded the hardened, whitish lump on his upper arm. No wonder it pained him so.

"Does it hurt very much?" she asked.

"Nay," he lied.

Lady Faithe shot him a skeptical look, got out of

bed, and flipped her hair behind her so she could sort through the keys on the chain she still wore around her neck. Her night shift laced up the front by means of a pink satin ribbon tied in a bow that fluttered in rhythm with her breathing. Luke bunched the covers more securely around his waist as a familiar heaviness arose in his lower body.

She lifted the lid of the chest at the foot of the bed, retrieved her medicine box, and unlocked it. "Here it is." Holding up a small ceramic vial, she returned to bed and uncorked it.

"What is it?" Luke asked, leaning toward her to inhale the vial's aromatic contents. "Perfume?"

"Spirit of rosemary. 'Tis good for bruising." Tilting the vial onto her fingers, she poured out a little clear, oily liquid. "Tell me if this hurts," she said in a comforting whisper as she tentatively touched the swelling on his upper arm.

"Nay," he said huskily. "It's fine." It did hurt, despite her airy touch, but he was loath to let her know that, for fear she'd cease her ministrations. She smoothed the liniment onto his battered flesh with featherlight strokes, taking seemingly great care not to hurt him. Except for a brief moment when her gaze seemed stolen by the wooden cross nestled in his chest hair, her attention appeared to be riveted on her work. He watched her fingertips draw careful circles all up and down the bruised skin, the slick fluid warming as she worked. A soothing heat soon encompassed his arm, spreading through his shoulder and down into his chest . . . and lower still.

"How does that feel?" she asked, so softly he hardly heard her.

He swallowed hard. "Fine. It feels fine."

She looked up at him through her lashes. "Does it hurt less than it did before?"

"Aye," he said truthfully. "Much less."

She grinned impishly. "I thought it didn't hurt before."

He smiled and shook his head. "Does it amuse you to lay your little traps?"

She stared at him, looking quietly stunned.

"What is it?" he asked.

"You . . . you smiled."

"Did you think I couldn't smile?"

She seemed to ponder that for a moment. "Yes. Yes, I suppose I did." An engaging grin lit her face. "I'm pleased to see I was mistaken."

As she reached toward the night table for the vial's cork, Luke caught a glimpse of dark marks on her inner wrist. She snatched up the cork, but before she could shove it back in the little bottle, he closed a hand over hers.

She gasped, her whole body tensing as he turned her fist so that he could inspect the marks. Clearly, his touch unnerved her, a fact that shamed him. Here he was on his wedding night, and his bride couldn't bear the feel of his hands on her.

Leaning over, his hair falling in his eyes, he ran a fingertip along the silken skin on the underside of her wrist—skin marred by shadowy bruises. She shivered.

He pried her fingers open to retrieve the cork, set it and the vial on the night table, then examined her other wrist, also bruised. She sat perfectly still as he held both her hands in his, stroking his thumbs over the marks. He recalled his brutal handling of her, his absurd accusation that she was trying to kill Alex, and felt only shame for having let the dark beast awaken, if only briefly.

"I . . ." He looked up and met her apprehensive gaze through errant strands of his hair. What could he tell her? That he'd never hurt her again? Who knew when the beast would next arise from its slumber? For the life of him, he couldn't think what to say to her.

How could he reassure her of his harmlessness when he couldn't reassure himself?

"It's all right," she said.

"I wish it were."

He felt the frantic pumping of her pulse through his thumbs as they caressed her wrists. Was it the same drumbeat of awareness that pounded through him—or fear? Letting her go, he dampened his fingers with the spirit of rosemary and lifted her right hand, cradling it in his palm.

"This isn't necessary," she protested as he gently massaged the liniment into her wrist.

"Does it cause you pain?"

"Nay."

"Then allow me this small indulgence."

She lapsed into silence as he ministered to her, his fingertips rough against her smooth skin, even through the film of warm oil. Her pulse still raced, and that pink satin ribbon fluttered continually.

Arousal thrummed within him as he released her right hand and went to work on her left. The urge to lower her onto her back and press his body into hers was almost irresistible. Lady Faithe was a beautiful woman, extraordinarily beautiful, and he'd been without the comfort of a woman's arms during his two months at St. Albans. He also thought he might like to have children, now that his life had taken on some semblance of normality. But he'd never bedded a woman who wasn't entirely and enthusiastically willing. Even whores were eager, if only for the coins in his purse. Not once had he even considered taking a woman who hadn't come to him of her own free will.

Until now.

With a mental shake, he reminded himself that she was his wife. He had every right to bed her. She would expect it. She'd think it strange if he didn't. And he wanted to. God knew he wanted to.

"My lord?"

He'd been sitting with her hand in his, lost in thought. Abruptly, he released her and dragged his fingers through his hair.

"I'll put this away." Recorking the vial, she got up and tucked it in her medicine box, then replaced the box in the big carved chest. Her keys clattered against the lid as she bent over to latch it. For a fleeting moment her gown dipped open, and he saw her breasts almost in their entirety—flawless ivory globes, too large to cup with a single hand.

When she returned to bed, Luke said, "Take that off."

She froze, her expression of alarm transforming to something else. Resignation? Anticipation? Raising a tremulous hand to the bodice of her nightgown, she began tugging on the pink ribbon.

"Not that." He stilled her hand with a touch, then hooked a finger under the chain hanging around her neck. "This. I don't care to listen to these keys jangling all night."

Her eyes flickered with something that might have been relief, or possibly just puzzlement. "As you wish, my lord." Ducking her head, she pulled the chain off and laid it on the night table, then shook out her lustrous hair.

As you wish, my lord. Luke had no doubt that, if he climbed on top of Lady Faithe, she would lie still for it. She would consider it her obligation to give in to her husband's needs, and she would grit her teeth and do so. Never mind that her husband was the dreaded Black Dragon, slayer of Saxons, and that she cringed at his very touch. She'd do her duty; if he wanted her, he could have her.

And oh, how he wanted her. But not if she acquiesced simply because she felt she had no choice—or, worse yet, out of fear.

Leaning over the side of the bed, he blew out the candle, immersing the chamber in moonlight. He lay down and adjusted the covers over himself, and Lady Faithe did the same.

For some time they lay side by side in the dark, the only sound their breathing. He absorbed her heat, her scent. He wondered what she was thinking, and how she would react if he took her in his arms.

"Are you afraid of me?" he asked quietly.

Long moments passed, and he began to wonder if she'd fallen asleep. Finally, she said, "A little."

A little was enough.

"Good night." He rolled away from her, punching his pillow.

"Good night, my lord," she said presently, and rolled in the other direction.

Chapter 5

Faithe awoke before dawn, which was not unusual for her, since she required little sleep and generally got up before her staff began rising. She'd thought perhaps she would sleep later this morning, given her wakefulness during the night, but like most farm creatures, she was ruled more by habit and instinct than rationality.

She dressed in the dark so as not to disturb her husband, fast asleep with his back to her. He'd spent a restless night as well; she'd heard him stirring next to her. The bed had felt too small for the two of them. It had never felt so with Caedmon, but then Caedmon, although a good-sized man, hadn't been as large as Sir Luke. Also, she and Caedmon had been used to sleeping together. She didn't know if she'd ever get used to sleeping with the Black Dragon. Once during the night, her foot accidentally brushed his leg, and they both quickly moved away from each other. She'd spent most of the night huddled at the edge of the bed to avoid touching him.

Lifting her keys off the night table slowly, so as to keep them from rattling, she looped the chain around her neck and pulled her hair out from beneath it. Faithe wished he hadn't ordered her to take them off last night. She hated being without them. They made her feel secure and capable. She might look like an unkempt girl, but when people saw the keys, they knew she was a person of consequence, and they treated her as such. Not wearing the keys made her feel incomplete.

She grabbed her medicine box and eased the door open, wondering if Alex had slept well, and whether his poultices had stayed on. He'd insisted that she not check up on him during the night. It was her wedding night, he'd said; she had better things to do than bother with him. And anyway, he was much improved, and would prefer to be left alone than awakened and fussed with. He'd been quite vehement on the subject. When Faithe stepped out onto the landing and looked down into the moonlit main hall, she saw why.

Alex was not alone. Sharing his pallet, as naked as he, was Blossom; Faithe knew it was she by her single disheveled braid. They were both asleep, she curled in his embrace with her back to him. The woolen blanket was drawn up only to their waists, revealing Alex's hand cradling one of her breasts. Her clothes lay strewn in the rushes, where they'd no doubt gotten tossed during the evening's frolics.

Faithe couldn't wrest her gaze from the sleeping couple as she descended the stairs and approached them. Blossom, although sound asleep, looked flushed and peaceful. Alex had his face against her hair, his mouth half open. The bandage had come off his head, but at least he was sleeping on his good side. Faithe was both impressed and appalled that he'd taken on Blossom in his condition. She hoped he hadn't done himself any permanent damage.

They looked like two of the barn kittens in their box, she thought, standing over them. Faithe missed that physical closeness, the animal comfort of curling up with another warm body. She envied those two that intimacy, regardless of its basis in simple lust.

Despite her misgivings at being wed to Sir Luke, part of her had been excited at the prospect of his bedding her. God help her, there was something strangely seductive about his predatory nature. He provoked the same thrill in her that she'd felt, as a child, when Orrik had tethered a boar to a tree and she'd challenged herself to see how close she could get to the enraged creature without flinching. She'd gotten near enough to stare into its monstrous black eyes, to tremble at its fearsome tusks and choke on its stink. And then, without warning, it had lunged for her, sending her squealing into Orrik's arms.

But there was more to the Black Dragon than the beast for whom he'd been named. There was a man as well, a man who could braid hair and massage liniment into bruised wrists, his touch roughly gentle and completely bewitching. He was a creature of contradictions—a fusion of man and beast. When Luke de Périgueux finally saw fit to claim his husbandly rights, she wondered which of the two would do the deed, the man or the beast.

Faithe uncovered and rebuilt the fire, lit a lantern, then leaned down and whispered Blossom's name until the young woman stirred, blinking. "Milady?" she muttered groggily.

" 'Tis best you get up and get dressed before everyone else is awake."

Nodding, Blossom stretched like a cat, her lush body quivering. Alex growled contentedly as Blossom arched against him, then he stretched, too. Their resemblance to a boxful of kittens was now complete.

Blossom sat up and tried to rise, but Alex, who hadn't yet opened his eyes, caught hold of her braid as it brushed across his face and pulled her down. Curling his arm once more around her, he tucked her into the curve of his body and pulled up the blanket. "Stay," he murmured.

"She can't stay," Faithe said. "She's got to help Cook get breakfast ready."

Alex squeezed one eye open. "Faithe?"

A smile quirked her lips.

He glanced at Blossom as she lifted his arm off her

and clambered to her feet, indifferent to her rather spectacular nudity. "Awfully sorry about this," he said, his gaze fixed wistfully on Blossom.

"No, you're not." Faithe plucked Blossom's undershift off the floor as she stood and handed it to the shivering wench.

"No." Alex grinned boyishly. "I'm not."

"I suppose it's too much to ask that your poultices have survived intact."

"Poultices?" Alex lifted the blanket and peeked beneath it. "I can't imagine what might have become of . . . ah." He fumbled beneath him and handed her the squashed remains of one of the herbal compresses.

"Thank you," she said dryly as she accepted the offering.

Blossom lowered her kirtle over her head, wriggling as she smoothed it down. Alex sighed and grabbed at the hem of her skirt, but she laughingly sidestepped him. Snatching her slippers out of the rushes, she balanced first on one foot and then the other to tug them on.

Faithe swiftly laced up the back of Blossom's kirtle. "Go bring me a bucket of water, and then see if Ardith needs you."

"Yes, milady."

Alex followed the kitchen wench with his eyes as she dashed out of the hall. "She's got a lot of . . . vitality. She and her sister both."

Faithe unlocked her medicine box. "How did you happen to choose Blossom over Bonnie?"

"I didn't. They chose for me. Drew straws or some such. From what I could gather of their conversation—it was all in English, of course—they intend to take turns."

"Seems rather sporting of them."

"Oh, they're very keen on sharing. Do you know, they wanted to have a go at me together?"

"No, really?" Faithe said dryly, the memory still

fresh in her mind of coming upon the twins and one of the more strapping plowmen disporting themselves in an empty stall of the barn last summer. "Seems a generous offer."

"Too generous. I turned it down." He grimaced as he shifted position on the pallet. "In my present condition, I doubt I would have lived through it."

"A prudent decision."

Blossom returned with the water, then departed, blowing Alex a cheery kiss. Faithe put the water on to warm and set about replacing Alex's poultices. They chatted amiably, but Faithe's mind was elsewhere. She kept thinking back to last night. The more she pondered it, the more perplexed she was that Sir Luke had chosen not to consummate the marriage. Several theories occurred to her, the most discomforting being that his affections lay elsewhere—that there was another woman somewhere to whom he was determined to remain faithful despite his marriage of property to Faithe.

Faithe cleared her throat as she smoothed down the poultice on Alex's hip. "I was wondering something about your brother."

"Aye?"

"He's . . . well, he's clearly a . . . well, quite a virile man, and not unattractive. I was thinking that if I were a woman . . . well, of course I'm a woman, but . . . that women must find him . . . that he must have had many . . . and probably still does . . . have at least one . . ."

"Are you asking whether he has a mistress?"

Faithe took a deep breathe and let it out. "Yes."

Alex shook his head. "He never has."

"Never?"

"He's a soldier, Faithe. Or was. Soldiers don't tend to stay in one place long enough to form alliances of that sort. Not that he's inexperienced with women . . . exactly. He's been with many women. But women of, well, a certain sort. Women who don't expect him to be there in the morning, if you understand my meaning."

"Ah."

Alex smiled. "Yes."

They spoke of other things as she treated the wound to his side, and then moved on to his head. Faithe waited for the opportunity to investigate her other theory about Sir Luke's reluctance to bed her, and when Alex mentioned their family in Périgueux, she pounced.

"Is your family very close?" she asked, easing into the rather awkward question at the heart of the matter.

"Not really. Except for Luke and me. Our mother died when I was very little, and we had a sister, Alienor, who died about ten years ago. I'm the youngest, then there are two sisters—three if you count Alienor—then Luke, then our eldest brother, Christien. Christien inherited our father's estate when he died at Christmastide." Alex executed a perfunctory sign of the cross. "And then there's the son of my father's second wife."

"Just the one child?"

"Aye. Lady Elise seemed to find the production of children distasteful in the extreme. No sooner did my father's seed quicken in her belly than she moved into separate quarters. He spent quite a long time trying to woo her back. Finally, he sought diversion elsewhere, but he wasn't happy about it. After years of lecturing his sons about fidelity in marriage, here he was with a mistress."

Faithe tied off the bandage, appalled at the idea that a woman would choose not to have babies, when she so longed for them. "Are all of your brothers and sisters . . . healthy?"

"For the most part. Alienor had been very ill before

she died. She suffered terribly. Our fool of a chaplain claimed she was possessed."

Faithe grew more alert. "Her mind was affected?"

"Aye, toward the end she was"—he shook his head grimly—"quite out of her senses, and in agony. 'Twas horrible, what she went through. The surgeon said 'twas a fever of the brain, and he bled her every day until my sire put a stop to it. Finally, he found a Moslem physician who seemed to know what was what. He said she had a lump growing inside her head." A knowing look narrowed his eyes. "Why are you interested in this? What are you digging for?"

"Nothing." She hastily packed up her things.

He guffawed, suddenly his old, carefree self again. "You're trying to find out whether there's madness in the family!"

She snapped down the lid of her medicine box. "That's absurd." It was also true. Father Paul had confided to her once that one reason he'd chosen a life of celibacy was to avoid passing on the lunacy that had ravaged his family. It was the only rationale Faithe could think of offhand for a landholding knight to opt for a celibate—and therefore childless—marriage. Most men in Sir Luke's position were eager for heirs.

"Rest assured," Alex gasped out through his laughter, "that the de Périgueux family is remarkably free of any and all interesting specimens, including madmen. Luke has tried to claim that distinction from time to time, but in fact he's the sanest of the whole dreary lot—which is probably why he's so sullen and miserable."

"That's reassuring," she said flatly.

"Aren't you a bit late with these inquiries? You've already gone and married him. There's no way to back out now—short of annulment."

Faithe stilled in the act of locking the medicine box. Annulment. Nonconsummation was grounds for annulment, wasn't it? Could it be that her husband regretted this hastily arranged marriage, and was even now maneuvering for release from his vows? If he refrained from exercising his marital rights, such release should be a simple formality, and then Faithe would be shipped off to some convent, and Hauekleah . . .

Hauekleah would be his. He'd simply take it from her, as he'd once threatened to. Then he could remarry if he chose. He could make some other woman mistress of Hauekleah. Some other woman would have everything she'd worked so hard to maintain, everything she'd vowed to keep from the Normans, everything she'd sacrificed herself for. She'd offered herself—her very body—to an infamously brutal Norman, and he didn't even want her because he could have Hauekleah without her. Eight hundred years, gone in a heartbeat.

"Faithe?" Alex was propped up on an elbow, studying her with a worried expression as she twisted the emerald ring around and around on her finger. "You've gone white. Are you ill?"

"Nay," she breathed, although she felt as if her insides had contracted into a single hot coal in her stomach.

"Do you need anything?" he asked solicitously. "Something to drink?"

"I need the truth," she said grimly. "Tell me the truth."

"Of course." He tried to sit up, but clenched his teeth and fell back onto the pallet. "The truth about what?"

"Your brother's plans. Has he spoken to you about ending this marriage? Is that why you mentioned annulment?"

Alex's expression sobered. "My brother is not without his faults, but he'd never enter into a marriage under false pretenses. He's an honorable man. Surely you can sense that."

She could. Despite his reputation and his fierce manner, Luke de Périgueux struck her as a man with scruples, the kind of man who wouldn't lower himself to such underhanded scheming. But why, then, was he disinclined to consummate their marriage?

Faithe prided herself on her ability to identify a problem and implement a solution, something she did a dozen times a day as part of her management of Hauekleah. What was this but one more problem to be solved? All that was needed was to analyze the situation dispassionately and formulate a strategy to deal with it.

She solved problems all the time. She was good at it. She could solve this one.

Alex smiled. "How ridiculous to think Luke would want to end a marriage to someone with a smile like yours. Whatever put the thought in your head?"

Scrambling for a response, she said, "I just thought perhaps he might choose to return to soldiering, once he's gotten a taste of farm life. And then he might petition for an annulment, rather than be burdened with Hauekleah."

"I can't see him ever considering Hauekleah a burden," Alex said.

Wait until he's seen how much work goes into farming, Faithe thought with a mental smirk. Sir Luke wanted Hauekleah very much—right now. But, like Thorgeirr, he would likely change his mind once he saw what he'd gotten into.

"Moreover," Alex continued, "annulments can't be had just for the asking. There have to be grounds."

Faithe rose and stirred the fire with a poker. From the corner of her eye she saw Alex regarding her with a speculative expression. She'd said too much; she could almost hear him adding up the pieces.

But when he spoke, all he said was, "Luke means

to make Hauekleah his home. He has no intention of returning to soldiering. I will, of course, once I'm recovered enough to handle a broadsword."

"That could take all summer," she said.

"If you're willing to have me underfoot for that long, I think I'd rather enjoy it."

"I'd love to have you, but are you sure you won't be bored here?"

His gaze lit on something out of Faithe's range of vision. She turned to see Bonnie—she recognized her by the two braids—coming through the front door with a flask of ale and a bowl of porridge. "Blossom told me you were awake," she said as she crossed to Alex and knelt at his side with a coy smile. "Some breakfast will help you get your strength back."

Alex met Faithe's gaze, anticipation sparking in his eyes. "Somehow, I don't think boredom will be a problem."

"Master Orrik's coming up the road!" called a red-haired boy from the doorway of Hauekleah Hall. Luke looked up from the bread and watered ale with which he was breaking his fast. "He's got a new cart!" the boy added excitedly.

Luke stood up from the table. "Where is Lady Faithe?" he asked the boy. She'd been absent from the hall when he'd awakened.

"In Middeltun, sire."

"Middeltun? Is that some town near here?"

Alex, propped up in a chair enjoying a shave by one of his twins, chuckled indulgently. "Don't know Hauekleah very well, do you? Middeltun is Faithe's demesne field—as opposed to the village's fields. It's the one she cultivates herself."

"They give their fields names?"

"So it seems." Alex tilted his chin up so that the wench attending to him could scrape the razor over his throat. How he would have laughed if he'd seen

Luke wrest that knife out of Lady Faithe's hand two days ago.

The buxom wench took Alex's face between her hands and gently altered the position of his head, cooing praise for his patience. The bondman called Firdolf, breakfasting at the other end of the hall, stared at the girl with great hound-eyes and glowered at Alex. If Luke's brother was aware of the young man's rabid jealousy, he gave no sign of it. Most likely he knew that, even in his wounded condition, he would triumph in a fair fight. Firdolf was big and young and brawny, but he moved a little too slowly and looked a little too harmless to be counted a threat.

"Can't you shave yourself?" Luke asked his brother.

Alex grinned as the wench planted a soft kiss on his forehead before proceeding with her work; Firdolf rose abruptly and stalked sluggishly from the hall. "Why would I want to?"

Why indeed? "How come you to know so much about Hauekleah?" Luke asked.

"She told me. We talk." Alex laughed. "Oh, don't look so sour, brother. I'm not trying to steal your wife out from under you."

"How reassuring," Luke said wryly.

" 'Twould be easy enough if I put my mind to it, though. Neglected brides are generally ripe for the picking." He tilted his head; the young woman ran the razor over his soapy cheek, dipped it in a bowl of water, and repeated the process.

"Neglected?" Luke couldn't believe she would have spoken to his brother about last night.

Alex shrugged elaborately. "I only meant it's the morning after your wedding, and you seem to have lost track of her already. A newly married couple ought not to emerge from the bedchamber till nones, and then they ought to need help walking."

"Thank you for your opinion," Luke ground out,

wishing his brother weren't quite so artlessly perceptive. He had no desire to share with anyone, even Alex, his ambivalence about bedding his bride.

"Shall I fetch Lady Faithe, milord?" the boy asked.

"Aye."

He raced out the door. Luke followed at an unhurried pace, squinting at the dazzling sunlight that greeted him when he emerged from Hauekleah Hall. He strolled through the gate of the stone wall that enclosed the house and peered down the road to watch the approach of a horse-drawn wooden cart with two oversize wheels. It was too far away for him to make out the driver. A flash of movement to his left caught Luke's attention; he watched the red-haired boy dart through a stand of trees by the side of the road.

Luke traced the boy's path through the trees. Beyond them he discovered an enormous, plowed field nestled in the crook of the river that curved through Hauekleah. Men and women dotted the field, broadcasting seed with great sweeps of their arms. To the east, beyond the river, sheep grazed in a pasture surrounded by rolling open meadows. The meadowland, punctuated by woodland patches and a network of rivulets, was a deep, saturated green, the cloudless sky an unearthly blue.

The sight literally stole Luke's breath. Not since his childhood in the Aquitaine countryside had he seen earth and sky meet in such jewel-toned splendor. Warm breezes caressed him, ruffling his unbound hair. He breathed deeply, filling his lungs with the perfume of his boyhood—fertile earth, spring grasses, a whiff of manure, and an underlying note of fruitiness. Scanning the landscape, he spied it, to the north on the opposite bank of the river—a vineyard planted in orderly rows. Now he truly felt as if he had come home.

One of the field workers—a woman, backlit by the morning sun—was walking toward him across the field, accompanied by a child. Only when Luke saw the child's bright head did he realize that this was the red-haired boy—and that the woman with him must be Lady Faithe.

She wore a broad-brimmed, conical straw hat over loose hair, and the same ankle-revealing kirtle that she'd had on when he met her. To his astonishment he saw that her feet were bare. Snugged up against her hip was a curved basket half filled with grain and secured by a leather strap looped over one shoulder.

"You were sowing grain?" he asked her incredulously.

She smiled, as if amused by his astonishment. "Winter wheat. The first planting goes in right after the spring crops are sown."

"Of all the sorts of work for you to be doing . . ." he began.

"Work is work," she said carelessly. " 'Tis all the same to me."

"Evidently."

"Sowing wheat is relaxing."

"Relaxing!"

He gazed over her shoulder at the field workers, each with a basket like hers, dispersing the sparkling grain in practiced arcs. A little girl scampered around a big open sack on the ground, scaring the crows away with a stick.

"It *is* relaxing," she said. "With other chores, I must always be thinking about what I'm doing. But with seeding, I get into a rhythm, and then my mind is free to venture elsewhere. I like to do it when I have things to think about, or problems to solve."

She ducked her head to fiddle with the strap on the basket, but not before he saw her face stain pink. Had she revealed more than she had intended? Was she thinking about last night? Had he, with his reluctance to consummate this marriage, been reduced to one of her problems to be solved?

"Your bailiff has returned," Luke said shortly.

"Orrik?" Lady Faithe looked up, instantly animated. She untied the hat and removed it, then lifted the strap of the basket over her head and handed it to the boy.

"Look, milady!" The boy pointed to the sky behind them. Luke and Lady Faithe shielded their eyes to peer overhead. "Three of 'em! That's your lucky sign, isn't it?"

"So it is," murmured Lady Faithe, her attention riveted on the three majestic hawks soaring in elegant circles over the field. Luke admired the ease with which she switched back and forth between French with him and English with the boy.

"What kind are they?" he asked, thinking he might take up hawking if he could raise the proper breeds.

"I can't tell from this distance," she said, still staring skyward. "There are so many different types around here. This region is known for them. That's how Hauekleah got its name. It means meadow of the hawks."

Luke's gaze shifted from the hawks to his wife, craning her neck, her eyes translucent in the morning sun, smiling with unabashed pleasure. God, she was beautiful—not in the way he'd come to associate with noble ladies. Her clothes were absurd, her hair untidy, as usual. And that hat! Yet, standing here with the verdant grandeur of her fields and pastures behind her, she looked so right, so perfect—a creature entirely in communion with her world.

It was a rare and precious world, a community intimately linked to the seasons, whose entire reason for being was to coax sustenance from the land. This woman's link to this land, Luke realized, had taken centuries to forge. No wonder she was so covetous of Hauekleah, so willing to offer herself as the spoils of war if only she could keep it.

"Good things will happen for you now, milady," the

boy announced gravely. "You've seen your lucky sign."

"Yes, well . . ." She ruffled his gleaming hair, then pointed to the seed basket. "Dump that back in the sack, Alfrith. Then help Cwen with the crows."

The boy's shoulders slumped in an exaggerated display of disappointment; clearly, crow duty was not his favorite chore.

"And at terce," she said, "you and Cwen may go to the kitchen and finish the rest of the hazelnut crumble from yest—"

"Oh, milady, thank you!" Alfrith raced toward the field with sudden determination. "I'll do a good job with the crows, I promise you."

"I'm sure you will." Chuckling, she turned and gestured for Luke to follow her back through the trees. "Come. I'll introduce you to Orrik."

The road was empty. "He must be coming to the back of the house," she said. Luke accompanied her back up the road and through the front gate of Hauekleah Hall. But instead of going inside, she led him around the side of the house, across a lawn planted with shade trees.

He couldn't help thinking what a strange pair they made. With her light-footed gait and her big, silly hat swinging to and fro in her hand, Lady Faithe looked the very image of pastoral innocence. Whereas Luke . . . he looked like what he was. An invader. An interloper. The black insect on the honey cake.

"You won't be able to speak your language with Orrik," she told him as they rounded the back of the house and proceeded up a flagstone walk through a kitchen garden that took up most of the walled croft. "He reads and writes Latin, but he refuses to learn French. He understands a little if it's spoken clearly, but he insists he'll never speak it himself."

"Eventually I'll expect all of Hauekleah's villeins to speak it—at least, those who answer directly to me."

She bristled slightly, but made no response. Past the garden, built up against the stone enclosure at the back of the croft, stood a cluster of small thatched structures. "The two in the right-hand corner are the storehouses," said Lady Faithe, pointing. "Vance is being held in the smaller one."

The flagstone walk terminated at a gate in the back of the stone wall; beyond it, he saw chickens pecking in the dirt. "There's a privy back there," she said, which he was glad to hear; he didn't care for chamber pots, and the woods were a bit far away for convenience. "Also the poultry house, barn, and stable."

The chickens shrieked and scattered in a panic. First one harnessed horse, and then another, came into view, followed by the cart, driven by a brawny man in a short, hooded cloak. The cart paused just outside the gate, and the man jumped down to swing it open.

"Isn't it rather early in the morning for him to be returning from such a distance?" Luke asked as they neared the gate.

"He probably spent the night with . . . a friend of his, down the road."

"A lady friend, I assume." These Saxons were the randiest people he'd ever met.

Faithe half smiled. "The Widow Aefentid. She has an inn on the other side of the woods."

By the time they got to the gate, a small crowd had gathered around the cart, but they moved aside to let Luke and Faithe pass. Lady Faithe walked up to the driver, who was unlatching and lowering the vehicle's leather-hinged back. "That's a fine cart, Orrik," she said.

Orrik lowered his hood as he turned toward her. "I thank you, my—" His expression turned grim when he noticed Luke.

He was older than Luke had anticipated, probably close to sixty, but with the solid build of a much younger man. He wore his silver gray hair twisted into a knot at his nape, and, like nearly all Saxon men, a beard—although, unlike most, his was neatly trimmed. His eyebrows were jet slashes over eyes that glowed like new steel against his tanned face. Luke knew immediately that this was not a man to dismiss lightly.

Orrik spared Luke only the most cursory glance. "So that's him, then." He spat into the dirt, then hauled a large key out of the cart and set it on the ground. Turning, he grabbed two small sacks. "I got those nails, and a hundred tallow candles. Got a good price on the quicklime and the tar. The salt was a bit dear, though."

Lady Faithe took a step toward her bailiff. "Orrik . . ."

"They tell me you already married the evil, murderous, stinking son of a—"

"Orrik!" Faithe shot a quick, wary look toward Luke and said, "He understands English."

Orrik cocked an eyebrow in Luke's direction and continued unloading his supplies.

"And we did get married," Faithe said, gripping her straw hat in her fists, "so he's my husband now, and lord of Hauekleah, so you mustn't say such things."

"I take back 'stinking.' " Orrik hauled out a bolt of brown wool and another of green and laid them on top of the keg. "He has no odor at all that I can discern. Doesn't seem quite natural. As far as I know, the rest still applies."

"Orrik, please."

"Nay, my lady," Luke said in English, keeping his voice level. "Let him talk. I like to know who I'm dealing with."

Orrik met Luke's gaze squarely for the first time. "You're dealing . . . *my lord* . . . with a man who saw firsthand what you bloodthirsty butchers did at Hastings. I saw hundreds—*hundreds*—of Englishmen mown down by your ungodly crossbows."

"I was at Hastings, too," Luke said. " 'Twas a battle, not a massacre. Both sides fought nobly."

"Nobly? You haven't heard what your William did to our king, then, after he'd been blinded by an arrow in the eye."

"I've heard it, but I don't believe it. All battles produce such tales."

"Granted," Orrik said, his voice soft with menace. "But in this case the tale is true, for I was among the men making that last stand with King Harold, and I saw it all from my ditch." The bystanders fell into silence. " 'Twas dusk when they rode up, your William and three of his men. They drew their swords, and all I could do was hold my tongue and watch, or they would have slain me, too. First William stabbed Harold in the chest, then the rest went to work on him. One cut his belly open and pulled out his innards, while another hacked off his head. The third man cut off his . . ." Orrik glanced at Lady Faithe. "Another part of him. And wrapped it up and tucked it in his saddlebag, for what purpose I can't begin to imagine." He drew in an unsteady breath, his face washed of color, clearly shaken by the memory.

Dear God, Luke thought, *he's telling the truth.* And the worst of it was, Luke wasn't even surprised. Although a natural leader, William had never struck him as a man of honor. Now he knew his instinct had been correct.

"Harold was a great king," Orrik said. "Strong and just and even-tempered. And that's the way your *noble* William chose to end his life." Spitting on the ground again, he wheeled around and hefted a stack of slate. "Justify that, if you can."

"I can't," Luke said. "Nor can I justify most of what I've seen during my years of soldiering—nor most of what I've done, for that matter."

"I daresay that's true." Orrik grunted as he dragged

four iron tires out of the cart. "Else they wouldn't call you the Black Dragon."

"They don't anymore," Lady Faithe interjected, her voice icy. "I won't allow it. From anyone." She exchanged a meaningful look with her bailiff, who grimaced and wiped his brow with the sleeve of his homespun tunic.

"Yes, my lady," he ground out.

She took a step toward him, her mouth set in a determined line. When she spoke again, very softly, it was in Latin, which Luke knew none of the onlookers could understand. "You must set an example for the others, Orrik. They look up to you."

"Milady, for God's—"

"Don't force me to try and decide what to do with you if you persist in this open disrespect. I've known you since I was born, and I love you like a father. You kept Hauekleah functioning while I was at St. Mary's, and I'll always be indebted to you for that. But Luke de Périgueux is my husband now, Orrik."

"Yes, but, milady—"

"He's my husband, and I can brook no insolence toward him from anyone, even you. Especially you. Do you understand?"

They stared each other down for several long moments, and then Orrik gritted his teeth and said, "I understand perfectly, my lady."

"Good," she whispered hoarsely.

Chapter 6

Looking down, Faithe saw that she'd crushed the brim of her straw hat in her fists. Prying her rigid fingers from the crumpled headgear, she handed it to the smithy's young daughter, standing nearby. "Would you give this to Moira to fix, Esme?"

"Yes, milady." The girl took the hat and ran off toward the manor house.

Overwhelmed with sorrow, for she'd never had to speak thusly to Orrik, she turned away from him, only to find Sir Luke staring at her with the oddest expression.

He'd observed her dressing-down of Orrik in silence, as if conceding this dubious privilege to her. Now he scrutinized her as if she were a thing he'd never seen before, his keen eyes tempered by a warmth that took her completely by surprise. He held her gaze for a moment, and then he nodded slightly, as if to say she'd done well.

She nodded back. Then, needing to flee Orrik's disapproving glare and the watchful eyes of her villeins, she walked back through the gate and into the croft. To her relief, Sir Luke came with her; she would not have wanted him alone with Orrik.

"Good morning, milady . . . milord," called Dunstan from the garden path. His nephew, little Felix, accompanied him, a horn of ale in one hand and a hunk of brown bread in the other. They paused at the door to the small storehouse. "Time for this sorry wretch to break his fast," Dunstan told Baldric, who was standing guard. Baldric withdrew a large key from his tunic.

"Did you have any trouble with him?" asked Sir Luke as he approached the storehouse, Faithe on his heels.

Dunstan shook his head as Baldric turned the key in the lock. "He went in easy enough. How was he during the night, Baldric?"

"Not a peep." Baldric swung the door open.

A fetid stench assaulted them, wafting out of the storehouse in a wave. Faithe's body reacted in advance of her mind, her gorge rising even before she'd put a name to the smell: Death.

Felix shrieked, the horn slipping from his fingers to soak the ground with ale. Dunstan hissed an Anglo-Saxon oath. Baldric, seemingly unmoved, looked on with an expression of vague curiosity.

Sir Luke stepped in front of her, blocking her view of the interior of the storehouse. When she tried to squeeze around him, he grabbed her shoulders and spun her away from the open doorway. "Nay, my lady," he said gruffly.

"I want to see—"

"No, you don't."

"Let go of me," Faithe demanded in a furious whisper, but he only held her tighter. She glanced toward Orrik and the others, filing into the croft to see why Felix had screamed. "They mustn't see me like this. You'll make me look weak in their eyes. Now, let me go."

His gaze searched hers. She thought she detected a trace of admiration on his part, mingled with foreboding. He closed his eyes, his jaw set, then grudgingly released her.

Sidestepping him, Faithe filled her lungs with air and strode up to the doorway. She hesitated when she heard the droning—a low, almost inaudible insect murmur—but she summoned her nerve and stepped inside.

The breath left her in a gust, one hand automatically covering her mouth while the other groped for the door frame. Sir Luke's strong hands wrapped around her waist from behind, supporting her. If not for him, she doubted her legs would have held her up.

"Have you seen enough?" he asked, his voice low and rough.

Christ, yes. But try as she might, she couldn't avert her gaze from the gruesome sight.

Vance hung suspended in a haze of dust motes, rotating slowly at the end of a noose tied to a ceiling beam. A ribbon of glittering sunlight shot through the vent hole near the ceiling to play over his lifeless body. His face, when it came into view, was dark and bloated.

But it wasn't the sight of his corpse, or even the noxious odor, that undid her. It was the flies. She didn't see them until the beam of light hit his face, and then she quickly squeezed her eyes shut, but the image remained. *God,* there were hundreds of them, crawling over his filmy eyes, swarming in his gaping, toothless mouth.

Her insides felt as if they were being slowly pulled up through her throat. Thank God she hadn't eaten breakfast; if she had food in her stomach, she would surely have lost it by now, in front of everybody.

"Come, my lady." Sir Luke pulled her gently back from the doorway, one arm encircling her.

"Nay." Faithe wrested away from him and braced an arm on the outside wall of the storehouse. "Don't hold on to me. They mustn't see." She closed her eyes and felt everything sway sickeningly, as if she were standing in a rowboat.

"For God's sake. They know you're human."

"They depend on me to be strong." Faithe raised a shaky hand to her forehead as sweat sprang out on her face. She felt curiously cold all over, as if the life were draining swiftly from her body . . .

Or as if she were getting ready to faint. She knew the feeling. She was prone to fainting in reaction to strong upsets; a physician had explained it as an imbalance in the bodily humors.

"Nay," she gasped, lurching away from her husband, away from Dunstan and Felix. She hated to faint in front of her people—to make a humiliatingly public display of her frailty.

"Come sit down." Sir Luke took her arm and tried to lead her to one of the benches at the edge of the kitchen garden, but she batted him away. She started for the house, then stopped in her tracks. The house would be full of people. No one must see. Turning, she walked on quaking legs in the other direction, back up the flagstone path toward the gate at the rear of the croft.

Clutching her skirt in quivering fists, she willed herself to remain upright and conscious—at least until she'd gotten to the barn, where she could be alone.

Orrik said her name, but she ignored him. The crowd stood aside for her as she bolted between them, walking toward the barn as quickly as she could without attracting undue attention. Her lips went numb; cold sweat trickled between her breasts. She could barely resist the urge to stop and put her head between her knees.

The doors to the barn stood open, thank God. She stumbled inside and leaned against a supporting post, her head down, breathless and trembling. It was cool in here, and dark, and smelled comfortingly of straw and livestock.

"My lady."

She raised her head to see a dark silhouette in the open doorway.

The Black Dragon, she mused, light-headed. *The Black Dragon has followed me here.*

"Go away." She pushed away from the post and tried to stand on her own, but things whirled drunkenly.

Faithe expected to feel the hard-packed earth slamming into her, but she felt his arms instead, banding around to crush her to his broad chest. She felt her feet lift off the ground, felt herself cradled against him like a child.

The Black Dragon is carrying me away, she thought in the graying moment before oblivion claimed her.

Faithe felt a shivery tickle on the toes of one foot, and wriggled them. The tickle was replaced by a series of soft, small blows, as if she were being attacked by some miniature creature, like a fairy . . .

She opened her eyes, baffled to find herself lying on her side in straw, and peered down toward her feet. A tiny, smoke-colored kitten—one of that spring's barn litter—batted eagerly at her toes while a shyer litter mate watched from the relative safety of its box.

Faithe realized she was in the empty stall reserved for the cats. She'd fainted, and Sir Luke must have brought her here. An awareness dawned, she felt a solid mass beneath her head, and saw a pair of long legs stretched out from that mass, and realized she was lying with her head in his lap! He must be leaning back against the mound of straw in the corner. The wool of his tunic, scratchy-soft beneath her cheek, did not mask the rock-hard muscles of his thighs. She sensed great strength held in check, which only magnified the intimacy of their positions.

Nonplussed, she lay very still and watched the smoky little kitten abandon her toes for the more tempting lure of Sir Luke's boot ties. Pouncing, the novice mouser furiously swatted a loose cord with its paws.

A large hand appeared in her field of vision as Luke

plucked up a piece of straw and tapped it on the knee of his chausses. The kitten stilled, then crouched behind the boot, staring at the jiggling straw with the fixed gaze of the natural-born hunter.

Smoky—for that's what she would name this kitten, she decided—crept stealthily onto Luke's legs, hunkered down, and finally leapt, attacking the piece of straw in a blur. Luke held it up, and Smoky rose on his hind legs to reach for it. This went on until the kitten managed to seize its quarry—or perhaps Luke simply let him have it—at which point it interested him no longer, inasmuch as it was defeated and obviously lifeless.

Reaching out slowly, Luke touched the tip of a finger to the little animal's throat and gently massaged it. Smoky settled down with an ecstatic purr, lifting his head to allow better access. Luke rubbed him between his eyes and behind his ears, his huge hand and long fingers surprisingly delicate in their movements. How, Faithe wondered, could the same hand that had dispatched God knew how many Saxons with his crossbow, handle a kitten so tenderly?

Eyes half closed, Smoky rubbed his head against Luke's hand, then lazily licked his fingertips. A deep, soft chuckle reverberated in Faithe's ear.

She turned and looked up at him. "Are you laughing?"

He marshaled his features. "You're awake. Good."

"Were you laughing?"

He regarded her solemnly. "I *am* capable of laughter, you know."

She raised an eyebrow at him. He raised one back at her, then stroked her cheek with a fingertip, just as he had stroked the kitten. "You're still pale. How do you feel?"

"Better. I think I'm fine now." She pushed herself up, squeezing her eyes shut against a surge of dizziness.

"I think not." Curling his arms around her, he drew her back against him, cupping her head with his enormous hand and pressing it to his shoulder. Not knowing what to do with her outside arm, she rested it on his chest, and felt, beneath the dense wall of muscle, the steady beating of his heart. He was so large, so *solid.* She inhaled his scent, already familiar to her, and felt oddly protected in the arms of this savage warrior.

"I've never seen anyone lose as much color as you did and stay on her feet," he said, his voice rumbling softly in his chest.

"I had to get away from them. I couldn't let them see."

A little amused huff shook his chest, just one. "In truth, I would have done the same thing."

She looked up at him. "Really?"

His expression softened into something that might almost have been a smile. "When one is in command of others, there's the tendency to want to appear invincible."

She nodded, pleased that he viewed them as alike in this way. Perhaps she shouldn't want to have anything to do with the Black Dragon, but he was, after all, her husband. It couldn't hurt to acknowledge some common ground. "I make it a point never to let them see that I'm tired or ill," she said. "Or out of sorts. They've never seen me upset about anything. They've never seen me cry. Not since I was a child, anyway."

"Even . . . when your husband died?" he asked quietly.

A slight pause. "I came here. I always come here when I need to be alone."

"What if there's already someone here?"

"They almost always leave right away. They know this is my refuge."

He seemed thoughtful for a moment. "A woman

shouldn't feel the need to be so . . . sewn up inside herself."

"Should a man?"

He didn't answer that, and they sat in silence. From this new vantage point, Faithe could see into the rough wooden box tucked into a corner of the stall. Clover, the slate gray mother cat, reclined in heavy-lidded contentment while most of her litter suckled energetically. Faithe wondered how it would feel to have a baby at her breast, drawing sustenance from her very body. How *complete* mothers must feel, how indispensable, how satisfied with their lot.

A pang of wanting burned through Faithe's belly. The greatest regret of her first marriage was that it had produced no children. Although she'd never said as much to Caedmon, she suspected the fault for their barrenness lay with him. He'd had several mistresses and numerous brief liaisons before wedding her, and yet no bastards had resulted from those unions.

Sir Luke began stroking her hair, his hand caressing her back as it glided downward again and again. The effect was hypnotic, and she nestled against him, wanting it to go on and on. Beneath her palm as it rested on his chest, she felt the quickening of his heart. It did not surprise her.

Something unspoken had coursed between them since the beginning, hiding behind their eyes, whispering softly in the background as they talked—knowledge, a sexual awareness, a hot pulsing beneath the cool surface. When he looked at her with those penetrating eyes, she felt as if he were looking *for* something, searching inside her. For what? Her feelings? Why should he care how she felt, about him or anything? He was the triumphant invader—her lord and master, her husband. All that was hers—her home, her lands, her livestock . . . herself—belonged to him now. He'd taken it all and mastered it. All except for her. He'd not claimed her body, not used her as was his right.

He wanted her, but hadn't taken her. Why not, when he had every right to do so? It didn't make sense, and that made her uneasy. Edging away from him, she said, "I need to return to my chores."

He tried to tug her back. "Nay, you're still white as a—"

"Please, my lord."

His eyes darkened at her use of the formal title. His jaw tightened. He looked as if there were something he wanted to say, but in the end he merely released her, his gaze remote and shadowed with melancholy.

She rose slowly on wobbly legs and quickly made her way out of the barn.

"A pity about Vance, but not exactly a surprise." Orrik paused midway through the apple orchard to run his hand over a scarred trunk while Lady Faithe inspected the tree's buds.

Luke regarded the bailiff and his young mistress thoughtfully as he rubbed his still sore arm. During the noon meal, when he'd ordered Orrik to give him a tour of Hauekleah, she had insisted on accompanying them, probably to make sure they didn't end up coming to blows. She needn't have worried—Luke had vowed to be civil to the man—but he let her come along anyway, after she'd managed to convince him that she'd recovered from this morning's fainting spell.

In truth, he relished her company. That she hardly relished his—as evidenced by her abrupt departure from the barn when his touch became too familiar—was sobering but understandable. It would take time for her to lose her innate fear of him and come of her own free will to their marriage bed. In the meantime, he must strive for patience. Tempting though it might be to simply throw her on her back and have his way with her, such lack of restraint would only reinforce his savagery in her eyes. He wanted her willing, not resigned—and certainly not fearful.

Luke asked the question Orrik clearly wanted him to ask. "Why is it not surprising that Vance took his own life?"

Orrik straightened slowly and continued down the tree-lined corridor without looking at Luke. "Might you not hang yourself, if the alternative was days of unrelenting torture, and you knew you'd still die by the noose?"

"But he wasn't going to be tortured," said Lady Faithe, hurrying to catch up to him. Luke followed them, his long legs quickly making up the distance.

Orrik snorted derisively. "The Normans torture all their prisoners before they execute them, my lady. 'Tis their way."

"But Sir Luke was going to try Vance in the hallmoot."

Orrik stopped at the east edge of the orchard and turned to Luke, his expression bemused. "Is that so?"

"It is."

"A ploy to ingratiate yourself with your villeins?"

"An attempt to see justice done," Luke said, "nothing more, nothing less."

"I wonder why he did kill himself, then," Lady Faithe said. "He'd been assured of mercy if he talked, and it seemed as if he had every intention of doing just that. Now we'll never find out why he and Hengist turned so murderous."

Orrik grunted and continued on, pointing out the beehives at the edge of a patch of woods to the north and the dovecote directly ahead.

"Straight through those woods to the east," Orrik said, "is Middeltun, the demesne field. It's worked partly by demesne staff and partly by bondmen owing week work to her ladyship. Middeltun's right in the elbow of the river. Within that horseshoe, you've also got Hauekleah Hall and the village proper. Then there's Norfeld and Surfeld."

Luke must have looked puzzled, because Lady Faithe said, "Those are the two fields that the villagers share. They're both on the other side of the river, accessible by bridges. One is north of the horseshoe, one south."

"Surfeld's right over here." Orrik led them to the edge of the river. On the south side lay a great expanse of unplowed earth.

"Why has this field not been planted?" Luke asked.

Orrik rolled his eyes.

"For the same reason half of Middeltun lies fallow," Lady Faithe explained. " 'Tis how the soil is kept fertile. Each season, one field is given a rest, while the other is divided up into furlongs and cultivated by the villagers."

Luke couldn't imagine his father having granted so much autonomy to his serfs. "And they cooperate in this with no supervision?"

Orrik grumbled something about soldiers playing farmer without learning the role properly.

"I oversee things to some extent," said Lady Faithe with a warning scowl in Orrik's direction. "But for the most part, they handle it all themselves. It works out rather well, actually. Last year we produced eighteen hundred bushels of barley—"

"And nine hundred of wheat," Luke interrupted, "plus a goodly harvest of oats, peas, and beans. I know. And I know prices were high last year. You got a shilling for a bushel of wheat, if I'm not mistaken."

Lady Faithe blinked at him. Orrik's poleaxed expression evolved into a grimace, and he looked away.

"The dairy produces about two hundred cheeses annually," Luke continued, "and a good deal of butter for the market. Fifty piglets, thirty goslings, and eighty chicks are born in the average year."

His wife was unnerved, but impressed; he could see

it in her eyes and in the smile that kept tugging at her lush mouth. He liked to see her smile; he especially liked to *make* her smile. "How many eggs?" she challenged.

"Four hundred. And you collect annual cash rents of twenty-six pounds."

"I take it Lord Alberic gave you this accounting when he offered you my hand in marriage," she said.

"Nay, I had to ask for it. He assumed I wouldn't care, but I do. This is my home now. Hauekleah is mine," he said pointedly, taking in both of them with his gaze, "and I want to find out everything I can about it."

Lady Faithe pressed her lips into a thin line and wrapped her arms around herself. So—she didn't like him referring to Hauekleah as his. Yet, by law and custom, it belonged to him now. Didn't she want him to show an interest in it? Would she prefer he governed her estate in ignorance?

"It's getting late, my lord," she said. "Orrik and I both have things to attend to before nightfall, if you've seen enough . . ."

My lord. "Enough for now," Luke said tightly. "I'm going to saddle up my mount and do a little exploring on my own. I'll be back in time for supper."

"As you wish, my lord."

Faithe picked at her supper of rabbit stew and toyed with the rim of her goblet, her husband's words from this afternoon echoing in her head: *Hauekleah is mine.*

She glanced at him as he distractedly sipped his wine.

He's too interested in Hauekleah, Orrik had said as they'd watched him walk away this afternoon. *I don't like it.*

She'd reminded Orrik that Caedmon had never been interested enough, and he hadn't liked that, either.

This is worse, he'd said. *Luke de Périgueux is a Norman, and they're a sly breed. It doesn't sit well, him coming in here like this and telling us how many eggs we produce, and what we got for wheat last year. Why does he need to know all that, if he's got you to keep running things for him?*

And then he had nodded slowly, his keen gaze narrowing on the spot where Sir Luke had disappeared into the orchard. *Unless he means to cast you aside.*

Faithe had stared at him, the blood chilling in her veins.

I'll wager that's exactly what he's got in mind, the shameless bastard.

Faithe had been preoccupied all afternoon, performing her chores numbly as she replayed Orrik's comments over and over in her mind. Despite the rage that had simmered within Orrik ever since Hastings, he was a wise man; Faithe had relied on his counsel for years, and he'd never let her down. She couldn't remember his ever having been wrong about anything.

Part of her still wanted to believe that Sir Luke was too honorable to stoop so low, yet how well did she really know him? The more she thought about it, in a panicky daze, the more likely it seemed that Orrik was right—that her husband meant to find out everything he could about Hauekleah, in preparation for the day when he would pack her off to a nunnery. By refusing to bed her, he was essentially stripping her of her rights as his wife. He could toss her aside at a moment's notice. She would have no security whatsoever. And she could lose Hauekleah.

She couldn't permit it, couldn't simply stand by and let him steal her ancestral home from her. Today's tour of Hauekleah only served to remind her of all she'd be giving up if she allowed that to happen.

Her problem was a simple one: Her husband was scheming to secure an annulment, and therefore steal Hauekleah from her, by refusing to bed her.

The solution? Force him to bed her. It was the only way to protect her rights.

"Why do you frown so?" asked Sir Luke.

She flinched. "Sorry." *Fool.* She sounded like some meek little child. Why shouldn't she frown, if she was so inclined?

"Is there something wrong with the ring?" he asked, eyeing the emerald encrusted band as she twirled it around her finger.

"Nothing." She released it. "Sorry." *Idiot.*

Force might not be the best approach. How did a mere female *force* a man of his size and strength to do anything? She smiled as it came to her. One place she'd never felt like a *mere* anything was in bed. It was during lovemaking with Caedmon that she'd discovered the true power of being a woman—the power to arouse and delight and finally satisfy. She'd learned to enjoy that power, to use it for her own pleasure and his. She'd learned how to be seductive.

She knew she was comely; she saw her beauty reflected in the eyes of nearly every man who looked at her. And in Sir Luke's eyes she saw not just attraction, but longing. The feeling, of course, was quite mutual; to deny it would be absurd. Every time he looked at her, with that probing gaze, her skin grew tight and shivery; her lungs felt as if they were being gently squeezed, leaving her starved for breath.

Faithe stole another glance at her husband, who was leaning forward to listen to some story his brother was telling. His gaze was focused, his eyes intent. He seemed to bring that fierce concentration to everything he did. She wondered if he would bring it to lovemaking as well.

She lifted her goblet with an unsteady hand and drained it, setting it down with a determined *thunk.*

That was it, then. There was no other solution to her problem. She'd have to make Sir Luke want her so badly that he *had* to bed her, regardless that it meant throwing aside his plans to take Hauekleah from her. She'd have to seduce her own husband.

She could do it tonight, when they retired to bed. She'd tease him a little, entice him a little . . . just enough to get under his skin. He wanted her already; it shouldn't take that much effort on her part for his simmering desire to escalate into a roiling boil. And then, when his need was too great to deny any longer, she could roll up her sleeves and finish the job.

A simple problem with a simple solution.

No great challenge, and she might—probably would—enjoy it quite a bit.

If she could stop this incessant shivering.

Don't be nervous, she chided herself. *You want him and he wants you. You're already married to him, for pity's sake. There's nothing to be afraid of.*

She could do this. This could work.

Chapter 7

"Milady's out of her bath now, milord."

"Thank you, Moira."

The stout maid bid Luke and Alex good night and left for her own home, leaving the two men alone in the vast and silent great hall. "Are your wounds healing well?" Luke asked his brother, reclining on his pallet in a shirt and loose braies.

"Very. That disgusting muck Faithe keeps slathering on seems to work."

Faithe. His wife and his brother had called each other by their Christian names since the beginning. Luke envied Alex his easy relationship with her.

"Now that you've expressed a measure of brotherly concern for my welfare," Alex said with a half smile, "I suggest you go upstairs and help that lovely bride of yours to dry off."

"I'm sure she can manage on her own."

"Perhaps not. Ladies tend to have trouble reaching the most interesting places—"

"I said she can manage," Luke bit out.

Alex fixed his all-too-knowing gaze on Luke. "This isn't right, brother."

Luke's hackles rose. "Who are you to scold me about right and wrong? I'll go up when I'm good and ready."

One of Alex's industrious twins emerged from the buttery, bearing a flagon and a cup. "Some brandy before bed, milord?" She glanced at Luke as she knelt at Alex's side, unable to completely disguise her disappointment at his presence. "I mean, milords. I can fetch another cup."

Alex turned doleful eyes on Luke as he rested a hand on the wench's bottom. "Are you good and ready yet?"

Luke rose from his bench. "It seems I am." He bid the couple a perfunctory good night. They were locked in an ardent embrace almost before he'd turned away. He took the stairs to the bedchamber slowly, letting Lady Faithe hear his footsteps so she'd know he was coming. When he got to the landing, he knocked softly.

"Enter," she said in French.

Luke opened the door. She sat on a stool next to the big wooden tub in the corner, a threadbare linen towel wrapped around her, pouring something from a green vial into her palm. Setting the vial on the floor, she rubbed her hands together, then leaned over and slid them up one leg from ankle to thigh, leaving a gleaming liquid trail.

Swallowing hard, Luke turned and shut the door, then stood facing it for a few moments to collect himself. She had extraordinary legs, as lithe and shapely as her arms, and surprisingly long. He almost wished he hadn't seen them, for the sight sorely undermined his resolve to keep his distance from her until she'd ceased to tremble at his touch.

Forcing himself to face her again, he saw that she'd finished her legs and was now rubbing the contents of the vial onto her arms. Her skin gleamed like polished ivory in the golden half-light from the oil lamps scattered around the room.

He cleared his throat and nodded toward the vial. "What is that?" he asked, just for something to say.

"An oil I use after bathing to keep my skin soft." Flipping her wet hair behind her, she tilted her head back and lazily worked the emollient into her throat and upper chest. The towel was so old and thin that he could almost, but not quite, see her nipples through it. "I extract the essence from almonds and thyme, and add a little to the oil. Not too much—just enough to lightly scent it." She held the vial toward him. "What do you think?"

He approached her almost warily and took the little bottle from her, bringing it to his nose. So this was the source of the enigmatic scent that always tickled his nerve endings when he was near her. Breathing in so much of her fragrance at once caused his senses to reel drunkenly. "It's quite nice."

He tried to hand the vial to her, but she stood up and turned her back to him, tugging the towel loose and lowering it. "I can't reach my back. Would you mind?"

Ladies have trouble reaching the most interesting places . . .

For a moment, he thought she was going to remove the towel entirely, but she wrapped it low around her hips, securing it—rather tenuously, he thought—with a quick tuck. Gathering her hair to one side, she draped it over her shoulder, then stood in expectant silence, her arms loose at her sides.

Her back was as sleek and well shaped as the rest of her, her waist exquisitely slender. The damp linen towel hugged a beguilingly dimpled derriere. Luke's hand twitched as he studied the spot where she'd tucked in the towel. All he'd have to do was pull it . . .

Glancing over her shoulder at him, Lady Faithe said, "I can do the front while you do the back." She lifted her hand, palm up. It took him a moment to realize what she wanted, and then he loosened his white-knuckled grip on the green vial and poured a bit of the oil into her palm. "Thank you." She rubbed her hands together, and then began smoothing them over her chest. He couldn't see what she was doing, of course, since her back was to him, but his imagination filled in the details. In his mind's eye he saw her breasts, slick with oil. He felt their weight and warmth as she stroked them . . .

"My lord?" she murmured. "Are you going to . . ."

He choked out some sort of response, then tilted the vial onto his palm and laid it hesitantly on her shoulder. Her skin felt hot to the touch, and slightly damp, and so incredibly smooth already that he couldn't imagine why she felt the need to soften it further. He moved his hand slowly, gliding it over an elegant shoulder blade and down along the inward curve toward her waist. As friction heated the oil, it released more of its intoxicating fragrance. He breathed the scent in deeply, letting it enter him, wreaking havoc with his equilibrium. He massaged her with firmer pressure, feeling the compact little muscles and smooth bones beneath the satin skin. He caressed her waist, her hips, reveling in her womanly contours and the sweet, feverish heat of her.

It was intimate to be touching her this way, astonishingly intimate. To be privy to her toilette was disarming enough; to participate in it implied an understanding, a sort of sexual promise. Luke's body reacted to that promise with a surge of arousal that stole his breath. His hand tightened reflexively around the curve of her hip as he swelled and rose beneath his tunic.

"My lord?" As she turned to face him, he thrust the vial in her hand and walked away. "Are you all right?"

"I'm fine." He strode to the edge of the bed and looked down on it, picturing her naked and luminous on the wolfskin blanket.

Fine? He was far from *fine.* He ached with need, he pulsated with it. She must know what she was doing to him. No woman could be this provocative unless she were deliberately trying to tempt a man. And yet, what did he know of women like her? The women he was used to were coarse creatures adept at firing a man's lust and dispatching it as quickly as possible. Highborn women, according to his father, were largely blind to the passion they inspired in men and ill-prepared to deal with its consequences—which was why the chivalrous man must learn self-control.

"Would you like me to undress you?" She came up behind him as he stood facing the bed.

God yes. "That won't be necessary."

He felt her hands brush the back of his neck as she untied the thong that secured his braid and unplaited it by trailing her fingers through his hair. His scalp tingled where she lightly grazed it.

She closed a hand over his shoulder and urged him to face her. Her damp hair hung down on either side of her chest, cloaking her breasts. His gaze stole downward, along her flat stomach with its delicate navel, and then further, to speculate on mysteries barely obscured by the swath of flimsy toweling that stopped at her calves.

"I'm your wife," she said in a near whisper. He met her gaze and she abruptly looked away. "A wife ought to . . . do these things for her husband."

These things? Just undressing him, or did she mean more? Regardless of what she meant, she was obviously uncomfortable—a wife performing her duty. Luke didn't know precisely what he wanted to be to Lady Faithe, but he knew for certain that he didn't want to be her *duty.* "You needn't—"

"I should." She reached for his belt, and he stilled. He was so hard, so inflamed. Her hands as she unbuckled him hovered so close to the source of his hunger, yet never directly touched it. The effect was maddening. He wanted to throw her onto the bed and drive himself into her. He wanted to race from the room, to protect her from his animal lust.

He closed his eyes and gritted his teeth, wondering if it were possible to go mad from sexual frustration.

She tossed his belt onto the bed. Then, before he could object, she gathered up his tunic and shirt and pulled them both over his head, laying them next to the belt.

"Your arm is better," she said, lightly trailing her fingers over the bruised flesh, "but you could use some more spirit of rosemary on it."

He remembered the fire her innocent, healing touch had kindled in him last night. It would probably be a good idea to discourage such ministrations tonight. All he wanted was for her to turn her back long enough for him to get out of his chausses—which did little to mask his state of arousal—and under the covers. " 'Twill heal well enough without more liniment," he said.

" 'Twill heal better with it." She dropped to her knees in front of him.

Luke stepped back and felt the bed behind him. "What are you—"

"Taking off your boots," she said matter-of-factly, although he thought her fingers looked inordinantly clumsy as she tugged at the laces.

"Stop that." Her head was an inch from his groin; thank God she was looking down. "I can do that."

"I don't mind—really." As she worked the laces loose, the top of her head brushed up against him, generating a subtle but insistent stimulation that made him even harder. He wanted it to go on and on; he wanted it to stop before he lost control. He tried to back up farther, but there was nowhere to go.

"Lift your foot." She pulled off a boot and set it aside. "Now this one."

He heard her draw in a slow breath, and then she reached for the cord at the waistband of his chausses.

"You don't need to do this," he rasped.

"I want to," she whispered unsteadily.

Was it possible she knew what she was doing? She had to notice his condition, but she didn't so much as blink as she wrestled with the knot he'd tied far too well. Luke's heart pounded in his ears. Her palms brushed his erection as she plucked at the cord. He sucked in a breath.

She looked up and met his gaze. He saw it in her eyes then, the resolution, the self-awareness. She knew exactly what she was doing.

Any lingering doubts vaporized when she closed a hand over his straining flesh through his chausses, lightly but deliberately, without breaking eye contact. He throbbed at her touch. Gripping her hand, he drew it up his length, molding it to him.

She *did* want him! She *did* know what she was asking for, and she wanted it as much as he did.

He noticed something then. She was shivering, very slightly from head to toe.

His ardor chilled instantly. She didn't want him at all—not really. She wanted to do her wifely duty. She wanted to consummate the marriage, because it was expected. But she didn't really want him at all. From all appearances, the prospect of giving herself to him unnerved her greatly.

He released her abruptly. "Get up."

She looked up sharply. "But . . . don't you want—"

"Nay." Not now, not like this. Not with her trembling like a hare in a trap. He seized her arms and pulled her to her feet.

"Your body wants it." She reached for him again, but he grabbed her wrist and held it tight.

"That's my body. My mind knows better. Get dressed."

"But—"

"Get dressed," he repeated, more harshly than he'd intended. He gentled his voice. "And we'll talk." His nerves were shattered, but he shouldn't take it out on her. She'd merely been doing her duty as she perceived it; she wasn't to blame. He wanted to explain things to her, wanted her to understand why he couldn't take her on these terms, but he couldn't hope to concentrate on what he had to say with her standing in front of him half naked.

She didn't move, except to lift her chin, her eyes blazing. "I won't let you do this to me," she said in a voice she seemed to be struggling to control.

The intensity of her anger, and its suddenness, took Luke by surprise. "I've done nothing to you," he said carefully.

Her hands fisted in the towel draped around her. "Precisely."

Christ, but he wished she'd put some clothes on. Then, perhaps he could *think.* Opening the chest at the foot of the bed, he pulled out what looked to be a night shift and handed it to her. It was a shift, he saw when she unfolded it, but an exceptionally delicate one of tissue-thin linen, lightly embroidered. She jerked her towel off, and he spun around, rubbing the back of his neck while she got dressed.

"Is this better, my lord?" she said acidly.

He turned around. The nightgown scooped low in front, exposing the upper slopes of her breasts—remarkably generous breasts for such a fine-boned woman. The gossamer fabric floated around her like a whisper, revealing as much as it concealed. He saw the rosy smudges of her nipples, and a shadowy hint of what lay between her legs.

His body stirred anew, but then she said, "I know why you won't bed me," and his arousal quickly waned.

"Why?"

Her chin rose higher; her fists quivered. He admired her pluck, despite this perplexing stand she seemed to be taking. "Consummating this marriage would make me your wife in every sense. I'd be protected against—"

"What?" A pressure began to swell behind his eyes.

"That's what this is about? That's why you want me to bed you? To protect yourself?"

"I married you in good faith," she said, her voice quavering. "As your wife, I have certain legal rights . . . the right not to be cast aside—"

"Legal rights?" he roared. Dear God, this was about *legal rights.* She hadn't wanted him at all. Nor had she been simply trying to do her wifely duty. She'd cold-bloodedly seduced him—or attempted to—in order to protect her legal position as his wife. Luke felt as if his head were going to burst.

He wheeled around, fists clenched, looking for something to smash. The depth of his anger unnerved him. Once the beast within him was fully wakened, God knew what it would do. An image flashed through his mind of the dead Saxon in the loft of that Cottwyk brothel. Luke had already committed murder; he was capable of anything.

"My lord—"

"Don't call me that!"

A spark of fear flared in her eyes before she banished it. She *should* be frightened. She'd roused the Black Dragon. She should be praying for mercy.

Instead, she had the temerity to take a step toward him. "I only want what any wife has the right to expect."

Seizing her roughly, he tossed her onto the bed, then leapt on top of her, his fair flying in his face. "Is this what you want?" He whipped her skirt up, watching himself as if from above, wondering how far he would go. "Is this what you expect?"

For a moment she just stared at him, her eyes widened in shock. "Nay," she gasped, scrambling backward across the bed.

"What's wrong?" He grabbed her hips to still her. Pinning her beneath him, he yanked her legs apart. "Isn't this what you've been asking for?" He thrust against her, although he'd never felt less aroused. It was not lust that drove him—the fear in her eyes would have vanquished that—but a darker, more uncontrollable passion.

She swung a fist, catching him on the nose. The burst of pain only fueled the demon within him. Grabbing her wrists, he held them down and thrust again. "An expedient fuck? Will that *protect your rights*? Perhaps we should call in witnesses."

"Nay!" She thrashed beneath him, striving to free herself. "Nay! My lord, please—"

"Call me by my name!"

"Just let me—"

"My name!" Two droplets of blood fell onto her cheek from his nose.

"Luke," she choked out. "Luke . . ." She stilled, breathless. "Don't do this. Don't do this, Luke, please."

He felt her heart thundering through her thin gown. Her eyes shimmered with unshed tears.

"Christ, don't cry," he said huskily.

"I won't. I wouldn't. Not in front of . . ." She looked away, struggling to compose herself.

Not in front of him. Of course not. He was the last person to whom she'd expose her soft underbelly—especially after this little display of savagery.

He could feel the rage dissipating in the face of her fear and helplessness, feel the beast retreating to its lair, deep within him. Thank God he'd managed to rein it in before it could vent the full measure of its fury. Never in the past had it been so easily subdued.

She returned her gaze to his. "Let me go, Luke. You don't want to . . . to . . ."

"God, no." Luke released her wrists and cupped her face with tremulous hands. He and Faithe were both shaking uncontrollably. "The last thing I'd ever want to do is hurt you. I'm sorry, my lady, I'm so—"

"Faithe," she whispered raggedly.

A drop of blood landed on her upper lip. He wiped it off with his thumb.

"Faithe," he breathed, loving the simplicity of her name, the soft feel of it in his mouth. He rubbed his thumb over the drops on her cheek.

Her gaze focused on his nose. "I'm sorry for that."

"You had every right to do that, and worse." He eased away from her, drawing her skirt down as he rolled to the side. "Christ." He threw an arm over his face. "I'm an animal. I should be locked up in a cage."

He felt her rise from the bed, and then he heard her soft footsteps in the rushes, and the sound of water being poured from the ewer into the washbasin. Presently, the mattress dipped as she sat next to him. Something cold touched his nose, and he flinched. "What—"

"Shh . . ."

She sat over him, dabbing gingerly at his nose and upper lip with a wet cloth, which quickly turned red. She dipped it in the basin, which she'd brought to the night table, and continued cleaning off the blood. Luke watched her as she tended to him, her forehead slightly creased with concentration, her eyes dark with concern.

For him. She obviously felt contrite for having hurt him—ludicrous, given the provocation—and now, ever the healer, she'd taken it upon herself to nurse him. The injury to his nose, although it still pulsed with pain, was inconsequential. Part of him wanted to reject her succor; he didn't deserve it. But another part wanted to stay like this forever, basking in her tender attentions. For her to take care of him this way, after what he'd done, humbled him.

"That's better." She rinsed the cloth thoroughly, wrung it out, and gently stroked it across his forehead. It felt so cool, so infinitely soothing. His eyes closed; his hands fell open limply at his sides. She bathed his face and throat and arms until he lay in dazed gratification, and then she dropped the cloth in the basin and curled up next to him.

Luke turned to her as naturally as if he'd done it a thousand times, and gathered her in his arms. She returned the embrace, gliding her arms around him and fitting her body to his. He stroked her hair as their heartbeats synchronized, breathing in the essence of almonds and thyme.

He felt the warmth of her body through her whisper-thin gown, felt her breasts crushed to his bare chest. Yet, curiously, he felt a far greater measure of contentment than desire. He couldn't remember the last time he'd held someone just for the comfort of it; in fact, he didn't think he ever had.

"I'm such an idiot," she whispered.

He pulled back a little to look upon her face. She wouldn't meet his eyes.

"I thought I knew why you didn't want to bed me," she said into his shoulder. "I thought you wanted to annul the marriage."

He rose onto an elbow. "Why, for God's sake?"

"So that you'd get Hauekleah without . . . having to be wed to me."

She thought he'd wanted to take her estate from her! No wonder she'd been so desperate as to resort to this bungled seduction. He understood now, but still, it stung to discover that her motives had nothing to do with him, and everything to do with Hauekleah. "I should have known your purpose in . . . tempting me that way . . . went deeper than mere duty. What kind of woman would voluntarily bed the Black Dragon, even if it *were* expected of her?"

"Luke . . ." Her eyes closed; she shook her head sadly. "I'm sorry."

He tucked a stray hair behind her ear. "For a moment there, I thought you actually wanted me." A grim chuckle escaped him. "You'd think I'd be old enough not to let wishful thinking influence my judgment."

Her arms tightened around him. "Luke . . ."

"It's been a very, very long time since there was anything good and pure in my life," he said quietly. "Now there's Hauekleah . . . and you." He took a deep, shuddering breath. "For once, I'm surrounded not by ugliness and death, but . . ." He trailed his fingertips lightly over her face; she closed her eyes and bit her lip. "I don't want to sully what I've been given. Our marriage may have been a coldhearted arrangement, but that doesn't mean it has to be a coldhearted marriage."

He shook his head in frustration at the inadequacy of words and flopped down on his back to study the network of massive timbers supporting the steeply pitched ceiling. "What I'm trying to say is, I don't want you on just any terms. I certainly don't want you if you're just submitting to me out of a sense of duty, or to protect your rights as my wife. And I don't want you if you fear me, even a little. When you give yourself to me—if you ever do—I want it to be because that's what you truly want."

"If I ever do?" she whispered.

Luke sat up and looked down at her. He knew what she was thinking. As long as their marriage went unconsummated, he'd be able to annul it and take Hauekleah from her. "I won't bed you just to ease your mind," he said softly. "God knows I want you, but not if that's the only way I can have you. You've got to learn to trust me. Until then, I'd just as soon sleep on the floor, if it's all the same to you."

She sat up next to him. "The floor!"

"I'm a soldier," he reminded her. "Or was. I can sleep anywhere."

"But why should you have to? Why should you suffer in the rushes, when you could sleep in comfort on a feather mattress?"

He rubbed his neck, his gaze wandering from her tousled hair to her flushed lips to the enticing swell of her breasts beneath the sheer gown. "I daresay I'll suffer more in your bed, my la—Faithe."

Hot color suffused her face. "As you wish . . . Luke."

"Wishes . . ." He smiled ruefully. "Aye, well, those are a different matter entirely."

Chapter 8

"Where are we, boy?" Orrik demanded of young Alfrith as his lackey, Baldric, hoisted the child atop a boulder at the edge of the forest known as Nortwalde.

"Th-the northernmost boundary of Hauekleah, Master Orrik."

Alfrith squeezed his eyes shut and hunched his shoulders. Faithe winced in sympathetic anticipation.

"Right you are," Orrik praised. Then he nodded at Baldric, who grabbed Alfrith by the front of his tunic and walloped him across the face.

"Thank you, master," the child muttered as the bailiff helped him down from the boulder and instructed Baldric to lift up the next body, young Bram.

"Where are we, boy?"

Bram ducked his head and mumbled something unintelligible.

"Is this really necessary?" Luke asked Faithe, whispering the question in her ear so that the many onlookers—nearly the entire population of Hauekleah—wouldn't hear.

He'd been quiet but observant all morning, as the villagers walked Hauekleah's perimeter in the annual ceremony that seared the borders into the memories of the next generation. Faithe had wondered what his reaction would be.

"The boys must be made to remember where our land ends and the neighbors' begins," she pointed out as Baldric pried Bram's hands from his face and gave him his ritual slap.

"Why? Why not just record the boundaries in writing?"

"There is a written charter," Faithe patiently explained, "but none of these people can understand it. Orrik and I are the only people at Hauekleah who can read and write."

"I can . . . to some extent."

"Yes," she said quickly. "I meant the three of us."

A lie, of course. In truth, although a fortnight had passed since her marriage to Luke, Faithe still had trouble thinking of him as the master of Hauekleah. Not that he hadn't made every effort to establish himself as such. He spent his days exploring the village and surrounding countryside, introducing himself to his new villeins and questioning them at length about the work they did and how they lived. He studied everything there was to study and inspected everything there was to inspect. He pored over Orrik's books detailing harvest yields, demesne production, rents, taxes, and fines. From all appearances, he embraced his new role with the greatest of zeal.

Still, Faithe couldn't help but feel that his enthusiasm would surely wane. Her Danish grandfather, Thorgeirr, had been much the same at first, according to Grandmother Hlynn. Setting aside his tools of war, he'd seemed devoted to Hauekleah. He'd even torn down the old, dark manor house and build enormous, sunny Hauekleah Hall in its place. But by the end of the summer, boredom had set in, and his hand had itched for the weight of the sword. One rainy September morning, he saddled up his warhorse and rode away, without so much as a word of farewell to his pregnant wife.

Soldiers are ill suited to farm life, Hlynn had explained to Faithe many times over the years. *Agents of death have no patience for making things grow.*

As a child, Faithe used to imagine an "agent of death" as a hulking, mail-clad brute with a horned helmet and a bloody sword in each fist. A fanciful image, to be sure. What, she wondered, did a real agent of death look like?

She contemplated her husband discreetly as he watched one boy after another accept his slap. Luke's gray tunic, though of good Sicilian wool, was simply cut and devoid of ornamentation. He wore no snippet of lambskin nor sword to indicate his rank, and although he was clean-shaven, his braided hair was as long as that of his Saxon villeins. He looked nothing like a Norman nobleman, but neither could he be mistaken for an Englishman. Like her, he didn't seem to fit neatly into any one world.

He stood with arms crossed, one hand resting across his mouth, his expression reflective as he observed the proceedings. When he grimaced, Faithe turned toward the boulder to see what had affected him so. Little Felix stood up there, his legs quaking as Baldric pried his hands off his face.

The quick slap seemed to momentarily stun the child, and then he burst into tears and held his arms out, crying, "Mummy! Mummy!" His mother scooped him up and patted his back as he sniffled wetly.

"Look at the baby!" Alfrith jeered. The other boys joined in, taunting little Felix with their usual insults. Felix was seven years old, but small for his age, and of a quiet and cautious nature. To make matters worse, after his father's death last year, he'd become strongly attached to his mother, causing the other boys to view him as infantile. They wanted nothing to do with him, except as an object of scorn. He was friendless and fatherless, and his dependence on his mother grew daily, inviting yet more ridicule—a vicious circle.

As Felix's crying worsened and the derision escalated, Luke regarded Faithe with a reproachful expression.

"I doubt he'll soon forget the northern boundary of Hauekleah," she said, but without much enthusiasm.

Luke just sighed and shook his head.

The huge assembly—over two hundred people—turned and walked in a southwesterly direction, toward the north curve of the river. Luke remained at her side, taking her hand at one point to help her over a fallen log. His touch made her heart race like a bird's. When she was safely past the obstruction, he released her. Could he sense her disappointment? Did it amuse him?

True to his word, he'd taken to sleeping on the floor of their bedchamber, wrapped up in a blanket in the rushes. They never again discussed that awful night; it was as if her misbegotten attempt to seduce him had been entirely forgotten, which was all for the good. It shamed her that she'd assigned such base motives to his reluctance to consummate the marriage.

If she was to believe him, he wouldn't accept her in his bed until she was unreservedly willing—no residual fear, no ambivalence. She had to care for him. She had to trust him. The paradox, of course, was that his refusal to bed her made it all that much harder to trust him, inasmuch as a platonic marriage could be readily annulled.

Nevertheless, Faithe knew that, in all likelihood, he'd never had any intention of casting her aside. She could remain at Hauekleah. But would he remain here with her? She had a hard time believing that someone like Luke de Périgueux could be happy spending the rest of his life on a farm. *Agents of death have no patience for making things grow . . .*

Would she lower her guard and learn to care for him, only to wake up one morning and find him gone, like Thorgeirr? Perhaps she could trust him not to steal Hauekleah from her, but could she trust him to be here next year, and the year after?

How ironic. Before he'd arrived, she'd prayed that

the Black Dragon would tire quickly of farm life and leave her in peace. Now, she found that possibility troubling.

When they got to the river, Faithe and Luke joined Orrik and Baldric on the wooden bridge next to the mill, while the rest of the villagers watched from the north bank.

Orrik called Alfrith onto the bridge. "Where are we, boy?"

Alfrith licked his lips nervously. "The western edge of Hauekleah, master."

The boy flinched as Baldric's hand neared him. "Relax, boy," Orrik soothed. "He's not going to hit you."

Alfrith's expression of gratitude was swiftly replaced by shock as Baldric laughingly lifted him in the air and hurled him over the side of the bridge. The boy sailed, screaming, into the water, landing with a loud splash and sinking like a stone.

A few long moments passed. Luke leaned over the edge of the bridge. "Is he all right?"

Alfrith bobbed to the surface, sputtering and thrashing his arms and legs, and awkwardly made his way ashore to the cheers of the spectators.

Bram had to be dragged onto the bridge, but he didn't resist when Baldric lifted him up, merely sucked in a giant breath and pinched his nose closed. As he was helped out of the water, a high-pitched shrieking commenced.

"Oh, dear," Faithe murmured as Felix's white-faced mother carried her writhing son toward the bridge.

"No!" the boy wailed. *"No, Mummy, please! No! No! No!"* The other boys laughed uproariously in the face of Felix's terror.

"Bring him forward," Orrik ordered the woman.

"If you please, Master Orrik," she said, "my Felix can't swim."

"Neither can the others."

"But he's just a wee thing, master, and he's so scared."

"All the better," Orrik said. " 'Twill fix this spot in his memory. Now, give him over."

Baldric wrested the frantic child out of his mother's arms and hauled him, flailing and screaming, onto the bridge.

"Oh, for pity's sake." Luke let go of Faithe's hand and held out his arms. "Give him here."

Baldric looked for guidance to Orrik, who glowered at his new master. "He'll do no such—"

"Yes, he will, Orrik," Lady Faithe said quietly, in Latin. "Don't force me to discipline you in front of the villagers."

Orrik's face flooded with purple. He barked a command at Baldric, who thrust the squirming Felix at Luke. Ducking his head, Luke settled the child on his broad shoulders. Felix became quiet and alert.

"Felix," Luke said gravely as he grasped the boy's feet, hanging down on either side of his chest.

"Aye, milord."

"I command you to remember, in future years, the morning when you were the tallest person in Hauekleah."

Felix gazed around at the multitude of faces looking up at him—including the other boys, clearly awed—and smiled.

"And when you remember this morning," Luke instructed, "you are to remember that this bridge marks the westernmost boundary of Hauekleah. Can you remember that?"

"Aye, milord!"

"Will you remember it always?"

"Forever, milord!"

"That suits me," Luke said, "if it suits my lady wife."

Faithe smiled broadly, disarmed, despite her misgivings about Luke, by his compassion for a terrified little boy. "It suits me quite well, my lord husband."

Something meltingly intimate glimmered in his eyes, and he almost smiled. "Good." He patted the boy's foot. "Are you hungry, Felix?"

"That I am, sire."

"Would you care to join me at my table for the noon meal?"

Felix gasped with astonished pleasure as the other boys exchanged looks of incredulity. "Can Mummy come?"

"Of course."

The boy leaned over to look Luke in the face and whispered, "Will you make me eat any turnips?"

"Felix!" his mother scolded.

" 'Tis a fair question," Luke told her. "I can't bear turnips myself," he assured Felix, "and I wouldn't dream of inflicting them on you. I understand there's to be some sort of sweetmeat for dessert, though. You might be called upon to eat some of that."

"I wouldn't mind that," the child confided.

"Excellent." With Felix on his shoulders and his hand held out to her, Luke looked the very antithesis of an agent of death. Faithe took his hand and let him lead her back toward Hauekleah Hall.

When she glanced behind her, she saw the rest of the villagers dispersing . . . except for Orrik, who stood alone on the bridge, glowering into the water.

"I don't quite know what to make of your brother," Faithe told Alex as she knelt that afternoon at the edge of her kitchen garden with her dibble and her seedlip full of beans.

Alex leaned forward on the bench, elbows on knees, twirling his cane between his palms. "You wouldn't be alone in that."

Faithe jabbed the dibble into the soil, plucked a

bean from the curved basket, and dropped it in the hole. "He's so . . ." She shook her head.

The young man chuckled. "Aye, he is that."

She planted three more beans. "It's just that I can't help wondering how . . . interested he's going to be in Hauekleah this time next year."

"Ah. You're afraid this is just a passing fancy of his. You still think he's planning on seeking an annulment, don't you?"

"Nay. That is, I'm almost certain he has no such plans." She couldn't be completely sure until he bedded her, but she had no intention of discussing these details with her brother by marriage.

Leaning over, Alex stuck his cane into the earth in the exact spot Faithe was going to dibble next. "Thank you," she said, and plunked in a bean.

"Why do you plant beans in your kitchen garden," he asked, using his cane to make a row of holes for her, "when you have furlongs devoted to them in your demesne field?"

"These beans are from the plants that were most productive last year," she explained. "I use this garden to experiment with different strains in the hope of producing better yields."

He chuckled as he scraped the dirt-encrusted tip of his cane on his boot. "Have I mentioned that I think my brother is a very lucky man?"

Faithe ducked her head so the brim of her straw hat would hide her blush. "Constantly."

"He knows it, too. He's grateful to have you."

"Has he told you this?"

"Nay. He hasn't had to. He's completely transparent to me."

"Transparent? Luke?" Faithe had never known a man more locked up inside himself.

"To me he is. I've known him all my life. Well, from the time I was six, at any rate."

Having finished that row of beans, Faithe moved

back and started another one. "I don't understand. He's six years older than you. Why didn't you know him before then?"

"Oh, I knew him, of course, but not well. I only saw him twice a year or so, when he was on holiday from the abbey."

She looked up.

"You didn't know he was brought up in a monastery?"

"Nay, I . . . we don't talk much."

"Evidently not." Alex sat back, his arms draped over the cane, which he balanced on his shoulders. "Luke was the second son, and as such, he was naturally destined for holy orders, just as I was destined for soldiering. Our father sent him to the abbey at Aurillac when he was very young so that he could get a good monastic education."

Faithe sat back on her heels. "I had no idea. Why didn't he become a priest, then? Or a monk?"

Alex grinned. "He hadn't quite the temperament for it. He had little patience for his lessons, and less for the holy offices. He had a disconcerting habit of breaking the rules, and rules are the backbone of cloistered life. He'd sleep through matins, skip Mass, sneak away and eat his meals in the fields . . ."

"Was he punished?"

"Not badly. Our father was a very powerful knight, and he'd made generous contributions to the abbey in return for Luke's education. It got to the point, though, where the abbot wrote to Father and gently suggested that perhaps Luke would be happier pursuing a secular vocation. And so, he was called home at the age of twelve, and trained in the arts of war alongside me. I concentrated on swordplay." Grinning, Alex held his cane by the handle and executed a series of thrusts and slashes that looked to be well practiced. "Luke preferred the crossbow. 'Tis a more impersonal method of killing. One doesn't have to look one's target in the eye. He never had the natural interest in soldiering that I did, but he embraced it as a preferable alternative to the Church."

"He seems to have embraced it very well," Faithe said, bending her head once more to her work, "to have become known as the Black Dragon."

After a pause, Alex said, "Luke is the type of person who, if he bothers to do something, wants to do it well. Look how he's thrown himself into the management of this farm. Your villeins respect him already—I can see it in their attitudes. Except for your bailiff, of course."

Faithe sighed. "I don't know if Orrik will ever accept a Norman as his master."

Alex tapped his cane thoughtfully on the ground. "I don't know as he has much choice, if he wants to remain bailiff here. I can't imagine Luke will put up with his insolence forever."

Faithe bit her lip. She'd not permit herself to contemplate the possibility that Luke might want to relieve Orrik of his duties. Orrik had served her family since long before she was born. He'd become a kind of father to her after her own father had succumbed to his chronic lung ailments. Orrik was mulish and frequently quarrelsome, but she loved him, in a way, and would be loath to replace him. She sincerely hoped he didn't persist in trying Luke's patience.

"Except for Orrik," Alex said, "I believe Luke finds life here quite agreeable. I don't think I've ever seen him so content." Leaning forward, he added, with a smile, "It seems to me his happiness must be at least partly due to his lovely wife."

"Don't be so sure," Faithe said, thinking about Luke rolled up in his blanket in the rushes night after night.

Alex waved a dismissive hand. "That will sort itself out in time."

"*What* will sort itself out?" Had Luke discussed their sleeping arrangements with his brother?

Alex cleared his throat. "I've got eyes and ears. I know how things are. Don't worry. These situations have a way of righting themselves. It's like steam building up in an untended kettle. There's nowhere for it to go, and the kettle trembles and shakes and threatens to erupt, but finally the top flies off all on its own, and the steam comes shooting out."

Somehow that imagery provided little in the way of reassurance. "So . . . I should just wait for the top to fly off?"

He shrugged, grinning carelessly. "Have you got a better idea?"

Luke awakened in the moonlit bedchamber, face-down in the rushes, his body quivering, hips flexing involuntarily, ready to explode.

Nay! Not again. He rolled over and sat up, drenched in sweat and painfully erect beneath his drawers.

It had happened once before, several nights ago, during one of his dreams about Faithe, naked and glistening and writhing in his arms. Only that time he'd awakened to find his pleasure already shuddering through him. He'd swallowed a groan as his seed discharged, then lay there breathless, praying that Faithe was still asleep. He hadn't been prone to this sort of thing since adolescence, and it shamed him to be subject to it now.

Standing, he approached the bed stealthily, so as not to awaken his wife.

Faithe lay on her back, her face turned toward him, mouth half open, arms and legs at odd angles. In deference to the warm night, she'd kicked the covers off, and her shift was rucked up around her thighs. Silvery moonlight caressed her lissome body, all too visible beneath the delicate linen. Her luxuriously round breasts rose and fell steadily. His palms tingled with the need to caress them.

Instead, his hand stole to the rigid shaft between his legs. It jerked at his touch; he clenched his jaw against the pulsing need that hovered just on the verge of erupting.

Not here. Yanking his chausses off their hook, he pulled them on and tied them, then tugged a shirt over his head. He'd go outside, find someplace private, and put an end to this excruciating ache himself.

Treading on silent feet to the door, he slowly opened it, stilling when he noticed movement down in the main hall. He squinted into the vast semidarkness.

Alex is awake, he thought. And then he saw that his brother was not alone. Two people occupied the pallet by the fire pit—Alex and one of his charmingly debauched twins.

They were naked, both of them, their bodies locked together as they sat facing each other, moving in a lazy, sensual rhythm. Alex smiled and whispered something to her; nodding, she slid her hand between them, to where they were joined. Even from this distance, Luke could see the glitter in Alex's half-closed eyes as he watched her pleasure herself, her head thrown back, her expression rapturous. Gripping her shoulders, he increased the tempo of his movements, every muscle in his body standing out in sharp relief.

Luke closed the door and pressed his forehead against it. His cock felt like red-hot steel. He lay on his back in the rushes without undressing.

Over the quiet breathing of his sleeping wife, Luke could just barely hear a series of soft, feminine cries from the main hall.

It was going to be a long night.

Chapter 9

She saw him as she strolled along the narrow path that led past the small sheep pasture tucked between the village and the river. The pasture was empty, the sheep having been gathered for shearing into the sheepfold, an open pen with a wooden shelter at one end, surrounded by a scattering of shade trees.

Her husband stood beneath an ancient oak, his back to her, his arms crossed, watching the annual shearing ritual. Even at this distance, Luke de Périgueux could not be mistaken for anyone else. His height, the breadth of his shoulders, and the uncommon stillness with which he held himself, distinguished him from other men.

Next to Luke, sitting on a stump with his cane across his lap, was his brother. Faithe was pleased that Alex had walked so far from the house. The wound to his side had knitted nicely, but the deep gash in his hip was healing more slowly, and with a dreadful scar. Even now, more than a month since the attack, it pained him to put his weight on that side. He walked with a limp, but Faithe hoped that wouldn't last.

It was a clear, sunny morning, and sultry for early June. The brothers de Périgueux were in shirtsleeves and chausses, having abandoned their tunics as a concession to the heat. As for Faithe, she'd chosen her lightweight, front-lacing russet kirtle and dispensed with an undershift altogether.

As she approached the men, Faithe noticed that

they weren't alone. Little Felix sat cross-legged in front of Luke, lining up his collection of clay soldiers in the grass. The fatherless boy had been Luke's shadow for the past three weeks, tagging along with him whenever his mother would permit it.

Alex pointed toward the sheepfold and said something to Luke, who nodded. Faithe knew what had caught their attention; a woman had taken up the shears, joining the half dozen men laboring industriously on the hard-packed earth outside the sheepfold to strip the animals of their wool.

"That's Elga Brewer," Faithe said, coming up behind the two men and dropping her satchel on the ground. They turned to greet her; Luke's expression of pleasure warmed her. "Elga takes time out from her ale making every June to help us with the shearing. Her father was a shepherd, so she grew up doing this."

Luke's dark eyes sparked with amusement. "Why aren't you pitching in yourself? I've seen you milk cows, rethatch roofs, weave wattle . . ."

"She was spreading manure yesterday," Alex put in with a grin. "I saw her."

"I'm not surprised." Luke smiled at her, something he did more and more recently. "Why draw the line at shearing?"

"Even if I had the skill, and I don't," Faithe said, "I'm not strong enough. Look at Elga." The brewer was as big as the biggest man, with arms of solid muscle from hauling around full kegs.

"She scares me," Felix said.

Luke chuckled. "She scares me a little, too."

They watched the shearing in silence from the tranquil shade of the old oak. Faithe smiled to herself. When the sheep were stripped of their winter coats, it meant that spring was drifting into summer, and there was no finer time of year than summer. Dunstan supervised the work, Orrik being off on one of his unexplained "errands." Faithe wished he'd just go ahead and marry the Widow Aefentid and move her into his house. These increasingly frequent visits to her under the guise of estate business took him away from Hauekleah at inconvenient times.

Not that Dunstan was unequal to the challenge of overseeing the workings of the farm. In fact, Orrik's recurrent absences had provided the young reeve with the opportunity to prove his mettle. Despite his youth, he was more than competent, and a natural leader. Just as important, unlike Orrik, he appeared to harbor no ill-will toward Luke. In fact, from all appearances, he'd come to hold his new master in as high a regard as he'd held Caedmon—possibly higher, for Luke took a far more active interest in the affairs of Hauekleah than Faithe's first husband had.

The young reeve strode back and forth, keeping tally on a wax tablet and calling out instructions over the bleating of the sheep. Each shearer had a child working alongside him, gathering the shorn wool into giant sacks and offering the workers ladlefuls of water from buckets.

"Why aren't you helping to collect the wool?" Faithe asked Felix.

The boy's shoulders slumped. "Uncle Dunstan wanted me to, and I tried, but I'm no good at it. The other boys . . . they said . . . well, I'm just no good at it."

Alfrith and Brad and the others had eased up some on their incessant taunting of Felix—a result of Luke's taking him under his wing—but it appeared they hadn't abandoned the sport altogether.

"You're just not as big as those other boys," Luke told him. "That's why you had trouble. You'll be better at it next year."

Felix shrugged and continued desultorily arranging his toy soldiers.

Alex grinned up at Luke. "What's stopping *you*

from helping with the shearing? You herded swine yesterday."

Faithe raised her eyebrows at her husband.

"I helped to gather up the pigs from the woods where they were foraging," Luke explained to her. "That's all."

"You're so keen on finding out how everything is done around here," Alex goaded. "Go on. Go ahead. Offer your services."

Luke hesitated.

"Perhaps you shouldn't," Faithe said. " 'Tis highly skilled work. An inexperienced shearer can cut a sheep pretty badly."

"He's done it before," Alex offered. "He told me."

"At the monastery where I was brought up," Luke explained. "But I was young, and they trusted me only with the wee ones. I was passably good at it, though."

"A grown sheep is a handful," Faithe said. "You're best off—"

"I'm best off seeing if I've still got the touch," Luke said, rolling up his sleeves.

Alex whooped. "That's the spirit!"

Luke nudged Felix with the toe of his boot. "What do you say, pup? Care to gather up my wool for me?"

Felix sprang to his feet and hopped up and down. "Can I? Oh, milord, thank you! I'll do a good job, I swear it!"

"I'm sure you will."

Luke walked up to the sheepfold, Felix in tow, and spoke briefly to Dunstan, who registered a fair measure of surprise.

Faithe chuckled. "They're not used to having a master who pitches in this way."

"Your husband didn't?" Alex asked.

Faithe expelled a long sigh. "Caedmon had other interests. He left the management of Hauekleah to me, and I was just as happy for it. I mean, I suppose I would have preferred if he'd at least cared about the land. But he didn't interfere with what I thought was best, and I was grateful for that."

"Do you resent Luke for coming in and taking over this way?"

Faithe thought about that. "Not really. 'Tis odd. I suppose I should. Perhaps I can accept it because he hasn't taken anything away from me, or tried to make me stop doing the things I did before."

"But you still think he's going to tire of Hauekleah and go back to soldiering, don't you?"

Faithe chewed her lip as she watched Luke drag a big ewe out of the sheepfold by her front legs, a look of determination on his face. "I don't know anymore."

The other shearers exchanged skeptical glances as Luke balanced the ewe between his legs, grasped her front hooves, and took the shears from Felix. He paused. His gaze flicked toward Faithe, just for a moment, and then he began cutting the wool away from the animal's belly.

Alex gave her a knowing smile. "He's trying to impress you, you know."

"Nonsense." But her cheeks grew warm.

Alex chuckled.

Luke alternatively clipped and pulled the wool from the sheep's body, exposing its creamy underbelly. He worked more slowly than the others, and a bit awkwardly. The wool came off in small, ragged pieces, which Felix grabbed eagerly and stuffed into his bag.

Gesturing Dunstan over, Luke asked him something. The reeve took the shears from him and neatly sliced the rest of the wool away from the ewe's belly.

"He's asking for advice," Alex murmured.

This display of humility would serve him well with the men, Faithe knew.

The other shearers watched this demonstration as they worked, still somewhat bemused, but interested. Taking back the shears, Luke turned the big ewe over and set to work on her back. His cuts were smoother than before, the wool pulling away in large sheets. Dunstan offered praise along with more instruction.

Tendrils of hair came loose from Luke's braid and stuck to his forehead, damp with sweat. His shirt stretched across his shoulders as he hunkered down over the writhing animal, struggling to control her while he stripped her of her wool. With every movement, the hard bands of muscle in his forearms bunched and flexed, veins standing out beneath the brown skin.

Luke wrapped a big hand around the ewe's snout and cut the wool away from her neck. Squatting down, a leg on either side of her, he sheared her hind end, tossing the filthy wool aside for Felix to lift gingerly and stuff into his bag.

Flipping the animal over, he sheared her side. Patches of sweat soaked the front and back of his shirt. Shearing was hard work, especially in this kind of heat.

Luke pulled the ewe up by her front legs, rolled her over onto her feet, and slapped her on her rump, sending her scrambling back into the sheepfold.

"Well?" Alex grinned at her. "Did he impress you?"

"He impressed the men." Cries of "Well done!" and "Good work, milord!" rose above the incessant bleating. Dunstan slapped Luke on the back. He deserved their praise. He'd shorn that sheep without so much as a nick, and had the good sense to ask for help—and take it.

Luke's gaze sought out Faithe. She saw the pride in his eyes, half hidden beneath something that might almost have been shyness, and smiled at him. He smiled back, then took the ladle Felix offered him and drained it in one tilt of his head. Whipping his shirt off, he tossed it onto the fence, then opened the gate and dragged out another ewe, this one a giant.

"He's a quick study," Faithe said as he propped the ewe between his legs and swiftly stripped her belly of its wool.

"I told you," Alex replied. "When my brother chooses to do a thing, he likes to do it well. He commits himself entirely to everything he does."

The fierce concentration in Luke's eyes attested to that. He worked faster than before, but with enormous grace and control. His movements were elegant in their economy, the very image of calculated strength. The wool came away in heavy mats, which Felix could barely squeeze into the bag.

Faithe couldn't wrest her gaze from Luke as he manipulated the huge animal, every part of his body coming into play to control her. His cross dangled down, getting in the way, so he flipped it behind him, then leaned down to straddle the ewe, immobilizing her with a firm grip on her front legs while he wielded the shears. Sweat dripped off his face, trickled down his bare chest and belly, soaked the waist of his chausses. The brown woolen hose clung to his legs, highlighting muscles taut with the effort of restraining the sheep.

A whisper of heat tickled Faithe as she watched her husband shear, his expression that of a man intent upon his work. He turned around as he tossed the animal onto her side, the muscles of his back and buttocks and thighs straining as he wrestled the big ewe.

He commits himself entirely to everything he does. Not for the first time, she wondered if he would bring that same intensity to their marriage bed, when the time came.

Faithe hadn't made any more sexual overtures since that night, and wasn't about to. Not only had she bungled her one invitation quite badly, but it seemed he truly meant it when he told her he didn't want her on just any terms. She had to learn to trust him; she had to give herself to him because she truly wanted him.

She'd made some progress in that direction. In her heart, she now knew that he wouldn't annul their marriage, regardless of whether it was consummated. One thing she'd learned about Luke de Périgueux in the five or six weeks since he'd been here was that he was, as Alex claimed, a man of honor.

But could she trust him to remain here once he'd gotten a thorough taste of farm life? He seemed committed to Hauekleah, but then, so had Thorgeirr, according to Grandmother Hlynn.

Having shorn the enormous ewe, Luke righted her and shoved her back into the sheepfold. The men cheered him enthusiastically. He accepted their accolades with what looked like a mixture of pride and embarrassment.

Faithe and Alex watched him shear two more sheep, and then Dunstan called a break for the noon meal. Luke turned Felix over to his mother, snatched his shirt off the fence, and strode back toward the oak tree.

Alex stood, leaning on his cane. "Well done, brother."

"Very well done," Faithe said, lifting her satchel off the ground.

"Thank you." Luke tilted his head toward the satchel. "What have you got there?"

"Some bread and cheese and wine," she said. "I need to inspect Norfeld and see how the crops are coming in, so I thought I'd eat my dinner in the field."

Luke wiped his face with the shirt and draped it around his neck. "I don't imagine you have enough food there for two."

"Ardith Cook packed it. If I know her, there's enough here for ten." Willing away an absurd wave of shyness, she said, "Would you care to join me?"

"If I may."

Faithe smiled, straining to keep her gaze from his bare torso, still damp with sweat. "I'd be glad of the company."

Luke turned to his brother. "If you were up to it, I'd ask you to join us."

Alex laughed. "Then you'd be a fool, giving up the

opportunity to have such an enchanting woman all to yourself."

Faithe rolled her eyes. Alex bid them good day and limped away in the direction of Hauekleah Hall. Luke and Faithe walked past the sheepfold to the river, strolling in silence along its grassy bank until they came to the bridge, on the other side of which lay Norfeld.

They were halfway across the bridge when Luke stopped and handed her his shirt. "If you don't mind, I think I'll wash off some of this sweat."

"No, not at all. I've never known a man to bathe as often as you, though." Every evening after supper, Luke disappeared for a while, always returning with his hair wet and slicked back.

He grinned as he squatted down to remove his boots. "I'm teaching Felix to swim."

"Truly?"

He stood and untied his chausses, stripping them off and giving them to her to hold. Beneath them he wore loose linen drawers with a drawstring waist. "I take him here and give him lessons. Soon I hope he'll have the courage to jump off this bridge. And next year, that boy won't scream when Orrik throws him into the river."

Faithe smiled to think of the Black Dragon taking such pains over an undersized little boy. "The others still tease him sometimes," she observed.

"The bullying instinct is very strong in young boys. But they're getting better." Ducking his head, he removed the cross on its leather thong and looped it around her neck, over her keys.

"Have you spoken to them?"

"Nay. 'Twould be a grave error to intercede openly on Felix's behalf. The others would view him as being under my protection, which would only make matters worse for him."

Faithe was impressed with the wisdom of the course

he'd chosen. But before she could compliment him on it, he braced his hands on the side of the bridge and leapt over it, jumping in with a loud splash. She watched him swim upriver, his vigorous strokes propelling him swiftly away from the bridge. He got smaller and smaller as he swam away, disappearing altogether when the river curved into the woods.

Faithe crossed to the opposite shore, laid Luke's clothes and her satchel on a boulder at the water's edge, then lifted her skirt up to her knees and tied it in a knot to keep it there. She sat on the boulder with her feet in the cool water and rummaged around in the satchel until she found a linen-wrapped bundle spotted with red juice. Laying the bundle in her lap, she untied it, grinning in delight at the first strawberries of the season. Ardith knew how she loved them.

She lifted one by its long stem and inhaled its fragrance, then popped it into her mouth.

"Mmm . . ." This was the taste she dreamed of all winter long and cherished during the brief few weeks of strawberry season. She ate her berries in luxurious contentment, savoring their summer-ripe flavor, the warm breezes that ruffled her hair, the bracing chill of the water that lapped around her ankles.

Luke reappeared around the bend and swam back toward her. When he was close enough to the shore to stand, he did so, walking slowly out of the river, his gaze trained first on her legs, and then her eyes.

She'd never seen a man move with such restrained, lethal grace. He stalked toward her like a cat approaching its prey—slowly, almost warily, never breaking eye contact. Water sluiced off his massive shoulders and long arms, ran in rivulets down his ridged stomach; the dark hair on his chest sparkled with tiny droplets. His waterlogged drawers hung low on his narrow hips, conforming all too well to his masculine contours.

A memory sprang into sharp focus, an image that

had obsessed her since the night of her ill-fated seduction attempt: Luke standing before her in nothing but his chausses, his arousal plainly evident as she knelt at his feet. She remembered the way he'd looked at her—the hunger in his eyes. She remembered touching him—the rigid heat beneath the tightly stretched wool, the desperate need just under the surface.

As he closed in on her, his gaze traveled slowly downward, until it lit on the open bundle in her lap.

"Strawberries?"

She nodded, lifting the best-looking one by the stem. "Would you like one?"

Luke took the berry from her, brought it to his nose, and smiled. He passed the small red fruit between his lips, his eyes closing as he bit it in half. Juice ran down his chin; he wiped it away with the back of his hand. "Perfect."

"That one was the ripest," she said.

"Then we should share it." Plucking the other half of the berry off the stem, he brought it to Faithe's mouth. Something about his feeding her this way struck her as so rawly intimate that, for a moment, she could do nothing but look at him.

He smiled into her eyes, then dropped his gaze to her mouth and nudged her lips open with the piece of fruit. She closed her mouth over it, unintentionally catching his fingertips between her lips as he withdrew them. His gaze flicked toward her eyes before settling once again on her mouth. A trickle of juice escaped her lips. He brushed it with his thumb, which he then brought to his own mouth and licked.

Their gazes met. He looked away and tossed the berry stem into the grass. Faithe busied herself retying the linen around the berries and stowing them in the satchel.

It had been this way in recent weeks. A hot current of awareness crackled between them, growing more charged with every word they spoke, every look they exchanged. Luke's desire for her was evident, yet every time she thought he'd act on it, he pulled back.

Perhaps he felt it was still too soon. By his own standards, he'd be right. He wanted her to lose her lingering doubts about him, but she still didn't quite believe that a ruthless professional soldier could be happy shearing sheep and herding swine for the rest of his life. Much as she'd come to care for Luke, she still held something back from him, and he seemed to sense this.

Perhaps he was looking for some sign from her that she'd overcome her initial fear of him and, moreover, learned to trust and even care for him. Was he waiting for her to make the first move? If so, he'd have a long wait, for she didn't think she'd ever work up the nerve to try and tempt him again.

In truth, Faithe found it rather odd, but touching, that this formidable warrior—who one would assume had a heart of pure ice—would bother about feelings in relation to the act of love. Yet he seemed to want some sort of union of the spirit before their bodies were joined. She wasn't used to taking sex so seriously. Caedmon certainly never did. He'd had appetites that needed appeasing, and she obliged him with enthusiasm. Their feelings for each other had gone no deeper than simple affection, and their love life reflected that. They'd tupped for no more profound reason than to entertain themselves.

She'd offered Luke that form of entertainment, but he didn't want her on those terms. Often she wished he did; she ached for him. Never in her life had she felt such constant yearning. Nothing in her experience had prepared her for this. Caedmon had wanted only her body. Luke de Périgueux wanted so much more; he wanted a piece of her soul. With a slight shock she realized that she was almost inclined to give it to him.

Backing up into the river, Luke said, "You should come for a swim."

"I can't swim."

"Come in anyway. 'Tisn't deep till you get to the middle. 'Twould cool you off."

"I don't want to. I'd get my kirtle wet."

He crossed his arms in a mock display of indignation. "A properly submissive wife would jump in simply because I commanded it."

"Then you should have married one of them."

"Are you afraid of the water?"

"Of course not."

"Good." He scooped his hands through the water, splashing her from head to toe.

She gasped. "You . . . you . . ."

He laughed, and she was struck by the way it transformed him, replacing his dark ferocity with something closer to Alex's boyishness. "What delicious outrage. You should see yourself." He splashed her again.

She looked down at her sodden kirtle. "Luke!"

"Aye?" He stood with careless grace in water up to his thighs, his hands resting on his lean hips, his chest shaking with amusement. His playfulness amazed her. Never had she seen this side of him, nor even suspected its existence. "Do I have to drag you in against your will?" He strode toward her.

When he was about a yard away, she kicked out, spraying him with water. "That does it!" He lunged for her.

She scrambled backward over the boulder, laughing nervously. He seized her ankles and dragged her toward him until she was snugged up against him, her legs flanking him. She felt his hands on her thighs, pulling her even closer, felt a heart-stopping thrill as he leaned down, his breath hot on her face, his voice a soft growl. "I must teach you a lesson in wifely obedience."

Bringing his hands to her shoulders, he trailed them lightly downward. She held her breath, her breasts seemed to swell in anticipation of his touch. But it never came. Instead, his fingers curled around the chain that held her keys and the leather thong to which his cross was attached, both of which he pulled off over her head and laid next to her on the boulder. As always, she felt vulnerable without her chatelaine's keys.

Grinning wickedly, he closed his hands around her waist, lifting her off the boulder.

"Luke! What are you—"

"Teaching you a lesson." He wrapped her legs around his waist and waded into the river. She squirmed and beat against his chest, but he just laughed.

His body was rock-solid, his arms immovable bands of steel; she was completely in his power. "Let me go!" she ordered amid helpless giggles.

"I don't think so." He waded deeper into the water.

"I demand that you let me go!"

He paused, waist-deep. "You demand it?"

"Yes!"

"Oh, in that case . . ." Lifting her off him, he hurled her, kicking and screaming, into the water. It closed over her head, immersing her completely.

Her instinct was to find her footing and stand. Instead, she located his legs beneath the surface and grabbed, yanking them out from beneath him. He flopped down into the water as she stood and began wading to the shore.

Halfway there, she heard him behind her. She let out an involuntarily little squeak of panic and tried to pick up her pace, but he was on her instantly, his big arms crushing her back against his chest and lifting her off her feet. "Sneaky Saxon wench!" he chuckled.

She hooked a foot around his leg, throwing him off balance and sending them both, into the shallow water at the edge of the river. They tussled together, laughing breathlessly, as she tried to elude his clutches. She managed to disentangle herself and clamber upright, but he sprang to his feet and seized her from behind before she could make her escape.

One of his hands inadvertently closed over a breast. There was a heartbeat's pause, and then he released her. She stumbled out of the water and turned around to look at him. His chest heaved as he appraised the length of her body, encased in a single layer of wet russet homespun and nothing else. She followed his gaze. The drenched kirtle molded itself to her breasts and waist and hips, and was still knotted in front, exposing her legs in their entirety.

He abruptly turned his back to her, skimming back loose strands of hair with both hands. "I'm going to change into my dry clothes," he said, a little gruffly. "I'll meet you in Norfeld."

"All right." Snatching up her satchel and keys, Faithe walked to the north, between a strip planted with barley and one of oats. Pausing, she twisted her hair to squeeze the water out, then bent over to untie and wring out her skirt. The drenched homespun would dry quickly in this hot sunshine, given its loose weave, in the meantime it would keep her cool. She stole a glance toward the river, and Luke.

He stood at the boulder with his back to her, completely naked as he twisted his drawers in his fists. She straightened, studying him unashamedly. He was the most beautifully proportioned man she had ever seen, his shoulders broad, hips lean, arms and legs long and sinewy. His body, packed with muscle, radiated resilient strength.

Tearing her gaze from him, she turned back around and walked between the two strips, pausing now and then to squat down and inspect the condition of the soil or pluck a weed. When she heard him coming up behind her, she looked down at herself; her hair covered her breasts, and already her drying kirtle had ceased to cling so indecently.

"Did you say you had wine in that bag of yours?"

he asked as he joined her, fully dressed in shirt, chausses, and boots.

"Indeed."

She retrieved the wineskin and handed it to him. He squeezed some into his mouth, then she did the same. They passed it back and forth between them as they slowly toured Norfeld, discussing the emerging crops and what they might bring at market. Luke seemed to like her idea of organizing the villagers into clearing a third community field next year. They discussed the project at length as they strolled west, to eat their meal in the untended meadow adjacent to Norfeld.

Blankets of wildflowers embellished the meadow with great sweeps of color, their fusion of scents perfuming the warm air. Faithe pointed to a patch of clover and they settled there. She unwrapped a loaf of white bread, a wheel of cheese, and the rest of the strawberries, laying the food out between them.

Dinner was a leisurely affair, accompanied by easy conversation. They talked about her plans for Hauekleah—*their* plans for Hauekleah, for he had ideas of his own, good ones. He praised her management of the estate, and she flushed with pride. They spoke in careful terms of the Norman occupation, and of what would happen to England under King William's rule. He questioned her at length about the customs of her people—their holidays and rituals—in a way that implied no disapproval, only a desire to learn.

If anyone had tried to tell Faithe, a month ago, that she would grow comfortable enough with the ferocious Black Dragon to relax with him in a wildflower meadow over cheese and wine, she would never have believed it.

As they finished the last of the berries and wine, she said, "You're an able man with the sheep shears. I was impressed."

He smiled a little self-consciously, clearly pleased with the compliment. The expression stripped years from his features. For the first time, she could almost believe he was but six-and-twenty. "Don't forget," he said, "it wasn't the first time I'd sheared. The monks taught me how, when I was a boy."

"Did you enjoy it?"

"I loved it." He reclined on his side in the clover, his head resting in his hand, and yawned, prompting Faithe to do the same; the warm sun and their full bellies were taking their toll. "Most of the abbey's farm work was done by lay brothers and serfs, but the monks and students were obligated to perform certain chores. To me, they weren't an obligation, but a joy. I was far more eager to tend sheep and pick grapes and harvest wheat—even milk cows—than to sit in some stuffy room and practice my Latin."

Faithe chuckled and plucked a perfect little violet that had sprung up among the clover. "I loved practicing my Latin."

"It shows. Your Latin is flawless. I can barely read it." He shrugged lazily, his eyes half closed. "That's all right. If I had that time to live over again, I'd still sneak away from class and spend my time in the fields. When I look back on those years . . ." His gaze grew wistful; he shook his head fractionally. "I can scarcely believe how happy I was then. Truly happy."

On impulse, Faithe slipped the violet into one of the eyelets through which the lacings of her still-damp kirtle were threaded. Luke watched her do this with heavy-lidded eyes. "Pretty," he murmured.

Faithe covered her awkwardness by gathering up the remnants of their meal and replacing them in her satchel. When she glanced back at Luke, he was fast asleep, still lying on his side, his arm cradling his head. His body had settled into the clover with such perfect grace that she couldn't take her eyes off him. He was uncommonly, breathtakingly beautiful.

With his face relaxed in sleep, he seemed even younger than before. She could visualize with ease what he'd looked like as a boy—dusky-skinned, black-haired, with enormous brown eyes that saw everything.

Using her satchel as a pillow, she lay on her back and gazed up at the endless expanse of blue overhead. Closing her eyes, she saw a little black-haired boy wading contentedly through gold-washed fields of ripening wheat beneath a cloudless Aquitaine sky.

Faithe awoke to a soft tremble of awareness—something touching the bare skin of her breast.

Bare? She opened her eyes, squinting against the afternoon sun. Blinking away her confusion, she looked toward the source of the sensation that had awakened her, then grew very still.

Luke sat over her as she lay on her back, delicately poking the stem of a violet into one of the eyelets on the bodice of her kirtle, now almost dry. Tiny purple flowers sprouted from half a dozen of the little holes; he'd been busy while she slept.

Hunching over her with an expression of intense concentration, he was apparently too absorbed in this undertaking to notice that she'd awakened. He probed the eyelet with great care, as if fearful of disturbing her. Finally, the stem slid through the hole, stroking the inner curve of a breast as he wriggled it into place. A warm shiver coursed through her; her nipples tightened beneath the homespun. Luke noticed this, and met her gaze.

His slow smile belied the heat in his eyes. "I couldn't help myself."

She sat up, delicately patting the row of tiny blossoms. "Perhaps I should take them out before we return to the house. What will people think?"

"They'll think we've had an extraordinarily pleasant outing. As, indeed, we have." Luke smiled warmly, then started to say something else, but stopped himself. Looking down, he spotted another violet and snapped it off. He tucked Faithe's hair behind her ear, and the flower with it. Very quietly, in a voice rough with feeling, he said, "I'm happy here."

She searched his eyes, so earnest, almost grave. "I know." She did; it was patently obvious.

"This"—he indicated all of Hauekleah with a small nod of his head—"is what I've been wanting, what I've needed for so long. I intend to spend the rest of my life here, Faithe. I'm not like your grandfather. I'm not going to ride off some morning and never return."

Faithe had never discussed Thorgeirr with Luke, nor hinted at her suspicions that he would abandon Hauekleah. "How did you know about—"

"Alex and I talk about everything."

Of course. Faithe ducked her head to hide her hot blush, but Like cupped her chin in his callused hand and lifted it, forcing her to look him in the eye. He brought his face close to hers; her pulse quickened.

"I'm not leaving here, Faithe," he said, softly but resolutely. "Never. I need you to know that."

She nodded. Presently, his expression softened, his gaze lighting on her hair, her mouth, the silly little flowers adorning her kirtle. "I'm happy here," he said. "Happier than I've been since . . ." Gently releasing her, he sat back and shrugged. "Happier than I've ever been, I think."

She took a deep breath. "I'm glad." She was. How strange to be glad that the Black Dragon had no intention of leaving, as she'd once prayed he would. How very remarkable. How astonishing and wonderful. Yet . . .

"Are you sure you're *completely* happy?" she asked him carefully. "What about Orrik?"

His expression clouded over. "Orrik. Aye, well . . ." He grimaced and shook his head. "Orrik is a problem.

The only real problem, but a serious one. I can't have a bailiff who's openly impertinent."

"I know. He'll come around, though. I'm sure of it."

Luke raised a doubtful eyebrow.

"Give him a chance, Luke," she pleaded, growing anxious. "I know he has faults, but he's been like a father to me my whole life. If you were to get rid of him, I'd be heartsick. Please, just give him a chance to get used to—"

"Shh." He reached out and stroked her hair. "I have no plans to dismiss him at present."

"Aye, but—"

"Faithe." He lowered his hand to cover both of hers as she twisted her ring around and around. She stilled. He tried for a wry smile, but his eyes were solemn. "You'll think this foolish, but it cuts me to the quick every time I see you doing that to your wedding ring. It's almost as if you want to yank it off and throw it in the river."

"N-nay, I . . . 'tis naught but a nervous habit."

"I shouldn't make you so nervous," he said quietly, leaning in close. There was something almost wounded in his expression. She saw with startling clarity how needful he was, how much he craved that piece of soul she denied him. "I've done everything I can to make you comfortable with me."

"I'm . . . I'm comfortable with . . ."

He chuckled as if at a fibbing child, and lifted her left hand, rubbing the ring with his thumb. "This little nervous habit says otherwise. When you've broken yourself of it, perhaps then I can believe you." Bringing her hand to his lips, he kissed her fingertips, lightly, sending hot chills coursing through her. "It's getting late. We should go back."

She nodded.

He stood without releasing her, then helped her to her feet and held her hand all the way back to Hauekleah Hall.

Chapter 10

"Milord! Are you up there?"

Recognizing Felix's voice, Luke slammed the last nail into the oaken tile and scooted to the edge of the roof. "Aye. Is she home already?" He'd instructed the boy to let him know the moment Faithe returned.

"Aye, milord. She's out back, tending to Daisy."

From Luke's perch on top of Hauekleah Hall, he had an excellent view of the entire estate. Shielding his eyes against the glaring afternoon sun, he scrutinized the stable and adjacent horse pasture. "There she is."

Faithe had her mare—a splendid chestnut with flaxen mane and tail—under a shade tree at the edge of the pasture. As he watched, she removed Daisy's bridle and draped it over the fence.

"Did she bring Master Orrik back with her?" Luke asked the boy.

"Nay, she came back just like she went out—alone."

Luke hissed a Frankish curse under his breath. Faithe had gone out in search of Orrik because the cookhouse had burned down that morning, and she felt he'd want to know about it as soon as possible. It wasn't a dire emergency—fires happened, especially in cookhouses, and this one had been extinguished before it had spread to the other outbuildings in the croft—but Orrik always insisted on being informed of such incidents immediately. Only it so happened the irascible bailiff had been off on one of his obscure "errands" since yesterday morning. Baldric, as usual, had professed ignorance as to his whereabouts. If he wasn't visiting the Widow Aefentid at her inn on the other side of the woods, then where the devil was he?

"Here." Luke handed his hammer to Dunstan, working alongside him to patch the roof, and descended the ladder.

"Can I come with you?" asked young Felix as Luke strode up the garden path toward the croft's rear gate. He was about to say yes, but then he thought better of it. It was difficult enough talking to Faithe about Orrik without an audience.

"I think not, Felix." The boy nodded, his gaze on the ground. "You look as if you can use an afternoon snack. Go to the kitchen and tell one of the girls I said to give you some bread and honey."

"Aye, milord!" Suddenly animated, Felix sprinted toward the Hall.

As Luke crossed the pasture toward Faithe, he wiped his sweaty face with his shirt and raked the stray hairs off his forehead. She saw him and nodded—a little uneasily, he thought. That was too bad. During the week that had passed since their outing by the river, they'd enjoyed such easy, congenial relations. He hated for her to show any sign of discomfort around him, even if it was that damned Orrik's fault and not his.

She had something in her hand—an iron hoof pick. Settling her weight against Daisy's shoulder, she leaned down and ran a hand along her mare's front leg. A light squeeze of the fetlock was all it took for the well-trained mare to lift her foot.

"Did she pick up a stone?" Luke patted the animal's flank.

"Probably. She started limping halfway home." Cradling Daisy's foot in one hand, Faithe used the pick to scrape dried mud from the hoof and shoe. She looked absurdly pretty performing this task, her expression serious, her hair falling in her eyes.

"I take it Orrik wasn't at the Widow Aefentid's inn?"

She shook her head without raising her eyes from her work. "There it is." She tapped the pick against a sizable pebble that had gotten lodged in one of the deep ridges on the bottom of the hoof.

He began undoing Daisy's saddle. "I won't bother asking why a stable boy can't take care of this."

She grinned crookedly. "I'm glad you're trying to ask fewer foolish questions."

He tugged her hair. "Insolent wench."

She looked up and smiled.

He lightly caressed her cheek, hot and flushed from her ride. "Did you ask the widow whether he'd been there?"

Her smile disappeared. Faithe bent her head to her work. "Aye. He hadn't." She gave the pick a twist and the pebble popped out. "There." Lowering Daisy's leg, she dug in her pocket for a chunk of carrot and fed it to the complacent animal. "Good girl."

Luke hauled the saddle and blanket off Daisy and carried them into the stable. Locating a currycomb, he brought it out and started brushing Daisy down where the saddle and girth had been. "Where do you suppose he's been since yesterday morning, then?"

"I have no idea." She drew in a deep breath and let it out shakily. "I asked Aefentid about those other times—all those other 'errands' Orrik went off on when I thought he was with her."

Luke stilled. "He wasn't with her?"

"Only for brief visits. He'd stop on his way back from . . . wherever he went off to. Sometimes he'd spend the night with her, but only at the end of his trips." She shook her head, her expression miserable.

"Then what's he been up to? Where's he been—"

"I wish I knew. I feel like an idiot for having just assumed he was with Aefentid. He was always discreet about her, because she's a respectable widow and runs her own inn. I thought this business about 'errands' was just his way of protecting her from gossip. I hate to think he's been doing something he feels he can't talk to me about."

"He'll damn well talk to *me* about it," Luke growled. He must have brushed the mare a little too hard; she whickered testily.

"Here, give me that." Faithe held her hand out, and Luke placed the currycomb in it. She set about brushing down the rest of the horse, her strokes leisurely, her brow furrowed. "Orrik hasn't always been this way—this bad-tempered and secretive. He never used to go away on mysterious trips before Hastings. But since then, he's seemed . . . haunted. The things he saw there—" She broke off, undoubtedly wary of bringing up such matters with her Norman husband.

"I know what he saw there," Luke said quietly—a tacit acknowledgment that Orrik had been truthful in his account of King Harold's mutilation at William's hands.

"And Caedmon's death affected him, too," she added quietly, without looking at him. She never spoke about her first husband. "Orrik cared a great deal for Caedmon, despite . . . their differences. He grieved sorely for him."

Luke moved closer to her as she brushed her way across Daisy's side to her rump. "What about you, Faithe? Did you grieve for him, too?"

Faithe glanced up at Luke, her eyes wide in the cool shade. She nodded. "Yes. I grieved for him. I went to the barn and cried into the straw. I cried until I had no more tears."

In a hushed voice, he asked, "Did you love him?"

Her eyes sought out his for a brief, penetrating moment, and then she dropped her gaze and began running the currycomb through Daisy's tail. "In a way. Not like . . . that is, we weren't . . . He was my husband. We'd spent nearly eight years together. He was good to me, despite everything."

"Despite," Luke murmured.

"Pardon?"

"You keep saying 'despite.' You and Orrik both cared for Caedmon despite . . . what?"

She brushed the tail with long, thoughtful strokes. "Caedmon . . . Well, to understand Caedmon, you've got to understand that he wasn't from the country. He'd been city-bred his whole life. He was brought up in Worcester, the ward of the bishop." She looked up and met his gaze squarely, as if making a point that she was not ashamed of what she said next. "Caedmon was the bastard son of an important man. A very important man, if you believe the rumors."

Luke followed her as she moved around to Daisy's other side. "How did you come to meet him, growing up in such different circumstances?"

Her shoulders lifted in a little shrug as she smoothed the brush downward. "I met him on our wedding day. Our marriage was negotiated through the bishop and my former overlord." She glanced briefly at Luke before going on. " 'Twas a good match for me."

"I'm sure it was." Luke felt ridiculously pleased that Faithe's first marriage had been an arranged union, and not one of love.

"He was landless, of course," Faithe continued, "but that was just as well, for I'd no desire to leave Hauekleah. His father, although he didn't claim him openly, had provided very well for him. Caedmon's wealth paid for improvements I'd been wanting to make."

"How did Caedmon feel about all this?"

"I think he was content here, despite . . ." That lopsided grin pulled at her mouth as Luke shot her a look of amusement. "*Despite* his lack of interest in the land. He took up hunting and hawking, and that kept him occupied while I . . ." She shrugged again.

"Continued to run Hauekleah," Luke supplied.

Another careless shrug. "So you see, he really couldn't help not caring. 'Twas the way he was raised."

"Did he care about *you*?" Luke asked.

Faithe ceased her brushing and looked directly at Luke. "He was no more in love with me than I was with him. Neither of us expected love when we got married. Arranged marriages aren't like that. They're . . ." Her face pinkened, and she looked away and began vigorously brushing out Daisy's mane. "They're about other things."

"They start out about other things." He leaned against Daisy's shoulder, his gaze trained on her, not looking away, despite her obvious discomfort. "They don't have to end up that way."

She nodded, color scorching her cheeks as she brushed.

"You're not still in mourning for Caedmon, are you?" he asked, knowing she wasn't, but wanting to hear it from her.

She shook her head. "I came to terms with it. Not that I'm happy about how he died."

"He died for a cause."

"A lost cause," she said crisply. She slipped the currycomb in one pocket and withdrew another piece of carrot from the other, offering it to Daisy, who lipped it off her palm.

"Faithe, the English who fell at Hastings died heroes' deaths. They fought well, for a cause they believed in. You should be proud, not bitter."

She looked at him strangely. "Caedmon didn't die at Hastings."

He blinked at her. "He didn't . . . I thought . . ."

"Not during the battle itself. He was captured."

"Captured."

She nodded. "Your army took him prisoner. He died later, of some illness. I'm not sure what kind."

"Ah." Luke rubbed his chin, wondering how to respond to this remarkable news—remarkable simply because no English prisoners were taken at the Battle of Hastings. Those who weren't killed all vanished into the woods. And if prisoners had been taken, their families would have been asked for ransom soon thereafter. Yet Faithe clearly believed her husband had died a prisoner of war.

"Who reported these matters to you?" Luke asked guardedly.

"Orrik. He and Dunstan and some of the others went to Hastings with Caedmon."

It was best, Luke decided, to question Orrik before he spoke further of this to Faithe. He rubbed the back of his neck. "I wish I knew when that . . . when Orrik will be back."

Faithe slapped Daisy on the rump to send her trotting out into the middle of the pasture, then clasped her hands tightly, her features contracted with worry. "Luke, please don't dismiss him. Please. 'Tis my greatest worry. I couldn't bear it."

He sighed. "I don't want to, Faithe. You must believe that. But he may push me until I have no choice."

"He'll get better," she said. "Give him time."

"How much time? I've been here for a month and a half, and still he treats me with complete contempt. Everyone else, including Dunstan, accepts me as their master. I think some of them are even coming to like me. But to Orrik I'm the enemy, and I'll always be the enemy, and there's nothing I'll ever be able to do to change that."

" 'Twas the shock of Hastings," she insisted. "Of losing Caedmon and seeing what happened to King Harold. He'll overcome his anger in time."

"Some types of anger can't be overcome," Luke said gravely. "Sometimes the best one can hope for is to . . . bury one's rage deep within. Although one always runs the risk that it will erupt without warning." Luke wished he didn't have reason for knowing this so well.

She regarded him curiously. His gaze dropped to her hands, still tightly clenched. Smiling, he reached out and pried them apart, taking one hand in each of his. "This hasn't been an easy conversation, but I haven't noticed you twisting your ring."

She looked down, a little shyly. "I've tried to break myself of the habit."

He squeezed her hands. "I'm glad of it." Releasing one hand, he trailed his fingertips down the side of her face. Her eyes drifted shut.

"Do you suppose," he said softly, "I could get a hot bath before bed?"

She opened her eyes. "I thought you liked to bathe in the river."

"Generally, yes. But I've been a bit stiff of late. Sleeping on the rushes has its disadvantages."

So quietly he almost couldn't hear her, she said, "The bed would be more comfortable."

"That it would." He smiled and ran a thumb over her lips, feeling the fluttery heat of her breath. "I must take it under very serious consideration."

She smiled back, a slow, immensely gratified smile. "That you should."

"Caedmon? He died of the pox." Orrik spat on the ground. "In some stinking Norman prison." He continued picking his way through the charred remains of the cookhouse by the rusty light of the setting sun.

When Felix had run in during supper with the announcement that Orrik was back from his mysterious errand, Luke had sent word for the bailiff to meet him here at compline. Faithe had wanted to come with him—she seemed to think they would beat each other senseless if left to their own devices—but he wouldn't let her. Assuring her he had no intention of either thrashing Orrik or dismissing him—yet—he insisted on going alone. This was one conversation he didn't care for her to listen in on.

Luke inspected the great oven, the only part of the cookhouse left standing, although its stone facade was dusky with soot from the fire, and the greasy odor of smoke clung to it. It would need a good scrubbing. "Funny. I was at Hastings. I don't remember any prisoners being taken."

Orrik rummaged through chunks of scorched wood and came up with a clay salt box. He lifted the lid. "Hah!" Tilting the full box toward Luke, he said, "Fire didn't get everything." Setting the box aside, he continued searching through the debris.

"The English all ran into the woods," Luke persisted.

"Except those whose bodies littered the field of battle," Orrik snarled.

"Alongside those of the Normans," Luke pointed out. "No English soldiers were taken prisoner at Hastings, Orrik."

"Is that a fact?" Orrik yanked a bent and blackened sieve from the rubble and tossed it aside with a dismissive grunt.

"That's a fact." Luke crossed his arms and leaned back against the oven, not caring whether his shirt, which was ready for the rag box, got soot on it. "Now, tell me what really happened to Caedmon."

"I've told you all I know."

"I think not."

"Are you calling me a liar?"

"Aye."

Wrath darkened Orrik's face. "You've got no call to accuse me of lying."

"In point of fact, I do, because you're not telling the truth."

"To hell with the truth, and to hell with you." Turning away, Orrik nudged a half-burned bench aside, uncovering an intact iron trivet. He bent and picked it up, setting it beside the salt box.

Luke didn't move from his indolent pose against the oven. "Lady Faithe may not share your lack of interest in the truth."

Orrik's steely eyes speared Luke. "What have you told her?"

"Nothing. Yet. I was waiting to talk to you. If you won't tell me what really happened, I'll get the facts from Dunstan, or someone else. But rest assured, I *will* get them."

Squatting down, Orrik dug a big flesh hook out of the ashes and turned it over and over in his soot-stained hands, his gaze unfocused. When he looked up, his eyes were full of sorrow. "I'll tell you what you want to know, but only so you don't go stirring things up, looking for your precious truth. Faithe doesn't need to know this, but she's a smart girl—she'll catch wind of it if you start asking questions. You must hear what I say and keep your mouth shut."

"You're overstepping yourself if you think you can tell me what to do," Luke said with menacing calm. "Just tell me what happened."

Muttering a Saxon oath, Orrik slammed the hook into a chunk of wood, then pried it loose. "We'd got word last summer that your Duke William meant to sail his army to England and steal the throne from King Harold. So we set out from here to join Harold's forces and await the invasion. There was Caedmon and Dunstan and me, plus a couple of men who didn't make it. Took a while for you bastards to get up the guts to come across, but we waited you out—right up till the fourteenth of October. We tried to stick together at Hastings, and we did, through most of the battle. All except for Caedmon. We lost track of him as soon as the fighting started, and we never saw him again."

"You didn't find his body afterward?"

Orrik stood, the flesh hook at his side. "Nay, and it wasn't like I didn't try. I searched among the corpses for hours, turning them over, looking into their faces . . ." He squeezed his eyes shut. "He wasn't there."

"He deserted?" Luke asked.

Orrik gripped the big hook in a shaking fist. "I didn't say that! I just said he wasn't there."

"Did you look for him? Try to find out where he—"

"What do you take me for? Of course I looked for him. I searched all of southern England for him. 'Twas Christmastide by the time I returned to Hauekleah. I didn't know what to tell Faithe. As it turned out, she took the problem out of my lap. She's the one came up with the notion that he'd been taken prisoner."

"And you let her believe it."

"What would you have done? I was just trying to spare her feelings." Orrik scratched his shoulder thoughtfully with the tip of the hook. "But like I said, she's a smart girl. She knew about ransom and such. She sent me to London in January to negotiate for his release."

"And you went?"

"Aye, well . . . not to London. I spent the time searching for Caedmon, then came back and told her they wouldn't let him go yet. She kept saying they'd set him free eventually, and I hated to think of her being disappointed. I kept looking for him, starting in Sussex and working my way north."

"No luck?"

"Not till Hocktide—the last day of Easter. If you can call it luck. I wasn't even looking for Caedmon at the time—just happened to be passing through this little village on my way to market. Stopped in an inn for a pint, and asked if anybody'd seen a fellow of Caedmon's description. They led me to a grave." A muscle jumped in his jaw. "I dug it up, to make sure. 'Twas him. He'd been dead a few weeks—" Orrik's voice broke; he crossed himself grimly. "I filled the grave in and came back to Hauekleah. Told Faithe her husband had died in prison. And there you have it."

Luke scrubbed his hand over his scratchy jaw. "You lied to her, then."

Orrik took a step toward Luke, white fire flashing in his eyes. "I love that girl like she was my own daughter! How could I tell her that her husband died in a shabby little Cottwyk brothel, fighting over a two-penny whore?" He blanched, clearly realizing he'd revealed more than he'd intended to.

Luke's scalp prickled with apprehension. *Nay . . . it can't be.* "Cottwyk?"

"Aye, 'tis a little hamlet not far from Foxhyrst."

"I know it," Luke said woodenly, pushing away from the oven. "And they told you . . . that's how he died?"

Orrik grimaced and rubbed his eyes. "Aye. They said he showed up during the winter and wandered around, sleeping here and there. Called himself Caedmon. They said he had red hair and a beard, all long and tangled-like. I dug him up, and it was him."

A picture materialized in Luke's mind—snarls of reddish hair, tattered clothes . . . Cold panic shivered through him. *Nay . . .*

"That he should have come to such an end," Orrik said dismally, "is something only the Lord Himself can understand." Reaching into his tunic, he produced something shiny. With a sick jolt, Luke recognized Alex's gold mantle pin with its white wolf insignia. "This belongs to the bastard that done it. There's writing on the back, in French. If it kills me, I'm going to find the murdering whoreson and stretch his filthy Norman neck."

Luke willed steadiness into his voice. "Find him? You're looking for the . . . killer? Is that what these 'errands' of yours are all about?"

Orrik nodded, rubbing the pin with his thumb.

"Aye. I've been looking for the bastard for over two months now—quietly, of course. Faithe mustn't discover what I'm up to. She mustn't find out how Caedmon died. But his death must be avenged, and I intend to be the instrument of that vengeance." He stepped closer to Luke, holding the flesh hook like a weapon. "Sear to me that you won't tell her how her husband died. Swear it!"

"Don't presume to command me," Luke managed. "Or threaten me. Ever again." Shouldering Orrik aside, he turned away and stalked back toward the house, deeply shaken.

Christ, I'd be the last person to tell her! God, don't let her find out . . . please . . .

"Don't worry," Alex kept repeating that night after Luke dragged him out to the kitchen garden to share what Orrik had revealed.

"For God's sake, Alex, I killed her husband!"

"Shh!"

Both men glanced back at the dark form of the house looming over them. The windows of the bedchamber Luke shared with Faithe were brightly lit, and people were moving around in there. Luke heard the splash of water. Faithe must be arranging for the bath he'd wanted this afternoon when he'd thought . . .

"Christ, what am I going to do?" Luke whispered.

"You're going to put it out of your mind," Alex said determinedly.

"How can you say that? 'Tis *your* mantle pin they've got."

"They've had it for months now. They haven't found me yet."

" 'They' is now Orrik. He's intelligent and very, very angry. A dangerous combination."

In the darkness, Luke saw Alex's teeth flash. "He hasn't found me yet, and I've been living under his nose since the first of May. Nobody here knows me as the White Wolf. I'm perfectly safe."

Luke shook his head. "You're too complacent, brother. You should be thinking up ways to protect yourself, not denying the existence of danger."

"Luke . . ."

"I won't let you be punished for a crime I committed, Alex. I won't. That's all there is to it."

Alex leaned heavily on his cane. "Nothing has changed, you know. If you turn yourself in, I'll take responsibility. I'll claim you're just trying to protect me."

Luke groaned. "This is madness. Madness."

Alex shrugged. "Life is mad. One learns to deal with it."

The men went back inside. One of Alex's twins—the one with two braids—poured each of them a cup of brandy. Luke accepted his gratefully and drank it in one burning gulp.

"Milord?" Moira descended the bedchamber stairs, followed by two serving boys bearing empty buckets. "Your bath is ready."

As Luke turned toward the stairs, his brother closed a hand over his shoulder and whispered in his ear, "Enjoy your bath . . . and your bride. And stop worrying."

Luke climbed the stairs and knocked softly on the bedchamber door. Faithe, in a shift and wrapper, opened it and ushered him toward the steaming tub. "Everything's ready. Would you like me to . . . stay and help?"

Was she blushing, or was that just a trick of the candlelight? "Nay, I . . . I can manage."

Disappointment shadowed her face for a brief moment, and then she said, "Very well." On her way out the door, she stopped and turned. "Did you ask Orrik about those errands of his?"

Damn. Luke rubbed the bridge of his nose, wishing he'd thought this all out a little better. "Nay . . ."

"Nay?"

"That is, I did. He . . . wouldn't tell me. He's very stubborn."

"That he is. Do you want me to question him?"

Luke's head shot up. "Nay!"

"We've always been close. Perhaps I can—"

"I said nay!"

Faithe grew horribly still in response to his harsh tone.

"I'm . . ." He shook his head. "I'm tired. 'Tisn't you."

She visibly relaxed and even smiled. "Let the boys know when you're ready for them to take the tub away," she said and closed the door behind her.

Luke undressed and sank into the water, hot and lightly scented with something pleasantly herbal. After unbraiding his hair, he leaned back against the big wooden tub, closed his eyes and let out a long, troubled sigh.

He killed her husband.

I went to the barn and cried into the straw.

"Christ."

Luke slid down until his head was submerged. Only when his lungs were on fire did he come back up, gasping.

He was the one. The dark creature—the murdering Norman beast whom Orrik pursued with such grim purpose.

He was my husband. We'd spent nearly eight years together. He was good to me.

And Luke slew him over a two-penny whore. An unforgivable crime, but one which he thought he'd put behind him, at least for the remainder of his mortal existence. However, the sin that haunted his memory and blackened his soul had now resurfaced to jeopardize all that he'd gained, to strip him of everything important to him . . . including Faithe. He'd come to care deeply for her—far more deeply than he would have thought possible just a short time ago. And she'd become the focal point around which he was building his new life—a bucolic life he'd grown quickly to treasure, and which was suddenly very much at risk.

The knowledge that he murdered her husband—with no provocation other than the savagery lurking deep inside him—changed everything. For weeks he'd imagined making love to her—gazing into her eyes as he was buried deep inside her. Now, he couldn't envision that without seeing her expression of love and longing replaced by shock and outrage when she discovered what he'd done . . . and that he was, underneath it all, a monster. He couldn't let that happen. Faithe had become a part of him; she'd gotten into his very soul. To lose her now would be like ripping out his heart.

He'd been disgusted that Orrik had lied to her. Now he must do so himself, by withholding the awful truth about her husband's death.

And, as for making love to her . . .

I cried until I had no more tears.

He'd made her a widow, then married her for her property. Guilt flowed red-hot in his veins. If he tried to bed her now, he doubted his body would even rouse to her.

Luke washed up and dried off, dressed for bed, and had the boys empty and remove the bathtub. Faithe came back in as he was settling down in his usual spot in the rushes. She hesitated in the doorway, her expression pensive, then closed the door, took off her wrapper, and blew out the candles. He heard the ropes supporting the mattress squeak as she got into bed.

"Faithe . . ."

"Aye?"

Oh, Christ. "Good night." He lay down with his back to her.

There came a long pause. "Good night, Luke."

Chapter 11

Luke seized the Saxon by his tunic and yanked him off the whore, her screams reverberating in his skull. His hand curled into a fist, which he aimed at the Saxon's head.

He hauled back and swung—

The impact jolted him awake.

"What—?" He sat up, his right arm shaking, his hand still tightly fisted.

With a groan, he buried his face in his hands. The images remained, though, playing themselves out in his mind's eye . . . the one mighty, war-hammer punch . . . the Saxon's head—*Caedmon's* head—whipping around . . . the limp body in the straw.

It was back, all of it, the whole dreadful nightmare, back in full force.

Tossing off his blanket, he stood and looked down at Faithe, fast asleep in the predawn half-light. As usual, her bedclothes were askew, her limbs at engagingly awkward angles. When she was sleeping, she reminded him of a newborn filly, a study in artless elegance.

Luke recalled his impression of the Saxon, Caedmon, as no more than a ragged savage. The details of his appearance were blurry—the herbs always impaired his memory—but he remembered that rank odor of his. How could a woman like Faithe have tolerated marriage to such a man, however indifferent the union? This was a man, after all, who'd deserted his army on the brink of battle, a man who'd lived like a wild thing all winter, frequenting whores instead of returning to the loving wife waiting patiently at home for him.

Her keys were on the night table, where she left them every night when she retired. He'd forced her to do so, although he knew she hated to be without them, even at night. He'd forced her to speak to him in his own language, even in private. He'd come to her country as an enemy invader and claimed her ancestral farmstead for his own.

And she'd adapted to all of it. Morever, she'd adapted with grace and intelligence and a strength of character he'd never seen the equal of, in a man or a woman. She'd not only come to accept him, but to care for him. He needed no words of endearment from her to know what she felt for him; it was no more than he felt for her, a deep connection that went beyond physical longing—although there was that, too.

She'd given him the life he'd hungered for during those bleak, bloody years of soldiering. She'd given him sunlight and green pastures, warmth and human affection, a place in the world to call his own.

And he'd betrayed her with an act of unspeakable savagery, a betrayal no less inexcusable for having transpired before they'd met. He should have known it would fall apart, sooner or later. He hadn't wanted to sully their marriage by bedding her too soon. As it turned out, he'd sullied it irretrievably before they'd even been joined in wedlock. And there was no way to undo what he'd done, to wash away the harm.

For a brief time, he'd been a happy man. He'd begun to think he could bury the Black Dragon once and for all, and forget the bloodthirsty creature had ever existed.

Fool, he thought, gazing with consuming sorrow at the innocent beauty of his sleeping wife. *You* are *the Black Dragon. You will never escape the beast.*

Luke dressed quietly, taking pains not to awaken Faithe, then pinned his mantle over his shoulders and slipped from the bedchamber. In the great hall, he found Alex curled up in naked contentment with his wench. Leaving by the back door, he made his way to the stable, saddled up his horse, and rode to the river.

Pausing his mount on the bridge that led north, he unfastened his mantle pin and studied it by the faint, early-morning glow from the east. He rubbed his thumb over the little onyx dragon imbedded in the golden disk, remembering the day his father had presented the mantle pins to his two younger sons. It had been just before Luke and Alex had left to join William's invasion of England.

Luke's normally stoic sire had been moved to tears that day, not only because he feared for his beloved sons' lives, but also because he knew he might never see them again even if they lived through the invasion. After all, their purpose in following William had been to gain English estates—and England was very, very far from Périgueux.

As fate would have it, he never did see them again. He died at Christmastide, and all Luke had to remember him by was this pin. It was Luke's most cherished possession. Unlike his brother, so careless with his belongings, he never let it out of his sight.

Turning it over, he read the words on the reverse side, the same parting wish that was inscribed on the back of Alex's mantle pin . . . which was now in the hands of Orrik.

Closing his fist tight around the pin, Luke whispered the message out loud: "Be strong and of good courage." And then he hauled back and hurled the pin as hard as he could over the side of the bridge. It sailed in an achingly perfect arc, submerging with a soft splash the moment it hit the water.

Luke watched the point of impact until the last telltale ripple had dissolved. And then he kicked his mount into a gallop and rode until he and the horse were both exhausted.

The sun was fully risen by the time he returned and handed his reins to the stable boy. Reentering Hauekleah Hall by the back door, he ducked into the kitchen for something to ease his thirst, only to find the big central table lined up with kitchen wenches plucking pigeons and tossing them into a giant pot. Most roasting and stewing generally took place in the cookhouse; in its absence, the kitchen had evidently been pressed into service.

"Milord!" Massive, ruddy-faced Ardith Cook emerged from the pantry, holding a slab of bacon in one hand and a cleaver in the other. "A pleasure to see you this mornin'. What is it you be needin'?"

"Some ale," he said. "And perhaps a bit of bread to break my fast."

"Bonnie!" Ardith bellowed. The wench who'd kept Alex warm last night jumped up from the table. "You heard his lordship. Bring 'im some bread and ale." She slammed the bacon down on a stone slab and imbedded the cleaver in the meat. "Ain't it a bit late in the mornin' to be breakin' your fast, milord?"

"I've been out riding."

Ardith nodded and yanked the cleaver out of the bacon, then proceeded to hack it up into pieces, grunting with the effort. "Lord Caedmon was much the same, rest his soul." She paused in her work to execute a cursory sign of the cross with the hand that held the cleaver. "He'd take those long rides first thing in the mornin', then show up here and eat everything that hadn't made it into the stew pot yet."

Her assistants chuckled in accord as they stripped the feathers off the little birds.

This wasn't the first time Luke had heard Hauekleah's villeins speak of their last master, but it was the first time he'd found himself interested in their comments. He tried to recall what had been said before, but all he could conjure up was a vague impression that Faithe's first husband had been well liked.

Again, he pictured in his mind the barbaric creature who'd appeared in the doorway of that Cottwyk brothel. How could that wretched soul and the respected Caedmon of Hauekleah have been one and the same?

Bonnie appeared with a hunk of white bread and a horn of ale, which she handed over with a coquettish smile. "Is there anything else your lordship might be needin'?" she asked from beneath lowered lashes.

"Nothing at all," he replied, just soberly enough so that she'd know he meant it. Alex would probably laugh if he knew one of "his" twins had decided to flirt with Luke. So would Faithe, for that matter; she struck him as being too self-assured to be much prone toward unreasonable jealousy. And it would be quite unreasonable. For one thing, Luke had taken his father's lectures on marital fidelity to heart; he had no intention of betraying Faithe with another woman, ever. And, although Bonnie and her sister had a certain voluptuous appeal, to be sure, they didn't . . . glow from within, as did their mistress. They didn't have golden skin and a magical smile and slippery hair that was always everywhere. They didn't laugh in that remarkable way that suddenly made everything clear as rain. They didn't smell like almonds and thyme. They didn't have gentle, knowing hazel eyes that looked right *into* him. They weren't Faithe.

"So," Luke said with deliberate nonchalance as he leaned against Ardith's worktable, "your late master liked to hunt and hawk, I understand."

"Aye." Ardith's huge body jiggled with every *thwack* of the cleaver. "He brung home plenty of game for the supper table, I'll say that for 'im."

"I hear naught but good things about him," Luke said around a mouthful of bread.

"Nor will you." Ardith scooped the diced bacon up

in her meaty hands and added it to the pigeons in the stew pot. Wiping her hands on her apron, she turned and heaved her great bulk toward the pantry. "He was a right agreeable sort, our Lord Caedmon."

"Right agreeable," one of the kitchen girls chirped.

"As goodly a master as ever lived," echoed another. There was a little flutter of movement as the wenches paused in their plucking to cross themselves.

"He was a red-haired fellow, yes?" Luke washed his bread down with a swallow of ale.

"Aye," Bonnie sighed. "And right handsome for one of that breed. Some of them are a bit . . . you know . . . milky-skinned and sickly-like, with wee little piggy eyes. Not our Lord Caedmon."

"A big fellow," someone else offered. "Not as sizable as your lordship, but good-sized, and vigorous."

"Never had a cross word for no one."

"Never."

"Always cheerful."

"Always."

"Really." Luke bit off some bread and chewed it thoughtfully. "Did he dress humbly, like her ladyship, or more in keeping with his station?"

"Oh, he liked his fine tunics and furs," Ardith offered, waddling back into the kitchen with an apron full of mushrooms, which she dumped onto the chopping stone. "Nothin' *too* fancy, mind you. He weren't one for jewels and that. He dressed simple, but *fine* simple, if you know what I mean. Always the best wool, the softest kid for his boots."

"Kept his beard trimmed nice," Bonnie said. "Took a tub bath twice a week!"

"He was city-bred," one of the girls explained.

"Brung up in Worcester."

"A ward of the bishop."

"They say his father was Lord Stigand, Archbishop of Canterbury."

One of the others laughed derisively. "Everyone knowed he was King Harold's bastard son."

"Twaddle!" Ardith raised her cleaver high. " 'Twas Pope Alexander himself sired our Lord Caedmon!" She attacked the mushrooms with a vengeance.

Luke drained his horn in one swift tilt. Next they'd be claiming he'd been the illegitimate son of the Lord God Himself.

Try as he might to superimpose their portrait of a well-scrubbed, urbane—and semidivine—Caedmon on his mental picture of the Saxon from the brothel, the images just didn't fit. Something was missing, some secret, some vital piece of information without which he'd never understand what had happened that stormy, half-remembered night. As he swallowed the last of the bread and bid the kitchen staff good day, he resolved to unearth that secret.

The bonfire, built atop the hill between the river and the vineyard, had died down some, but still lit up the night sky. Several dozen villagers continued to dance around it—to the accompaniment of reed flutes, cowbells, and makeshift tambourines—in ale-soaked celebration of St. John's Eve, the twenty-fourth of June. The men carried torches; the women wore their hair loose and crowned with floral wreaths. Boys darted among them, flourishing their glowing brands.

Faithe was gratified to see Felix among their number, waving his brand and laughing along with the rest of them. The turning point had come one afternoon last week, when the other boys had stumbled upon Felix taking a solitary swim in the river. That he knew how to swim amazed and impressed them; that he was willing to teach them how elevated his status from pariah to comrade in the blink of an eye.

Faithe, sitting with Luke in a secluded spot against a moss-covered outcropping of rock, watched the revelers through half-closed eyes, her feet moving in rhythm to the music. They'd done their dancing, she and Luke. Earlier, when it seemed as if every soul in Hauekleah had joined the circle around the bonfire, he'd let her coax him into it. She'd been impressed with his restrained grace as he executed the simple movements of the traditional dance, and gratified that he'd joined in just to please her. Gratified and a little surprised, for he'd been out of sorts for several days now.

It began the day the cookhouse burned down and she'd gone searching unsuccessfully for Orrik. She remembered her conversation with him in the horse pasture. He'd remarked that she'd stopped twisting her wedding ring. They'd spoken of hot baths and comfortable beds. She'd thought they were going to make love that night.

They hadn't. His choice, not hers. He'd withdrawn from her that evening, and remained that way since, buckled back into that armor she'd thought he was shedding. For a while, he'd seemed so relaxed and happy. Now, he was much as he'd been when he first arrived at Hauekleah. He rarely smiled. On the infrequent occasions when they spoke, she had the impression that he was preoccupied with things she knew nothing about. His thoughts seemed focused, not on the world around him, but deep within himself.

A niggling thought had begun insinuating itself into her mind whenever she contemplated Luke's renewed detachment. Perhaps he *was* like Thorgeirr, after all. Perhaps, despite his best intentions, life at Hauekleah had begun to wear on him, and he was mentally removing himself from everything about it, including her, in preparation for the day he left.

Except that sometimes, often, when she looked in his direction, she found him studying her with extraordinary intensity. At such times, she fancied a hint of something almost like fear in his eyes, mingled with the yearning that he couldn't hope to disguise.

Whatever the cause of his reticence with her, she hated it. The rapport they'd established had been such a precious thing to her, a thrilling gift, unexpected and full of possibilities. And now it was gone. She didn't know why, only that its absence filled her with sadness.

Stealing a glance at him, she saw that he was staring off at something beyond the bonfire. Tracking his riveted gaze, she discovered the object of his interest to be his brother, lounging on the other side of the fire with Bonnie and Blossom cuddled up on either side. Faithe did not deceive herself that it was Alex who had so captured Luke's attention. All men liked to stare at beautiful women, especially when they came in matched pairs. The sisters were mirror images of each other, remarkably similar in every respect. Their own mother, now dead, hadn't been able to tell them apart; it was she who'd trained the girls to distinguish themselves by how they braided their hair.

Luke wasn't the only man staring at the threesome. Firdolf had spent most of the evening gazing at them sullenly from the other side of the fire as he steadily emptied a wineskin. It was, of course, Blossom—she of the single braid—on whom his attention was fixed. Earlier, he had asked her to join him in dancing with the others, but she had refused. Alex had grinned and shrugged at him, whereupon he'd stalked away to get quietly sotted all by himself.

The flesh around Luke's eyes tightened in concentration as he gazed upon the girls. "Caedmon didn't have a twin brother, by any chance?" he asked, without taking his eyes off the threesome beyond the fire. They were the first words he'd spoken to her in quite a long time.

Puzzled, Faithe said, "Nay. What on earth would make you think that?"

"Did he have *any* brothers?"

"None that were raised in Worcester with him. He

quite possibly had half brothers, and perhaps half sisters. I suppose we'll never be certain, since no one knows for sure who his father was. All the likeliest candidates have legitimate heirs, so I suppose it's possible."

"A half brother . . ." Luke shook his head slightly, his brows drawn together. "Nay, I think not."

"What makes you think Caedmon had a brother?" she asked, perplexed by his interest in her late husband, but eager to keep him talking.

"I just thought it was"—he shrugged—"a possibility. I was just wondering. I don't really know why." He still hadn't looked at her.

They sat in silence for a time, then she said, quietly, "We can talk about Caedmon if you want to."

He did look at her then, turning his head toward her, his eyes huge in the dark.

"Moira told me you were asking about him yesterday," she said. " 'Tis natural that you'd be curious about the man I was married to for eight years. If there are things you want to know about him, you can ask me."

He lifted the flask of ale to his mouth and drank from it, then gazed at the dancers with such a taciturn expression that she decided she'd somehow disturbed or insulted him. Finally, he said, "They tell me he was a good man."

"He was," she said. "Everyone liked him." She decided to elaborate on that, since she was in a better position than her people to be objective about the matter. "In truth, that was partly because he didn't exercise any real authority with the villeins. He rarely ordered them to do anything, and never disciplined them. That was all left up to me, which, of course, was how I preferred it."

"And it never troubled you that he was so uninterested in Hauekleah?"

"Oh, from time to time I wished he'd care more.

But one can't have everything. As I've said, he was good to me. He never struck me. I'm sure he was faithful. And, although he never really fit in here, he tried to make the best of it. He found pastimes that amused him. All in all, despite our differences, we got along better than most married couples." She watched the dancers cavorting around the fire, remembering this same celebration last summer. Caedmon had lifted her up and spun her around and around until she shrieked with laughter. "In some ways, he was . . . this may sound silly to you."

"Nay. What?"

"He was like a big brother." Except in bed, of course, but she had no intention of sharing such matters with Luke. "I liked him. I was looking forward to growing old with him."

Luke turned his face from her; a muscle stood out in his jaw.

Faithe took off her chaplet of tiny ivory roses, which was beginning to irritate her scalp. Laying it in her lap, she brushed the silken petals with her fingertips, enjoying their sweet perfume mingled with acrid wood smoke. "But then word came last summer that your army was planning on crossing the Channel and challenging King Harold," she said softly, "and Caedmon knew he'd have to join Harold's forces. He didn't relish the idea, I can tell you that."

Luke seemed suddenly more alert. "Nay?"

"He wasn't a soldier, he was . . . well, not a soldier. He hadn't been trained in fighting, although of course he could shoot an arrow and handle a sword passably well. I could tell he was anxious."

Luke nodded, seeming intently interested.

"Don't misunderstand me," she said quickly. "He wasn't cowardly. I don't mean to imply that. He didn't deny his duty or try and get out of it. It's just that he . . . would rather not have had to go. Caedmon was a man of peace. The skills of war come naturally to some men, but not to others. Dunstan was much the same—willing to go, but not happy about it. Orrik was the only man among them who seemed truly eager for battle."

Luke snorted, as if this didn't surprise him.

"It took a few weeks to gather up the supplies and weapons they'd need before they could set out to join Harold. I was so worried for Caedmon. He . . . changed. He'd be belligerent one moment and terribly melancholy the next. He lost his appetite. He refused to speak to me of his fears, although I knew he felt them. He'd get these dreadful headaches. When the vomiting started, I called in a surgeon. He told me this sort of thing happens to some men before they go into battle, and not to worry overmuch. So I tried not to."

Luke was very quiet, listening attentively.

"They left almost exactly a year ago," she said. "You know the rest. He was taken prisoner and died over the winter. I never saw him again."

Luke took her hand, the first he'd touched her in days. "I'm sorry."

She forced a small smile. " 'Twasn't your doing."

He seemed to stiffen; his hand left hers.

"There he is!" a young voice cried out. It was Felix, running toward them with his brand, followed by Alfrith and the others.

" 'Tis the Black Dragon!"

The pack of boys converged on Luke and laughingly waved their brands at him. "Go away, Black Dragon!"

"Get out of here!"

"Go back to where you came from!"

Faithe laughed along with the boys, until she noticed Luke's nonplussed expression. He seemed almost to shrink back against the mossy stone, staring at the taunting children as if he truly didn't know what to make of them. She laid a hand on his arm. "They're supposed to be driving away dragons," she explained.

" 'Tis all part of St. John's Eve. And, you being the Black Dragon . . ."

He nodded stiffly, his mouth forming a smile that never reached his eyes.

"Well done, boys," Faithe said, "but I think perhaps we'll keep this particular dragon here at Hauekleah with us. I've grown rather fond of him." From the corner of her eye she saw Luke look at her. "What do you think? Shall we keep him? Perhaps he'll scare away the bears."

"I vote we keep him!" Felix exclaimed.

"Aye! Let's keep him!"

"But that's not to say we want to encourage other dragons to make their home here," Faithe said. "You'd best go make sure there are no more left in the area."

"Aye, milady!"

"We'll run them into the river, milady!"

"Excellent!" she said.

The boys raced away. Looking down, Faithe saw that she still had her hand resting lightly on Luke's arm. She could feel the ropy muscles beneath the soft linen of his shirt. He felt warm and solid and thoroughly masculine, and she wanted him unbearably. Her desire for him—his body, his heart—had swelled into a kind of exquisite anguish. She felt it all day, every day, from the moment she woke up in the morning and saw him, curled on his side in the rushes, his face softened from sleep, his lips parted, strands of raven hair falling over his forehead.

Faithe lifted her hand to his scratchy cheek. He closed his eyes and tilted his head, pushing lightly against her caress, like a cat.

Opening his eyes, he looked at her—looked directly into her eyes—for the first time in days. She felt dizzy from the effect and breathed his name.

He looked at her mouth. She felt a flittering in her

chest, as if a small bird were trapped there. Did she only imagine him moving infinitesimally closer?

Raising his hand slowly—so slowly—to her mouth, he touched a tentative fingertip to her bottom lip.

Steam hissed. They turned toward the sound to see the villagers extinguishing their torches and brands in the river. Felix and Alfrith filled buckets with water and ran up the hill with them, dousing the bonfire with great drama.

Luke moved away from her, bending his head to rub at the back of his neck. "I take it the evening's festivities have come to an end."

"Aye. Luke?"

"Aye?"

"What's wrong?"

He took too long answering. "Nothing."

"You've been so—"

"Nothing's wrong," he said shortly. Standing, he held his hand out. "Shall we?"

She took his hand and allowed him to help her to her feet. He released it, and they walked back to Hauekleah Hall in silence.

Chapter 12

Faithe found Sunday Mass interminable, as usual. All she could think about during the lengthy service was the many outdoor chores she might be completing on this glorious morning, if only Mass didn't have to take quite so long.

When it was finally over, she left Luke talking to Father Paul in the dark little church and stepped out, with the others, into the dazzling sunshine. In the center of the village green—an irregular patch of grass encircled by the church, smithy, fulling mill, and other public buildings—was the community well. Orrik sat on the edge of the well, talking to Baldric, who stood before him. When he saw her, he rose, dismissing Baldric with a wave of his hand, and came toward her.

"Could I have a word with you, milady?"

"Of course."

Orrik glanced toward the church, and then all around them, as if to make sure they weren't being overheard. "It's come to my attention that . . . *his lordship* has taken to nosing around about matters that are none of his concern."

Faithe just stared at him.

A group of women drifted in their direction. He guided her by the arm several yards away.

"I don't understand, Orrik. What are you saying?"

The bailiff cleared his throat. "Your husband, he's been asking questions of late."

"Questions about Caedmon," she said.

He nodded. "Baldric told me you knew about it. It ain't right."

"Luke is curious about his predecessor. I see nothing objectionable in that."

Orrik grimaced and shook his head. "That man's a Norman soldier, milady. The enemy. We must never forget that."

"*That man* is my husband and your master," she said icily, her temper rising. "Don't you forget that, Orrik."

Spots of color rose on Orrik's cheeks. "He shouldn't go stirring things up."

"What's there to stir up?"

Normally a man who was never at a loss for words, Orrik appeared to be groping for them. "Nothing, nothing at all. It's just . . . it sits wrong with me, is all. I don't like the idea of him trying to dig around in Caedmon's life the way he's doing. If he starts asking you about him, I hope you'll tell him to go to the devil."

"You're too late, Orrik. I've already told him everything he wanted to know."

Orrik's mouth went tight; something like alarm sparked in his eyes. "What? What did you tell him?"

"What business is that of yours, and why does it matter? He's making some casual inquiries, out of curiosity."

Orrik grunted derisively. "Those Norman bastards don't do anything casually. I don't like him poking around this way. Don't like it one little bit."

Faithe lifted her chin and forced herself to gaze steadily into Orrik's white-hot eyes. "Your master's actions aren't subject to your approval or disapproval, Orrik. You'd best remember that."

"Milady, I just don't like—"

" 'Tis not your place to like or dislike what he does." She moved a step closer, lowering her voice. "I've told you before, I've *begged* you not to force me to decide what to do with you if you can't manage to accept Luke as lord of Hauekleah."

"But—"

"I cannot align myself with you, Orrik, no matter how badly you want me to. Can you imagine what it would mean for Hauekleah to have a master and mistress who were at odds with each other?"

That her motivation in all this was ultimately for the good of Hauekleah appeared to give him pause. He hesitated, frowning. "Aye, but—"

"Don't put me in the position of choosing between loyalty to you or loyalty to Sir Luke. Because I will choose him every time. He's my husband and master of this estate. And he can question anyone at Hauekleah about anything he wishes. And you have naught to say on the matter."

The spots of pink had blossomed and spread to encompass his entire face. With an insolent little bow, he growled, "I will obey your dictates, milady."

"See that you do." She turned and stalked away.

"Where's your Uncle Dunstan?" Faithe asked Felix that afternoon as he helped her weed her kitchen garden. "I haven't seen him lately."

Felix yanked a weed out of the earth and dropped it in the shallow basket held by Faithe, who stood over him. "Master Orrik sent him to Winstow to visit with my Aunt Audris and Uncle Synn."

Faithe frowned at him. "When?"

The boy screwed up his face as he thought about it. "Day before yesterday? My aunt's been sick."

Faithe knew that Dunstan's sister, the wife of a Winstow oil merchant, had been ill of late, but Orrik hadn't wanted the young reeve to visit her, inasmuch as it would take him away from Hauekleah during the growing season. She wondered what had changed his mind.

"How long will your uncle be in Winstow?" Faithe asked.

"A month, perhaps two."

The basket slipped out of Faithe's fingers, strewing their little heap of weeds all over the flagstone walk. She squatted down to gather them up. *"Two months?"* During the summer? Had Orrik taken leave of his senses?

"My aunt's sick," the boy said, as if she hadn't heard him the first time.

Yes, but she had a husband to take care of her. And why on earth Dunstan should have to spend two months there was beyond Faithe. Winstow was only half a day's ride from Hauekleah. If he absolutely had to see his sister, he could visit for a few days and come back.

Faithe sat back on her heels, the scattered weeds forgotten. It didn't make sense, Orrik sending Dunstan away like this.

Or perhaps it did.

Early the next morning, Faithe saddled up Daisy and rode west. By noon she was in Winstow, a sizable town compared to the village of Hauekleah, but small enough so that she had no trouble locating its only oil merchant.

She found Dunstan outside the oil shop, helping his brother-in-law unload barrels from a cart. It was a hot day, and their shirts were soaked through with perspiration.

"Milady!" He finger-combed his damp hair, his expression one of blank surprise. "What brings you to Winstow?"

"I came looking for you." She glanced at the other man. Dunstan introduced her to Synn, then invited her inside for a meal.

He led her through the shop and up a narrow stairway to a little upstairs kitchen, where he invited her to sit. If it was hot outside, it was stifling here in this dark, close little chamber. Through an open doorway to another room, she saw an emaciated young woman sleeping on a pallet. Dunstan excused himself to dampen a cloth and lay it on her forehead, then closed the leather curtain that served as a door.

"'Tis a wasting disease," he said softly, so as not to awaken his sister. "There's naught to be done for Audris but pray, I'm afraid."

"I'm sorry," Faithe whispered, sincerely.

Dunstan dished her out some stew and a tankard of ale. "Is anything amiss at Hauekleah? Do you need me to come back?"

The stew looked badly overcooked; she wondered whether Dunstan had made it himself. "Nothing's wrong, precisely," she said carefully. "But there are some matters I'm curious about."

"Aye?" He fetched some stew and ale for himself and sat across from her.

She prodded the unidentifiable stew meat with her eating knife. "To begin with, I'm not quite sure why you felt the need for such a long visit to your sister. I understand she's very ill, and I'm sorry, truly I am. But Felix told me you were planning on being here for a month, possibly two. I don't know that we can do without you for that long at this time of year, Dunstan."

Dunstan swallowed a bite of stew and shrugged. "That's exactly what I told Master Orrik, but he insisted. I confess, it didn't make much sense to me, either."

Her mouth fell open. "Do you mean to say this trip was Orrik's idea?"

"Aye. Nay. In a manner of speaking. I'd been asking for leave to visit Audris ever since she took ill. But what I had in mind was two or three days. All along, Orrik's been telling me I can't be spared. All right, I says. Let me know when I can go. All of a sudden, late last week, he tells me to pack my things. He's sending me to Winstow, and I needn't return till harvest time."

Faithe choked on her ale. "Till harvest time! What was he thinking of?"

Dunstan shook his head in evident bewilderment. "Can't rightly say, milady. He claimed I wasn't needed because of how well Sir Luke's been pitching in. Now, I know his lordship's been making himself right useful, and he's game to try anything, that he is. But . . ." He trailed off sheepishly.

"But he can't take the place of an experienced reeve," Faithe supplied. Dunstan had served Orrik—and served him well—for years. He was irreplaceable, and indispensable. As Orrik well knew.

Why had Orrik sent him to Winstow? What was so important to him that he was willing to jeopardize the welfare of Hauekleah to accomplish it?

"Was there anything he asked you to do here?" she asked. "Any assignment, any task?" She nibbled experimentally at the grayish meat, washing it down with a quick swig of ale.

"Nothing at all, milady," he said between mouthfuls. "I was to visit with my sister and put Hauekleah out of my mind."

Then Orrik's purpose in sending Dunstan here was simply to remove him from Hauekleah. Why?

Faithe gave up on the stew and drank her ale in silence. "Orrik's been acting strangely of late."

"Aye?"

"He's very put out by questions Sir Luke has been asking."

"Questions?"

"About Caedmon."

Dunstan tensed, looking everywhere but at Faithe. She lifted her tankard to her mouth, watching him over the rim as he fidgeted. Never had she known a man who was easier to read. And she'd never known him to be able to keep a secret. Whenever there was gossip circulating at Hauekleah, she always went to Dunstan. She could invariably coax him into revealing what no one else would tell her. Was that why Orrik had sent him away? Because there was something he didn't trust Dunstan to keep his counsel about if pressed?

"You and Orrik are the only men at Hauekleah who survived Hastings," she said speculatively.

"Do you want some more ale?" he asked, rising.

"Nay. I want you to tell me whatever it is Orrik doesn't want revealed."

He sat back down slowly. "I . . . I don't know what you're—"

"I think you do," she said quietly.

"Milady . . . I can't. Master Orrik, he made me promise I wouldn't tell."

"Wouldn't tell what? Something about Caedmon? Does it have to do with Hastings?"

"Milady, please. He said it was for your own good, and it is. He said it would hurt you too much to know—"

"Hurt *me*?" Faithe gripped the edge of the table. "You two have been keeping something from me? What?"

"Milady—"

"Hear me, Dunstan. Orrik was wrong to swear you to silence. I'm not a child, and I don't need protection from unpleasant truths."

"Aye, but—"

"And I assure you I don't appreciate such protection. I hate to make threats, but you must know that I can't have a reeve who withholds information from me."

The color washed from Dunstan's face. "Milady . . ."

She leaned toward him, fixing him with a resolute look. "Just tell me what it is that's been kept from me, and all will be forgiven."

His head sank into his hands. Presently, he rose from the table and stood facing the tiny opening that served as the room's only window. She heard him draw in a breath, and then let it out in a gust. He wrapped his arms around himself. "After we left here last summer, me and Orrik and Caedmon and them other fellows, to join King Harold . . . well, your husband, he wasn't himself, milady."

"I know."

"He was . . . ah, there's no point in going into all that."

"Did something happen while you were waiting for the Normans? Something I should know about?"

Dunstan stood very still for a few moments, as if contemplating what to tell her. "The important thing, the thing Orrik told me not to tell you, is what happened once the battle started."

Faithe knew he was withholding something—something that had occurred during those long months of waiting for William to lead his army across the Channel. Perhaps it was something that would reflect badly on Caedmon, and that was why Dunstan hesitated to share it. Swiftly surveying the possibilities, she voiced the one that rose to the surface. "Was there . . . a woman?"

Dunstan spun around. "How did you know?"

She gritted her teeth. She hated this. She would have hated it worse, she knew, if she'd had stronger feelings for Caedmon, but she hated it anyway. Her marriage might have been passionless in most respects, but they'd both enjoyed the sex—so much so that it never occurred to her that he'd want to seek more of it elsewhere. Disillusionment, flavored with betrayal, burned in her stomach.

At the same time, she felt a sense of relief that she'd uncovered at least one of the secrets being withheld from her. Not wanting Dunstan to see how shaken she was, she gathered herself together and said, "I didn't know for sure, but it stands to reason there would have been—" Her voice snagged; she took a sip of ale, trying to ignore Dunstan's expression of compassion. "We'd never been separated for that long. Caedmon was . . . well, he was a man, with a man's needs. And he was anxious about the fighting. I'm not surprised." She forced herself to ask, "Was he in love with her?"

"Oh, nay, milady, 'twas nothing like that. They were, well . . ."

"They?"

"Aye, well, you know. They were . . . common women."

Prostitutes. Of course. She shouldn't care. She really shouldn't. Such liaisons were quick and impersonal. But then she pictured Caedmon in some strange bed somewhere, doing with some faceless whore what she'd thought he only did with her, and it seemed very personal, indeed.

"I gather he just wanted a bit of comfort," Dunstan assured her. "Except that once, well . . ."

"What?"

He chewed his lip, then wheeled back around and leaned on the windowsill. "Nothing, milady. 'Tis of no importance."

She closed a hand over her keys, willing confidence from them. "Tell me. Tell me everything."

"I'll tell you what happened when the battle started." He was still keeping something from her, she knew, something about some prostitute, but before she could demand the rest of that story, he said, "Your husband wasn't taken prisoner, like you were told, milady."

Faithe stood slowly. "What do you mean? Was he killed during the battle? Then why—"

"He disappeared," Dunstan said, "just as the fighting started."

"What do you mean, 'disappeared'?"

Dunstan shook his head, expelling a ragged breath. "I was the last to see him. I've never told anybody this, not even Orrik. As far as he knows, Caedmon just vanished. But I saw him, right as the horns sounded and the war cries were raised. He was crouching at the edge of the woods, howling and rocking back and forth with his arms over his head."

Faithe was speechless. She clutched her keys so hard that they bit into her palm.

Dunstan turned to face her, his eyes glimmering in the dark little room. "I'm not sure what happened, milady. I think he finally just . . ." He raised his shoulders slightly. "Orrik called me and asked me if I'd seen Caedmon. When I looked back, he was gone. I lied. I told him I hadn't seen him. Maybe 'twas wrong, but I just couldn't . . . I couldn't tell Orrik how he'd been, like a terrified animal. I just couldn't."

Faithe swallowed down the anguish in her throat. "He deserted, then."

Dunstan looked down. That was answer enough.

Her head felt numb, wobbly. "That's what Orrik didn't want me to know."

He nodded. "Orrik searched for him till Christmastide, and then he'd use any excuse he could to get away and look for him some more."

"Of course," Faithe whispered. "Of course."

"He found him at Hocktide. Found his body, that is, in a grave in Cottwyk."

"How did he die?" Faithe asked shakily.

Dunstan looked distressed. "Nay, milady. You don't need to know—"

"Don't tell me what I don't need to know!" Her eyes burned. Caedmon had killed himself; that must be it. He'd taken his own life and would be condemned to hell for it. She knew it, but she had to hear it from Dunstan's own lips. *"Just tell me how he died!"*

A moan came from beyond the leather curtain.

"Audris." Dunstan started for the doorway.

Faithe grabbed him by his shirt. "Tell me!"

Another moan, followed by a thready voice calling, "Dunstan? Synn?"

"Please!" Dunstan tried to pry her hands loose. "My sister needs me. Please let me—"

She shook him. "Tell me!"

The voice again: "Dunstan?"

"He was murdered!"

She stared at him.

Dunstan squeezed his eyes shut. "I'm sorry, milady. He was killed over a . . . woman. Some Norman soldier, they think. I didn't want to—"

"Go to your sister," she rasped, releasing him.

"Milady—"

"Go!" She turned abruptly, before he could see her tears, and raced downstairs and out of the shop.

Luke could smell the coming storm. As he secured the last of the fresh reed thatch to the rooftop of the parish church, he wondered for the hundredth time where Faithe was, and when she'd be home. She tended to go her own way, rarely reporting her comings and goings, and it had never troubled him. But storm clouds had been gathering all afternoon, gradually dimming the light by which he thatched, and he found himself preoccupied by her whereabouts and anxious for her return.

Glancing overhead, he found that the clouds had congealed into a solid blanket the color of old steel. The warm, saturated air squeezed in all around him, and the hairs on his arms stood on end. Summer storms could be hellish. If she wasn't home soon, he hoped she'd find shelter.

"Looks like you finished up just in time, milord!" young Alfrith called up to him as he and the other boys gathered the reeds scattered about on the ground.

"Look, milord!" Felix pointed toward the road,

where it emerged from the woods. Luke could make out the distant figure of a woman on horseback, riding their way. "Is that her?"

"That's her," he breathed in relief. Climbing down the ladder, he withdrew a handful of pennies from the pocket of his loose braies and handed them out to the boys, who chorused their thanks. "Clean up as much of this thatch as you can before it starts raining," he instructed, grabbing his shirt off the bottom rung of the ladder and shrugging it on. "If you hear thunder, go home."

He'd hoped to intercept her on the road, but by the time he got there, she'd already passed by—at a gallop! Perhaps she didn't want to get caught in the rain when it began. Still, she'd torn up the road as if she were being chased by demons.

He saw her ride around to the back of Hauekleah Hall. When he got to the stable, Daisy was in her stall, being curried by a stable boy. This struck Luke as odd; Faithe always did this herself.

"Where's your mistress?" Luke asked the lad.

"I saw her go into the barn, milord."

"The barn?"

"Aye, and the fellow who was workin' in there, he come out and shut the door, so's she could be alone. She looked like she'd been . . ." The boy hesitated uncertainly, as if worried that he was saying too much.

"Go on."

"Crying. Her eyes were all red. Kind of wet, too, and she hurried away so quick. Me mum . . . well, she says milady likes to do her crying in the barn so she thinks we don't know what she's about."

"Is that so," Luke said dryly. On his way out he said, "Finish up quickly and get home before the storm comes."

He paused outside the door to the barn. Faithe had gone there to be alone—to hide her weakness from others, evidently fooling no one. She hated for people to see her cry. Everyone at Hauekleah knew it, and respected her desire for privacy. Luke should respect it, too, especially considering the recent chill in their relations—a chill for which he had no one to blame but himself.

He hadn't wanted to withdraw from her so completely—to undo the intimacy they'd managed, against all odds, to establish—but how could it be otherwise? He'd killed her husband. He'd made her a widow and then married her for Hauekleah. Every time he looked at her, a knife blade of remorse slid deep into his heart. He was a beast. How could he even think about touching her . . . and more . . . considering what he'd done? Considering what he *was*?

If he disturbed her now, she would probably order him away. Most likely, she'd be annoyed with him, even angry. And he would deserve that anger, for intruding on her precious solitude. He should leave.

Yet he didn't. He stood outside the door until he began to feel foolish, and then he pushed it open, slowly and silently, and stepped inside, closing it behind him. It was dark in the barn. From behind the closed gates of the stalls on either side of the central aisle, he heard the snufflings and restless movements of the livestock. He wondered where Faithe had secreted herself.

As if in answer, a half-grown kitten padded out of an open stall at the far end and looked at him. This was the grayish kitten Faithe had dubbed Smoky.

As he approached the open stall, he heard a sound—a soft, scratchy inhalation. Presently there came another. Luke's chest tightened. *Don't let her send me away. I know I deserve it, but I couldn't bear it.*

When he saw her, curled up with her face buried in the straw, her back shaking, the tightness squeezed him from inside. He whispered her name. She didn't hear him.

Taking a step toward her, he said, "Faithe?"

She looked up, startled. Her face was wet; she was trembling.

"Are you all right?" he asked softly. She looked surprised, and a little puzzled. It came to him why—he'd spoken to her in English. He always conversed with her in his native French—always. It was a way of asserting his authority, and she knew it. He'd never begun a conversation with her in her own language—until now.

He took another step toward her. Again in English, and as tenderly as he could, he said, "Faithe, what's wrong? Talk to me."

She closed her eyes, tears spilling down her cheeks as she hitched in a breath. Sitting up, she looked at him, her eyes filled with pain, her face crumpling, and held out her arms.

His world spun. She wanted him, she needed him.

He crossed to her in one long stride and sank into the straw, gathering her in his arms and murmuring words of solace, endearments—all in English. He whispered her name over and over as he kissed her hair and rubbed her back and reveled in the almond-sweet scent of her and the damp, heartbreaking heat of her face and the lush pressure of her body against his.

"Faithe." The tension in his chest pounded away at him, making him shake. "My sweet, sweet Faithe. Don't cry. It's all right. It's all right. Everything's all right."

"Nay," she murmured, her voice like wet rust.

He threaded his fingers through her hair, pulled her close against him. "Nothing could be this bad."

She nodded, her face wet in the crook of his neck. "It is. I don't understand anything anymore. I thought I knew how everything was. But I didn't know anything. I didn't know anything . . ."

She wasn't making any sense. "Shh . . . it's all right, now. It's all right."

"Oh, God, I wish it were. I'd give anything it if were."

"It is. Faithe, look at me." Pulling back just a bit, he cupped her damp face in one hand and tilted it up. "Tell me what has you so distraught."

Fresh tears pooled in her eyes. "I went to Winstow to see Dunstan. Orrik sent him there so that he wouldn't tell me . . ." She closed her eyes; the tears overflowed.

"Tell you what?" he gently pressed as he blotted her face with his sleeve.

"That Caedmon . . . that he deserted the field of battle. He didn't die in prison, Luke. He was murdered." She broke off in sobs, her face pressed against his chest.

Luke held her with arms deadened from shock. "Oh, God." *She knows. Oh, God, she knows.*

She cried for just a moment, then quieted. "He was killed over a woman."

Steady, now. She needs you. "Faithe. I'm so sorry, I—"

" 'Tisn't your fault."

He squeezed his eyes shut, gritted his teeth. "Faithe . . . oh, God."

"I shouldn't be reacting this way."

"How could you not?" He kissed the top of her head. "Go ahead and cry. Go ahead. You have every right." And it would be just punishment for him to have to hold her while she did so—comfort her while she grieved over that which he had brought to pass.

She cried until the tears were all wrung out of her and she lay limp in his arms. Thunder rolled softly in the distance; an eerie sort of twilight had descended, although it was just late afternoon.

"We should go back," he said quietly.

Faithe tightened her arms around him. "Nay.

Please. Not yet. I can't face them yet." She looked up at him, her eyes enormous in the strange, purplish light. "Please, Luke. I need you."

Luke felt dizzy. *I need you.* He buried his hand in her hair, gripped the back of her head. *I need you . . .*

"Ah, Faithe . . ." He pressed his mouth to her temple, felt the frantic pulsing beneath the hot skin. "I'm lost," he whispered, so quietly he could barely hear it himself. "Lost." He touched her wet cheekbone with his lips.

"Not lost," she said on a sigh. "I've found you." She stroked his face with trembling fingertips. "We've found each other."

"Faithe . . ." Her lips beckoned him. He felt their heat, was drawn to it, bent his head to her. "Faithe, forgive me," he breathed against her mouth as his eyes closed.

A light gust of laughter tickled his lips. "Foolish man." He thought she whispered these words, and then she moved her head, deliberately, slowly, stroking the hot silk of her lips against his.

A sound escaped him, an exhalation of pure delight. He joined in, caressing her lips with his, lightly, teasingly, savoring the sweet, heartbreaking pleasure of it.

Framing her face with his hands to still her movements, he covered her mouth with his and kissed her, a deep kiss of wild longing, a kiss they'd waited too long to share. He felt her hands on his back, his shoulders, his neck, urging him closer, raking his hair. He clutched at her. He reeled from the intensity of it.

A rumble of thunder startled them both. They broke the kiss, gasping for air, and held each other tight.

"Luke," she said, "I've wanted you to do that. I've wanted it so much."

He smiled, gratified in spite of everything by the pleasure she took in him, her frank desire for him. "So have I."

She kissed his throat, whispering against it, "What else have you wanted?"

Her soft query spawned a fierce rush of arousal within Luke. Bracing himself on an elbow, he eased Faithe onto her back in the straw and spent a moment just looking at her. Even with her face all tearstained and straw tangled up in her hair, she was the most exquisite thing he'd ever seen. The odd, dusky light made her skin look translucent, incandescent. Her lips were puffy, and a deep, bruised red. There was something potently erotic about lips dark and swollen from kissing. He touched them; they were feverishly hot. He wanted to lick them; he wanted to bite them. He was lost.

"What else," she repeated patiently, "have you wanted?"

Drawing in a shuddering breath, he allowed his gaze to travel downward. She wore the russet kirtle that she preferred on warm days. He could tell by the unencumbered fleshiness of her breasts beneath the rough homespun that she hadn't bothered with an undershift. Unlike most of her gowns, this one laced up the front. Every time he saw her in it, he wanted to untie the cord.

Lowering his hand, he did just that.

Chapter 13

Luke saw her out of the corner of his eye, watching him as he tugged at the cord, loosening the bow in which it was tied. She studied his eyes as if something in them fascinated her. He concentrated on keeping his hand steady as he pulled the cord slowly through the top pair of eyelets . . . and then the next . . . and the next. Her chest rose and fell rapidly; the thin homespun trembled with her heartbeats.

Those keys of hers were in the way. He lifted them, and she tensed slightly. Instead of removing them, as he had intended, he merely moved them to the side. She smiled, and then closed a hand over the arm on which he braced himself. The heat of her touch seemed to burn right through his linen shirt.

Thunder murmured distantly as he continued unlacing the kirtle. From the surrounding stalls came the low fretting of the animals as it grew forebodingly dark. The very air seemed to swell and press in.

Luke drew the cord through the bottom pair of eyelets, just below her navel, leaving her kirtle unlaced but still closed. One end of the cord was softly frayed. He brushed it lazily over her throat, along her jaw, and around the dainty edge of an ear. He swept it across her lips, over her chin, and down her throat again. She closed her eyes, smiling as if this were the greatest sensual pleasure imaginable. Tossing the cord aside, he replaced it with his hand.

She sighed at the first rough touch of his fingertips

on her throat. He traced the shape of her face, caressed its delicate contours—forehead, eyelids, cheeks, nose, those blood-flushed lips, still hot to the touch.

To touch her in this slow, hypnotic way, as if he had all the time in the world, was the greatest indulgence imaginable. He'd never taken his time with a woman, prolonging the preliminaries just for the elemental pleasure of it.

I'm truly lost, he thought as he lowered his hand. The loosely woven homespun grazed his fingertips as he trailed them over the rise of a breast. He felt an erratic thudding through the supple flesh; his own heartbeat thundered in his ears.

Very gently he rested his hand on her breast. Her grip tightened on his arm. He felt an insistent nudging against his palm as her nipple hardened through the rough fabric. His body echoed her response, as if they were a single being; he stiffened beneath his braies, straining toward her against the confines of the loose trousers.

Everything seemed to be happening so slowly in this unnatural and expectant semidarkness. He *was* lost, cast adrift with Faithe in a kind of bewitched haze. It was as if there were no past and no future—just the two of them, alone together, now and forever, in this nest of fragrant straw. Time was suspended, if only temporarily; and so were his sins. What had gone before did not exist. All he could hear was the deafening pulse of his heart, all he could see was Faithe, her head back, her eyes half closed, her smile one of dreamy anticipation.

Luke moved his hand languidly over the heavy cushion of her breast, cupping it, thumbing the rigid nipple until she arched her back, her fingers digging into his arm. Leaning down, he closed his mouth over hers, stealing her sigh as he slipped his hand beneath the open gown. He glided his fingertips over the silken underside of her breast; the skin there was like the finest, sleekest satin, but warm. She moaned into his mouth when he caressed the resilient flesh with a firmer touch, gasped when he gently tugged her nipple. Withdrawing from the kiss, she writhed in delicious abandon. He'd never beheld anything as sweetly, irresistibly provocative. He had to see more of her.

Sitting up, he swept her open kirtle aside with both hands, exposing her from the waist up. Faithe drew in a quick, startled, breath, but lay still as he gazed at her. Her body was an exquisite contradiction. Those voluptuous breasts belonged on a rounder, more ample woman, not this fine-boned creature with her slender waist and flat stomach. The juxtaposition should have looked wrong, but it couldn't have been more enticing.

He ached—quite literally—with the need to possess her. If he'd ever been more aroused than at this moment, he couldn't remember it. All his former doubts and misgivings evaporated in the scalding heat of their mutual need. The urge to untie his braies and take what they both wanted was powerful, but stronger still was the need to prolong this temporary respite, this isolated moment in time—to rejoice in this wonderment, this sense of revelation, to let the magic spin itself out. A quick coupling wouldn't do. He wanted to discover her, consume her, join with her . . . make love to her, body and mind, heart and soul.

And, too, Faithe of Hauekleah wasn't one of his whores, accustomed to taking the full, violent measure of a man's animal passions. She might not look and act like a highborn lady, but that's exactly what she was, and he must heed his father's counsel and take her with care. He had no idea how it had been between her and Caedmon, but he could surmise that she'd not been ill used sexually. Although her feelings toward her first husband seemed lukewarm, she regarded him, still, with sisterly affection. Most likely he'd been very much the gentleman in bed, and so

Luke must endeavor to be the same. After all they'd been through, he was not disposed to jeopardize this delicate moment by venting his lust like some rutting beast.

He skimmed his hands lightly over her face, her throat, her breasts. Faithe breathed his name, and other words he couldn't make out. Drawn, for some reason, to her delicate little navel, he probed the tiny indentation with a fingertip. A kind of kittenish growl rose from her, and her hips moved—just slightly, but enough to spark a hot, answering pulse in his loins.

"What else?" she whispered. His confusion must have shown on his face, because she added, "What else have you wanted?"

He met her gaze for a long, breathless moment, and then he smoothed his hand downward, over her lower belly, until he felt, beneath the homespun, a subtle swell. She bit her lip as he moved his hand slowly—so slowly—over this place of heady mystery. His breath and hers came faster and faster. He felt the little ridge of bone beneath the soft flesh, traced the tight cleft with his fingertips.

She was damp; he felt it even through the kirtle. Suddenly impatient, he whipped her skirt up and lay next to her; she turned to face him. Luke pushed a thigh between hers to urge them apart, and they locked their legs together as naturally as longtime lovers. He searched her eyes as he slid his fingers deep into her exceedingly narrow entrance. Her gaze lost its focus, and she sucked in a tremulous breath. He stroked her with slow, inquisitive fingers, enthralled by her slippery heat.

Curving his other hand around the back of her neck, he coaxed her closer and took her mouth in a hungry, lingering kiss, all the whole caressing her intimately, reveling in her breathless sighs, her little gasps of pleasure. He felt her hand fluttering between them, untying his shirt all the way down the front. She glided her fingers through the dense mat of hair on his chest and whispered against his lips, "What else, Luke?"

He hesitated only briefly, loath to ask too much of her, but so desirous of her touch. Taking her free hand in his, he guided it between his legs, pressing it to his aching shaft, hoping it wouldn't offend her. Although she'd touched him this way once before, that had been playacting—part of her misguided effort to seduce him. To his relief and gratification, her fingers curled automatically around him through his thin braies; he wore no drawers, because of the heat. A spasm of pleasure sucked the breath from his lungs. He was as hard as a column of steel. She drew her hand up and down his length, squeezing with just the right pressure, and he groaned helplessly.

"Ah, Faithe . . ." Luke rocked his hips in time with her caress. "Yes." He explored her until she moved in rhythm with him. With his free arm, he pulled her to him, crushing her breasts, warm and heavy and damp with sweat, against his chest. He buried his face in her hair, inhaling her scent, moaning her name as his body tightened, strained, trembled.

She trembled, too. Her legs, tangled with his, quivered like bowstrings, and her breath came in soft pants. "Luke . . . oh, God, Luke."

Now. He rolled her onto her back in the straw, cradled between her legs.

"Yes!" She slid her hands down to his waist and pulled him against her. Her responsiveness surprised and delighted him. Holding himself stiff-armed above her, he went to undo the drawstring of his braies just as she did. Their hands fumbled together, and they laughed in breathy frustration.

"Let me," he said hoarsely. She nodded and sank into the straw, her eyes closed, her bare chest heaving. Luke didn't think he'd ever seen a more alluring sight.

He reached for the drawstring as a volley of thunder shook the barn and lightning illuminated their little stall. The cold white light flickered over the face of the woman lying before him. An ugly memory stabbed Luke in the gut, and he stumbled backward, squeezing his eyes shut. "Jesu!"

His mind's eye conjured the face in the straw, adding a trickle of blood from the slack mouth. He saw the tangled red hair, the beard, the lifeless, half-open eyes—a fleeting image, there and gone in a blink of lightning. He smelled the dead Saxon, felt, all over again, the sick jolt of realization. *What have I done?*

"Nay." He ground his fists against his forehead, as if that would obliterate the image of the man he had slain—of Caedmon, a good man fallen victim to the Black Dragon's ungovernable rage. *I grieved for him . . . I cried until I had no more tears.* "Nay . . ."

Why now, in this timeless, enchanted moment, when he thought he'd been granted a brief reprieve from his greatest sin, did he have to relive it? Cruel timing, just when he was about to . . . *had been* about to . . .

"Christ." It would be a pointless effort now, his erection having waned.

"Luke?"

He opened his eyes and saw her sitting up and looking at him, her gaze full of concern. With one hand she held her kirtle closed; the other reached for him. He instinctively recoiled from her touch.

"Luke?" Thunder exploded again, accompanied by a burst of lightning. Her beautiful face tightened with worry. She moved toward him, her arm outstretched.

He stood abruptly. "I have to go."

Her eyes were huge. "Go?"

"Faithe . . ." He dragged his hand through his hair, loosening it from its braid. What could he say? How could he possibly make this all right?

For an endless moment she stared at him, wide-eyed in the heavy darkness. And then her face took on a horrible stillness. The light left her eyes, her throat moved convulsively.

"Faithe." Why was this happening? What could he do? What could he possibly say? He went to her and knelt in the straw, reaching out to gather her up while his mind raced to find words, any words, to explain why he couldn't do this.

"Nay!" She jerked away from him, backing up hurriedly and gaining her feet as she clutched the bodice of her kirtle with both hands. "Don't touch me." It wasn't her anger that twisted the knife in his gut, but the chill in her gaze, a detachment that had never been there before. He'd pushed her too far. She was closing herself off to him.

"Oh, God, Faithe." Luke rose on unsteady legs, raking the hair out of his eyes. He'd never begged in his life, but he begged now, in a raw, choked voice. "Don't do this. Please. I couldn't bear it. I need you."

"You need no one. You've never needed anyone, least of all me."

His chest shook with a kind of tragic laughter. Not need her? She'd given him his heart; she *was* his heart. She'd made him human again. Without her, he'd revert into the beast he'd once been. "Dear God, Faithe, if you knew how untrue that was . . ."

"Then why can't you—" Her voice caught in her throat. "Why?" Her chin wobbled; her eyes shimmered. "Why? I don't understand. Explain it to me. Can you just explain it to me?"

"Don't cry," he said gruffly, taking a wary step toward her.

She sidestepped him and lifted her chin, making a heartbreaking effort to compose herself. "Fear not, my lord. I'll make every effort not to cry in front of you again."

"Faithe . . ." He buried his face in his hands. *God, think of something to say. You can't lose her. You can't let this happen.*

"You wanted me to trust you," she said in a wavering voice. When he uncovered his face, she was studying him with that dreadfully remote gaze, one fist keeping her kirtle together, the other clutching her skirt. Unshed tears pooled in her eyes. "You didn't want me on just any terms. You wanted me willing. You wanted me to want you. You said . . . you said our marriage may have been a coldhearted arrangement, but that didn't mean it had to be a coldhearted marriage. And I believed you." A huff of bleak laughter escaped her.

"Faithe . . ."

"Fool that I am, I believed you. I thought you wanted . . ." She faltered, covering her mouth with her hand as tears slid from her eyes.

"I did. I do." Luke took a step toward her, and she took a step back.

She rubbed her cheeks with her sleeve. "Perhaps you actually believe that. But I'm not so deluded, not anymore. How can our marriage be aught but coldhearted? You haven't got it in you to make it otherwise."

"You're wrong, Faithe."

"Am I? I took you at your word, Luke. I took a chance. I opened myself to you. I gave you everything that was in me, more than I've ever given anyone, simply because you asked for it. You made me take off my armor, but yours is welded on tight. That's why you can't . . ." She glanced toward the nest of straw where they had lain. "You don't want me that close to you. Deep inside you, there's a place I'll never touch. But you touched me, Luke." Fresh tears spilled down her cheeks, hated tears that she couldn't bear to shed in his presence, but couldn't seem to stop. "You made me fall in love with you."

She loved him. She loved him! Joy and despair warred dizzily within him.

"That was cruel of you," she added grimly. "You didn't have to make me love you." She tried to sweep past him. He grabbed her arm. "Let me go!"

"I can't." He knew if he let her go now, it would never be the same between them. They would have crossed a line, shattered the fragile bond they'd forged. That bond was all he had; his whole world was built around it. He couldn't lose it.

"What do you want from me, Luke?" She tried to wrestle out of his grasp. "How much more do you mean to take from me? When will it be enough?"

"Faithe, be still. Let me try to explain—"

"Your words mean naught to me. Actions are more telling by far."

He nodded slowly. "You're right. I've been a fool." His sins be damned. Caedmon be damned. All Luke had been and done, all his remorse and torment, all that had gone before be damned and forgotten. The only thing that mattered now was Faithe and him, and he could think of only one way to renew their delicate bond. Why resist anymore what he wanted so desperately—what they both wanted? Banding his arms around her, he bent his head to kiss her, but she wrested it to the side.

"Save your kisses. Let me go!"

"Nay. You're not leaving here until I've convinced you—"

A thunderclap crashed overhead, accompanied by a sputter of lightning; they both started. Faithe took advantage of the diversion to extract herself from his grip. Turning, she fled toward the entrance to the stall, but Luke leapt upon her before she could slip through.

"Let me go!" She fought him, lashing out wildly, raining frenzied punches on him until he pinioned her arms. Her fury took him aback; he must have mishandled things very badly to have driven her to this. Now he had to try and repair the damage, if only she would let him.

"Stop this!" he demanded, but she squirmed and kicked until he lost his balance, toppling over with his arms locked around her. He deliberately twisted as they went down, landing on his back in order to take the brunt of the fall himself, but the gesture was lost on her. She was like a savage thing, enraged and determined to get free.

He wrapped an arm around her waist and grabbed both flailing fists in one of his as she grappled with him. Her kirtle fell open as she struggled to rise off him, her breasts brushing heavily against his bare chest, along with the cold scrape of the keys. As she thrashed to get free, her hair fell across his face, inundating him with her scent; her hips ground against his. His body responded with a mindless resurgence of arousal, but she didn't seem to notice.

"Be still!" he growled.

"Burn in hell!"

"I'm quite sure I will." He rolled her onto her back and pressed her into the straw. Pinning her wrists above her head with one hand, he closed the other around her face, forcing her to look him in the eye. "Faithe, listen to me."

She whipped back and forth beneath him, oblivious to the effect this was having on him. He was painfully erect beneath his braies, and it was all he could do to keep from thrusting against her.

"Let me go! I hate you!"

He brought his face close to hers to be heard over the rumbling of the thunder. The soft weight of her breasts, the silk of her skin, the scent and warmth of her, nearly robbed him of his self-control. "I love you."

That seemed to confound her for a moment. She gazed searchingly into his eyes, then shook her head. "You don't love me."

"God help me, I do," he rasped. "I do."

"You don't know the meaning of love."

"Not before, perhaps, but I do now. I love you, Faithe, and I can't let you leave here thinking otherwise. I can't lose you now. Christ, 'twould kill me."

He kissed her quickly, before she could object, a fierce kiss of possession that she didn't return.

"Words," she ground out, trying vainly to free her imprisoned hands. "Words and kisses. They mean nothing. Let me go."

He released her. She blinked in surprise when he raised her skirt and knelt between her legs, whispered his name in disbelief when he yanked open his braies and fell upon her.

"Why are you doing this?" she gasped, pushing futilely against his shoulders. "Because you think *I* want it?"

"We both want it. We both need it." Luke wished she could rise above her rage and hurt long enough to see that.

"Nay, 'tis naught but an act of pity. Let me go!" She struck out with her fists. He grabbed them and held them tight as she bucked beneath him.

"Don't make me hold you down, Faithe."

"Let me go!"

He shifted to position himself between her legs. "This"—he nudged her with his organ's broad tip—"was hardly born of pity." She felt slick and hot and very tight against him. She grew very still and closed her eyes.

Thunder reverberated as he whispered her name. She couldn't have heard him, yet she opened her eyes and met his gaze as quavering flashes of lightning played over her. There was a clear-eyed calm about her—an understanding, an acceptance. *Thank God.*

Squeezing her hands, he flexed his hips, driving himself deep, deep inside her with one long thrust. Another blast of thunder swallowed up his shuddering groan. Faithe might have cried out; he couldn't hear her. She threw her head back, her expression unreadable in the dark.

For one long, heart-stopping moment she lay inert beneath him, gripping his hands as tightly as he gripped hers. She felt impossibly snug where he was buried within her, and hot. How he'd hungered for this; how often he'd awakened, soaked with sweat and shivering on the edge of ecstasy, after dreaming of this. *'Tis no dream this time. 'Tis very, very real.*

"I love you, Faithe," he said shakily. "I do, I swear it to God." He released her hands slowly, experimentally. *Let her want this,* Luke silently prayed. *Please let her want this.*

A crack of thunder made them both flinch. She wrapped her arms around him, holding him close, her damp face pressed into the crook of his neck. Slipping an arm beneath her shoulders and curling the other around her head, he breathed incoherent words of comfort into her hair amid a flurry of kisses. *She wants this. I know she wants this.*

Lightning flared as the sky burst open. Rain sizzled onto the thatch—a hard, steady, cleansing rain that drained the sodden heaviness from the air. Within moments, it felt lighter, cooler; Luke could breathe deeply for the first time all day.

Faithe's chest rose and fell slowly. She untucked her face to look at him. Her hazel eyes were transparent in the stormy half-light. Threads of rusty gold feathered out from her enormous pupils, like veins of precious ore trapped in polished crystals. The effect was striking, but it was the human warmth in their crystalline depths—the tender reassurance—that squeezed his throat with emotion.

She raised a tentative hand to his cheek and rubbed it lightly; his stubble rasped against her palm. His eyes stung suddenly; he shut them and lowered his forehead to hers. He tried to say her name, but choked on the simple word.

"Shh." She slid her hands beneath his shirt and rubbed his back and shoulders. "Shh."

He sank on top of her, inhaling the tranquil scents of rain and straw, almonds and thyme . . . listening to the rhythmic hush of her breathing, the constant pattering on the thatch . . . basking in the sweet, warm, limitless comfort of her body.

To lie so peacefully within a woman's arms, while intimately connected with her, was a novel experience for Luke. Sex had always been a quick, primitive labor of lust. None of the women he'd paid to release that lust had ever stroked his back with cool, gentle hands, or whispered soothingly into his ear. None of them had loved him. Nor had he loved them. He'd never truly made love to a woman, although he had, on occasion, called it that. He'd never lain united in quiet contentment with a woman as their breathing synchronized and their hearts beat as one. He'd never been a part of anyone else, until now.

Her fingers drew soft, languorous circles over his shoulders and back, down the length of his spine, and beneath his loosened braies, over the slope of his buttocks. The airy massage was both pacifying and stimulating. His skin tingled all over; his body felt heavy, yet charged with sensation. As she continued this feathery touch, that sensation gravitated to where they were joined. His senses focused in on his body penetrating hers. Deep inside her, within her warmth and softness, he felt her heart pulsing in time with his.

The pulses became a steady throb. Still unmoving, he felt his ardor quicken, felt himself grow harder still, within her. She noticed this; her hands stopped moving. Her hot, damp tissues seemed to swell around him.

"Would you tell me again?" she asked, very quietly.

He knew what she meant. Lifting himself up on an elbow, he brushed her hair off her face and whispered, just loudly enough to be heard over the rain, "I love you, Faithe." He lowered his mouth to hers and kissed her tenderly. "I love you." He kissed her again, and again, breathing words of love and need upon her lips, as his body strained and quivered inside her.

There was something exquisitely maddening about lying perfectly still while his craving for release grew more intense, more undeniable, with every moment that passed. The source of that craving, sheathed within her, vibrated with the need to push, and push, and push again.

He trailed his hand down from her face to a breast, fondling its silken weight until her breath came fast. When he took her nipple between thumb and forefinger and pressed, she gasped. A spasm rippled through her from within, clenching him.

Enough. Closing his hand around her hip, and still braced on his elbow, he slowly pulled out of her. He paused at the snug little opening, willing himself to go slowly, to be gentle and solicitous.

Curling his hand beneath her to lift her hips, he pressed inward, gradually this time, gritting his teeth against the astonishing pleasure, against the urge to plunge hard and fast. She sighed as he seated himself within her, and again as he slid out and in, out and in, taking his time, his entire body taut with desire.

Faithe kissed his throat as he rocked slowly within her, all his muscles tensed and shivering. She closed her hands over his shoulders and met his measured thrusts with sinuous grace. The rhythmic crush of straw beneath them provided counterpoint to the rain's cool, steady hiss.

"You feel wonderful inside me," she murmured, snaking her hands down to his hips.

"You feel . . . oh, God. I can hardly bear it." He felt as if his heart were going to burst; every beat pummeled him from within. Her body milked him like a hot fist. With each partial withdrawal, it seemed to pull him back in. It was too much; at this rate, he'd explode within moments, and he didn't want this to end yet.

He altered his thrusts to make himself last, penetrating her again and again with a rotating movement that coaxed soft moans from her. Sliding his hand out from under her hip, he caressed her breasts, teasing the nipples in a way she seemed to like. Her breathing turned ragged. "Yes . . . oh, Luke."

Just hearing her whisper his name as she writhed in his arms fired his loins. *Truly, I'm lost,* he thought as he spiraled inexorably toward orgasm, his thrusts accelerating despite his desire to go slowly for Faithe's sake. Her body took over, tightening and lunging, ramming deep, deep . . .

Faithe's expression of easy delight soon fled. Looking almost pained, she grew rigid beneath him, her fingers digging into his hips. Her body trembled; she arched, grinding herself against him, her head rolling back in the straw. He heard a low, whimpering cry as her body bucked and shuddered. Her internal muscles pumped him frantically.

"Oh, God." His body recognized what was happening before his mind did, responding to her climax by driving into her with savage urgency. Animal instinct propelled him, tearing a roar of fulfillment from him as tremors shot like lightning up his extremities, meeting and igniting in his groin, shooting out of him with blissful violence. The intensity of it blinded and deafened him. Amid the delirious frenzy of release, he felt Faithe's arms and legs lock around him, holding him tight even as her own crisis ran its course.

I was lost, he thought dazedly as the convulsive pleasure crested and then slowly ebbed, racking him with its aftershocks. *But Faithe has found me. I'm lost no more.*

Chapter 14

Faithe lay sated and drowsy in Luke's arms, absorbing his heat, reveling in his quiet strength. His chest hair felt springy, cushioning her cheek against the rock-solid muscle underneath. She breathed deeply, savoring the damp, tangy smell of him—of both of them. Hard work and sex were a heady combination, one that affected her like strong wine. Directly beneath her ear, his heart thudded with steady resonance.

The straw underneath them crackled softly as he shifted. He'd not retied his shirt, nor his braies, although he'd pulled them up. Her clothing was similarly disheveled. She had no idea what became of the cord that had laced up her kirtle, once, long ago, in what felt like another lifetime. Where the gown parted, she felt his warm torso against her bare breasts. Her skirt was tucked around her thighs, and her legs were comfortably intertwined with his.

Rain still whispered against the thatch. The livestock had quieted, save for the occasional contented grunt. In the aftermath of the storm's worst fury, the light had lost its strange, purplish cast and taken on a silvery radiance, enhancing the mystic aura surrounding them. Never had Faithe felt more at peace. The day's distressing revelations about Caedmon—although she would have to find a way to deal with them—seemed for the time being to recede into the distant past. She felt a happy sense of fruition mingled with hope.

"This is a perfect moment," she murmured, nestling against her husband as she slid her fingers through his chest hair. "Everything is good. We love each other . . . we have each other. Naught is amiss."

Luke's heart hammered erratically for a few moments; she felt him tense.

"Is anything wrong?" she asked, lifting her head to find him frowning.

When he met her gaze, she saw that unsettled look that had so troubled her during the past few days. He looked away quickly; she felt his chest expand, and then he let out a lengthy sigh. He looked back at her, and she saw a fierce determination in his eyes. "It matters not. Nothing matters save for us. Nothing can touch us. I won't let it."

She studied him; there was something vaguely desolate about him "What's wrong, Luke? You can tell me."

A hot, liquid sadness shimmered in his eyes. "Nay, I can't," he whispered rawly. "I can't. I wish to God—" His words caught in his throat. He looked everywhere but at her, his eyes shining, his mouth set in a grim line. "Have you ever wished," he said unsteadily, "that you could go back in time and undo something you've done?"

"Of course. Everyone has." She settled back on his chest, facing away from him, since he didn't seem to want to look her in the eye. "What is it you want to undo, Luke?"

After a long pause he said, "Something I can't tell you. Something I can never tell you."

"Have you told a priest?"

"Aye, I've made confession and spent two months doing penance at St. Albans. But there are some sins that blacken the soul irretrievably, and this is one of them."

Faithe sorted through the possibilities. Her stomach clenched. Closing her eyes, she forced the words out slowly. "The Norman soldiers . . . some of them, when they want a woman . . ." She swallowed down her dread, recalling how barbaric Luke had seemed just a short time ago, pinning her hands to either side of her as he crushed her into the straw . . . *Don't make me hold you down, Faithe.* "They just take her," she finished in a quivery whisper.

A heartbeat passed, and then Luke rose abruptly onto an elbow. Cupping her chin, he turned her to face him. The intensity of his gaze robbed her of breath. "I'm guilty of many sins," he said, "grievous sins, for which I'll surely suffer the flames of hell. But rape is not one of them." His fingers pressed hard into her chin. "Never."

"Truly?" she asked, wanting so badly to believe.

He hesitated, and she began to fear the worst, but then he said, "If you're thinking about . . . before . . . with us . . ."

"N-nay, I . . ."

"I would have lost you. 'Twas the only way I knew to show you . . . to keep you . . ."

"I understand," she assured him, meaning it. "I understood then." Reaching up, she caressed his scratchy cheek. "And I believe you. You're a good man, Luke de Périgueux."

His mouth quirked. "I've been called many things in my life, but never that." He fell back again in the straw, and Faithe lowered her head onto his chest.

They lay together contentedly, listening to the rain and each other's breathing. Faithe lifted Luke's rough cross from its nest of chest hair and brought it close to her face. It was fairly large and carved of dark wood. She hadn't noticed before, but it was actually a crucifix. A crude figure of Christ was sculpted on the surface of the cross. It was primitive work, but there was something endearing about it.

"I should think a man of your noble birth would wear a golden crucifix," she said, "if he wears one at all."

She felt a gentle plucking at her hair; he must be picking straw out. "I made that."

She turned to look at him. "Did you?"

"Put your head back where it was," he scolded amiably. Pressing her down with firm hands, he continued idly grooming her hair. "I made it at the abbey at Aurillac, when I was a child."

She smiled at the image of a dark young boy taking a knife to a block of wood, his attention fixed on his work to the exclusion of everything around him. *He commits himself entirely to everything he does,* Alex had said of his brother. Luke's lovemaking had borne out the truth of that. Awed at first by his single-minded intensity, she'd soon found herself swept up in the same fierce passion. She's been transported, not just physically, but spiritually. It was as if they'd lost themselves in each other, merging as one into a domain of pure ecstasy.

Rubbing her fingertips over the uneven surface of the crucifix, she said, "And you've worn it ever since?"

There came a pause; she sensed he was smiling. "This may surprise you, but I've got this absurd streak of piety in me that I can't seem to eradicate—a souvenir from my monastic upbringing, I suppose. I actually enjoy Mass."

"It doesn't surprise me in the least," she said. "I'd already discerned it. And I don't think it's absurd at all." She hesitated before asking, "Did you really mean it when you said . . . do you really think you're . . . damned to hell?"

He left off extracting straw from her hair and tightened his arms around her. "I'm afraid there's little question of that," he said softly.

"Why? Because of this mysterious sin you can't undo?"

He hesitated. "Partly, yes. Mostly. But then there are all my years of soldiering."

Faithe reclined next to him, looking down; he wouldn't meet her eyes. "Luke, even the priests say 'tis no sin to serve your king in battle."

"Not all soldiers embrace warfare with quite the enthusiasm I did," he said hollowly.

"Nor is it any sin to want to do a thing well."

"Nay. 'Twas more than that." He sat up with his back to her and raked his fingers through his hair, groaning in exasperation when he yanked yet more loose strands from the braid. Faithe murmured something pacifying and set about unwrapping the leather thong that bound his hair and gliding her fingers through the plaits.

He sighed. "I was twelve when I was sent home from the abbey for failure to apply myself to my studies. My father gave me a simple choice. Return to Aurillac and commit myself to my education so that I could take holy orders, or remain at Périgueux and learn the arts of soldiering along with little Alex. I made my choice. Now, I regret it with all my heart. Although"—he glanced over his shoulder at her, his expression softening—"if I'd become a monk or a priest, I never would have married you. So perhaps 'twas worth it."

"How can you say that, when you believe you're damned for having been a soldier?"

Quietly he said, "I will certainly suffer the pains of hell one day, but until then, I get to spend the rest of my earthly life with you. That's worth more to me than you'll ever know." His expression sobered, and he turned away again, his elbows resting on his updrawn knees. "I didn't want to disappoint my sire a second time, so I threw myself into my training. When I was called upon to fight for real, in a private war in

Aquitaine, I was like a machine. I sent many men to heaven with my crossbow that day. We vanquished the enemy. My father's overlord had me kneel in the blood-soaked mud, and he knighted me right there in the field. That's when they started calling me the Black Dragon. My father was very proud."

Faithe drew her fingers slowly through his hair. "As well he should have been. You did nothing wrong, Luke."

"I was so young, so . . . unthinking. I had not a care for my own mortality, much less the state of my soul. And I spared not a moment's remorse for those I killed."

"They would have killed you if they could have," she said.

"That's not the point," he remonstrated gently. "I was so brutally callous. I'd chosen the crossbow because I could kill from a distance. I never had to look in the eyes of the men I slew, so I never thought of them as real. They were . . . the enemy. Animated suits of mail. And I dispatched them by the score. God alone knows how many lives I took." He rubbed his forehead.

Faithe rested her face on his back, feeling the strain in him through his shirt. "That's why you feel such torment? Because you didn't care about the men you killed? Does Alex care?"

"Alex has always known they were flesh and blood. He's had no choice. Killing with the sword is very . . . personal. The first time he killed in battle, he wept afterward. I held him."

"Oh." Faithe slid her arms around Luke's back.

"He eventually came to terms with it—and in a way I never had to. He grew into an acceptance of the killing, knowing full well he was taking another man's life. I never developed that type of wisdom. I just kept on killing, easily and thoughtlessly. Until one day . . ."

She lifted her face from his back. "Yes?"

"An engagement had just ended. I remember standing in a castle courtyard, surrounded by the bodies of my enemy, many with my own crossbow bolts piercing their armor. The sun was setting. 'Twas one of those fiery sunsets that casts a sort of otherworldly glow on everything it touches."

Faithe closed her eyes, picturing the scene, and nodded.

"It looked so different, so unreal . . . that for the first time, it actually did seem real to me. Does that make any sense to you?"

"Aye. A great deal of sense."

"It hit me like a cudgel. 'Twas as if I suddenly realized what I'd been doing. The next few days were a nightmare for me. I dreaded having to go into battle again. I didn't think I'd have the stomach to aim my crossbow at someone. I didn't know if I should." His back expanded as he took a deep breath. "I confided in a friend of mine, an archer. He told me that sort of thing happens from time to time, but that there was a cure for it. He gave me . . ." Luke shook his head and swore softly under his breath.

"What did he give you?"

Luke sat in silence for several long moments. "Herbs," he said tonelessly. "A mixture of them, to chew before battle. Catnip, mostly."

"Catnip. 'Tis a vile plant. 'Twill make you—"

"A monster. Or rather, more of a monster than I already was." He shook his head. " 'Twas most effective. It roused the blood-thirst within me, and to a degree I'd never imagined before. Now, not only did I not care about the killing, I couldn't even remember it afterward. But the men would tell me what I'd done, how wild I'd been, how ferocious. To hear them tell it, I was the ultimate soldier—a hero. But I never felt much like a hero in my bloody chain mail, shaking from the aftereffects of a battle I couldn't even recall."

She made a sound of disgust. "A loathsome plant, catnip. And dangerous. It incites madness."

"In me, it merely reawakened the madness lurking deep inside. I've always harbored a beast in my breast. The herbs simply unlocked it from its cage."

"Nonsense."

He turned and stared at her incredulously. "I beg your—"

"Complete nonsense. Catnip's notorious for taking sane men and turning them into murderous animals. Other herbs do much the same, and no doubt they were all in that mixture. What you became was the product of the herbs you chewed. It came from outside of you, not from within."

"Nay, I'd always been without scruples on the battlefield."

"Until that day in the castle courtyard," she pointed out. "You'd matured. You'd developed a conscience, an awareness of yourself and your actions. You'd changed."

Luke looked in her direction, but not *at* her. His gaze was preoccupied, as if he were spinning her words around in his mind, examining them from every angle.

"You didn't want to go on," she said, "but then you started chewing the catnip and you had no choice. It imposed the blood-thirst on you after you'd grown out of it."

He met her gaze. " 'Twould be comforting to accept what you say, but 'twould be false consolation, I fear. My soul is as black as pitch."

"Truly? How is it, then, that I've managed to fall in love with such a demon?"

He blinked at her.

"I've never been much drawn to black-hearted beasts before," she added, caressing his scratchy jaw.

"Aye, well, I've managed to keep my darker nature in check since coming to Hauekleah."

"Your darker nature has not emerged," she said, "because it's long gone. And you no longer chew those despicable herbs, so your own good nature—your true nature—has finally had the opportunity to assert itself."

He closed his eyes and tilted his head, rubbing his face against her palm. "I'd love to believe you."

"Believe me," she whispered. "And ease your mind. You *are* a good man, else I wouldn't care for you as I do. I wouldn't want to give myself to you. I wouldn't want to have your children, and grow old with you."

"Ah, Faithe." Luke slid a hand around her neck and drew her close, kissing her until she grew light-headed. He lowered her into the straw and they kissed endlessly, caressing each other with slow, dreamy hands.

When at last they drew apart, breathless, she said, "You see? All is well. All is wonderful. 'Tis just as I said before. Naught is amiss. The past is gone. There is no more Black Dragon. There's just us."

"Just us," he whispered, lightly stroking her face. "Nothing matters but us."

"Whatever you were in the past, whatever the herbs turned you into, whatever they made you do, no longer exists."

He closed his eyes, his forehead creased, his jaw tight.

"Anything you did under their influence," she said, "cannot blacken your soul. God is merciful. He understands all."

Luke sighed heavily and wrapped his arms around her, tucking her up against him. "That's why I like Mass. I can immerse myself in the ritual and feel almost worthy of redemption. I can feel at one with God."

She nodded. "That's how I feel when I look out over Hauekleah's pastures and meadows in the late afternoon, when the sun is low and the shadows are long. I'm afraid I find Mass an utter waste of time."

"Aye, I can tell from the way you squirm about on your bench, forever turning to look out the door, as if the day is passing you by."

"That's precisely how I feel in church."

"I know. I know everything about you."

"What do you know about me?"

"I know that you like it when I do this." He plucked her nipple, sparking a current of arousal between her legs.

"Luke!" she gasped, pushing his hand away. "Don't do that. I won't be able to talk to you, and I like talking to you."

"I like it, too. But I like other things, as well." His hands roamed over her, through her unkempt kirtle and beneath it. "You're very . . . passionate. I hadn't expected . . . that is, I've never been with a woman who . . . well, who . . ."

She laid her palm on his cheek, hot as an oven. "Are you blushing?"

He turned his head, smiling in an engagingly grudging way.

"You are," she exclaimed with delight, rising on her elbows to look down upon him. "How perfectly splendid! I've made Luke de Périgueux blush!"

His broad chest shook with laughter; he encircled her with his arms. "It's just that I've never known a lady to speak so openly of such matters."

"Does it displease you?" she asked, honestly wanting to know.

He shook his head slightly, never losing eye contact. "It intrigues me," he said softly. "Everything about you intrigues me."

She smiled. "Everything?"

"Everything. What's in here . . ." Luke lightly tapped a finger against her forehead. "And here." He pressed his hand over the inner curve of her left breast, where her heart was, and then grinned. "And under here." Snaking his hand up under her skirt, he burrowed his fingers through the hair at the juncture of her thighs.

"Mmm." Faithe stretched with delight as he stroked the moist seam with a whisper-light touch. She was instantly breathless. "I like your fingers. They're a little rough. When you touch me there, I want to jump out of my skin."

He smiled slowly as he continued his wispy caress. "You're so responsive. It's very exciting. I thought I was going to scream, at the end, when you . . . well . . ."

She glided a fingertip down his nose. "When I came?"

"God's bones, woman." He laughed in evident astonishment.

"You did scream."

"Did I?" His fingers stilled, and then continued brushing her cleft with patient fingertips; she felt her sensitized flesh swell and open.

" 'Twas more of a sort of very loud groan. I loved it. I wished it could go on and on and on. I wished I could come forever and ever, with you inside me."

"I can't think I'd object to the situation," he said wryly, "if you could think of some way to arrange it."

She chuckled, trying to keep her mind on their banter even as she reveled in his touch. "I shall put my mind to the matter."

"I've never been with a woman when . . . that happened to her."

"Never? Alex said you'd been with many women."

He grimaced, but she sensed amusement in his eyes. "I must have a talk with Alex. Yes, I've been with many women. Most soldiers have."

"Prostitutes," she said.

He nodded. "They like to get things over with and get their coins. There's little pleasure in it for them, from what I've been able to gather. Nor do they seek it. 'Twould only slow things down."

"How sad."

He seemed to ponder that. "Yes, I suppose it is sad. I never thought about it much at the time. I mean, I knew they were missing something by not . . . finishing. But it never occurred to me that I was missing something as well. I reckoned 'twas enough that I took my pleasure. I never knew how it could feel to be inside a woman when she . . ." His eyes grew dark, his blush deepened.

"What are you thinking?"

"I'm thinking I'd like to feel it again."

"Would you?"

"Oh, yes." Luke nudged her slightly. She felt an insistent stirring against her thigh, and her heart sped up.

She'd never known anyone so thoroughly masculine. His body thrilled and intrigued her—especially now that he'd been inside her. He was sizable everywhere, she now knew, including that part of him steadily hardening against her.

"Tell me how to touch you," he said, rolling her onto her back, "to make it happen."

Faithe covered his big hand with hers and guided a fingertip to the half-hidden little knot of flesh where her desire was concentrated. She sucked in a breath when he stroked it.

"Here?" he breathed raggedly. "Like this?"

"Mmm . . . but perhaps a little softer, and to the side a bit. You need barely . . . *yes* . . ."

He caressed her until she writhed, handfuls of straw clutched in her trembling fists. "Like that. Yes."

"And this?" he asked, circling the little nub with quickening fingers. "Is this—"

"Yes!" A tempest of sensation gathered inside her, like a storm ready to explode from the heavens. Insensible with pleasure, she moaned unself-consciously.

"Oh, Faithe." He kicked off his braies. "Not yet. I want to feel it when it happens." She thought he was going to mount her, but instead, he lay on his side next to her. Draping her outside leg over his, he pushed into her, just enough to stretch her open, all the while pleasuring her with his hand.

Her body expanded around him as he entered her by maddening degrees, enhancing the stimulation. Her breath came in harsh gasps; her head rolled back and forth in the straw. "Luke . . . Luke . . ."

"Now," he gasped, sliding in to the hilt. "Come for me now." Luke touched the little knot directly, and her body convulsed around him, rioting with pleasure. "Oh, God." He grabbed her hips, pounding into her, his head thrown back. With every stabbing thrust, he groaned harshly, until the groans merged into a single strangled cry of fulfillment. His body tightened as he rammed himself deep inside her, his seed pumping against her womb.

Gasping for air, Faithe collapsed in the straw. Dull thunder filled her ears, overpowering all her other senses. Presently, she became aware of trembling fingertips on her face. "Are you all right?"

She growled contentedly. "Oh, yes."

He sighed in evident relief and drew himself out of her, gathering her up in his arms. "I was too . . . rough at the end. 'Twas wonderful." He dragged a shaky hand through her hair and kissed her forehead. "Too wonderful. I was afraid I'd hurt you, or . . . upset you." Shaking his head, he added, "I shouldn't have lost control like that."

"Foolish man." She curled into his embrace. "You're supposed to lose control. That's the point. We're supposed to lose control together."

He chuckled breathily. "You do have a way of putting things."

"You could never hurt me—or upset me."

He stiffened slightly. "I've spent a lifetime hurting and upsetting people. 'Tis a difficult habit to break."

"That wasn't you," she said resolutely. " 'Twas the Black Dragon, and he doesn't exist anymore. He vanished when you ceased chewing those herbs of yours."

He lay quietly for a moment, lightly rubbing her arm. "Perhaps. Still, I dread what might happen if I don't keep myself reined in."

She pulled back to look at him. "Even when you're inside me?"

"Especially then. You're not like . . . the women I'm used to. I'm not quite sure how to make love to someone like you."

"You seem to have managed fairly well so far," she said dryly.

He snorted. "Merely because you're so forgiving of my lack of delicacy."

She laughed outright. "There are many things I might want from you in bed, Luke de Périgueux, but delicacy isn't one of them!"

"Exasperating wench!" He chuckled. "You know what I mean."

"Unfortunately, yes. And I want none of it. Lovemaking should be joyous and without restraint."

"I've trained myself to exercise restraint," he said. "I'm afraid to abandon it now. You mean too much to me."

"Foolish, foolish, foolish man." Rising onto an elbow, she ran a light fingertip down his forehead and nose; when it reached his lips, he kissed it. "One of these days," she threatened softly, "I shall have to seize those reins you've got such a tight grip on, and show you what it's like to let go of them."

His gaze darkened. "Are you sure that would be a good idea?"

Smiling, she lowered her mouth to his, whispering against his lips, "Quite sure."

Chapter 15

Luke came awake slowly, as if he were drifting to the surface of a warm, clear pool, drifting toward the sunlight . . .

He blinked and yawned. It *was* sunny, more so than when he usually awoke. He'd slept late, then. Little wonder, since he and Faithe had spent the night—most of it, anyway—making slow, spellbinding love while the rest of Hauekleah slept soundly.

A glance at Faithe's side of the bed revealed that she'd already awakened and gone downstairs. He'd never known her to sleep past dawn.

He stretched luxuriously, growling with contentment. The linen sheets shifting over his bare flesh reminded him that he was naked; his nakedness reminded him of last night—and yesterday afternoon in the barn.

Luke smiled. He was going to like being married to Faithe of Hauekleah.

He washed and dressed quickly, eager to see his wife again, to put his arms around her and feel her arms around him. Such need, such desire, such euphoria. It was like a drunkenness of the soul—a state of ecstatic inebriation. He couldn't wait to be with her, to touch her, to bury his face in her hair and inhale her very essence.

I'm lost, he thought as he descended the stairs into the main hall, *and I'm glad of it.*

Joy rose within him when he saw her standing near

a window, inspecting something in her hand. His cheer faded when he saw that Orrik was with her, pointing to what she held and saying something Luke couldn't bear. Baldric, his arms crossed, leaned against the wall.

His brother sat on a bench nearby, getting a haircut from one of his twins—to the obvious displeasure of young Firdolf, who eyed them sulkily as he stacked firewood on the hearth. Of course, it was the twin with one braid, the one of whom he was so enamored, Blossom. Luke wondered why he'd taken a fancy to just the one and not the other, since they were so very much alike. Love, he decided, knew no logic nor reason.

Alex grinned when he saw Luke. "Good day to you, brother. You've awakened just in time for the midday meal." Alex's eyes sparkled with secret humor, as if he could guess why Luke had slept so late.

Faithe smiled with unabashed pleasure when she noticed Luke. He smiled back, feeling, already, that tingle of gratification he felt whenever he was near her. She waved him over, and he crossed to her.

"What do you make of this?" she asked, holding out the shiny object in her palm.

Luke reached for it, stilling when he saw what it was—a golden disk inset with tiny pearls in the shape of a wolf's head. Alex's mantle pin. He cut his eyes toward his brother, who met his gaze with a fleeting quirk of the mouth, a twitch of an eyebrow.

He finds this amusing, Luke realized, summoning enough presence of mind to take the pin and make a show of examining it.

Orrik scowled. "That belonged to the Norman devil who murdered Caedmon." The bailiff cast an uncomfortable look in Faithe's direction, and received a rather chilly gaze in return. Faithe had told Luke of her intention to dress Orrik down for keeping the truth from her all these months; it appeared she had already done so.

Alex gestured toward the pin. " 'Tis of Frankish origin."

Luke glared at his brother, appalled that he would offer any such helpful insight.

"Well, it is," Alex said nonchalantly. "Anyone can see that."

"He's right," Orrik agreed. " 'Tisn't English-made. That was obvious just from the design. And there's that inscription in French on the back."

Luke turned the pin over numbly, knowing perfectly well what was inscribed there: *To my youngest son: Be strong and of good courage.*

"It looks like *your* mantle pin," Faithe said.

Luke stared at her.

"Does it?" Orrik asked, his voice soft, his silvery eyes glinting.

"So it does," Alex said easily as he brushed bits of snipped hair off his face. He smiled mischievously at Luke, who glowered back. "They're the same size and shape, and the design around the edge is nearly identical. We should compare the two. Where is yours?"

At the bottom of the river, as you know very well. "I've lost it," Luke ground out, vexed by his brother's flippant attitude. This was all a game to him, though clearly both Orrik and Faithe took it very seriously.

"You lost your mantle pin?" Faithe asked, reaching out to touch Luke's arm. "The one your father gave you? I'm so sorry. I'll tell everyone to look for it. 'Twill turn up."

I sincerely hope not. For the two pins to be compared would be disastrous. "That would be . . . good," he said, guilt twisting in his stomach. "Thank you."

"It matters not whether we find your pin," Orrik snapped. "This one"—he jabbed a finger at the wolf pin—"is Frankish for sure."

"For sure," Baldric echoed.

"Aye," Faithe said, "and most likely it came off the mantle of a Norman soldier. After all, 'twas found in a . . ." Her composure faltered slightly, just for a moment. "In a brothel," she said briskly. "Soldiers frequent such places, do they not?"

She paused, looking around at the four men. They all cleared their throats and muttered in the affirmative.

"All we know about this pin's owner," she said, "is that he's someone's youngest son."

"And that he's a whorin' murderer," Orrik snarled.

Faithe's cheeks stained pink, and Luke guessed why: If the murderer had been whoring that night, so had his victim. One of the many regrets consuming him of late was that this gentle, loving woman had been forced to confront the unsavory circumstances of her husband's death.

Faithe took the pin out of Luke's hand and flipped it over thoughtfully. "I mean to find the man who lost this," she said, softly but firmly.

Luke glanced toward Alex to see a flicker of unease in response to Faithe's quiet resolve.

She looked up and met Luke's gaze, her expression sad and intent. "He was my husband, Luke. I can't let this pass. I have to find the man who killed him. I couldn't live with myself if I didn't."

"I understand," he said, because it was clearly what she wanted to hear. She needed his approval. She needed to know that he accepted her decision to apprehend the man who'd murdered her first husband. That Luke himself was the man she sought was a fact he intended to keep from her at all costs. It would devastate her; it would ruin him. And he would lose her.

He would lose her. He couldn't let that happen. All that mattered now was keeping the truth from her, though doing so would only further tarnish his soul.

"I must find out why Caedmon disappeared from

Hastings," she said, "and why he lived . . . and died . . . as he did. And I must and will bring his killer to justice. Nothing will deter me."

Luke risked another glance at his brother. Alex's subtly arched eyebrow conveyed no humor this time, and his mouth was set in a grim line that Luke didn't often see on the affable young man's face. It was clear that he discerned, as Luke did, the very real threat behind Faithe's quiet resolve, so different from Orrik's fierce but unfocused bluster. Her determination could not be dismissed, and should not be ignored.

"I will continue my inquiries," Orrik said. "I'll show that pin in every village the Normans have passed through—"

"Isn't that what you've been doing all along?" Faithe asked.

"Aye, well, I'll step up my efforts. I'll talk to every Englishman between here and—"

"Every Englishman?" Faithe asked.

"Aye. Every man, woman, and—"

"Why not the Normans?"

"The Normans! The soldiers?"

"Aye."

"You mean for me to question Norman soldiers?"

"You're looking for a Norman soldier, are you not? Who better to identify the man who wore the insignia of the white wolf than one of his colleagues?" Faithe spoke quietly, but there was a layer of steel underlying her words.

"Milady, I—"

"If you've restricted your efforts to the English, 'tis little wonder you've been unsuccessful."

"I'll be damned if I'll go begging information from those bastards. 'Tisn't worth it."

"It is to me," Faithe said softly.

The bailiff's face grew dark. "What makes you think they'd cooperate? Why should they implicate one of their own in the murder of a Saxon?"

"There are ways to get information from unfriendly people. But you didn't even try."

"And I won't. Even for you, milady."

Luke took a deep breath. "I will."

Everyone looked at him. Alex's eyebrows shot up.

He thought fast. "I'm one of them. They'll talk to me. And I'm expendable here. It matters not if I'm away from Hauekleah from time to time, but Orrik is indispensable, especially with Dunstan away."

Alex nodded slowly, clearly perceiving the reason for Luke's offer. If Luke did the investigating, he'd have control over what was discovered—and revealed. Engaging in this charade would only compound his guilt over misleading Faithe, but what choice did he have? Left to her own devices, she could ferret out the truth, and he mustn't let that happen.

Faithe stepped toward him and laid a hand on his chest. "You would do that for me?"

Contrition flowed hot through Luke's veins. "Aye. Of course."

She touched his cheek. "You're a good man, Luke. Thank you."

Christ. All he could do was nod.

"Perhaps you could start by questioning Lord Alberic's men at Foxhyrst," she suggested. "Those men were your friends—you fought alongside them. Surely they'll tell you who the pin belonged to."

"If they know," Luke said. "There are thousands of Norman soldiers in England, Faithe. Trying to locate one based on nothing more than a mantle pin . . ." He shrugged, hoping he seemed convincing.

Faithe turned the gleaming object over and over in her hand. "Perhaps if we knew more about the pin itself, its origins . . ."

Orrik snorted. "It came from France. We know that."

"The Frankish Empire is huge," Faithe said. "This could have been made in Normandy, Anjou, Poitou . . .

anywhere. If we knew where it was made, that would help us to identify its owner."

She was smart. Too smart. "An excellent suggestion," Luke allowed, "but I couldn't begin to tell you where it came from. I don't know anyone who could."

"I do," she said thoughtfully.

Luke sighed. "Do you?"

"He's a goldsmith with a shop in Foxhyrst," she said. "I commissioned this from him." She fingered the chain around her neck.

Baldric frowned and cleared his throat to get Orrik's attention. "The only goldsmith I know of in Foxhyrst is an old Jew."

"That's the one," Faithe said. "Isaac Ben Ravid is his name."

Orrik shook his head. "Nay. We don't need help from infidels."

"This particular infidel," she said icily, "happens to have been quite a renowned jeweler in his day. He served most of the royal houses of Europe before he got too old to travel."

"How do you know this?" Orrik demanded.

"We talk whenever I go marketing in Foxhyrst," she said defiantly. "I like him. He told me every region has its own distinct style—that the differences between a brooch from Paris and one from Rouen might be subtle, but they were there. He said he'd gotten to where he could pinpoint not only the city of origin of a piece, but sometimes the craftsman who'd made it."

Luke exchanged another uneasy glance with his brother. Faithe noticed. "Don't tell me *you* refuse to talk to Jews!"

"Of course not," he answered automatically. "I'll go to Foxhyrst on the morrow." Best to get this out of the way. He could simply stay the night in an inn and return the next day, claiming he'd had no success.

"And while we're there, we can question the soldiers garrisoned at Lord Alberic's castle."

Damn. "We?"

"Of course. I'm going with you."

"That's really not necessary," Luke said.

"Nay, but 'twould help. Isaac knows me. He might be more forthcoming with me than with a stranger. And I . . . I need to do this. I need to be a part of this. Can you understand that?"

Luke admitted truthfully that he could, knowing that nothing he could say would persuade her not to accompany him. The apprehension of Caedmon's murderer had become a crusade with her. Her eyes glittered with determination. He respected her for it; it showed the fortitude of character he'd come to love in her. And it heartened him to think that if he were the one found dead in some dark little loft somewhere, she wouldn't rest until she'd avenged him.

But it chilled him to the bone to think of that vengeance directed toward him.

Luke couldn't get to sleep that night. The lovemaking that should have left him pleasantly exhausted only deepened his remorse over the deceit he was perpetuating against Faithe. After several sleepless hours, he rose and opened the window shutters, letting the watery moonlight bathe him. He breathed deeply of cool night breezes perfumed with the mingled scents of Hauekleah, and thought, *I can't lose this. I can't lose Faithe.*

Turning, he gazed on her, asleep on her back with the sheet pushed down to her hips, as naked as he. No—not completely naked; last night, he'd told her he wouldn't object if she wanted to resume wearing her chatelaine's keys to bed, and she'd taken him at his word. Now, as he studied the golden chain looped securely around her neck, the keys nestled between her lush breasts, he regretted that magnanimous gesture.

She'd locked up Alex's wolf pin in the little cabinet in which she kept her jewelry. In the morning she would retrieve it, and they would take it to Foxhyrst to be examined and speculated upon. Had her keys been lying on the little table next to the bed, it would be a simple matter to unlock the cabinet, take the pin, and hurl it into the river to rest alongside his. The theft would be investigated, but no one would ever suspect him—and the pin could not then be taken to Foxhyrst and shown to this Isaac Ben Ravid.

Luke crossed to the bed and sat carefully, looking down upon his sleeping wife. Holding his breath, he reached out and gently slid his fingers beneath the keys clustered on the end of the chain. The back of his hand brushed the silken resilience of a breast. She sighed and arched her back; Luke closed his hand around the keys to silence them, even as his loins stirred.

He shook his head ruefully, awed at her power to rouse him even in sleep. Tempted as he was to awaken her with a kiss, he forced himself to keep still until her breathing had become steady again. Gripping the keys with one hand, he slowly—so slowly—eased the chain upward, over her head. Could he disentangle it from her hair and slide it out from beneath her without disturbing her?

The question became moot, for the chain grazed her ear and she stirred. "Luke?" she murmured in a sleepy rasp.

"Aye." Distracting her with a kiss, he carefully lowered the keys to her chest. What had made him think he could take them without waking her up? A pointless attempt, born of desperation and tainted with guilt. He loathed this deception, especially in light of their newfound intimacy.

"I dreamed you touched me," she whispered against

his lips, then took his hand and pressed it to her breast. "Here."

"I did."

"Mmm." Her nipples puckered in response to his caresses. Leaning over, he took one in his mouth and suckled—an elemental act, both comforting and stimulating. His teeth grazed her, and she gasped.

"Are you all right?" he asked, drawing away.

She groaned. "You *must* stop asking me that."

"Do I ask it so often?"

"Far too often." She sat up and cupped his beard-roughened face. "Luke, I'm not the fragile creature you think I am. You must stop being so careful with me." She kissed him again, lightly. "You must stop holding back when we're making love. You're so . . . restrained, always keeping yourself in check. I hate it. The only time you give in to it is at the very end."

"It's because I care for you. I love you. I can't just unleash my lust on you like some mindless beast."

She made that kittenish little growl he loved so much. "I might like that."

Luke thought about all those quick, violent couplings with coarse women whom he thought of as little more than receptacles. He touched a fingertip to her nose. "You mustn't encourage me to give vent to my animal nature. You might not appreciate the results as much as you seem to think."

"You keep using those words—animal, beast . . . That's the problem, you know. You still think there's a savage creature curled up inside you, and that if you let down your guard for a moment, 'twill break free, and I'll run screaming from you."

The image made Luke smile. Try as he might, he could not imagine Faithe running screaming from anything or anyone.

"That creature is gone," she insisted. " 'Twas a creation of those herbs, and now it's dead and buried. Is that so hard to believe?"

"You have a way of making me want to believe it," he said, "and of making it sound like the truth."

She nodded. "I think you believe in here"—she touched his forehead—"but not in here." She rested a hand over his heart and kissed him softly.

Luke deepened the kiss, folding his arms around her and lowering her onto the rumpled sheets. He moved against her, growing harder with every slow thrust.

She broke the kiss with a yawn. "We'll be setting out early tomorrow. We should really get some sleep."

"You're absolutely right." Parting her legs, he glided into her with one long stroke, eliciting a soft exhalation of pleasure from her. "You go ahead and sleep. I'll join you when I'm done here."

Faithe chuckled, and he felt the vibrations deep inside her. Somehow that seemed as intimate, and erotic, as feeling her climax. She wrapped her legs around his hips, forcing him deeper still into her damp heat.

"I thought you were sleepy," he murmured as they rocked together languidly.

She smiled. " 'Twould be rude not to stay awake and keep you company until you've done."

"How thoughtful of you," he breathed, his mouth descending on hers.

"Think nothing of it."

It was late in the morning by the time Faithe spied Foxhyrst Castle rising above the rolling meadows and cultivated fields through which she and Luke rode. A disquiet had settled over her husband, she noticed. He held himself stiff in his saddle, answering her attempts at conversation with cursory responses. Perhaps it discomforted him to return to the place that had been his home base while he'd served as a soldier under Lord Alberic's nominal command. Given his repentance of that service, such discomfort would be understandable.

As they rode closer, Faithe could make out the oblong shape of the walled town, as large as a small city. The castle was nestled in the northwest corner, surrounded by its own curtain walls. Built up against the inside of those walls, Faithe knew, were dozens of barracks housing hundreds of soldiers. Surely one of those men would recognize the owner of the white wolf pin. After all, it had been found in Cottwyk, which wasn't far from here. The soldier who lost it might have been one of Lord Alberic's men-at-arms. For all she knew, he might be serving under the sheriff still.

"Luke," she said as they rode through the town's south gate, "what if he's there? At the castle? What if we find him today?"

"Who?" Luke asked distractedly.

"The . . . the man who killed Caedmon. What if someone points him out and says, 'There's the fellow who lost that pin.' What will we do then?"

"That won't happen." Luke stared stonily ahead as he led them up Butcher Lane, a narrow ribbon of packed earth on either side of which thatch-roofed timber dwellings leaned drunkenly toward each other. So grimly certain did he seem that Faithe questioned him no further.

They rode north and then east through the crowded little streets, their progress toward the Jewish quarter slowed by a moving sea of pedestrians, horsemen, carts, dogs, pigs, goats, and chickens, all either dodging or dining on the many scattered piles of offal. It smelled like . . . a town—a place in which too many people and animals lived far too close together, with no proper way to dispose of their waste. Faithe always felt as if she could never quite get a full breath when she was in a town.

Most of the mounted men they passed were Norman soldiers, Luke's former comrades. Some seemed to recognize Luke; several waved to him and called his name, but Luke pointedly ignored them.

"Perhaps you should talk to them," Faithe said. "We could show them the pin and ask them if—"

"Later," he said softly. "First let's deal with this goldsmith."

As they rode east, the crowds thinned. The streets widened, and the houses that lined them were built of stone, not wood, and roofed with tile. A group of bearded men in dark robes and exotic, peaked hats passed them, glancing up curiously as they rode by; otherwise, not a soul was to be seen. It was always quieter in the Jewish quarter, but today it seemed as if the world had come to a halt. Faithe wondered why.

"He lives here," Faithe said, pausing in front of a corner house with large, shuttered windows.

They dismounted, and Luke knocked on the oaken door. After a few minutes he knocked again. "He's not home."

Faithe peered through a window shutter and saw shadowy movement. "Someone is." She rapped on the door.

"He won't answer," came a heavily accented voice from behind them. They turned to see a young man, beardless but wearing the peculiar hat, watching them from the street.

"Why not?" Luke asked.

" 'Tis the sabbath. Old Isaac never comes to the door on the sabbath."

Faithe and Luke exchanged a perplexed look. " 'Tis Saturday," she said. "The sabbath is tomorrow."

The youth started to smile, and then seemed to think better of it. He tucked his hands in his sleeves. "Our sabbath is today. Isaac can't see customers on the sabbath."

"We're not customers," Faithe corrected. "We just want to ask him something."

"He won't do business of any kind today."

" 'Tisn't really business."

"If you're not family," he assured them, firmly but with an apologetic smile, "it's business. Come back tomorrow."

"But we're only here for the day," Faithe said. Luke had made it clear that he wished to be home by supper. He'd refused to consider staying overnight in an inn. Those in Foxhyrst, he'd said, were "not just inns anymore," given the influx of soldiers, and he'd never dream of letting her spend the night in one.

The fellow shrugged elaborately. "You can knock all you like, but he won't answer." He turned and walked away.

"That's that," Luke said. If Faithe hadn't known better, she would almost have thought he looked pleased. "No point in staying here." He remounted, and Faithe followed suit.

"What shall we do?" she asked.

"We'll go back to Hauekleah," he said. "I'll return by myself on Monday and speak to this goldsmith. And I can question the soldiers then, too."

"If you're going to come back on Monday, I'll come with you," she said.

He shook his head. "Let me handle this. You're needed at Hauekleah."

"Luke, I thought you understood," she said quietly.

"I do, I just . . ." Luke rubbed the back of his neck and sighed. He looked away, and then he looked back. "Isn't there a holiday next week?"

She nodded. "St. Swithun's Day—the fifteenth of July. There's to be a grand feast in the sheep meadow, with music and dancing. The abbot of Ramsey sent word that he might come."

"Don't you have to supervise the preparations?"

He was right. She bit her lip. "Perhaps Moira . . . or Orrik . . ."

"You never leave this sort of thing to others. If you

try to do it this time, you'll be fretting over it all the while you're gone. And with the abbot coming, don't you want to make sure—"

"Perhaps we can come back to Foxhyrst next week, after the feast."

"The soldiers might be dispatched on some engagement by then," he said, "and I'd lose the chance to question them. Nay, 'tis best that I return on Monday, alone." Leaning over, he took her hand. "I know you like to be involved in everything. But I promise I won't mishandle things."

She squeezed his hand. "I trust you, Luke. Did you think I didn't?"

Distress shadowed his eyes. Releasing her hand, he raked his fingers through his hair, which he wore loose that day.

"Luke, what's the matter?"

"I'm hungry, that's all," he said without looking at her.

"So am I. My stomach's been growling like a bear."

"Come." He flicked his reins, and Faithe followed him toward the center of town. "Let's find something to eat and drink, and then we can be on our way."

Luke bought curd cheese pasties wrapped in parchment from a peddler on Butcher Lane, near the south gate. Pointing, he said, "There's a tavern. I'll get our flask refilled with ale, and then we can eat as we travel."

Faithe waited on horseback outside the alehouse as Luke jumped down from his horse. He'd almost gotten to the door when a voice boomed out, "By the blood of Christ, if it isn't the Black Dragon!"

Luke and Faithe both turned to find a mounted procession filing into town through the gate. Riding up front, surrounded by a cluster of soldiers—one of whom was the man who'd called out to Luke—was Lord Alberic, in his brocades and furs. A lady's maid rode behind, followed by a curtained litter suspended between a pair of creamy mares, which no doubt housed Alberic's wife. More soldiers leading unmounted horses brought up the rear.

"My lady." Alberic inclined his head toward Faithe, who was glad she'd chosen a silk kirtle for the trip, and taken the time to braid and veil her hair, like a proper gentlewoman. "Sir Luke. What an unexpected pleasure." The sheriff's frigid gaze belied the empty courtesy.

Faithe managed a smile, despite Alberic's chilly demeanor and her discomfort at being virtually surrounded by Normans; some instincts were hard to shake. "Good day, Lord Alberic."

"My lord." Luke turned to the soldier who had called out to him. "Griswold, good to see you."

"I didn't think I'd ever lay eyes on you again," Griswold bellowed. He was fair-haired and burly, with a great square face marred by a deep scar that ran from the outer edge of one eye to the cleft in his chin. He nodded toward Faithe. " 'Tis little wonder you've got no use for your old mates, what with this pretty young wife to keep you company. This *is* your lady wife, is it not?"

Luke introduced Faithe—rather stiffly—to Griswold and several other men, whose names she knew she would never recall. They all greeted her with genial respect, which surprised her at first, given that she was a Saxon and they were in the business of subduing her kind. The reason for their deference, she realized, was that she had married a Norman—not just any Norman, but the celebrated Black Dragon—so she'd essentially become Norman by default. Her chagrin at being welcomed into the ranks of a people she still considered her enemy was overwhelmed, however, by relief at not having to deal with their animosity on top of everything else.

The litter's curtain parted, and Lady Bertrade peeked out. "Lady Faithe!" she exclaimed with seemingly genuine delight. "How very lovely to see you! And Sir Luke! Did you come to visit us? I *am* sorry we weren't home. We've been in Norfolk, buying horses. How unfortunate for you to ride all this way and find us not at home."

"Ah, well . . ." Faithe darted a quick, helpless glance in Luke's direction.

"We were most disappointed, my lady," Luke said with a small bow, "particularly because we missed seeing *you.*"

Lady Bertrada's face, a fleshy moon framed by an elaborately draped and twisted veil, reddened with gratification. Faithe suspected that she wasn't used to such kind remarks; no doubt they did not come frequently to her husband's lips. "You must accompany us back to the castle," her ladyship offered excitedly, "and join us for dinner. We've just gotten in a barrel of aromatic wine from the Rhineland, and it's exquisite. You've never tasted its equal, I assure you."

"That's most kind of you," Luke said tightly. "But I'm afraid we were just on our way home."

"But surely you can delay your return. You can stay the night with us and ride back in the morning, when you're fresh." She looked expectantly toward her husband in an obvious attempt to elicit support for her invitation.

"Do come," said Lord Alberic, his tone devoid of inflection. It was more of a summons than a request.

Luke dragged his hand through his hair.

"Aye!" roared Griswold. "We can catch up on old times!"

Faithe caught Luke's eye. "Wouldn't it be good to have this chance to talk to your old friends, my lord husband?" she asked pointedly.

"Aye, but . . ."

"And tomorrow we can go together to visit the other gentleman we were unable to see today." She tried to convey her eagerness in her expression; they could question the soldiers *and* Isaac Ben Ravid together, without Luke's having to make a second trip. "Her ladyship's invitation solves all of our problems!"

Luke held her gaze for a long moment, and then closed his eyes briefly. When he opened them, they were filled with resignation. "In that case," he said, remounting his horse with an attitude of surrender, "how can we turn it down?"

Foxhyrst Castle was much as Faithe remembered it from visits to the Saxon lord and lady who had occupied it before William's invasion. One of the few stone keeps in this area of England, it was well-fortified behind thick walls, which was undoubtedly why it had been given over to Lord Alberic and his men. But despite its importance, it was a distinctly humble, even crude edifice, comprised of a single hall no larger than the great hall in her own home. One end of it was screened off, presumably to serve as a makeshift bedchamber for Foxhyrst's new lord and lady. The rest was one dark, damp, rush-strewn cavern with a fire pit in the middle. Faithe noticed the stack of straw pallets in the corner and realized they would spend the night sleeping on the floor amid strangers, never a welcome prospect.

On their arrival, servants scrambled to erect a great many long trestle tables, which they draped with white linen cloths, an incongruously luxurious touch in the dank old hall. Soldiers and other retainers filed in and took their seats for the midday meal, and soon the hall was abuzz with conversation.

Lady Bertrada apologized repeatedly for the modest accommodations, insisting that they would be tearing the keep down and constructing "a proper Norman one" as soon as King William granted permission. Foxhyrst would be vulnerable during the rebuilding, their liege had pointed out, and therefore they must wait until the locals could be trusted not to stage a sneak attack.

"Don't know as that day will ever come," Lord Alberic grumbled as they took their seats at the high table. "Damn Saxons are a devious lot—sly, tricky. They'll turn on you in an instant."

Luke stiffened next to her. "Have a care how you speak in my wife's presence, my lord," he murmured menacingly.

Alberic, sitting across from them, paled. Nodding woodenly to Faithe, he muttered some cursory apology, and then avoided talking to them for the remainder of the meal; his loquacious wife made up for his silence.

Faithe stole a glance at her husband, grimly slicing into his roast stag with raisin sauce, and smiled. It wasn't that long ago that he had called her people "sneaky" to her face, and meant it, yet now he had the temerity to take his overlord to task for making the very same observation.

Dessert was almond cream with loganberries and crystallized violets. As Faithe glanced surreptitiously around the table, trying to determine whether others were actually eating the flowers or pushing them to the side, as she was wont to do, the soldier called Griswold came over and slapped Luke on the back. "So, old friend. How are you adapting to farm life?"

Luke gazed steadily across the table toward Lord Alberic. "I've never been happier."

A muscle jumped in Alberic's jaw. Faithe knew that he and Luke couldn't stand each other, although she wasn't sure why. She also knew that Alberic had granted Hauekleah to Luke more out of spite then generosity, thinking a working farm an insultingly humble alternative to the grand estates that most of the Norman knights coveted. For Luke to proclaim his happiness with the grant amounted to rubbing Alberic's nose in his own misjudgment; what he'd intended as a punishment had turned out to be a blessing.

" 'Tis an exceptionally fertile and productive farmstead," Luke said, ostensibly to Griswold, but surely for Alberic's benefit. "The people are hardworking and cooperative. Hauekleah Hall is sizable and in good repair. And my bride"—he smiled and took her hand—"is young and beautiful."

Alberic's gaze slid toward his rotund lady wife, tucking into her second bowl of almond cream, oblivious to the drama of wills being enacted at her dinner table. Faithe wondered whether it was such a good idea for Luke to goad his overlord this way. Alberic, after all, was a powerful man who had already proven himself inclined toward spitefulness. Not that she didn't respect Luke for his unwillingness to defer to such a man. She just hoped that tendency didn't come back to haunt him some day.

Chapter 16

Luke watched with interest as his lordship's gaze shifted from his plump little pigeon of a wife to Faithe, captivating in emerald silk, and then back to him. Alberic's eyes narrowed; his nostrils flared. Luke could have laughed out loud.

Instead, he turned toward Griswold, standing behind him, and said, "My brother mentioned you the other day."

"Alexandre?" Griswold exclaimed. "Heard a dozen Saxons jumped you and him in the woods a while back."

A dozen. Luke grinned. "There were only two, but they came out of nowhere. One of them had a spiked mallet, and he did a fairly thorough job of it on Alex."

"How *is* the White—"

"Fine," Luke said quickly. "He's fine. Much improved. He's walking without a cane now, and he can ride again. He's planning on returning to the sheriff's service in the fall."

"So, what did he say about me?" Griswold asked.

"He said, 'Can't say as I miss Griswold. That fellow didn't know when to keep his mouth shut. Never could stand to be around him.' "

Griswold brayed with laughter.

"Except," Luke amended, "he didn't say 'fellow.' I can't repeat what he really called you, because there are ladies present."

That produced a chuckle from everyone except Alberic, who appeared to be pointedly ignoring the conversation.

"I must say, Luke," Griswold began, "you're in remarkably good spirits. I never knew you to seem so . . . at ease."

"Hauekleah suits me." He gave Faithe's hand a gentle squeeze, which elicited an engaging smile from her.

Griswold shook his head disbelievingly. "Well, now, that's something I never thought to hear you say. Not that I'm disputing the truth of it, mind you. I've seen some strange things in my day, but few stranger than the Black Dragon exchanging his crossbow for a plow—and liking it."

"I've always been partial to farming," Luke said.

"And to beautiful woman, eh?" Griswold grinned. " 'Tis easy to see why you're so content with your lot."

From the corner of his eye, Luke saw Lady Bertrada whisper something in Alberic's ear while pointing to his almond cream. Grimacing, he shoved the bowl at her, and she attacked it with zest.

" 'Twas a most agreeable match," Luke said for his lordship's benefit. "I'm grateful to Lord Alberic for arranging it."

"Never thought to see the day when you'd settle down with one woman," Griswold said. "Wouldn't have pegged you for the marrying type at all." He caught Luke's eye and winked.

A tickle of apprehension crawled up Luke's scalp. Griswold, one of his fellow crossbowmen, had been famous for his zealous wenching. No matter where the corps was dispatched, he always seemed to find the whores. Whenever Luke was in need of their services—usually right after a battle, when the bloodthirst, fueled by those loathsome herbs, still hummed in his veins, and he craved release—he would ask Griswold where to go.

"I've been trying to remember when I last saw

you," Griswold said with a mischievous grin. " 'Twas four or five months ago, wasn't it? Was it the day we took Cottwyk Castle?"

He knew very well that it was. Luke let go of Faithe's hand and reached for his cup of brandy. "That's right."

Griswold scratched his scar. "Nasty siege, that. They set vats of tar on fire and poured it on us from the battlements, remember?"

Luke hadn't remembered that—not until just now. Suddenly, his nostrils were filled with the stench of burning pitch, his ears with the screams of men writhing in agony. He'd gotten off some good shots and hit three of the Saxons on the battlements. One of them, though merely wounded in the arm, fell to the ground outside the curtain wall. He landed faceup; he was young, little more than a boy, and his eyes widened in terror as half a dozen Norman soldiers closed in on him. Luke's comrades eviscerated the youth as he lay helpless and shrieking, then left him alive to die slowly amid the mayhem of the siege. And then . . .

Enough! Luke drained his brandy in one gulp. He would remember no more. Damn Griswold for making him remember any of it.

To Faithe, Griswold said, "Your husband was the fiercest warrior I ever knew, my lady. A legend, and that's the truth. The enemy trembled when they heard his war cries."

"So I understand," Faithe said quietly. Luke gritted his teeth.

"Aye, 'twas a bloody siege, that," Griswold continued. "And afterward, you were desperately in need of a good—"

Luke shot him a look.

"—stiff brandy, as I recall," Griswold finished with a grin.

I need a good tupping, Luke had told him, still buckled into his blood-spattered chain mail and quivering from head to toe.

I know a place, Griswold had said. *'Tis as close to a brothel as you're going to find in these parts. About half a mile into the woods. There's just the one wench, and she's not much, but she'll spread her legs for anyone with tuppence and a hard cock—even a hard* Norman *cock. Most of these Saxon bitches run and hide when they see us coming.*

"Do you remember?" Griswold asked him laughingly, with sly glances at Faithe.

"Nay," Luke lied. In truth, he hadn't remembered any of it clearly—until now. Although Griswold was just having a bit of fun at his expense, Luke found himself unamused. He didn't want to be reminded of the events of that bloody awful day, especially in the presence of Faithe.

Eager to put an end to this conversation, Luke said, "Do you lazy curs still spend your afternoons playing ninepins outside the barracks?"

The garrulous soldier laughed. "That we do. Why? You in the mood to lose some silver?"

Luke rose. "Nay, I was thinking 'twould amuse me to empty *your* purse." To Faithe he added, "If my lady doesn't mind, that is."

She smiled up at him. "Of course not."

The hot sun was a blessed relief from the chill and gloom of that hall. Griswold slapped Luke on the back as they strode across the bailey toward the soldiers' barracks. " 'Tis good to see you, Luke. I missed you after you disappeared the day of the Cottwyk siege. Somebody told me you became a monk, but I never did credit that. Can't quite see you taking a vow of chastity, that's for sure."

It struck Luke that the subject of sex must comprise a goodly portion of Griswold's waking thoughts.

"Luke!" He turned to find Faithe walking briskly toward him from the keep.

He rested a hand on her arm when she joined him. "Is everything all right?"

Nodding, she glanced at Griswold and then reached into the little pouch on her girdle. Too late, Luke realized what she was retrieving—Alex's mantle pin.

Luke snatched it from her, but not before Griswold saw it. "Say! Isn't that—"

"We have no idea who it belongs to," Luke said, spearing Griswold with a look of warning while he squeezed the golden disk in his fist.

Griswold blinked at them both. "But isn't that . . ." He reached toward Luke. "Let me see it. I think it's—"

"If you know who it belongs to, we'd be most interested," Luke said slowly, fixing Griswold in his gaze and not letting him go. "We don't know whose it is."

"The man who owns that pin," Faithe explained to the mystified soldier, "is a murderer. We're searching for him."

Griswold looked back and forth between them. "A murderer."

"So it would appear," Luke said carefully.

"Luke." Faithe touched his tightly clenched fist. "Show him the pin. Perhaps he knows who it belongs to."

Luke stared unblinkingly at Griswold. "I'm sure he doesn't."

Griswold arched an eyebrow, a slow grin spreading across his face. "How do you know unless you let me see it?" He held his hand open. "Come. What are you afraid of?"

The bastard's eyes glinted with mischief. Luke's jaw ached from grinding his teeth together. After holding Griswold's gaze for several more long moments, Luke dropped the pin into his palm.

Griswold examined the pin from all angles as the sun glinted off it. "Well, I'll be damned."

Luke cursed inwardly.

Faithe clasped her hands together. "Do you recognize it?"

"I should say so!"

Her eyes grew wide. Luke squeezed his shut.

"Well?" Faithe prodded.

" 'Tis a wolf!" Griswold said.

Luke opened his eyes.

"Yes, of course it's a wolf," Faithe said. "But—"

"Very clever." Griswold brought the pin close to his face and squinted at it. "Up close, you can't really make out the shape. But from a distance"—he held it out and peered at it—"it couldn't be anything else."

Faithe wrung her hands. "But who—"

"And it's all done with those tiny little pearls. There must be over a hundred of them."

"Yes," Faithe said impatiently, "but who does it belong to?"

"Who does it belong to?" Griswold echoed.

"Aye."

Luke held his breath.

"Can't say I know." Griswold handed the pin back to her. "Sorry." He grinned at Luke.

Luke let his breath out in a rush. "Let me have that." He reached for the pin. Faithe handed it to him with a look of melancholy that sent a little dagger of shame into his chest. "I'll show it to the other men." The bald lie only shoved the dagger deeper.

"All right," Faithe said. "Thank you, Luke." Faithe gave his arm a grateful squeeze, then turned and walked away. Luke followed her with his eyes until she entered the keep.

Griswold studied him as he stared at the door through which she'd disappeared. "Ready for that game of ninepins?"

"Indeed I am," Luke said, grateful that his old friend knew better than to demand explanations. They continued their stroll toward the barracks.

"Care to triple our usual bet?" Griswold asked.

"Have you got that much on you?"

"Nay, but you probably do." He flashed a cocky grin. "And you're going to let me win."

Luke couldn't suppress a grin. It was a small enough price to pay.

The whore screamed as thunder roared in his ears. Why was she screaming?

Luke struggled to his feet, the dark little cottage whirling drunkenly. He climbed the ladder as the wench's screams grew louder and louder.

Why is she screaming?

It was dark in the loft—until lightning pulsed through the window, and he saw the young Saxon in the straw. He was little more than a boy, and his guts had been torn right out of his belly to lie strewn about him like purple serpents. It was he who'd been screaming.

And then . . .

Panting in terror and agony, the youth looked at the crossbow in Luke's hand, then met his gaze. He had hazel eyes, like Faithe's—soft English eyes. "Please," he mouthed in the Anglo-Saxon tongue.

Luke's comrades jeered the boy's plea for mercy.

"Please."

Luke turned and walked away. The Black Dragon had no interest in mercy.

"Nay!" Luke sat up, shaking and yanking at the scratchy blanket that covered him. His heart pounded in his ears.

"Luke?" came a gentle whisper in the dark.

"Faithe?" Luke looked around frantically, disoriented. He could see nothing, but he knew he wasn't in his own bed.

Soothing hands found him and stroked his sweat-dampened brow. Warm breath fanned his face. "We're in the great hall of Foxhyrst Castle. Remember? We're staying the night."

He ran a shaky hand through his hair. "Aye. I remember." They'd had to bed down in this gigantic chamber with at least twenty others—visitors, servants, and a few soldiers for whom there was no room in the barracks. Luke had chosen a relatively isolated corner and positioned Faithe's pallet between his and the wall, to offer her a measure of privacy. She slept in her green silk kirtle, he in his shirt and chausses, having removed his tunic.

"Were you having a nightmare?" she whispered.

"Aye." Luke heard a soft whisper of silk as she left her pallet and joined him on his. He wrapped his arms around her gratefully and pulled her down to lie next to him.

She kissed his neck. "Do you want to talk about it?"

Images swam in the darkness. He sorted through them, knowing he couldn't tell her everything, wishing desperately that he could. "There was a boy . . ."

"Aye?"

"I didn't remember him," Luke said softly, so as not to awaken the others, "until this afternoon, when Griswold reminded me about that day . . . the day we took Cottwyk Castle." Drawing in a fortifying breath, Luke said, "He was a Saxon. I wounded him, and he fell to the ground about ten yards from me. Some of the others, they . . ." He shuddered. "You don't want to hear this."

"Tell me," she whispered firmly.

"Oh, Christ. They ripped off his chain mail and disemboweled him."

Her arms tightened around him reflexively.

"I told you you didn't want to hear this," he said.

"What happened then?"

Luke rubbed his chin on the top of her head. "I hadn't wanted to remember the rest. I'd stopped myself from remembering all of it this afternoon, but it came back in my dream, what happened after that."

She waited patiently.

"He looked at me, the boy. First he looked at my crossbow, and then he looked at me, and he said—well, I couldn't hear him, but he looked right at me and said, in English, 'Please.' "

"Oh."

"He was begging me to kill him, Faithe."

"Yes."

"And I didn't."

"Oh, Luke."

"I turned and walked away."

"Why?"

"Because I was a monster, without conscience or pity. I was less than human."

"You were under the influence of those herbs. You could never do that today."

That was true enough. He was incapable of such cavalier brutality today. "You've tamed me."

"I didn't have to. 'Twas the herbs that made you walk away from that body, not your own nature."

Luke nodded. The herbs. They'd surged through him, taken him over, like a demon inhabiting the shell of his body.

"I'm sorry you were forced to remember that," she murmured.

"Being here, among my old mates, talking to Griswold . . . I'm remembering more and more of what happened that day." *Why was the whore screaming?* "I'm not sure what to make of it all."

"Don't try to make sense of things you did or experienced while you were chewing those herbs. 'Twould be like trying to find reason in madness. Put it out of your mind."

More truth—more good sense. But that awful day, shrouded in a bloodred haze, wouldn't let him put it out of his mind. The haze was slowly burning off, like fog. As it dissipated, and the events of that day were clearly revealed to him, yet more questions arose to torment him.

Why was she screaming? Why?

"Think no more of this tonight," she whispered, holding him close. "Try and get some sleep."

"I doubt I'll be able to sleep now." He quivered with tension.

"Then let's make love."

"What?" he chuckled. "Here?"

"Aye. Here." She licked his throat, one hand snaking down to his hips to pull him toward her.

"We can't," he protested, even as his body insisted that it most assuredly could.

"Why not?" She moved against him in a frankly sexual way that aroused him intensely. To look at her, one would never guess that she could be so sweetly wanton. The contrast between the demeanor she presented to the world and the sensual creature she became in bed had the power to flood his loins with heat.

"How can you even ask why not?" he demanded in an incredulous whisper. "Stop that." He banded his arms around her to still her.

"Don't you like it?" Insinuating a hand between them, she molded it to his erection; he sucked in a breath. "You do," she accused in a whispery little giggle. "I can tell."

"Of course I do," he growled low in his throat. "But we're not alone here."

"They're asleep."

"We'll wake them up."

"Not if we're quiet." She massaged his turgid flesh through his chausses.

"Don't do that," he said hoarsely, but he couldn't quite bring himself to stop her.

"Don't do this?" She stroked him firmly, just the way he liked.

"Oh, God." Luke found himself on his back, with her hovering over him. He heard a silken rustle, sensed her raising her skirts, felt her knees on either side of his hips as she straddled him. "Faithe, no. Not here."

Leaning down, she breathed into his ear, "Have you never done this with others nearby?"

"Aye." Of course he'd tupped women in the presence of others. He couldn't count the number of times he'd shared a woman with his comrades, or found himself in a brothel with enough wenches to go around, but only one room. But he'd been a soldier then, eager for nothing more than physical release, and the wenches had been . . . "They weren't like you, those women. You're—"

"Highborn and refined," she finished, mocking him with laughter in her voice as she untied his chausses. "Convent-bred. Easily disturbed. Easily shocked."

"Does nothing shock you?"

She laughed softly. "I rather enjoy a little shock from time to time. It keeps the bodily humors in balance."

He moaned softly at the first touch of her bare hand on his throbbing organ. Her fingertips slid over the little drop of moisture at the tip. "You're ready for me," she said. "I'm ready for you, too." She found his hand in the dark and pressed it between her legs. He probed her slick heat and heard her breath quicken.

"Let's go outside." He wrapped his hands around her waist, but she seized them and forced them onto the pallet on either side of his head.

"Don't make me hold you down," she whispered laughingly.

They'd been his words, that stormy afternoon in the barn, words meant to subdue, to control. Her turning them around this way took him aback, and he stopped struggling for a moment—long enough for her to maneuver him into her, just a bit.

"Oh, Faithe. Don't . . ."

"Don't what?" Holding his wrists down, she lowered herself onto him, taking his full length inside her. He felt her hot flesh close around him, felt the delicious, intoxicating pressure of her body squeezing him . . .

He moaned.

"Shh."

"I cannot believe you're doing this."

"Lie still. Don't talk." He felt the soft glide of her hair on his face, her warm lips against his. "Don't talk."

She kissed him, her tongue mimicking the slow, steady rocking of her hips. He did lie still, although it would have been an easy matter to wrest his hands from her and pull her off him. Something in her tone and manner had stripped him of his will in this matter, absolved him of accountability, and he found, to his astonishment, that he liked it.

He liked having her hold him down and take him, almost but not quite against his will. He liked lying motionless in the dark, with strangers sleeping nearby, and letting his gentle, well-bred wife tup him senseless. He liked the tight little bands of her hands around his wrists, the hot luxury of her mouth plundering his, the slippery-snug embrace of her most intimate flesh. Each lazy stroke coaxed him closer and closer to completion.

He arched his hips to meet her thrusts. Instantly, she raised herself until they almost uncoupled. "Nay!" he whispered.

"Don't move," she reminded him. "And don't speak."

He forced himself to lie still, with his loins on fire and his heart on the verge of exploding. She resumed her maddeningly slow lovemaking. He felt her body tighten, heard her breath come swiftly as her own climax approached.

"Faster," he whispered desperately, his body taut and shuddering.

"Shh."

"Oh, God, Faithe." It pained him to lie unmoving while this mounting urgency consumed him. His chest heaved. He was drowning, submerging in this intolerable pleasure.

He groaned.

"Don't—"

Swearing harshly, he whipped his hands out of her grasp. She tried to rise off him, but he seized her hips and rammed her down hard. They moaned in union. Her fingers bit into his shoulders.

He thrust upward as he worked her hips, whispering her name, wild curses, things that made no sense. She whimpered as her body contracted around him, setting off his own sudden, frenzied climax. Pleasure erupted from him, consumed him entirely. He forced what might have become a scream into a low, ragged growl of gratification.

Breathless and shaking, they held each other tight until the last of the tremors coursed through them. And then they kissed and kissed, stroking each other's hair, laughing softly into each other's mouth, breathing endearments and declarations of love against each other's lips.

Faithe grew heavy in his arms; he pulled his blanket over both of them. The other day in the barn, she'd threatened to seize the reins he held so tightly and show him what it would be like to let go of them—and that's exactly what she'd just done. She was wise in strange and mysterious ways, his sweet little Saxon bride. She'd turned the tables on him, exercised a sexual authority he'd thought to be his exclusive domain.

She'd shocked him. And he liked it.

As he drifted off to sleep, he reflected with a smile that his bodily humors had never felt more perfectly in balance.

Chapter 17

"Aquitaine," said Isaac Ben Ravid in his guttural accent the instant Faithe removed the mantle pin from her pouch. " 'Tis from Aquitaine."

Damn. Luke closed his eyes and rubbed the bridge of his nose.

"Aquitaine? Are you sure?" Faithe asked.

Isaac's warm gaze grew chilly for the briefest moment, as if she'd insulted him.

"I don't mean to doubt you," she said. "But you barely saw it. Are you sure—"

"Put it here." The old man pointed to one of several anvils on the huge, scarred table in the middle of his workshop—a large room at the rear of his house. Morning sunlight poured into the chamber from two tall windows behind him, which flanked a small furnace. His handiwork, in various stages of completion, was displayed on shelves all around the perimeter of the room. There were gold and silver caskets, cups, circlets, girdles, brooches . . . even a few items, like a large silver chalice, that had obviously been commissioned by an officer of the Church.

Isaac sat at the table and picked up a tiny hammer, one gnarled hand automatically tucking his long white beard into his robe to keep it out of the way. He leaned over the brooch, so that all that could be seen of him was the top of his strange, pointed hat.

"This design around the edge," he said, pointing with the slender handle of the little hammer, "is typical of the southern regions of the Frankish empire, as is the way the gold has been burnished."

"But why Aquitaine?" Luke managed. "Why not Tolouse or Gascony?"

Old Isaac smiled a bit condescendingly. "There's a world of difference between a mantle pin from Tolouse and one from Aquitaine. This"—he tapped the pin with a fingertip—"reminds me of the kind of thing I saw in the cities of Ventadour and Périgueux. The jeweler who created this piece is from that area."

"Périgueux?" Faithe said. "It's from Périgueux?"

Luke clenched his jaw until it hurt.

"Aye." The old goldsmith lifted the pin and inspected it closely. "Or Ventadour, or perhaps Brive-la-Gaillard. Somewhere in that area." Turning the pin over, he read the inscription out loud " 'To my youngest son. Be strong and of good courage.' Did this pin belong to a soldier?"

"That's what we think," Faithe answered.

Isaac nodded. "Those sound like the words a father would say to his son when he sends him off to war." He rubbed his thumb thoughtfully over the piece and then handed it back to Faithe. "Why are you looking for him?"

She tucked the pin back into her pouch. "He murdered someone. My first husband."

The old man's expression sobered. "Then he should pay."

"I intend to see that he does," Faithe said quietly.

"Périgueux, eh?" Orrik's gaze narrowed on the pin he held.

"Or Ventadour or Brive-la-Gaillard," Luke quickly put in. "Somewhere in the area of Aquitaine."

"He seemed very sure of it," Faithe added, gratefully accepting the horn of ale Bonnie handed her. She'd had no time to rest up from her exhausting trip to Foxhyrst, nor to change out of the dusty, rumpled kirtle she'd slept in last night. No sooner had she and Luke entered Hauekleah Hall than Orrik had appeared and begun hammering them with questions.

Alex joined them and took the pin from Orrik. "I suppose it might have come from Aquitaine." He glanced at his brother. "It does look something like yours, after all. We already knew that."

Luke accepted his own horn and drained it swiftly.

"Périgueux . . ." Orrik scratched his beard.

"Or any city of Aquitaine," Luke repeated testily.

"That might be helpful," Orrik said. "Folks from down there tend to be darker than those from the north. You two are perfect examples."

Luke and Alex exchanged sober looks. Wondering at the cause of it, Faithe asked, "Do you know of someone? Another soldier from Aquitaine?"

"Nay!" they said in unison.

She sighed. " 'Tisn't much to go on . . . a soldier with dark coloring."

"But 'twill help," Orrik said. "We can enlist some men to help us make inquiries. Baldric can be spared, and his brother, Nyle, and there are three or four others, all good men."

"How do you propose we use these men?" Faithe asked.

"They can start in Cottwyk and work their way out from there," the bailiff replied, "visiting every single hamlet and farm and city in the area until someone identifies the man we've looking for. 'Twill be a much more thorough search than I was able to perform on my own. We have more information to go on now, and we can get half a dozen men to help us. One of them is bound to turn up something."

Faithe handed her empty horn to Bonnie and turned to her husband. "What think you, Luke?"

He shook his head. "I don't like it."

Orrik rolled his eyes. "I suppose you have a better idea."

"I'm going to send those men to Hastings," Luke said.

There was a heavy moment of silence.

"Hastings," Orrik said tonelessly.

Luke cleared his throat. " 'Tis wiser to start from the beginning—from Caedmon's disappearance last October. I mean to investigate the reason for that disappearance, and track his movements through the winter."

Faithe let Orrik ask it, not wanting to appear to doubt Luke, especially in front of the others, but not understanding, either. "Why? 'Tis his death we're investigating, not why he left Hastings, or what happened to him during the winter."

Luke rubbed the bridge of his nose. Alex turned and looked out the window, leaning on the sill.

"The more we find out about what drove him away from Hastings," Luke said, "and how he lived, the better we'll be able to piece together the events that led to his death."

Orrik shook his head. "I don't see it."

"Perhaps the circumstances surrounding the killing aren't what they seem. Perhaps that's why you've had so little luck in finding the man responsible, because you've *assumed* that Caedmon was killed over a . . ." He glanced uncomfortably toward Faithe.

"It's all right," she said quietly, touching his sleeve.

"But what if that's not the way it was at all?" Luke continued. "What if Caedmon knew his killer? What if it had naught to do with the woman? What if—"

"What if, what if, what if," Orrik growled. "This is absurd. Caedmon died because some Norman cur couldn't wait his turn. I'm sorry, Faithe." He'd gone red in the face, as he always did when he was upset. "But, for God's sake! We know how he died, we know why he died, and it doesn't have a damn thing to do with his disappearance from Hastings."

"I think it does," Luke said calmly.

"Then you're a fool," Orrik spat out.

"Orrik!" Faithe gasped. Alex turned around.

"And frankly," Orrik ground out, seemingly oblivious to Faithe's outrage, "I'm more than a little curious as to why you seem so determined to detour this investigation away from the time and place of Caedmon's death. Sending those men to Hastings would be a waste of time, as you must be aware."

"Obviously I disagree with you," Luke said.

"And that should be enough to silence you," Faithe told Orrik. "Luke is in charge here, not you. If he wants to send those men to Hastings, they'll go to Hastings, and you have naught to say about it."

Orrik shook his head disgustedly. "Do you know who the killer is, de Périgueux? Is that why you're trying to lead us away from him?"

Faithe fisted her hands in her skirt. "Orrik! That's enough!"

"Is he an old friend of yours?" Orrik persisted.

"For God's sake, Orrik!"

"Think about it, my lady," Orrik said. "That man"—he stabbed a finger toward Luke—"comes from the same region, perhaps even the same city, as the murderer. They might have known each other, might even have grown up together. Why else would he be sending those men on this pointless trip to Hastings, when—"

"You've overstepped yourself, Orrik," she said in a low, wavering voice. "Badly."

"But, my lady—"

"Not another word," she added grimly, "or I'll dismiss you myself."

Silence rang in the hall.

"As you wish, my lady," Orrik ground out as he executed an arrogant little bow. Turning on his heel, he left Hauekleah Hall.

Luke rubbed his forehead. Alex looked uncharacteristically grave.

"I need some air," Faithe said wearily, "and I've been meaning to see how the vineyard is doing. I'll be back by suppertime."

It came to her as she strolled through the fragrant rows of vines, absently inspecting leaves and stems and roots while she basked in the low sun slanting over the surrounding pastures and meadows.

She knew what she had to do.

Luke wouldn't like it. He hadn't wanted her to go to Foxhyrst; he'd probably find this even more objectionable. But the more she thought about it, the more she knew she had to do it.

She walked slowly as the sun gradually settled onto the hilltops, relishing this time to herself. Privacy was a precious commodity in her life; so was silence.

When she spied the distant figure of a man walking toward her, she sighed in irritation. But then she recognized his distinctive, long-legged gait, graceful in its restrained power. She noticed his height, and the soldierly way he held his arms in relaxed readiness. Just watching him walk was enough to make her ache for him. She smiled and walked toward him.

They stepped into each other's arms and embraced as the sun dipped below the hills, casting the vineyard in an ethereal twilight. He felt so large and warm and solid. She breathed in the wool of his tunic mingled with his familiar, masculine scent, and felt a sense of perfect communion with her world. He'd done that for her; he'd completed her. They'd both been lost, but now they'd found each other, and all was in harmony.

"You are so beautiful, Faithe," he said, his soft, deep voice resonating against her ear. He kissed the top of her head.

She smiled against his shoulder. "I was just thinking the same thing about you."

His chest vibrated with silent laughter. "I'm a great hulking brute."

She shook her head. "You're a beautiful man, Luke of Hauekleah, and I love you very much."

"Luke of Hauekleah," he murmured. "I like the sound of that."

She looked up at him and said archly. "You're supposed to say, 'I love you, too.' "

He laughed. "I do. So much . . ." His amusement seemed to fade. He brushed her hair off her face. "So much it frightens me sometimes."

"Why should love frighten you?"

"Not love," he said. "The loss of it. The possibility that . . . it won't always be there. That you'll stop loving me. I think that would kill me."

"Nothing could ever make me stop loving you, Luke. Nothing." Faithe wrapped her arms around him and held him close. "What put such a thought in your head?"

After a long pause he said, with a nonchalance that seemed forced, "I'm just out of sorts from being hungry. I've been sent to fetch you back for supper."

"Right this instant?"

"It's on the table."

Tell him now. Tightening her arms around him, she said, softly, "I'm going to go to Cottwyk." Not *I want to go. I'm going to go.*

She felt the tension course through him. He held her at arm's length and looked down at her, his brow furrowed. "Why?"

Choosing her words carefully, she said, "I've never seen his grave, Luke. I need to see it."

He frowned as if he wanted to argue with her, but could think of nothing to say.

"And there are other reasons," she continued. "I know you don't think there are answers to be had there, but I think . . . perhaps there are. I wouldn't have said this in front of the others, but I do think 'twould serve us well to question the local people, and . . . see for ourselves . . . where it happened."

His gaze burned through her; his hands clenched her shoulders. "You mean to go to that . . ."

"Brothel. Aye."

"Nay!"

She bristled.

Very quickly he said, "I know I can't prevent you from doing this if you've set your mind to it. You're used to making your own decisions and going your own way. I respect that. But . . ." Releasing her, he turned away and rubbed the back of his neck. "For you to even think about setting foot in a place like that . . ."

"I'm not a blushing maid, remember? I feel certain I can pay a visit to a house of prostitution without swooning."

"But why should you?"

"To see the place where Caedmon died," she said. "I may be able to learn something. Perhaps there will be clues about what happened that night."

"I assume Orrik's already been there. Why should you subject yourself to all this?"

"Perhaps Orrik missed something. I'd be looking at things with fresh eyes. And as for *subjecting* myself to this, I've told you—I'm not so very fragile. I'll be fine. And I'll feel as if I'm doing some good." She approached him and stroked his face lightly. "I need that."

"I know," he said huskily, dragging both hands through his hair. "I know. When do you propose to make this trip?"

"I'll be busy all this week with the feast of St. Swithun, so 'twill have to be next week. Monday, perhaps."

He closed his eyes briefly. "Is there anything I can say to talk you out of going?"

"I shouldn't think so."

Sighing heavily, he said, "Then I'm going with you."

She smiled and slid her arms around his waist. "I was hoping you'd say that. I'll be glad to have your company."

He grunted softly, and she thought she heard him say, "Aye, 'twill be quite the jolly outing."

Before she could respond, he withdrew from the embrace and took her hand. "Come. Our supper is getting cold."

Chapter 18

"That's it," said the fat priest, pointing to the other side of the churchyard from where they stood. "That's where we buried him."

"That's where we buried him," repeated the innkeeper, a red-faced fellow in a greasy apron.

Luke didn't look where they pointed. He looked at Faithe, alert and still, staring at the place where her husband had been laid to rest. Finally, she crossed the churchyard, weaving between the weathered headstones until she stood next to the newest-looking one—a crude wooden slab on which had been carved one word: Caedmon. The grave was isolated from the others at the very edge of the patch of consecrated ground, and the earth over it had not yet had time to settle; it rose in an oblong mound and sprouted a melancholy assortment of weeds and grasses.

Luke glanced uneasily at his brother, who'd insisted on accompanying them to Cottwyk. The journey had clearly taken a toll on Alex; he hadn't ridden that far since before he was wounded. He leaned heavily against a tree trunk, his expression taut.

"You shouldn't have come," Luke told him—in French, so the handful of Saxons standing behind them couldn't eavesdrop on their conversation. Lately, however, he'd taken to speaking English even with Alex, to encourage him to become more fluent in it.

"After three months of lazing about on that pallet, I needed a bit of exercise." The note of strain in

Alex's voice belied his lighthearted tone; he was in pain.

"You didn't come for the exercise," Luke accused without wresting his gaze from Faithe, kneeling at the side of Caedmon's grave. "You came because you were worried about me."

Alex grinned humorlessly. "The last time we were here, you caused a bit of a stir, as I recall."

Luke grunted. *A bit of a stir, indeed.*

"When we rode away from here that morning," Alex said, " 'twas one step ahead of these good citizens standing behind us right now. They were waving pickaxes and reaping hooks and looking for a Norman to hang—after some rather inventive punishments, no doubt."

"They wouldn't mind hanging one still, I don't imagine." Luke and Alex had been received with civility by the citizenry of Cottwyk only because they were accompanied by a beautiful young Saxon noblewoman, who also happened to be the widow of the mysterious "Caedmon" who occupied the lonely grave at the outskirts of the churchyard. Luke had a vivid mental picture of these same men standing in the mist over the whore's burnt remains that morning, brandishing their crude weapons and promising retribution. He hadn't remembered that clearly until now. This visit to Cottwyk was bound to drag long dormant memories to the surface, just as his visit to Foxhyrst had; he'd best steel himself for them.

"Aye, they'd be ripe for a hanging," Alex agreed. "Which is precisely why I chose today for my reintroduction to the saddle." Alex moved his sword aside to rub his hip.

"Sit down." Luke pointed to a stump; Alex sat.

Faithe crossed herself and set about plucking the weeds from the ill-tended grave.

"No one will recognize us," Luke said, unused to

offering reassurance to Alex; usually it was the other way around.

"Nay, no one saw us."

Rather, everyone who'd seen them was dead. Luke had killed Caedmon, then the wench had tried to escape him, only to be felled by lightning.

"We're in no danger here," Luke said as he watched Faithe tidy up the grave of the man he'd slain.

"None." But Alex's hand stole to the hilt of his sword and remained there.

When the grave was finally stripped of weeds, Faithe painstakingly patted down the earth. Luke's heart twisted in his chest as he watched her.

She rose and returned to them, brushing the dirt from her hands and kirtle. "Those weeds will be back within days," she said. "I don't know why I bothered."

But Luke did. She couldn't bear to think of the man she'd shared her life with for eight years spending eternity in such a piteous resting place. Retrieving his purse, he shook out a handful of silver and gave it to the priest, Father Tedmund. "I want that wooden marker replaced with a proper headstone," he said in English. "A big one, with carvings. An important man is buried there."

Father Tedmund eyed the coins with an expression of awe. "I'll order it on the morrow, milord!"

"And see that the grave is properly tended," Luke instructed. "Have someone keep the weeds off it and put flowers there on holy days."

" 'Twill be done as you bid, milord."

Faithe reached out and took Luke's hand. When he looked down, she gave him a watery little smile and glanced away.

Luke addressed himself to all the men. "We have some questions about the man in that grave."

"There was another fellow askin' about 'im," said a big man in a leather apron, whom Luke took to be the village smithy. "A ways back. Older gentleman. He even dug up the grave."

Faithe nodded. "Orrik."

"Aye, that was his name. We told him everything we know."

"Well, now you're going to tell us," Luke said. "When did Caedmon first arrive here?"

" 'Twas at the end of Christmastide," Father Tedmund said. "I found him on the morning of Twelfth Day, sleeping in the back of the church."

"Did he tell you anything about himself? Where he came from? How he happened to be in Cottwyk?"

All the men shook their heads. "He didn't talk much about himself," the priest said. "But I gather he'd been wandering around for some time, and just happened upon Cottwyk. We . . . put up with him, and he stayed."

"Where did he live?" Luke asked.

The men exchanged looks; several glanced anxiously at Faithe. Father Tedmund cleared his throat. "Some nights he slept in the church."

"And the other nights?"

The priest's corpulent face turned pink. "Perhaps milady would like to take her ease in Byrtwold's inn while we talk." He fixed Luke with a meaningful look.

"I'd rather stay out here," Faithe said.

"Er . . ." Byrtwold, the innkeeper, fingered his ruddy jowls. "My wife brews the finest ale in this part of Cambridgeshire, milady. And you must be tired after your long ride."

"I'm not tired," she said. "I'm staying here."

"They won't speak candidly with you here," Luke told her in French.

"I'll tell them they may speak frankly."

"Aye, but they won't. They'll want to protect your feelings. We won't learn anything."

Alex hauled himself up from his stump. "Come to

the inn with me, Faithe. *I'm* tired, even if you're not, and thirsty as well. I don't want to sit there all alone."

She hesitated, frowning.

"Luke is right," Alex told her. "They won't talk about . . . certain things with you here."

"Fine," she said with a decided lack of grace. "But you must remember everything they say, Luke, and tell me later."

"Of course."

Alex escorted her across the road to the humble inn on the other side. Luke turned back to the men. "I take it Caedmon stayed with a woman."

"Helig," the smithy said, "the whore what was struck by lightning. But only sometimes, when she didn't have no other customers."

"She felt sorry for 'im," Byrtwold explained. "Used to let him sleep by the fire."

Luke rubbed his jaw. "What did he do with his days?"

"Roamed here and there," said Father Tedmund. "Did odd jobs sometimes for meals when he was . . . himself. Other times, he'd beg for whatever could be spared. And when he was at his worst, someone would always give him something to eat, or buy him a pint."

"We never guessed he was a man of consequence," a gaunt fellow in the back put in.

"Never," the priest concurred.

"What do you mean," Luke asked him, " 'when he was himself'?"

Father Tedmund looked very ill at ease. "How well did you know this man?"

"Not at all," Luke answered. "He was my wife's first husband."

The priest nodded. "Good. 'Twould be harder if you'd been a mate of his, to tell you how he was."

"How he was?" Luke said.

The smithy crossed his arms. "He were mad, that one."

"Not all the time," someone corrected. "They came and went, those spells of his."

"Aye, but toward the end, he was mad as a ferret."

" 'Twas those headaches of his that did it to him," Byrtwold said.

The priest nodded. "Aye, he'd get the most hellish pains. He'd grab his head and start screaming and rocking back and forth. Especially when there was any kind of loud noise or a lot of activity."

"He did it during the plow race the day after Epiphany, and then again on Shrove Tuesday, when we was all out playing games on the green."

"Aye, he set up such a fierce howlin' we had to drag him away."

An unwanted memory ambushed Luke. He saw his sister, Alienor—once such a quiet, gentle creature—tearing out her hair and shrieking, "There's something in there! I can feel it!" And, according to the Moslem physician who'd treated her, there was, indeed, a lump growing in her brain. She became wild, striking out at her sire, her siblings, the servants. In the end, they'd had to tie her down.

"He'd talk nonsense, that Caedmon," the innkeeper said. "Prattle on and on about angels and devils and whatnot. We got to where we didn't pay him no mind."

"Kept on about the demon inside his skull," said Father Tedmund.

"Demon?" Luke said.

"Aye, a demon trying to get out. He'd hit his head with his fists, slam it against walls."

"Sometimes he'd hit us."

"Aye, well, he was mad. He couldn't help it. And I think he was sorry, after. He'd get real quiet and stay that way for days."

Thinking back to Alienor, Luke strained to remember details from those final, nightmarish months, details he'd spent years trying to forget. "Did Caedmon ever have seizures?"

"Like fits?" the smith asked; Luke nodded. All the men murmured affirmatively. "Happened from time to time. He never remembered them once they was over."

"Did he complain of double vision?" Luke pressed.

"Aye, he'd get dizzy and see two or three of a thing."

"Perhaps there *was* a demon inside him," the fat priest allowed. "But in between the bad times, he could be . . . almost normal. And you could tell he was a good man—or had been, before the madness struck. I suppose that's why we took him in the way we did, and tolerated his spells."

"You liked him," Luke said quietly.

Father Tedmund pondered that a moment. "We liked the man he'd once been, when we caught glimpses of him, and we felt sorry for what he'd become."

"And he never spoke about his past?" Luke asked.

The men all shook their heads, except for Byrtwold, who said, "Once he did. He was in his cups, he was. He'd spent all afternoon in my inn, drinkin' and mutterin' to himself. When I told him 'twas time for him to leave, he set up quite the hue and cry. Punched me in the face he did. Bloodied my nose. But then he sees that blood and he starts blubberin' like a baby. Starts goin' on about how he can't go home no more. He can never go home, on account of he don't want his wife seein' what's become of him."

Luke took a deep breath and let it out slowly. "I see."

"I felt right sorry for him, I did," the innkeeper said. "He didn't ask to go mad. God works in mysterious ways, and the Devil, too."

" 'Tweren't his fault," someone else agreed.

"He hated what he was. You could see it in his eyes."

Christ. "Thank you," Luke said. "You've been helpful."

"Ill?" Faithe whispered. "How ill?"

"Very ill, from what they told me." Luke glanced uneasily at Alex, sitting beside him, and reached across the table in the dim little inn to take Faithe's hand. "It sounds as if he may have had the same malady of the brain that killed my sister, Alienor."

Alex grew alert.

Luke wondered how to tell her the rest. "He was . . . he'd become—"

Alex kicked him under the table. When Luke looked in his direction, he surreptitiously shook his head. Although he'd been but ten years old when their sister had been taken, he remembered the nightmare all too vividly, Luke knew. He and Alienor had been very close, and her death, preceded by months of escalating insanity, had affected him deeply at the time.

Apparently Alex didn't want Luke to tell Faithe of Caedmon's dementia. Was he right? Would the news devastate her, as Alex feared? She was a grown woman, not a child, and strong. Still, what woman would want to find out that her husband had become a raving madman toward the end of his life? How could he tell her that Caedmon had spent the winter begging for scraps between fits of violent lunacy, getting by on the Christian charity of the good people of Cottwyk? Instead, he cleared his throat and said, "He got headaches."

"Aye." She nodded distractedly. "Aye. He'd been getting them before he left for Hastings. Awful headaches."

"That's right," Luke said. "He must have been sick already."

"What else?" Faithe asked. "It must have been more than just headaches."

Luke bought a moment by taking a sip of his ale. "Seizures," he said. "He had seizures. And sometimes he'd see double."

Faithe looked mystified. "Why didn't he come home, so I could take care of him? Why did he stay here? I don't understand."

Alex spoke up, quietly. "Perhaps he didn't want to burden you with his illness."

A perceptive observation on his brother's part, but then Alex had always been gifted with the ability to look through a person and see the workings within.

"Do you think that was it?" she asked Luke.

"I'm certain that was it," he said, squeezing her hand. "He was trying to spare you."

"I wish he hadn't." She stared at something on the table that he couldn't see, her eyes glimmering in the darkness. "I wish he'd come home."

"From what I can tell, the people here were good to him," Luke assured her gently. "They fed him and took care of him. They liked him."

Faithe started to say something, but choked on the words, her face crumpling. She closed a hand over her mouth as tears welled in her eyes.

"Oh, Faithe." Rising, he circled the table and sat next to her, gathering her in his arms and pressing her face to his chest. "Sweet Faithe," he murmured, stroking her hair as she cried silently, gratified that she could expose her vulnerable side, even as his heart ached for her. "My love. My sweet love. It's all right. Everything will be all right. Let's go home."

She looked up. He blotted her wet face with the sleeve of his tunic.

"We can't go home yet," she said hoarsely.

"Faithe—"

"We haven't been . . . to that place. We haven't seen where it happened."

"You're in no state to go there."

"I'm fine." She raised her chin gamely, sniffing away the last of her tears. "I'm going."

"Nay," he said firmly. "I'm putting a stop to this. This has gone far enough. We're going home."

She closed her hand over her chatelaine's keys, again seeking strength from them. "You two are welcome to return to Hauekleah. I'll join you when I've finished here."

Alex grinned and downed his ale. "She sounds very determined, brother. I can't think of any way to make her leave with you."

Neither could Luke, short of tying her up and throwing her over his saddle, and he suspected that would be a mistake. "All right," he conceded grudgingly. "We'll take you where you want to go."

She stood, followed by Luke and Alex. "Did you ask them how to get there?"

"Aye," he lied as he ducked through the doorway. "It's to the north, through the woods."

"This is it?" Faithe asked dubiously when they rode into the clearing and she saw the humble little cottage.

"This is it." *It's not much of a whorehouse,* Luke had said the first time he'd seen it. He'd barely been able to make it out against the shadowy woods that ringed it. *At least it's shelter,* Alex had said. *'Twill rain soon, and I'd rather be in there than out here when it does.* Shivering from the effects of the herbs, Luke had told himself to ride it out, that a good, hard tupping was all he needed to set him right.

How wrong he'd been. And how it chilled him to recall these long-forgotten details. How much more would he recall before this day was over?

The wattle-and-daub hovel looked even more dismal in the light of day than it had that ill-fated night four months ago. The thatch was decayed, the deerskin over the door partly rotted, and there were gaps in the crumbling clay walls big enough to shove a fist through. Chickens scratched in the hard-packed earth surrounding the cottage; there must have been over a hundred. Luke didn't remember the chickens—or the crude poultry house at the edge of the woods—but then his memory of this place and what had transpired here was blurred and patchy.

"How can you be so sure this is the right place?" Faithe asked. "Perhaps their directions were poor. This doesn't look like . . . one of those places."

Alex grinned at her. "And what would you know of such places, Faithe? This is it." He dismounted, and Luke and Faithe followed suit.

The deerskin moved; the dirt-smeared face of a child peeked through, and then the skin abruptly fell back into place.

Luke, Faithe, and Alex blinked at each other. From within the cottage came a shrill cry of "Mummy! Mummy!"

The deerskin parted again, and this time there appeared the large, befreckled face of a woman. A froth of coppery hair blossomed from beneath the rag tied around her head. Luke felt a jolt of recognition, but shook it off. This wasn't the whore who'd been struck by lightning. That woman was dead. This was someone else, another redheaded woman.

She blinked back at her three visitors, and then opened the skin wider. Her belly was swollen with child, and an infant slept openmouthed against her hip, cocooned in a sling tied over her shoulder. Several children's faces popped out around her. One tried to squeeze around her bulky form, but she yanked him back by his tangled hair, producing a yowl of pain.

Luke knew that this was no whore.

"What you be wantin'?" the woman asked, eyeing them distrustfully. No doubt she rarely had callers, and she would assume they were all Normans, which would make her even warier.

Luke began to speak, but Faithe touched his arm and stepped forward. "I'm Faithe of Hauekleah," she said. Surprise—that Faithe was a Saxon, no doubt—widened the woman's eyes fleetingly. "These men," Faithe continued, "are my husband, Luke of Hauekleah, and my brother by marriage, Alexandre de Périgueux."

"My name is Aefrid," the woman said. "These youngsters"—she nodded toward the many little faces pressing between her and the doorframe—"is mine."

Luke was glad she didn't try to name them one by one. There were an alarming number of them, pushing and squirming and struggling to get a look at the visitors.

"I wonder if we might . . . come inside?" Faithe asked.

Aefrid hesitated, as if she couldn't imagine why such highborn folk would want to come into her home. "You hungry? All's I got is porridge, but you're welcome to it. Ain't got no ale, but the water comes from a clean spring."

Faithe smiled warmly. "Some spring water would be lovely."

The red-haired woman frowned in evident puzzlement at the notion of water being lovely.

"Mind if we stable our horses in back?" Luke instantly regretted his loose tongue.

Aefrid regarded him curiously. "How'd you know I have a byre round back?"

"I . . . assumed it, since I see no separate barn or stable for your livestock."

Aefrid snorted. "The only *livestock* as I can lay claim to is these godforsaken fowl." She kicked one of the chickens into a feathery riot. "Dumb as mud, and evil-tempered to boot, but they lays me enough eggs to make a livin'."

"Are you a widow?" Faithe inquired as Aefrid guided them around back to the attached byre, into which they led their mounts. Children swarmed after her, scurrying to keep up and clutching at her ragged skirts. Luke tried to count the children, but they all looked alike, with their round, freckled faces and rusty hair, and they skittered about too quickly to keep track of.

"A widow? Me?" Aefrid guffawed as she kicked chickens aside to make room for their horses. "Naw, my Gimm run off soon as I tells him I'm cookin' us up another wee one." She patted her big belly as she led them through the low doorway that connected the byre to the cottage. "Couldn't take it no more, I reckon. Just wandered off down the road, cryin' like a babe."

Luke tripped over something as he entered the cottage—whether a child or a chicken he knew not, for the dark, musty dwelling was packed to the rafters with both. A miasma of unbathed humanity and live poultry made his nostrils flare and his throat close up.

"My," Faithe murmured; a rather eloquent understatement, to Luke's way of thinking.

"How many children do you have?" Alex asked their hostess, amusement, and something like awe, in his voice.

Aefrid looked sheepish. "I never was much good at counting." She reached out and seized two little girls by their braids. "Dita! Run to the spring and fetch a bucket of water. Hildy, you try and find some cups ain't too dirty."

Faithe studied the interior of the gloomy little cottage, as if trying to imagine it as a house of sin. Luke followed her line of sight, his gaze coming to rest on the fire pit, over which a kettle of porridge bubbled thickly. A memory assaulted him: Alex sleeping on one side, he on the other, both wrapped in their mantles. He remembered the hallucinatory dreams, the waking delusions, and shivered as he had that night.

Alex lifted a tiny girl from a bench, sat down, and

settled the child on his lap. She slid two filthy fingers into her mouth and stared up at him with eyes like wagon wheels. "How long have you lived here?" he asked the child's mother.

"Since March," Aefrid answered, accepting three cups from little Hildy and setting them on the table with a *thunk.* "This was my sister's place, rest her soul." She crossed herself and wiped the cups down with a handful of skirt. "Felled by a bolt of lightning, she was. God's vengeance for her wicked ways."

"She was a . . . sinner?" Faithe asked.

"A traitor to her people," Aefrid spat out. "She consorted with—" Cutting herself off abruptly, she shot uneasy glances toward Luke and Alex.

Alex grinned at Luke. So it wasn't Helig's having spread her legs for a living that Aefrid objected to, but her having spread them for Normans.

"I see." Faithe appeared to be biting her lip.

"Aye, well, here's Dita with your water." Aefrid set the bucket on the table and dipped their cups in one by one.

Luke accepted his, and seeing nothing crawling within, downed it in one thirsty gulp. It was sweet and cold.

Aefrid stroked her belly with one hand, the baby cradled against her hip with the other. "Gimm run off at the beginning of February. Candlemas, it was. Left me a shoemakin' business, but I ain't no cobbler, for one thing, and I gots these little ones to care for." She shook her head. "We lived in one room over the shop in Slepe. Not even any little croft to plant a few turnips in. Did a lot of prayin' and a fair measure of starvin' during the month of February. Then I got word they done found Helig . . ." She broke off, her eyes shining in the murky half-light, clearly not as unmoved by her sister's death as she'd made out.

A picture flashed in Luke's mind: a woman's body faceup in the cold morning drizzle, her bright hair singed, her feet charred, her exposed skin imprinted with strange, fernlike burns . . .

Her eyes wide open, staring up into the rain.

Alex looked at him, his expression grave. He remembered, too. Luke wished he hadn't come here. He wished he were anywhere other than here in this stinking clay hut having scenes from his worst nightmare dragged out into the light of day.

"Well"—Aefrid sniffed and patted her sleeping babe—"God has His ways, that He does. Helig's ill fortune was a blessing for us, inasmuch as we came into this here cottage. By rights it should have gone to my brother, Ham, but he lives at Foxhyrst Castle—he's the sheriff's hangman—and he didn't need it. So he give it to me. Sold the shoe business and bought me some chickens and brung 'em here. Now, I sell eggs in Cottwyk and sometimes in Foxhyrst, on market days. We may not be rich, but we don't go hungry, and there's plenty of folks can't say that."

"You should be proud of yourself," Faithe told Aefrid, to her red-faced gratification. Setting her cup down carefully on the table, Faithe said, "I should tell you why we're here."

"I thought," Aefrid said hesitantly, "you was travelin' and got thirsty."

Faithe took a step toward the woman and said, "Someone else died here that night—the night your sister was struck by lightning."

Aefrid nodded cautiously, clearly trying to sort out where this was leading. "Aye, fellow name of Caedmon. They say he wasn't quite—"

"Wasn't quite well," Luke said quickly, pinning Aefrid with his darkest gaze. "That's right. He was ill. Had been for some time. That was before you moved here, of course."

"Aye, but they told me all about 'im," Aefrid said. "And I could swear they said he was—"

"He was the lord of a great farmstead." Alex stood,

balancing the little girl on his hip while she patted his close-cropped hair, giggling. "And he was Lady Faithe's husband."

Aefrid gaped at Faithe. "Oh, milady, I'm . . ." She glanced warily at Luke and Alex. "I'm sorry for your loss."

"I'm sure you are." Luke withdrew his purse. "Our purpose in coming here was to see where Lord Caedmon died and find out whatever you may know about that night." He shook all the rest of his silver into Aefrid's palm, to her apparent stupefaction. "Understand," he added, meeting her gaze meaningfully, "that we're not asking what you've heard about him personally, but whether you know anything about his murder. Any help you can offer us would be most appreciated."

"Lord," she whispered, pouring the coins from one hand to another as her children squeezed around to watch—and grab. "I ain't *never* seen this much silver in one place, milord. And never in *my* hand, I can tell you that!"

"Can you tell us anything about the murder?" Faithe asked her.

"Only what the townsfolk told me," Aefrid said. "Someone come here that morning lookin' for . . . my sister . . . and found the cottage empty save for the body upstairs in the loft. They put him on a litter and went lookin' for Helig, and found her dead on the road."

Faithe was staring up at the loft.

"Thank you," Luke said. "You've been most helpful." He took his wife's arm and guided her into a corner. "There's nothing to be found out here, Faithe. It's time to—"

"We should go up there," she said.

"There's no point to that, Faithe," he said as gently as he could. "We're not going to learn anything by poking around here. Any clues Caedmon's killer might have left behind—except for that mantle pin—are long gone."

"I know," she said, "but I have to go up there, anyway. Don't you see? For so long I thought I knew how Caedmon had died, and then I found out everything I knew was wrong. Now, I just want to understand. I want to . . . see where it happened. I have to shut the door on this."

"Ah, Faithe." He did understand. He wished he could just drag her out of here for her own good—and his—but he couldn't justify that, so he just said, "I'll go up first."

The ladder squeaked as he climbed it. He recalled the Saxon, Caedmon, hauling himself up it unsteadily that night. Luke had thought the man who'd stolen the whore from him was merely drunk, but he wasn't. He was sick, probably dying.

Despite his ill-health, he'd managed to get what he'd come for. Luke remembered waking up from a violent nightmare to groans and the rhythmic crackling of straw from the loft. He'd tried to rouse his brother so they could leave, but Alex could sleep through anything, so he'd drunk all the whore's brandy and passed out by the fire pit.

The next time he awoke, it was to screaming.

He paused at the top of the ladder, peering into the loft, seeing it but not seeing it.

The whore screamed while thunder crashed overhead. Why was she screaming?

He'd lurched to his feet . . .

"Luke?" came Faithe's voice from behind him on the ladder.

"Aye." Luke climbed up the rest of the way and entered the loft, crouching. He heard Faithe come up behind him, but didn't turn around.

He recalled, vividly, awakening to the whore's screams and racing up here to find—

Christ. The Saxon was beating her. She was trying to fight him off, but he just kept slamming his fist into her face, calling her a betrayer, a Judas.

"Luke? Are you all right?"

Luke was on his knees in the straw, his head in his hands.

Luke had seized the Saxon by his tunic, yanked him off the shrieking woman. The Saxon's eyes blazed with something untamed, uncontrollable. He made a fist and hauled back, but Luke landed a clean punch to the bastard's head, sending him sprawling.

"Luke?" He felt himself being shaken, but he was somewhere else entirely.

The whore was already down the ladder, sobbing. Luke looked down at the Saxon, on his back in the straw, his eyes half open, and felt the cramped little space whirl and spin . . .

"Alex! Alex, something's wrong with Luke!"

Luke crouched in the straw, whispering, "My God, my God . . ."

"Faithe." Alex's voice, from behind. "Go downstairs."

"But something's—"

"Go out back, you and the woman, and fetch our mounts."

"But—"

"We have to leave. Do it—please."

After a pause, she said, "All right."

Luke felt Alex's hand on his back. "She's gone. She's getting the horses."

Luke managed a nod.

"What happened?"

He looked up. He saw his brother's face, familiar and comforting, and felt things slip back into place.

"I killed him."

"Yes, I know. I shouldn't have let you come up here."

"Nay." Luke grabbed the front of his brother's tunic. "You don't understand. I killed him, but . . . I didn't mean to. 'Twas just one punch, just the one punch, and he . . ." Luke studied the spot in the straw where Caedmon had lain, as if he might materialize there.

"He was ill," Alex said, "and probably frailer than he looked. That's why he died from the one punch."

Luke nodded. "Aye."

Alex closed a hand over Luke's shoulder. "Let's go downstairs. Let's get away from here. We never should have come."

Luke shook his head. "Nay . . . we should have come a long time ago. I should have."

"What are you talking about?"

"He was beating her."

"Caedmon? He was beating the whore?"

"Aye, I didn't remember it till just now. The herbs . . . all that brandy. But he was . . . he was like an animal. She was screaming. I came up here to—"

"To stop him," Alex finished. "To save her."

"I didn't save her."

"You saved her from *him.*" Alex squeezed Luke's shoulder, smiling in the dark. "You couldn't stop the lightning, but you stopped him. You weren't fighting over her, you were trying to protect her."

"Aye . . . thank God."

The crime that had blackened Luke's soul had been no crime at all, just an ill-fated effort to do the right thing, the honorable thing.

"Father would have been proud of you," Alex said.

Luke nodded. "I need to tell Faithe, to make her understand."

"Christ, that's the last thing you should do!"

" 'Tis the right thing. I'm sick to death of doing the wrong thing, keeping everything hidden."

" 'Twould be a mistake, Luke. A dreadful mistake."

"No more secrets," Luke growled.

"Just one," Alex said. "This one."

Luke shook his head and started to rise.

Alex grabbed his arm. "Luke, think about it. Even if you could make Faithe understand, and I'm not sure you could, why bring this trouble down on your head? And it could be very big trouble, brother. You'll be admitting to killing a man in a brothel. No matter how you explain it away, it won't look good."

"I'll explain it by telling exactly what happened. How Caedmon was attacking that woman—"

"And how do you think that will make Faithe feel?"

Luke thought about that and swore rawly.

"You've gone to some pains to keep the truth of Caedmon's madness from her," Alex said, "because you don't want to hurt her. And now you want to—"

"Nay! I don't want to, but I'm sick at heart from lying to her."

"Just one lie," Alex said, "a lie of omission. If you don't admit to killing Caedmon, no one will ever suspect you. No one will ever know, Luke. No one. Faithe will never find out, which is all for the best. Why cause her that kind of pain? Why let her know what kind of creature her husband had become at the end?"

Luke closed his eyes. "I hate this."

"I know, brother. But at least now you don't have to bear the burden of all that guilt. You can go on with things, knowing you did nothing wrong. On the contrary, you acted nobly."

Luke rubbed his neck. That was some consolation. A great deal of consolation, if the truth be told. He had never been quite the monster he'd thought himself, even at his worst, even with the blood lust thrumming in his veins and those damned herbs clouding his mind. Beneath it all, he'd been—and still was—a good man, a man who deserved a good life—a man worthy of Faithe of Hauekleah.

"You're smiling," Alex said.

"Am I?" Luke felt as if the storm cloud that had hung over him for months was finally dissipating, leaving the sky pure and blue.

"Come." Alex thumped him on the shoulder. "Let's get out of here."

"Gladly."

Chapter 19

Faithe sat in her warm bath, basking in the late afternoon sun streaming through the slats of the window shutters, her head resting against the smoothly curved lip of the tub, her eyes closed, her mind and body drifting . . .

The ride back from Cottwyk had been uneventful, even relaxed, despite Luke's distress in the loft. Alex had explained it away as an attack of dizziness, and assured her that Luke had recovered, Indeed, he'd seemed fine on the way home. More than fine; she couldn't remember his ever having been in better spirits. So gratifying was it to see him laughing and engaging in careless banter with his brother that Faithe was able to forget, for the duration of the journey home, her purpose in going to Cottwyk.

The more she explored the secrets of Caedmon's final months and brutal murder, the more impenetrable the mystery became. Her visit to that dismal little cottage had served one important function, however; it forced her to confront the unsavory truth. At the end of his life, Caedmon had been sick and alone, dependent for his food and drink and shelter on the goodwill of people he barely knew. And he'd died in a stinking little hut, fighting over a whore.

Self-delusion not being one of Faithe's weaknesses, she had to admit to herself that she didn't particularly care to be confronted with yet more heart-wrenching details about how Caedmon had died—and, more important, had lived. It broke her heart to think of him stumbling along like the village leper, holding his hat open for scraps, for God's sake!

Her marriage to him had been passionless but amicable. She'd liked him, and he'd liked her. He'd been like a slightly galling but essentially agreeable big brother, and her memories of him and their years together were by and large happy.

Closing her eyes, she thought back to last year's revelry around the St. John's Eve bonfire. She recalled how Caedmon had lifted her up and swung her around and around as she'd squealed and laughed.

That was how she wanted to remember him, she decided. That was who he'd been to her and how she would always think of him. She didn't need to learn anything new about him that would sully that comforting memory. What would be the point?

She heard the door hinges creak. Slitting her eyes open, she saw Luke duck through the doorway, which was too short for him and barely wide enough for his shoulders, and close the door behind him. He was so large and powerful that he dwarfed the enormous bed chamber, yet he moved with exquisitely controlled grace.

Something loosened inside her, like a knot coming undone. For the first time since she'd found out how Caedmon had died, she felt truly at ease, truly content. Caedmon was in the past. Her future was standing in front of her. It was time to let go of what had gone before and embrace what was yet to be.

"Luke, I've been thinking about something."

His gaze lingered on her wet hair, her face, her breasts cresting the surface of the water. "So have I. All the way back from Cottwyk."

She grinned indulgently. "Not that. I've been thinking about Caedmon."

His smile faded. She sat up and wrapped her arms around her updrawn knees.

"The men you've appointed to investigate his murder," she said. "They're to leave for Hastings on the morrow, is that not right?"

"In the morning, aye."

She shrugged. "Perhaps we oughtn't to send them. Perhaps we ought to"—she let out a long sigh—"simply let the dead rest. Let Caedmon rest. Let the whole thing go."

He stared at her for a long moment, and then he came and squatted down next to the tub. Running a finger along her chin, he asked, "Why this change of heart?"

"I found out everything I needed to know today in Cottwyk."

"But we didn't find out anything, not really."

Smiling into his eyes, she cupped his beard-roughened cheek with her wet hand. "I saw where he died, and I found out that I didn't want to know any more. I don't need to seek out his killer and see that he's punished. God will exact His own vengeance. 'Tis time for me to leave the matter in His hands and get on with my life—with our life."

Luke closed his eyes and leaned into her palm, whispering something.

She leaned closer. "What?"

"I love you." He took her face between his big hands and kissed her. "I love you." Smiling, he pressed his forehead to hers and whispered, "I love you so much, and I'm so happy. I used to think I didn't deserve such happiness. But now I think perhaps I do, and that makes it all the better."

They kissed again, sweet and slow. When they drew apart, Luke looked down and said, "Is that water still warm?"

"Aye. I'm finished here if you want a bath."

Gaining his feet, he unbuckled his belt and hung it on a hook. "I'd like one." He whipped off his tunic, shirt, and crucifix and hung them next to the belt. The muscles in his back and shoulders flexed as he moved. Unshaven, his hair loose and disheveled, and wearing only his chausses and boots, he looked savage and virile and incredibly provocative. Heat pulsed in her lower belly; she didn't think she'd ever grow tired of looking at him.

Faithe stood and twisted the water out of her hair. He paused in the act of untying his chausses and stared at her—her breasts, hips, arms, and legs—his dark gaze caressing her until her skin erupted in gooseflesh and her nipples tightened.

"Cold?" He lifted her towel from the stool next to the bathtub and shook it out. "But it's so warm in here."

She stepped out of the tub, the rushes crackling beneath the soles of her bare feet. "I'm not cold, but I wouldn't mind getting dried off."

"I'm at your service." Crossing to her, he wrapped her in the towel and rubbed her arms and back through it. He pulled her toward him, kneading her with his strong hands until she sighed with gratification.

"Mmm. I like that."

"So do I." He kissed her as he massaged her breasts through the damp linen, then lowered his hands to her bottom. "I love touching you."

Dropping to his knees in front of her, he stroked the towel over her legs, his breath hot on her most sensitive flesh. He passed the towel between her thighs, dried the wet curls there. The soft friction was sweetly maddening. Did he know the effect this was having on her? She smoothed wayward strands of hair off his forehead, the better to see his eyes.

He looked up at her. He knew.

Draping the towel over his shoulders, he opened her with gentle fingers, studying her intently, as if he'd never seen a woman's mysteries this close before.

Perhaps he never had, given what he'd told her

about his sexual past—the swift couplings with anonymous whores.

He drew closer, his breath coming in quickening rushes of heat that made her tingle. He looked up at her again, almost bashfully. "Would it be all right if I . . ."

"Yes," she breathed, burying her hands in his hair to urge him closer still.

"Tell me if I'm doing it wrong."

She chuckled breathlessly. "I don't think it can be done wrong."

Closing his eyes, he touched his lips to her very softly, almost tentatively. She gasped at the hot tickle of pleasure. Looking up sharply, he opened his mouth to speak, but stopped himself and smiled. She returned the smile. "Yes, I'm all right," she murmured.

"I know. I'm learning." Closing his hands over her hips, he glided his tongue over her aching flesh until she moaned and clutched at his hair. He kissed her, suckled her, even nipped her lightly with his teeth. Her climax approached swiftly, exploding with luxuriant intensity as he continued to pleasure her, gripping her hips tightly to hold her still.

He nuzzled her lightly as the blood slowed in her veins and her breathing steadied.

"Are you certain you've never done that before?" she breathed as he stood and took her in his arms.

"I think I would have remembered." He kissed her, and she tasted herself on his lips.

"Would you like me to do that to you?" she asked him.

He chuckled deep in his chest. "Yes, and possibly a few other things—all in good time. Right now I'd like to know where you keep that oil that smells like almonds and thyme."

She pointed to the green vial on the floor near the tub. Bending to retrieve it, he removed the cork and poured some of the fragrant balm into both palms.

Standing behind her, he slid his rough, oily hands over her back and hips and waist, working it in with lazy, circular strokes.

"You're using too much oil," she murmured.

"You can wash it off."

"You mean to tell me I'll have to bathe all over again?"

"Indulge me."

She felt like indulging him. If the visit to Cottwyk had altered her outlook, it had, from all appearances, done the same to him. He seemed changed, at peace with himself. She sensed a deep and real contentment in him that only served to reinforce her own sense of rightness, and she treasured it as much as she treasured her own happiness.

Luke glided his slick hands around to the front and upward, until they touched the undersides of her breasts. He paused while her heart pounded in her chest, and then he circled each breast slowly, caressing the pliant flesh with strong fingers.

The hair on his chest prickled her back; she felt the dampness of the towel over his shoulders and the slightly scratchy wool of his chausses against her bare bottom and legs. He lowered his head, his breath tickling her ear. "I've wanted to do this ever since that night."

She knew which night he meant—the night she'd tried to seduce him. The night she'd teased him by asking him to rub oil into her back.

"I was wild with wanting you that night," he rasped as he caressed her breasts with a firmer touch, circling closer and closer to their rigid tips.

"What did you want to do to me?" she breathed, closing her eyes and letting herself back fall onto his shoulder as he stroked her languidly, getting closer, closer . . .

"This." Capturing each nipple, he pinched them slowly, until she moaned his name like a plea.

"And this." He molded himself against her from behind, smoothing one hand down her belly until a slippery finger probed her damp folds.

"Oh, God." Reaching behind her, she pressed her hands to his wool-clad hips as they rocked against her. With every thrust she felt the thick column of his erection against her bottom. He curled a finger inside her, and then another, caressing her from within as his breath came hot and ragged in her ear.

"What else?" she asked as a second climax gathered inside her.

"I wanted to take you," he said gruffly. "I wanted to bury myself in you, possess you. Again and again. I wanted you every way a man can want a woman."

"How do you want me now?" she asked, teetering on the edge of fulfillment. "Tell me."

His heart thundered against her back. "From behind." He whipped the towel off his shoulders and flung it onto the rushes. "Right here."

He urged her downward until she knelt on the rushes with her knees apart, then bent her forward, curling her hands over the edge of the tub. There came a moment's pause, when all she could hear was his breathing, and she knew he was untying his chausses. Grasping her hips with both hands, he pushed into her, moaning with the effort. He felt so immense, so hot and sweet and perfect inside her, that a raw sob tore from her lungs.

He didn't say *Are you all right?* He didn't stop, or even slow down. He drove into her, over and over, faster and faster, groaning harshly with each fierce stroke. She held on tight to the edge of the tub, one shoulder thudding against it repeatedly as he pounded into her, feeling the blissful panic of impending orgasm.

Luke wrapped his strong arms around her, his hair falling over her face, his body pumping against her in a delirious frenzy. He was engulfed in sensation, she realized. He'd given himself up to it, handed over the reins and let it command him. Never before had he loved her with such violent abandon, and she found that it thrilled her in a deep and primal way.

He squeezed a breast with one hand, while the other slid between her legs to the quivering little knot of pleasure there. She cried out at the first rough touch, her body convulsing beneath him as her climax erupted.

Through the riot of sensation that gripped her, she felt him bite her neck, just hard enough to restrain her while he forced himself deep, deep inside her. She knew then that he was truly lost in his animal passion.

He stilled, every muscle in his body rigid, a low, guttural sound emerged from deep in his chest. And then she felt the hot, frantic pulsing within her, and she smiled as tears stung her eyes.

They collapsed into the rushes together, slick with oil and sweat. He wiped her tears away with a shaky hand and whispered breathlessly, "Why are you crying?"

"This is perfect. A perfect moment."

He chuckled tolerantly as he drew himself out of her and gathered her in his arms. "That's what you said after the first time, in the barn."

"I was wrong. That was a very good moment—excellent. But this is perfect. Everything is wonderful. Naught is amiss."

"You're right," he said wonderingly. "Everything *is* perfect—or as close as one could reasonably hope for. And 'twill remain that way. Now and forever."

"Now and forever," she murmured against his lips.

Things remained perfect for another twelve days.

Chapter 20

After supper on the last day of July, as Faithe's house staff and the village children busied themselves decorating Hauekleah Hall for tomorrow's Lammas Day songfest, little Felix appeared in the doorway.

Luke could tell he'd been swimming, which he did more and more by himself lately, ever since Luke taught him how. His hair was wet, and his clothes clung damply to his small body. Grinning excitedly, he scanned the activity in the great hall until his gaze lit on Luke, at the rear, enjoying a game of draughts with Alex.

"Milord!" the boy shouted over the commotion and waved a small object in the air. "Look what I found!"

Luke squinted at the object, which gleamed in the early evening sun streaming in through the doorway.

"I found it at the bottom of the river! I saw it shining!"

"Luke!" Alex hissed.

Luke stood. He held out his hand. With all the calm at his disposal, he called out, "Bring it to me, Felix."

Luke held his breath as Felix darted between two groups of children sitting on the floor, tying ribbons around sheaves of wheat. Waving to Alfrith and Bram, he jumped over several long garlands of midsummer blossoms stretched out across the floor waiting to be wound around posts and hung from rafters.

As he passed Faithe, strewing mint and wormwood among the rushes, he paused.

"Nay," Alex whispered.

"Felix, bring it here!" Luke demanded loudly. He couldn't hear Faithe's voice from across the huge, crowded room, but he could read her lips: "What have you got there?"

"Look." Felix handed her the mantle pin.

Orrik came up behind Faithe and peered down over her shoulder.

Alex stood up. His right hand automatically touched his hip, where the hilt of his sword would have been had he been wearing it.

Luke muttered a brief, heartfelt prayer.

Faithe smiled when she saw what it was she held, and ruffled Felix's wet hair. The other boys gathered around him, stealing glances at the pin and patting him on the back. "Good work," Orrik said. Felix puffed up his little chest with pride.

Luke's gaze was riveted on Faithe as she studied the onyx dragon imbedded in the golden disk, her smile never wavering. Meeting his eyes across the room, she held it up and cupped her hand around her mouth. "Look what Felix found!"

Luke circled the table and strode toward her through the preholiday mayhem, his hand outstretched. "I'll take that."

As he watched, she turned the pin over and held it close to her face. Halfway across the hall to her, Luke paused and glanced back at Alex, still standing next to the table where they'd been playing draughts. He held Luke's gaze for a grim moment and then lifted his cup of brandy and drained it.

When Luke looked back at Faithe, he saw that her smile had turned into a frown of puzzlement. Her lips moved slowly as she read the inscription—identical to that on the white wolf pin, save for the words that prefaced the quote. Luke's was inscribed *To my middle son,* Alex's *To my youngest son.*

Luke felt starved for air.

She looked up at him. The bewilderment in her eyes made his heart splinter into a thousand fragments. He crossed to her until they were close enough to touch, but he didn't touch her. Around them, Faithe's *famuli*—mostly kitchen wenches and serving girls—stopped what they were doing to stare at their lord and lady. The tapestry of chatter became muffled and then faded away. Orrik snagged Baldric by his tunic and whispered something in his ear. Baldric grinned maliciously and raced out the back door.

" 'Tis a quotation from Deuteronomy," Luke said, very softly, knowing she didn't care about that, but not knowing what else to say. "Moses' counsel to the people of Israel. 'Be strong and of good courage. Have no fear or dread, for the Lord your God goes with you. He will not fail you or forsake you.' "

She just stared at him.

"My father was a pious man. He . . ."

She was shaking her head. "I don't understand."

The young boys gaped, clearly sensing that something momentous was happening, but not sure what it was—except for Felix, who looked back and forth between Luke and Faithe with a heartbreakingly flustered expression. A few of the serving girls, including Bonnie and Blossom, edged closer, straining for a look at what Faithe held in her hand.

"Faithe." He took a step toward her, but she backed up, and he knew then that she did understand. God help him, she understood perfectly. "Faithe . . ."

"I don't understand," she repeated, her voice wavering. "Explain it to me. Just explain it to me, please!" Desperation glittered in her eyes.

Luke closed his eyes briefly. "I'm sorry, Faithe. Whatever happens, know that I love you, and that I'm—"

"Explain it!" Her face turned a scalding pink; her eyes were wild. "Tell me this isn't what it looks like. Please! Tell me that other pin isn't Alex's!"

"Yes, do." Orrik crossed his arms, his eyes like newly minted silver shillings.

"It's my pin."

Luke turned to find Alex behind him.

"I'm the man you were looking for, Faithe," Alex said.

Faithe shook her head again. "No, Alex."

" 'Tisn't how it seems," Luke said.

Orrik snorted disgustedly.

"Then tell me how it is," she demanded shakily. "Explain it."

Luke scoured his mind for the right words. Felix sniffled pathetically.

"Oh, God." She fisted her quivering hands in her skirt. "Alex, please tell me you didn't . . . *please*!"

"We can't talk about it here," Luke said, indicating their audience. "Let's go outside and—"

"I'm sure you'd like that." Orrik nodded toward the herd of brawny men being led through the back door by Baldric. They'd been rebuilding the cookhouse, and they still gripped their tools in their meaty fists. Luke saw augers, chisels, and various axes, hammers, and saws of all shapes and sizes. "See that this murdering cur"—he pointed to Alex—"doesn't go anywhere."

Faithe opened her mouth to speak, but seemed at a complete loss; Luke had never seen her look so helpless. The men blinked at Orrik and exchanged looks. Alex was well liked by everyone at Hauekleah.

Obviously sensing their hesitation, Orrik said, " 'Twas he who murdered our Lord Caedmon. He all but admitted it."

The men murmured darkly. One of them grabbed Alex by the arm and held a carpenter's axe to the back of his neck.

Pulling herself together, Faithe ordered her staff and the children out of the great hall. They all dropped what they were doing and left quickly, save for Bonnie and Blossom, weeping piteously, and Felix, who lingered unnoticed behind Orrik.

"You"—Orrik jabbed Firdolf on the arm—"go fetch a good, strong length of rope, and tie it into a noose. Bring it back here."

Firdolf's mouth dropped open.

"Do it!"

The young bondman backed up slowly, glancing back and forth between Blossom and Alex.

"Now!" Orrik ordered.

Firdolf turned and lumbered off to do the bailiff's bidding.

"Nay!" Bonnie, crying hysterically, clutched the front of Orrik's tunic. "Let him go! He didn't do it! He couldn't have!"

"Stop this!" Orrik slapped the young woman's face.

"Orrik!" Faithe gasped.

"You bastard!" Alex screamed, leaping toward the bailiff. Three of the men seized him and wrestled him back. "Don't you touch her!"

Orrik sneered at Alex's rage. "Nyle! Baldric! Take these wenches outside."

The two brothers grabbed the twins, who began to struggle frantically, biting and lashing out with their fists. Blossom broke free and hurled herself toward Alex. Baldric pounced on her and lifted her roughly off her feet. She kicked him in the shin. He yanked her braid, causing her to howl in pain.

"Stop it!" Alex bellowed. The girls quieted; their captors held on tight. "Bonnie . . . Blossom. Go home."

They shook their heads, tears streaming down their crimson faces.

"Aye," Alex insisted, quietly but firmly. "Go into

your house and wait there. There's naught you can do to help, and—"

They both burst into fresh tears.

"And this isn't as bad as it seems," he lied. " 'Tis a misunderstanding, nothing more. Go home. Go."

They nodded limply. The men let them go, and they lurched from the hall, holding on to each other.

"You've quite a way with the wenches," Orrik observed. "But 'twill take more than sweet words to keep me from stretching your filthy, murdering neck this evening."

"He didn't do it," Luke said.

Alex shook his head. "Luke . . ."

Luke looked directly at Faithe and said quietly, "I did."

She stared mutely, stricken by his confession. Dimly Luke was aware of Orrik barking orders, someone's big hand closing around his arm, a sharp pressure at his back, through his tunic. Alex tried to intercede, but they held on to him, three or four of them.

"He's lying to protect me!" Alex claimed. "I did it. 'Twas my pin you found there, wasn't it?"

"All that means," Orrik told him, "is you were there with him when he did it. If I have to choose which one of the two of you is more likely to do murder, it's got to be the Black Dragon. He's the one that did it. I know it in my bones. 'Tis an act of brutality perfectly in keeping with his nature."

How convenient for Orrik, Luke thought, to have such a good excuse for disposing of the Norman master he never wanted in the first place, and had always despised.

Faithe never wrested her gaze from Luke's. "Why?" she choked out. "You must have had a reason. I know you must have had a reason."

The time for deceit—even in the name of kindness—was over. Luke's position as master of Hauekleah wouldn't save him from Orrik's unreasoning fury. His only hope for salvation was the truth. "I didn't just murder him in cold blood, Faithe. I swear it. And I didn't kill him fighting over . . . the woman."

"Doesn't matter what clever lies you come up with, de Périgueux," Orrik threatened. "As God is my witness, you're going to swing from my noose this night."

"Nay!" Faithe exclaimed. "There will be no hanging. I won't permit it."

"God's bones, woman, do you mean to just let the man walk free?" Orrik demanded. "He killed Caedmon—he said so himself! He murdered your husband, and you propose to—"

"I didn't murder him," Luke interjected.

"Liar!" Orrik rammed his fist into Luke's stomach. A sickening burst of pain doubled him over. Hands grabbed him and yanked him upright.

Faithe and Alex were both screaming at Orrik. Orrik screamed back, "He's a murderer, and he's got to hang!" He snatched a small saw out of someone's hand. "I'll cut his stinking Norman throat before I let him go free."

"Then the Normans will hang *you,*" Faithe warned.

" 'Twill be worth it," Orrik said. "I'll go to the hangman willingly, knowing I've seen justice done."

"You call this justice?" Faithe demanded. "Hanging a man without a trial?"

Orrik grunted dismissively. "We've no authority to try him. Only his king can do that, and you can't tell me we can expect real justice from him. Even if he *were* found guilty, the great and mighty Black Dragon would never hang for killing a lowly Saxon. Worst that'll happen to him is a whipping. The only way to see justice served is for us to hang the bastard ourselves, even if we have to do it in the dead of night and burn the body afterward."

Baldric grunted in agreement. The others seemed taken aback—even appalled—by what the bailiff was proposing. Unfortunately Luke knew that all Orrik needed in order to implement his threat was the cover of darkness.

"I forbid this," Faithe announced, scanning the faces of the men surrounding them. "Do you hear me? I won't have it."

All the men, even Orrik, murmured their assent, but Luke detected a predatory gleam in the bailiff's eye, a mulish set to his jaw, and knew, even if Faithe didn't, that she couldn't hope to control him. Not for a moment did Luke believe Orrik would willingly hand him over to the Normans, no matter what pacifying assurances he offered now. Alex's severe expression indicated that he knew this, too.

Faith turned to Luke. "What happened that night? Tell me the truth this time. You've lied to me for months, one way or another."

Luke didn't deny it.

"No more lies," she said. "What really happened?"

Luke drew in a steadying breath. "I was trying to protect . . . that woman. Helig. She was upstairs in the loft, with Caedmon. I'm sorry, Faithe. I didn't want to tell you this. I didn't want you to find out what happened that night."

"I daresay *that's* true," Orrik snarled.

Faithe sliced a look of warning toward Orrik, then returned her attention to Luke. "Go on."

"They were upstairs together. I was asleep downstairs." No point in offering all the sordid details—the herbs, the nightmares, the madness. They would muddy things and only hurt his cause. "I woke up to screams, the woman's screams. I went up there, and . . . I'm sorry, Faithe. He was attacking her."

She looked at Luke as if he'd said he'd seen fish flying in the sky.

"Lying pig!" Orrik slammed his fist into the side of Luke's head. Pain erupted in a white-hot flash.

More screaming . . . he shook his head to clear it as the hands tightened around his arms. His ears rang.

All he could hear was Felix wailing, amid uncontrollable sobs, "I'm sorry, milord! I found the pin. 'Tis all my fault."

"Listen to Luke!" Alex was yelling. "Won't you just listen to him? He's telling the truth."

"It's impossible," Faithe murmured, her bright flush draining quickly—too quickly.

Luke tried to approach her, but the hands held him back. Hot blood trickled into his eye, and he could feel the stinging flesh begin to swell. "I'm sorry, Faithe, truly I am. But he was . . . hitting her. Over and over again."

"He's never done anything like that," she said woodenly. "Never."

Luke implored her with his eyes to look at him. "I wouldn't lie to you, Faithe."

"Hah!" Orrik spat out.

"Not anymore," he amended, feeling as if he were skidding down a perilous and deadly slope. "You've got to believe me."

"I . . . want to . . ." But she didn't. Of course not. She didn't want to believe the man she'd been married to for eight years was capable of such savagery.

"He was . . . his illness, it made him . . ." Luke groped for the words to explain it to her, but her eyes were becoming glassy, unfocused, and he didn't think she really heard him. She wavered slightly on her feet, and he knew then that the shock was too much for her. This was exactly how she'd looked after finding Vance's corpse hanging in the storeroom that morning, before she'd run away to faint in the blessed solitude of the barn.

"Faithe . . ." Luke said, but she just turned away with dreamlike listlessness. "Someone help her. Moira!"

"I'm . . . I'm . . ." Sweat gleamed on Faithe's bleached face. Moira tried to put her arm around her, but she swatted the plump maid away. "Nay," she said hoarsely. "Leave me be."

She stumbled away, and out the back door.

"See what your lies have done?" Orrik demanded, rage flaring in his eyes. "She's like my own daughter, that girl. Look what you've done to her."

"Here it is, Master Orrik." It was Firdolf, returning with the noose he'd fashioned from a length of thick hemp rope.

"You've done naught but damage since you came here," Orrik charged, trading his saw for the noose and snapping it to test its strength. "Now I mean to do a little damage myself. An eye for an eye, as they say."

"Your mistress has forbidden this!" Alex reminded him.

"My mistress has been taken in by the smooth Norman ways of her husband." Orrik draped the noose around Luke's head and pulled it tight. "She's not thinking straight. It falls to me to do her thinking for her."

"Nay! Nay!" Felix pummeled Orrik with his little fists. Orrik backhanded him across the face, and he sprawled into the rushes.

"Go away, Felix," Luke ordered. "You can't help me." And he didn't want the boy to have to watch him hang. He had enough on his conscience.

"But 'tis my fault, milord!" Felix whimpered. "I've got to help you."

"You can help me by going home to your mother, so I don't have to worry about you. Now, go!"

The boy got to his feet, but hesitated.

"Get out of here!" Luke roared.

He sprinted out the front door.

Orrik seemed grimly amused. "Shall we get on with things?" He tugged on the rope, jerking Luke's head to the side. "That big oak outside the sheepfold has a good, sturdy branch high up. 'Twill do quite nicely for our purposes, I think."

"Listen to me, all of you," Alex exhorted the men, straining against the arms that held him. "Orrik has no authority to do this. You heard Lady Faithe. She expressly forbade this!"

Orrik grabbed a sledgehammer from the man next to him.

"No!" Luke screamed.

Hauling back, Orrik whipped the hammer's handle across Alex's forehead. The impact jolted him; he slumped over unconscious, supported by the men who held onto him. Blood dripped from his head into the rushes.

Orrik caught Firdolf's eye and pointed to Alex. "Get him out of here."

Firdolf took Alex from the men who held him, hooking his hands beneath his shoulders to drag him away. Orrik grabbed him by the tunic and whispered something in his ear. Firdolf gaped at Orrik and then at Alex. "But, Master Orrik, if I leave him there, he'll—"

"Just do it!" Orrik put his mouth near Firdolf's ear and muttered something else. Luke thought he heard the word "Blossom." Most likely he was reminding the lovesick young man that, with Alex out of the way, he'd have the object of his desire all to himself.

Firdolf nodded slowly and, seeming to steel himself, continued dragging Alex out of the hall.

"Don't do it!" Luke yelled at him, not knowing where he was taking Alex, but not liking Firdolf's hesitation. "Alex has committed no crime. Orrik has no right to order this!"

Firdolf stubbornly refused to look up or react in any way to these desperate pleas, but Luke saw the consternation in his eyes.

"I'd save my breath if I were you," Orrik snickered. "You'll soon need all the breath you can get."

"Alex was right," Luke told the men gathered around. "Orrik is acting on his own in this. He's going against Lady Faithe's orders."

There commenced a great deal of muttering and whispering.

"I'm avenging Caedmon!" Orrik insisted.

"Your vengeance is misplaced," Luke said, loud enough for everyone to hear. "What happened to Caedmon was a tragedy, but he was dying anyway. He was sick, very sick. I think he had a kind of growth in his brain. 'Twas the same malady that killed my sister."

"Lies!"

"It made him mad in the end. He'd have spells of uncontrollable violence. That's why he attacked that woman. He was—"

"Damn you to hell!" Orrik swung the sledgehammer handle again.

A dull explosion went off in Luke's head, and then nothingness swallowed him up.

Chapter 21

Faithe awoke in darkness to the familiar, comforting scent of straw. She sat up, and a wave of vertigo washed over her.

I fainted. That's right. I came to the barn and fainted.

And then she remembered why she fainted—Luke's terrible confession, and the things he'd said about Caedmon. *He was hitting her . . . over and over again.*

"Nay." She pressed her hands to her forehead to make everything stop spinning. "Nay . . ."

As God is my witness, Orrik had told Luke, *you're going to swing from my noose this night.*

"Christ." Lurching to her feet, she staggered out of the barn. Smears of red and purple bruised the sky. How long had she been out? Had Orrik followed through on his threat? Had he gone against her order and hanged Luke? He'd never broken a promise to her before, but he was a changed man since Hastings, and she wasn't sure what to expect of him anymore.

Clutching her skirts, she ran on jittery legs to the rear gate of the croft. Someone was standing just inside it, arms crossed, watching her approach.

Orrik.

"Whoa!" He grabbed her by the shoulders. "Slow down, my lady! No need to—"

"Did you do it?" she gasped, her chest heaving, everything whirling. "Tell me you didn't—"

"Steady, my dear. Do what? What do you think—"

"Hang him. You didn't hang Luke. Tell me you didn't—"

"Of course not!" His eyes widened in indignation, their pupils contracting to make them look even more silvery than usual in this eerie twilight. "Did you think I'd go back on my word to you?"

"I . . . I don't . . ." Relief made her dizzy. He tried to gather her up for a fatherly embrace, but she backed away from him, murmuring, "I was so scared. I came to in the barn, and I remembered how you'd threatened to hang him—"

"And then I swore not to, didn't I?" He reached out and tilted her chin up. "Didn't I?"

"Aye, but . . . aye."

"You ordered me not to, and that was good enough for me. Have I ever broken my word to you?"

Beyond Orrik's shoulder Faithe could see Baldric standing a few paces away, outside the small storehouse. Even in the semidarkness, she could make out his slyly mysterious smile. She still felt light-headed from her fainting spell, and her thoughts were blurry and confused, but she had the sense that things were not quite as they seemed. Foreboding itched at her.

"Where is he, then?" she asked, wrapping her fist around her keys. "Where is Luke?"

"Right in there." Orrik cocked his head toward the storehouse. "Where we keep all knaves and cutthroats until we can deal with them properly," he added with a scowl.

Ah. So that was it. Baldric was standing guard over his own master, imprisoned like a common bandit in the same place where Vance had inexplicably hanged himself. He nodded in her direction. She wondered what he knew that she didn't. She could demand the full truth from Orrik, but she knew from experience he was too smart and too obdurate to reveal more than he cared to about any matter of importance to him. And Baldric would be no more forthcoming; he was entirely Orrik's creature.

But there was someone who might speak frankly to her, someone she wanted to talk to anyway, *needed* to talk to.

"I'd like to speak to my husband," she said. "Who has the key to the storehouse?"

Baldric heard her; he withdrew the key from his tunic, but Orrik held up a restraining hand before he could insert it in the lock.

"Begging your pardon, my lady," Orrik said, "but that's a damned foolish notion, if you don't mind me saying so."

"Actually," she informed him coolly, straining for composure despite her wooziness, "I do. I mind it very much. He'd my husband, and I'm going to speak to him."

She tried to brush past him toward the storehouse, but he seized her arm; his grip was surprisingly steely for a man his age.

"He's a vicious murderer," Orrik said. "A man of ungovernable rages—no better than a mad dog. And now that he's been caught and locked up, he may have snapped completely."

"Oh, for God's sake, Orrik." She tried to push past him, but he held her tight.

"I'd hate to have it on my conscience if anything happened to you."

"I absolve you from responsibility," she said. "Now, get out of my way."

"He'll poison your mind," Orrik warned. "Twist the truth."

"You ought to know a thing or two about that," she replied archly.

Orrik glowered. "If you insist on going in there, I'm going with you."

"Absolutely not. I'm not some child who needs—"

"I'll brook no argument about it, Faithe." His hand

tightened painfully on her arm; his metallic gaze bored into hers. He only used her Christian name when he was really upset about something. "You're my responsibility, whether you realize it or not. Always have been, always will be. I *will not* allow you to go in there alone."

She swallowed hard. "Your fingers are digging into my arm."

He looked down at his hand and blinked, then released her abruptly. "I mean it. I'm not letting you go in there by yourself, Faithe."

Faithe willed calm into her voice. " 'Tisn't your place to *let* me or not *let* me do anything, Orrik. Now, stand aside."

They held each other's gaze for a charged moment, and then he abruptly turned away. "Do as you please."

Clutching her skirt, she stalked up to Baldric. "Give me the key."

Baldric looked toward Orrik, who nodded sullenly, then handed over the key. She twisted it in the lock and pushed the door open. No sound came from within the storehouse.

Faithe took a hesitant step inside. "Luke?" Looking down, she saw him lying on his side on the earthen floor, his back to her, his hands tied together with rope. "Luke." Kneeling, she touched his shoulder; he didn't respond. She shook him. "Luke!"

"He's not dead," Orrik assured her from the doorway.

Faithe untied the ropes that bound Luke's hands.

Orrik made a sound of disgust. "I'll just have to find some more and tie him up again when you leave."

"You won't be here when I leave. I'm relieving you of all responsibility in this matter."

"What?"

"You're to go home and go to bed. You and Baldric

both. Neither of you is permitted anywhere near the storehouse or Luke."

"Who's to stand guard then?"

"He doesn't need a guard. Look at him." He still hadn't moved or responded in any way to her touch.

"He'll come to eventually. I can't let you leave the man unguarded, Faithe."

Faithe sighed, knowing Orrik would just sneak back here unless she posted a man. "I'll have Nyle stand watch. I can trust him."

"You can't trust me?"

"After you tried to hang Luke?" Gently turning her husband onto his back, she saw that one of his eyes was badly swollen and that he had an ugly wound on his forehead. "Look what you did to him. You had no right to do this."

Orrik snorted contemptuously. " 'Twas less than he deserved. How can you bring yourself to ask after him? How can you want to speak to him? The man butchered your husband in a jealous rage."

She peeled strands of hair from the dried blood on Luke's forehead. "That's not the way Luke tells it."

Orrik rolled his eyes. "All that blather about how Caedmon was attacking that woman—beating her savagely? Think about it, Faithe. No one knew Caedmon better than you did. Search your soul. Was he capable of that kind of viciousness toward a woman?"

"The Caedmon I knew," she said, "could never have done that. He never once struck me in the entire time we were together. He never even seemed tempted. He had no temper to speak of."

"You see?" Orrik crossed his arms, his expression smug.

"But he'd been ill."

"According to whom?"

"The people of Cottwyk."

"Did they tell you this?"

"Nay. Luke did."

"Aye." He nodded, as if a point had been proven—and indeed, there was a certain heartless logic to his reasoning. "And after you left the hall this afternoon, he started humming a different melody. Claimed Caedmon was mad."

"Mad!"

"A raving lunatic, to hear your *lord husband* tell it."

"Mad . . ." Faithe murmured. She *had* to speak to Luke; it was imperative that she sort through all the hearsay and find out what really happened, and why. Two weeks ago, after returning from that troubling visit to Cottwyk, she'd lost interest in the details of Caedmon's death; all she'd cared about was Luke and moving forward. Now she was forced to confront the ugly past again, and dig and dig until she found the truth.

"Sickened me to hear our Caedmon maligned that way, in front of the men, yet." Orrik shook his head disgustedly. "The man's dead, by de Périgueux's own hand, and he still can't let him rest in peace! Has to sully his character for all to hear. But I'll tell you what'll *really* do some damage—that's if we let those Norman bastards try your precious Sir Luke, and he comes out and makes these claims publicly. Then we can just kiss Caedmon's good name good-bye and be done with it!"

"What are you saying?" Faithe rose to her feet, suddenly suspicious. "Wasn't your intention to hand Luke over to the Normans for trial?"

"Is that really what you want?"

"Is there a choice?" A fair trial would resolve things once and for all. Matters that had been cloaked in secrecy for long months would be examined out in the open, and her heart told her that Luke would be found innocent of wrongdoing, regardless of Orrik's cold-blooded logic.

"There is a choice," Orrik said, lowering his voice as he steered her by the arm past the door and out of earshot of Baldric. "There need never be a trial. This entire business could be over by tomorrow morning."

"What do you mean?"

He closed a hand over her shoulder. "I mean there's Norman justice, such as it is . . . and then there's Saxon justice."

The only way to see justice served, Orrik had said after Luke confessed to the killing, *is for us to hang the bastard ourselves, even if we have to do it in the dead of night and burn the body afterward.*

She twisted out of his grip. "You can't mean—"

"You need have naught to do with it," he said, his voice reasonable, even gentle, like a father telling his little girl that Papa would take care of everything. "You'll know nothing about it."

"I already know about it," she reminded him.

"Put it out of your mind," he soothed. "Go to sleep tonight, and in the morning 'twill all be—"

"For God's sake, Orrik, have you no decency left at all? I used to be able to trust you, and now—"

"You can trust me!" He looked genuinely stung. "I'm the only one you *can* trust. I'm the only one who looks after you, who makes sure things are taken care of."

He seized her arm; she shook him off. Baldric was staring at them. Orrik noticed this and glared at him; he hurriedly looked away.

He rubbed his eyes. "Faithe," he said wearily. "I'm sorry, truly I am. I know I shouldn't talk of taking matters into my own hands. 'Tis just so vexing to see my little girl ill-used and be powerless to set things right. That Norman bastard"—he jabbed a finger toward the storehouse—"murdered Caedmon and then deceived you about it. I can't help but want to punish him. Perhaps I'm overzealous."

She began to speak, but he cut her off. "I *am* overzealous. I'm half mad with outrage, if the truth be told, but only because of my concern for you. I hate to see you hurt."

He chucked her under the chin, as he used to do when she was little. "You're my fair-haired lass, my wee Faithe. The child I never had. Perhaps I go too far at times, but it's only because I care for you. Please believe that."

"I do." She did. Orrik had always been there for her, the most rock-solid presence in her life, especially after her father died. She would have been alone if not for him. He did take care of her, completely. He'd represented her interests with their overlord, arranging for her convent education and helping to negotiate her marriage to Caedmon. He'd kept Hauekleah productive and efficient during her years at St. Mary's, and relinquished control willingly when she returned. But it was the little things that had earned her undying affection. It was the time he'd taught her how to ride, leading her pony around by the reins for weeks until she felt confident enough for him to let go. It was the way he would put aside his work to play blindman's buff with her when she was bored. It was the tales of romance and adventure he'd spin for her when she was too wound up to get to sleep.

He *had* been like a father to her, truly. But those years were over. She'd warned him many times not to force her to choose between loyalty to him and loyalty to Luke. He hadn't heeded her, though, and now the bond of affection they'd shared was irretrievably broken.

"Where is Alex?" she asked. "Did you lock him up somewhere else?"

Orrik's smile thinned out. "Nay."

"Where is he, then?"

Orrik pulled on his beard and avoided her gaze. "He saddled up and rode off."

Faithe let go of the gate. "Rode off. Left? He just—"

"Just left." Orrik cleared his throat. "Probably scared we'd lock him up, too, but he's not the one who did murder."

"Did he say where he was going?"

Orrik shook his head. "Just rode off into the woods to the west."

"Oh." The idea of Alex abandoning his brother to his fate didn't sit right with Faithe. An uneasiness gnawed at her.

"There, there." Orrik chucked her under the chin again. "You look exhausted. It's been a trying evening all around. Why don't you go to bed and get some sleep?"

Her gaze stole to the storehouse, which Baldric was relocking. "I couldn't possibly sleep with him in there." Faithe wanted to stay here and watch over Luke, but she also felt an obligation to find out what really happened to Alex. She must saddle up and ride west as hard as she could. If he'd simply ridden away, as Orrik claimed, she might overtake him. But if she didn't, and if she could find no one in that direction who'd seen him pass, perhaps Orrik was lying to her and some other fate had befallen him.

Faithe ordered Orrik and Baldric to go home and assigned Nyle the job of guarding the storehouse. "Put some straw in there," she told him. "I'll bring him a wineskin and something to eat when he's awake."

"Yes, milady."

Come to me. Please, Faithe . . .

Luke paced the storeroom like a caged beast. His head throbbed from the blow Orrik had dealt him, and his left eye was swollen shut, but otherwise he was unharmed. He'd been surprised to wake up in this place, and with no noose around his neck.

Pride kept him from pounding on this door and screaming for Faithe. He didn't want to plead with her to talk to him if she didn't want to, and he certainly didn't want her to see him like this—held prisoner by the very men he had commanded that morning. But deep inside, in a dark and needy place where there was no room for dignity, he'd begged her. *Please come to me, Faithe. Talk to me. Please.*

It was quite possible, even likely, that she hated him now. Not only had he admitted to killing her husband, but God knew what Orrik was telling her. And after the shock of Luke's confession, she'd be in a vulnerable state . . .

"Christ."

He had to explain things to her, had to make her understand. He never should have withheld the truth in the first place. She was strong; she could have handled it if he'd explained it right. After all, what happened to Caedmon wasn't a murder, but a tragedy. Luke had been the instrument of his death, but in a way he'd died of the thing growing inside his head, for that's what had driven him to attack that whore.

But he hadn't trusted her to understand. He'd underestimated her, and by doing so made himself vulnerable to Orrik's vengeance. In a way, it was his own fault that he'd ended up in this storehouse, awaiting his uncertain fate.

There wasn't much room for him to move around in here. The walls of the cool stone hut were lined with barrels and bundles and sacks: malt, flour, dried fish, salted pork, honey, wax, cheeses, ale . . . Just dim shapes against the walls, for the only light came from the vent hole—an opening on the back wall rather like an arrow slit on its side, up high near the raftered ceiling. And that light wasn't much, with night falling. Soon it would be black as pitch in here. There was straw to lie on, but sleeping would be out of the question.

Stopping in his tracks, he turned and rammed a fist against the door. "Guard! Who's out there?"

A pause, and then, " 'Tis me, milord, Nyle."

"Why am I not dead? Why didn't the bastard hang me when he had the chance?"

"He wanted to, sire," Nyle replied. "After he knocked you out, he tried to get us to drag you out to the big oak outside the sheepfold. Only one sorry cur was willing to do it, and I'm ashamed to say 'twas my own crawlin' louse of a brother, Baldric."

Luke grunted, unsurprised.

"Anyways," Nyle continued, "the rest of us, we put a stop to it. We thought you deserved a fair trial, 'specially after what you said, about disobeying Lady Faithe, and Caedmon bein' out of his senses and all—"

"Hold your tongue," came a muted voice, accompanied by footsteps—Orrik. "Didn't Lady Faithe warn you not to talk to him?"

"N-nay, she didn't say nothin' about talkin'."

Another voice, Baldric's: "You haven't got the sense of a squirrel, Nyle. Listenin' to his lies . . ."

Luke swore softly, discouraged by the appearance of Orrik and his minion. This could only bode ill.

"We don't know as they're lies," Nyle said defiantly. "We don't know nothin'. Lord Caedmon may well have gone mad. Folks do. We don't—"

Baldric muttered something else; Luke thought he heard the words ". . . hang him anyways."

"He's to stand trial," Nyle insisted. "Orrik promised."

"Not if he turns up danglin' from them rafters in the mornin'." Baldric snickered.

Luke looked up at the beams that supported the roof of the storehouse and remembered the morning they'd found Vance, dead and bloated and crawling with flies. He'd wondered at the time why Vance would hang himself when he'd been assured of a fair trial by his Saxon peers. *I'll tell you everything,* a grateful Vance had promised. *I'll tell you why we done what we done.*

Suspicion tickled Luke's scalp. When Luke first threatened to hand Vance over to Alberic's hangman for torture, the bandit had asked for Orrik . . . *He'll see things are done right.*

Was it possible the bandits had ambushed Luke and Alex on Orrik's orders—or more likely, in exchange for Orrik's silver? The Saxon bailiff had been outraged at the prospect of a Norman master, and Luke was certain he wouldn't stop short of murder to achieve his ends.

If Orrik *had* arranged for the attack, he would want to keep his involvement a secret at all costs, knowing how the Normans would punish him if he were found out. Vance would have to have been eliminated before he could testify at the hallmoot.

Luke hadn't suspected Orrik of killing Vance at the time, because he wasn't anywhere near Hauekleah that night . . . or was he? According to what the Widow Aefentid had told Faithe, Orrik often spent the night with her on the way home from his trips. Her inn was just on the other side of the woods. Baldric could easily have ridden there and reported Vance's capture to Orrik. Who was to say the bailiff hadn't sneaked back to Hauekleah in the dead of night, hanged Vance, and returned to the widow's inn, only to drive his new cart back in the morning as if he hadn't been here in days? Baldric might have helped him execute the ugly deed, or perhaps he'd merely stood guard; Orrik was strong enough and vicious enough to hang a man all by himself, especially if he knocked him unconscious first.

Luke shook his head, disgusted with himself for not having figured it out sooner. Of course Vance's "suicide" was Orrik's doing; it was the only explanation that made all the pieces fall into place. Perhaps if he'd come to this conclusion sooner, he'd not be waiting here for Orrik to come back in the middle of the night and attempt the same thing with him.

He brought his ear close to the door again. "I'm tellin' you, Sir Luke wouldn't take his own life!" Nyle was saying. " 'Tis a mortal sin, and anyway, he ain't the type for it."

Baldric just laughed, as if tickled by his brother's naiveté. Indeed, Nyle was good-hearted, but rather simple, and far too trusting.

"Nyle, you go home," Orrik said. "Baldric will keep guard tonight."

Damn. Nyle would have been far easier to manipulate than his brother.

"But . . . Lady Faithe told me to—"

"She's changed her mind," Orrik said smoothly. "She sent me to replace you with Baldric."

Luke doubted that, but Nyle accepted it without question. He bid his brother and the bailiff good night, and then Luke heard his footsteps retreating up the garden walk.

When it was quiet once more, Orrik said, "I'll be back around matins. With rope."

Baldric chuckled.

"He's a shrewd bastard," Orrik warned him. "Don't *you* talk to him, and don't open that door for any reason, do you hear me?"

"Of course not." Baldric sounded genuinely offended.

Orrik lowered his voice ominously, so that Luke had to strain to hear it. "Because if he isn't here when I get back at matins, 'tis you they'll find hanging from that ceiling in the morning. And don't doubt that I'll do it."

"I won't open the door, I swear it!" Baldric promised. "And I won't listen to a word he says. He'll be here."

"See that he is."

Orrik's footsteps faded away.

Chapter 22

Luke took advantage of the last few moments of light to survey his surroundings. He kicked sacks and rolled barrels aside, looking for anything heavy or sharp, anything to use as a weapon. No doubt Orrik had searched the storehouse before they'd left him here; nothing of any use was left behind.

He stamped a foot against the earthen floor. It was packed almost as hard as stone from decades of having heavy goods piled atop it, but he might be able to dig beneath the wall . . . that is, if he had a tool to dig with, and a day or more to accomplish the task.

He went up to the door. "Baldric!"

No answer.

"I'm thirsty. There wasn't enough wine in that skin. My throat's parched."

Silence.

"Be a good fellow and bring me some water."

Nothing. Baldric was having none of it. He was smart to be cautious, for Luke had no interest in assuaging his thirst; it was freedom he sought. And he had every confidence that he could take Baldric easily. Clearly, Baldric knew this, too, for his entreaties were met with stony silence.

"I understand," Luke called through the door. "Orrik doesn't want you opening this door. But I really am desperately thirsty. I'll tell you what. I've got a purse full of silver in my tunic. You can have it if only you bring me a cup of water."

A long pause, then: "How much silver?"

"My purse is bulging with it," Luke lied; he had naught but a few pennies on his person. "You should take it now, before Orrik comes back. That way you won't have to split it with him. You'll have it all to yourself. And all I ask is a bit of water."

Luke wasn't under the illusion that Baldric would actually bring him any water, but the opportunity to steal a purseful of silver might be worth the risk of opening the door. The knave would probably arm himself first, but Luke had disarmed his share of men.

"Nay," Baldric finally said. "Ain't worth Orrik's wrath if something goes wrong."

Luke continued in this vein for a while longer, despite the silence from the other side of the door. He finally gave up when it became apparent that Baldric had no intention of responding to him anymore.

Time passed slowly. Night fell, plunging Luke's makeshift prison into complete darkness save for a ribbon of moonlight filtering in from the vent hole. As Luke paced restlessly, he wondered about Alex. Where had Firdolf taken him, and why had he been so hesitant to do so? Unless Luke could get out of this storehouse, he strongly suspected that neither he nor his brother would see another dawn.

He'd never hold Faithe again, never smell her enigmatic almond-thyme scent, never feel her laugh while he was inside her, never explain any of this. He'd never have the chance to make her understand, to make her love him again. All that would remain of him would be a tragic memory of the man who'd slain her husband then deceived her.

Somehow that tormented him even more than the notion of dying. As a soldier, he'd come to grips a long time ago with his own mortality. In fact, at one time he might have been able to give himself up to death and feel as if there was a certain justice in it, given the Black Dragon's many sins. But he wasn't the Black Dragon anymore. Through Faithe, he'd discovered that he could be like other men; he could live a normal life, could love and be loved. No longer did he feel a murderous monster clawing from within, trying to get out. He didn't deserve to die, not this way, and not without reconciling with Faithe.

A faint sound drew his attention to the back wall. He stood beneath the vent hole and listened. There it was again, a kind of scraping from outside, a soft grunt . . .

Whispering?

Yes, someone was whispering. It was a high-pitched voice; Luke's heart seized up. "Faithe?" he called softly.

"Nay, milord." A little face appeared in the vent hole. " 'Tis I!"

"Felix? How did you get up there? Do you have a ladder?"

"Nay, milord. I'm standing on Alfrith's shoulders, and Alfrith's standing on Bram's shoulders."

"What if Baldric finds you here?"

"We sneaked around back. He didn't see us. I mean to get you out of there. The other boys said they'd help."

"Nay, 'tis too dangerous. Go home, all of you."

Felix shook his head resolutely. "If it wasn't for me, you wouldn't be in this fix."

Luke actually laughed, so absurd was the notion of his troubles being the fault of this well-meaning child. "I'm perfectly capable of mucking things up all on my own, Felix. What are you doing?"

Felix had squeezed his little head through the vent hole and was in the process of jimmying his arms and shoulders through. "I've got something for you."

"You'll get yourself killed. Go back."

"Milord," he grunted as he wriggled through, "if you wouldn't mind catching me . . ."

Luke had little choice, as Felix was already halfway

through the hole. Grabbing the child, he lowered him to the floor. He could scarcely believe he'd fit through that narrow opening; for once his size had served him well.

Felix reached behind him and pulled something out of his belt, handing it to Luke with an expression of pride. It was a short pickaxe, the type stonecutters used.

"I found it out by the cookhouse," Felix explained. " 'Twas the best I could do by way of a weapon."

"You did well." The pickaxe's iron spike could pierce a skull. "You're a handy man to have around." For all the good it did. Luke had a weapon, but Baldric seemed very determined not to open that door. "Now, let me give you a boost so you can get out of here."

"That won't be necessary, sire."

"You're not staying here, and that's—"

"Baldric!" came a boy's frantic cry from outside. "He's dead! Sir Luke, he's—"

"What's this?" Baldric exclaimed. "What are you little beasts up to? Begone, or I'll—"

"He's dead!"

"Who's dead?"

"Sir Luke! He's gone and kilt himself!"

Luke looked down at Felix, barely visible in the darkness save for his wide, toothy grin. "Your idea?"

"Aye. You might want this." He groped around for the pickaxe and pressed it into Luke's hand.

"Get away from the door," Luke ordered him. "Take that rope and wait in the corner there."

The boy obeyed.

Luke stood to the side of the door.

"What makes you think he's dead?" Baldric demanded.

"We saw him! We climbed up to the vent hole—"

"You *what*? You little—"

"Just to see 'im," the boy said. "But he was

sprawled out on the floor with his eyes half open and a dagger sticking out of his throat."

"He don't have no dagger," Baldric said.

"He must have had it hidden somewheres," said a second boy, sounding remarkably convincing. "Or else someone slipped it to him. But he's dead as a stone."

"As a stone," piped up another voice.

"There's blood everywhere."

"Everywhere."

"Christ's bones," Baldric growled.

"You don't need that knife," one of the boys said loudly, obviously for Luke's benefit. "I told you, he's dead as—"

"Hush!"

Luke heard a metallic jiggling in the lock and braced himself. The door opened slowly. A dark shape eased through. Luke made out an outstretched hand, the glint of steel.

Gripping the pickaxe by its head, Luke slammed the wooden shaft down on Baldric's arm. He dropped the knife and howled in pain. Luke grabbed Baldric by his tunic and yanked him into the storehouse, where he stumbled and fell. He tried to rise, but Luke was already on top of him, the pickaxe's iron spike pressing into the cur's throat.

Baldric sucked in a panicked breath and rasped, "Don't kill me!"

"Kill him! Kill him!" the boys chorused.

Luke cocked his head toward the youngsters. "*They* think I should kill you."

"Nay, please. Please!" Baldric was trembling all over. "I'm begging you, milord!"

"*Milord?* Was I your *lord* when you tied my hands behind my back and locked me in here?"

"I'm sorry, sire, truly I am!" Baldric's eyes were filling with tears.

"Kill him!" the boys demanded, crowding the doorway.

"Perhaps I should hand you over to *them,*" Luke suggested, to spirited agreement from his young audience. "That might be amusing to watch."

"Sire, please!" Baldric wailed. "What can I say? What can I do?"

"You can tell me where my brother is."

Baldric's mouth gulped air; he looked like a carp in a barrel, waiting for the cook. "I . . . I don't rightly know."

Luke turned to the boys. "He's all yours."

"Nay!" Baldric screamed as the boys crowded around. "I mean, I know what Orrik told Firdolf to do with him, I just—"

"What?" Luke demanded. "What were Orrik's orders?"

Baldric's throat bobbed. "Firdolf was to tie him up and gag him, and then dump him in the woods."

Luke swore harshly. With Alex immobilized, and smelling of blood from his head wound, he'd be irresistible prey for the forest predators. "I take it Orrik expected the wolves to finish what he started and didn't have the guts to finish himself."

"Orrik did say as how there wouldn't be much left of him come morning."

"Exactly where did Firdolf leave him?"

"I . . . I don't know, sire. He was to take him deep in the forest, where no one would find him till . . . till there was nothin' left to find."

Luke pressed the spike deeper into Baldric's throat; he gagged and choked. "Don't! Don't kill me!"

"You deserve to die." Slowly, Luke eased up on the pressure. "But I don't deserve to have my conscience sullied with the death of an insect like you."

"Oh, thank you, thank—"

"Felix," Luke said, flopping Baldric onto his stomach, "bring that rope over here. Bram, Alfrith, find me some rags."

Luke tied Baldric's hands and feet, then gagged him

securely. "Mustn't have you drawing undue attention to yourself."

Taking the key off Baldric's belt, and retrieving his knife, Luke shooed the boys out of the storehouse and locked it, then hung the key on the door handle where it would be easily found.

"We'll stand guard over him," Alfrith offered.

"He doesn't need a guard," said Luke. "And I don't want Orrik coming back and finding you here. You're not to speak of this to anybody, do you hear? I don't want any harm coming to you because you helped me."

They grudgingly agreed to keep mum.

"Did any of you see Firdolf take my brother away?"

The boys all nodded. "We all seen him," Alfrith said. "Everyone was watchin'. He trussed Sir Alex up and threw him over a packhorse and took him on down the road into the woods. Them two wenches, the twins—"

"Bonnie and Blossom," one of the older boys supplied with a dreamily lecherous grin.

"They run after him till they couldn't see him no more, then they just sat in the road and cried."

"Has Firdolf returned?"

"Aye," Felix said. "He come back around nightfall."

"Where does he live?"

"In that little hut by the fish pond, the one that's half belowground."

"You're brave and clever fellows," Luke said, "the lot of you."

" 'Twas Felix who planned the whole thing," Bram said, "and talked us into goin' along with it. We reckoned if the runt of the litter"—he slapped his youngest confederate on the back—"had the ballocks for it, we did, too!"

Felix laughed along with the rest of them, his metamorphosis from pariah to comrade now fully realized. In fact, from all appearances, he'd fallen comfortably into the role of leader, despite his size and ignominious history.

"Excellent work, Felix," Luke said. "I'm lucky to have a man with your talents at my disposal."

Felix's chest expanded to twice its size. "Thank you, milord!"

Luke ordered the boys back to their own homes, watching as they dispersed to make sure none of them lingered around the storehouse to "stand guard." Letting Orrik get his hands on them would ill repay them for effecting his escape.

For a few long moments he gazed up at the shuttered windows of Faithe's bedchamber, wondering if it would ever be *their* bedchamber again. He actually took a step toward the house before drawing himself up shortly.

Luke wanted to see her—needed to see her—but now was not the time. Although he was fairly sure he could slip into the house undetected, Alex was out in the middle of the woods somewhere, bound and gagged and waiting for the wolves. They might even have come by now. Getting to him had to take priority over seeing Faithe.

Turning on his heels, Luke sprinted to the fish pond, keeping to the shadows and creating as little noise as possible, and located the sunken hut Felix had directed him to. Only the thatched roof and about two feet of wall were aboveground. Dim light filtered between the ill-fitting slats of wood with which the humble dwelling was constructed. He heard voices from within, and the jabbering of a baby.

Squatting down, Luke whipped aside the bearskin covering the doorway. A woman shrieked; the baby in her arms started crying; a dog barked. Half a dozen faces looked up from bowls of something—it smelled like leeks—that they were eating around the fire pit. None of the faces belonged to Firdolf.

"Milord!" someone said—a man of middle years.

Luke recognized him as Eldred Woodward, Firdolf's father. He grabbed the dog, an enormous black beast—as it tried to lunge for the doorway. Luke had taken a step down into the hut, but backed up swiftly; he'd stay right where he was.

"Where's your son?" Luke demanded, looking from Eldred to his wife, Meghan, busily unlacing her kirtle as she shushed the shrieking infant.

"Beggin' your pardon, milord," Eldred said as he struggled to hold tight to the rope around the snarling cur's neck, "but I thought you was locked up in the storehouse."

"Not anymore."

Eldred smiled and nodded, seeming perfectly satisfied with that answer. "That's a right ugly eye you got there, sire."

"Where's Firdolf?" Luke repeated.

"Dunno," Eldred said.

"I know he's been back."

"Aye, he come back," Meghan said as she withdrew a ripe breast and shoved the nipple into the babe's mouth, instantly quieting him. "But then his sweetheart come for him, and he went out again."

"She ain't his sweetheart," a young girl said with an elaborate roll of her eyes. "He just wishes she was." She snickered, and her siblings joined in.

"Are you talking about . . ." Which twin was it that Firdolf had taken a fancy to?

"Blossom," the girl supplied. "She wears the one braid."

"Aye, that's the one." Meghan leaned over her suckling babe to spoon some soup into her mouth.

"When did she come for him?" Luke asked, shifting his weight as he squatted in the doorway.

"Right after he come back," Eldred said.

The dog writhed and growled, baring long, discolored teeth. It had yellow eyes, like a wolf. Luke thought about Alex lying in the dark woods, bound and gagged, and shivered.

"He up and left in the blink of an eye," the girl said, grinning.

"I would too, if she'd of come for me," Eldred muttered under his breath. Meghan lifted her skirt and shot a foot out, catching him in the shin. "Ow!"

"Do you know where they went?"

There came a flurry of shaking heads.

"He were gone just like that," Meghan said.

"Just like that," her daughter echoed.

Luke sighed. "Where do they live, the twins?"

"They've got a place all their own," Meghan said, "on account of their parents is dead and their older sisters is all married off. 'Tis back behind Hauekleah Hall, near the punfold, where the stray animals are kept. They've got flowers growin' in a trough out front."

Luke retraced his steps swiftly, cursing every moment's delay in getting to Alex. He gave Hauekleah Hall as wide a berth as possible as he darted quietly among the house servants' cottages until he came to the one Meghan had described.

Through the cottage's open window he saw the twin with two braids, Bonnie, stuffing bread and cheese and fruit into a satchel by the light of a lantern as she stood at a table.

He entered the cottage without knocking. Bonnie squealed and dropped the satchel. "Oh, 'tis you, milord!" she whispered. "How'd you get out of the storehouse? Oh, look at your poor eye!"

"Where's your sister?"

She pressed a finger to her lips and cut her eyes toward a curtain stretched across the width of the cottage, dividing it in half.

"In there? Is he with her?"

"You mean Firdolf? Aye, but—"

Luke strode toward the curtain, but she grabbed him by the tunic.

"Let me go!" He twisted out of her grasp. "I'm going to make him tell me where he left Alex."

Bonnie coughed delicately. "Blossom's already set herself to that task, milord."

A muffled moan came from beyond the curtain, a man's moan. Bed ropes squeaked.

"Ah," Luke said.

"He didn't want to tell her what he done with Sir Alex, 'cause Orrik told him not to, and he's afraid of Orrik." She gazed up at him through lowered lashes. "But Blossom can usually change a fellow's mind about things."

Feminine whispers floated through the curtain.

"Oh," Firdolf groaned. "Oh . . . oh God."

Bonnie took a step toward Luke and reached up to gingerly touch the stinging flesh around his eye. "What a nasty thing to do to such a lovely eye," she cooed. "Does it hurt?"

"Nay," he lied, backing up until he felt the table behind him.

She made tsking sounds as she drew closer. "You mustn't deny it. I know how it must pain you. I'd dearly love to make it better."

Her hands stole up to rest on his shoulders. He took them and lowered them to her sides. "The Lady Faithe tends to my wounds. Just her."

Bonnie smiled slowly. "How lucky for her," she murmured.

"Oh, yes!" Firdolf gasped. "Yes! Oh my God, Blossom!" The squeaking quickened, keeping time with his harsh breathing.

Bonnie continued to smile at Luke. He slid sideways to put some distance between them. Turning, he indicated the satchel full of food. "Do you mean to take that to Alex?"

"Aye, soon as we find out where he is."

"Hold still," Firdolf growled. "Yes . . . yes . . ."

"I should think you'll have your answer soon," Luke observed.

"What are you doing?" Firdolf explained in breathless outrage. "Come back here! Blossom, for God's sake, I'm just about to—"

"I don't know, Firdy. I just don't feel right enjoying myself like this, knowin' Sir Alex is out there in the middle of the woods somewheres . . ."

Firdolf made a sound between a groan and a whimper. "Blossom, please. You can't stop now."

"I wouldn't, if I knew I could go fetch him after we're done here, but I don't even know where to find him, and you won't tell me. Perhaps if you told me . . ."

"He's in the woods to the southwest. In a clearing. I'll tell you how to get there, just please finish—" He sucked in a breath. "Oh! Yes . . ." The bed ropes set up a furious racket, and presently Firdolf let out an ecstatic howl the likes of which Luke had never heard before.

Moments later, the curtain flew open. Blossom stood there, wearing a dressing gown that hid little, inasmuch as it was open down the front. On a large bed behind her, Firdolf sprawled naked, his eyes closed, his chest still heaving.

Blossom smiled with delight when she saw Luke. "Milord! You got out!"

Firdolf bolted upright, gaping at Luke and clutching the sheet between his legs.

"You poor thing," Blossom purred as she approached Luke. "Look at your eye."

Bonnie cleared her throat and indicated her sister's open robe. "Blossom, sweetie . . ."

"Oh. Right." Blossom's movements were unhurried as she covered herself and tied the sash. "Good news. Firdolf's agreed to tell us where he put Sir Alex." She turned toward her bed partner, who continued to stare at Luke in abject terror. "Ain't that right, Firdy?"

The young man appeared to be nodding his head, but he might have just been shaking.

"Firdy?" Luke prompted.

"Right!" he croaked, bobbing his head up and down. "I'm sorry, sire, I was only doin' what Orrik told me. I didn't want to . . ."

Luke strode toward him purposefully, causing him to shield his head with an arm. "Just tell me where he is," Luke said.

"In . . . in the woods southwest of here."

"I know that. How do I find him?"

"T-take the road till you come to the second stream, and follow it south. When it b-branches, go right. When you see the stand of birch, leave the stream and ride straight for the tall boulder. There's a kind of clearing beyond there that dips down, like a little valley. That's where I put him."

Turning away, Luke grabbed the satchel off the table on his way out the door, ignoring Firdolf's litany of apologies and the twins' pleading to come with him. "Don't tell anyone I was here."

The stable was close by, and blessedly deserted. Saddling up his mount and Alex's, which he led by the reins, he followed Firdolf's directions through the woods, guiding himself by the bright moonlight.

Relief consumed him when he spied the tall boulder that marked the drop-off to the clearing where Firdolf had left Alex.

And then he heard the growls.

Chapter 23

The silvery beasts slinked in the moonlight, circling their quarry as wolves were wont to do. Luke had to strain to make out the dark form in their midst, obscured as he was by tall grasses. Alex lay on his side, his hands and feet tied, a white cloth wrapped around his mouth. The grassy hollow was larger than Luke had expected; his brother was a good hundred yards away.

As Luke rode forward, a wolf broke away from the pack and lunged for Alex, only to retreat when his prey kicked out with his bound feet. They'd probably been harrying him this way for some time—feinting in and out while they worked up their collective courage to attack; although ruthless hunters, wolves tended to be wary of men.

The largest one, less cautious than the others, rushed in and closed its jaws around Alex's leg before he could respond. Luke kicked his horse into a gallop as the wolf pulled and tugged, ripping Alex's chausses; Luke saw dark smears of blood on his brother's calf. This success emboldened some of the others; they pounced on their helpless victim with ravenous growls.

The animals who'd hung back to watch all scattered when Luke reined in his mount and jumped down. The four who'd closed in on Alex merely bared their fangs, their hackles raised, low rumbles of warning issuing from them.

"Over here!" Luke yelled, waving his arms. The

large one took a few lazy, menacing steps toward him. He withdrew Baldric's knife—an inadequate weapon, but all he had—and held it at the ready. "Come on! Come on, you godforsaken curs!"

The big wolf leapt; Luke ducked and rolled, slashing out with the knife. A canine yelp told him he'd done at least a little damage. A ripping sound, along with a hot sting of pain on his shoulder, told him the damage wasn't one-sided.

The great beast turned and charged again. Luke dropped the useless knife and wrapped his hands around a big rock, slamming it into the wolf's head as it leapt. A chilling howl rose from it as it staggered back. Heaving the rock overhead, Luke delivered a final, mortal blow; the animal trembled and went slack.

Still holding the bloodied rock, Luke turned to face the three remaining wolves, all stealthily retreating. He lifted it high, roaring at the top of his lungs for good measure. The wolves darted away, three streaks of silver dissolving into the night.

Throwing down the rock, Luke located the knife and slid it beneath his brother's gag, slicing it off with one stroke.

"That's six," Alex said.

"Six what?" Luke cut through the ropes knotted around Alex's wrists and ankles.

"Six times you've saved my life. And I haven't saved yours once." Alex sat up awkwardly, with a little help from Luke. "You'll have to slow down, so I have a chance to catch up."

"If I slow down," Luke observed, "you'll end up dead, and you never will have the chance to catch up."

Alex grinned crookedly. "Good point. Anyway, thanks." He clapped Luke on the shoulder, igniting a jolt of pain that made him gasp. "Damn," Alex muttered, looking at the blood on his hand. "Son of a bitch got you."

"You, too." Luke peeled aside the shredded remnants of wool clinging to the gash on his brother's calf. Luckily, it was shallow.

"Then there's Orrik's handiwork," Alex said, indicating Luke's head wound and swollen eye and the purpling knot on his own forehead.

"I wouldn't mind paying him back for that," Luke grunted as he got to his feet.

"And I can't say I'd mind helping you." Alex let Luke help him to stand up and mount his horse. He laughed like the Devil when Luke told him how Blossom had coaxed his whereabouts out of Firdolf. "He's been sniffing around her all summer."

"You're not jealous?" Luke asked as they rode across the clearing toward the woods.

"Serves me right. I've been greedy, keeping both girls for myself. Besides, she did it for me, and I actually think she's a little sweet on that fellow. Of course," he added with a grin, "she's a little sweet on just about anything in chausses. She and her sister both. Don't tell me they haven't rubbed up against *you* from time to time."

"I won't," Luke said dryly.

Alex laughed again. "But I take it you resisted their charms."

"I'm married."

"You sound like Father," Alex said, his voice quietly mocking. Before Luke could retort, he added, "That's a compliment. He was a good man, and he knew what was important in life. There are worse fates than being like him." As they entered the woods, he asked, "Where to now, brother?"

"Foxhyrst," Luke answered immediately. "I'll turn myself over to Alberic and demand to be taken to London for trial by King William."

Alex made a face. "Wouldn't you rather go back to Hauekleah and give Orrik a spoonful of his own tonic?"

"And then what? I've admitted publicly that I killed Caedmon. Do you think Faithe can simply go on as if nothing has happened? I've deceived her horribly. I've got to make up for all the lying and covering up, got to undo the damage and win her back."

Alex shook his head in resignation. "All right, but why put yourself in Alberic's hands? The man despises you. Why not ride to London on your own and present yourself to the king?"

"Protocol demands that I surrender myself to the sheriff and that he brings me to the king. Don't worry. Alberic hates me, it's true, but he would never risk William's wrath by taking matters into his own hands."

"I hope you're right."

"I'm going to do everything the proper way for once, so that there can be no question of my good intentions. I've got to get everything out in the open—be tried in the king's court, explain things, and be officially exonerated." He took a deep breath. "When all of that is behind me, I can work on . . . winning Faithe back. Regaining her love."

"Assuming you've lost it."

"Any other assumption," Luke said grimly, "would be the most pathetic wishful thinking."

Upon returning to Hauekleah, Faithe woke up young Bert, who slept in the stable. He blinked in drowsy confusion when he saw her standing over him in the dark, holding her mare's reins. "Milady! Is that you?"

"Tend to Daisy." She handed him the reins. "I rode her too hard."

"Wh-what hour is it, milady?" Bert asked as she walked away.

"Nearly matins, I should think." *Nearly matins,* she reflected as she made her way by moonlight to Hauekleah Hall. It was the middle of the night, and she was as exhausted as her horse, and greatly troubled. She'd covered many miles searching for Alex, only to find no evidence that he'd been that way. This did not bode well.

Detouring to the kitchen, she procured a wineskin and some bread, then lit a lantern and carried it out the back door to the moonlit croft. As she approached the storehouse, she hesitated. Nyle was nowhere to be seen. When she saw the keys dangling from the door handle, she was truly puzzled.

She knocked on the door. "Luke?"

No answer came.

"Luke?"

Dread crept up her spine. She couldn't shake the image of Vance hanging from the rafters of this very storehouse. Her fingers shook as she turned the key in the lock and pushed the door open.

Holding the lantern before her like a talisman, she stepped into the storehouse. "Luke?"

Faithe dropped the wine and bread when she saw him, bound and gagged on the dirt floor. The realization that he wasn't Luke but Baldric, brought a moment's relief, but . . .

"Where is Luke?"

Baldric, thrashed and grunted. Setting the lantern down, she pulled off his gag and began untying him. "Where is my husband? What's happened to him?"

"Obviously," intoned a voice from behind her, "he's escaped."

Faithe turned to find Orrik blocking the doorway, his hands fisted on his hips, his eerily luminous eyes fixed on Baldric.

"I . . . I'm sorry, Master Orrik, truly I am, but he tricked me! He used them kids. They told me—"

"You whine like a weasel, Baldric. Have you no shame?"

Baldric stood and rubbed his wrists, looking terrified. " 'Twasn't my fault, master, I swear it!"

"Of course it was your fault," Orrik said with deadly calm. "Didn't I tell you not to talk to him? Didn't I tell you not to open the door?"

"Aye, but I just . . ."

"You *just* disobeyed me. And now our prisoner has escaped. And it's all your fault."

"I . . . I can explain! Truly I—"

"Go," Orrik commanded, and pinned Baldric with his steely gaze. "I'll deal with you on the morrow."

The bailiff stood aside just enough for Baldric to creep through the doorway.

"What was Baldric doing here?" Faithe demanded. "I specifically told you he wasn't to come anywhere near—"

"Nyle fell down on the job," Orrik said. "I had to replace him, and Baldric was the only man available."

"I'm sick to death of your lies, Orrik!"

"My lady—"

"What have you done with Luke? Did you hang him?"

Orrik's face darkened. "On my mother's soul, I did no such thing. I haven't laid eyes on him since I locked him up in here. And I daresay I never will again. Neither will you." He nodded knowingly. "Aye, we've seen the last of your *lord husband,* I'll wager. He's well on his way to Bulverhythe Harbor by now. By the time the sun has risen, he'll be on a boat, crossing the Channel. A man can disappear very easily on the Continent. He'll never be brought to justice now, but the Normans would have mucked up the job anyway. 'Tis just as well this way." He spat on the ground. "Good riddance to—"

"Shut up, Orrik."

He stiffened his stance, but gentled his voice. "Now, my lady, don't be getting all—"

"All what?" she demanded in an unsteady voice. "My husband has . . . has disappeared, and all you can say is—"

"He didn't disappear, Faithe. He escaped. There's a difference."

"And what of Alex?" she demanded. "What happened to him?"

"I already told you. He got on his horse and rode—"

"I've spent half the night riding west, Orrik, and there was no sign of him."

Orrik looked momentarily stunned. "You didn't believe me? You went out at this time of night, alone—"

"Of course. I have no reason to believe you anymore. What really happened to Alex, Orrik?"

He thrust his jaw out. "He rode away, just like I said. If you didn't find him, 'twas merely because he was fleeing like a rat, worried I'd change my mind and come after him."

She sighed heavily. "I'll never find out the truth from you—about Alex *or* Luke."

"Your husband escaped, and that *is* the truth."

"I'm sick of listening to you."

She lifted her lantern and tried to squeeze past him through the doorway, but he blocked the way. "He tricked Baldric and escaped, and do you want to know why?"

"Shut up! I'm tired of your explanations, your . . . your heartless logic."

"The truth can be heartless, my dear, but it *is* the truth, and it bears a little respect now and then. Luke de Périgueux escaped because he couldn't face the king's court. He knew that if his vicious crime were scrutinized in the open, he'd be found out for what he is—a murdering beast, without conscience or remorse."

"Shut up!"

"Not that his beloved King William would have meted out the punishment he deserved for such an offense. He might not have even been found guilty—officially. But they would have known. They all would have found out what he really is. That's what he fears. That's why he escaped."

"Shut up!" She slammed a fist into his chest, but he didn't even flinch.

"Don't you see? That he escaped proves his guilt. He's afraid to stand trial."

"Perhaps he's merely afraid of what you'll do when my back is turned."

Orrik shook his head. "I can't believe you're still defending him. He admitted killing Caedmon, yet you still think him the beleaguered innocent. You still want to give him the opportunity to avoid punishment for what he did."

"I want to see justice served."

"So do I," Orrik said solemnly. "But it's too late for that. Luke de Périgueux has eluded justice." He closed his hands over her shoulders and said quietly. "All we can do now is go on with our lives. In a way, he's done you a favor by sneaking off this way. You'll never see him again. You can put him out of your mind. Forget he was ever here."

Forget Luke? The notion was too ludicrous to contemplate. She could no more put him out of her mind than she could forget to breathe. He'd become a part of her. Everything he was, everything he'd done, was intimately connected with her now.

"I need to find out the truth," she told Orrik.

"You need to forget," he said. "But for now, you need to sleep. 'Tis late. You're tired. We'll talk again in the morning, when you're rested. I'll come by around terce."

By terce she'd be halfway to Winstow, looking for the truth, but it would be the height of folly to share her plans with Orrik. "I'll see you then," she said and went upstairs to her chamber to wait out the rest of the night.

It was midday by the time she arrived at the oil merchant's shop. She found Dunstan upstairs, tending to his sister. The poor woman's wasting disease had transformed her into a virtual skeleton covered in skin the color of yellowed parchment.

" 'Tis only a matter of days now," Dunstan whispered as he closed the curtain that separated Audris's sickroom from the kitchen.

"I'm sorry," Faithe said as she took a seat at the table.

"I pray that God will take her soon." He poured them each a tankard of ale. "I've made some soup."

"I'm not hungry," she lied, remembering the stew.

"Is all well at Hauekleah?" he asked.

"Hardly." Faithe told Dunstan about the discovery of the pin, Luke's horrible confession, and his subsequent escape from the storeroom. The young reeve appeared deeply shaken by this news. "When I was here last," she said, "you told me many things . . . but you kept some to yourself. I know you were trying to protect my feelings, but I need to know everything now."

"Nay, milady . . ."

"Something happened while you and Caedmon and Orrik were waiting for William's forces to cross the Channel. I think it had something to do with . . . a woman. A prostitute. You wouldn't tell me then. You must tell me now."

" 'Twould tarnish his memory," Dunstan said. "The man was . . . he was ill."

"Was he mad?"

Dunstan stared into his ale. "Some diseases ravage the mind as well as the body. I've seen it with Audris. The things she says, when she manages to talk to me . . . most of the time, they make no sense. Caedmon . . . he was getting that way. Those headaches maddened him."

"I understand he suffered from seizures and double vision."

"Aye, but 'twas more than that. He'd complain of the oddest things, like not being able to taste his food.

He seemed drunk a lot of the time, even if he hadn't had a drop."

Faithe leaned across the table. "Tell me. I appreciate that you want to safeguard Caedmon's memory, but he's dead, and Luke is alive. I need to understand what happened that night in Cottwyk, for his sake as well as my own. If what you're keeping from me has a bearing on that—"

"It may." Dunstan took a deep, unsteady breath. " 'Twas about a fortnight before Hastings. King Harold and most of his men were in the north, fighting the Danes who invaded right before William, but he'd commanded some of us to remain in the south. We were spending the night at an inn in a tiny village—Ixbridge, I think it was. We all slept downstairs, but Lord Caedmon, because of his rank, got a private chamber upstairs. There was a woman there, a woman who . . . sold herself. Her name was Matfrid. He spent the night with her." Dunstan looked at her inquiringly, as if asking whether she wanted him to go on.

Faithe nodded. *Hear this out. Don't let him see how this affects you, or he'll never tell you the rest.*

"During the night, we heard screams. Horrible . . ." He shook his head. "We went upstairs to Caedmon's room, and . . ."

"He was attacking her?" Faithe asked in a choked whisper.

Dunstan nodded. "With a knife."

"Oh, my God."

"We got it away from him. He'd cut her face."

Faithe covered her mouth with a hand and squeezed her eyes shut.

"We had to pay her two shillings and move on," Dunstan said. "That was the only time he'd been like that. I mean, he'd been more hostile than usual before that, picking fights with us and all, but after Ixbridge . . . well, we knew then that something was very wrong with him."

"Orrik was there that night?"

Dunstan nodded. "He ordered us to keep quiet about it. Caedmon was subdued after that. He didn't call much attention to himself till he disappeared from Hastings."

Faithe let out a pent-up breath and rubbed her forehead.

" 'Twas wrong to keep it a secret, I know that now. But you must understand, Orrik was only thinking of you. He loves you like a daughter. If he's made mistakes, it's been for that reason only."

"I know," she said. "That's what makes all this so hard."

Orrik was waiting for Faithe in the doorway of Hauekleah Hall upon her return that afternoon, a folded sheet of parchment in his hand. "Where have you been, milady? I've been worried about you."

"You worry about me far too much," she said meaningfully. "I know about Ixbridge."

His eyes widened and then closed. "Faithe . . ."

"You had no business keeping that from me, Orrik—especially in light of what Luke said about Caedmon. If he attacked a woman once, he could do it again. Luke was telling the truth about what happened in Cottwyk. You knew it, but you said nothing. Why, Orrik?"

At length he opened his eyes. He looked more melancholy than she'd ever seen him. "I was only thinking of you, Faithe. De Périgueux means nothing to me, less than nothing. He's the enemy. You're . . ." He took a step toward her, arms outstretched; she stepped back. "You're my little girl, Faithe. My wee lass. I didn't want you to be hurt."

"Losing Luke would hurt me, Orrik—worse even than finding out . . . what Caedmon did. Caedmon was sick, and his illness drove him mad. Didn't you think I could understand that?"

"I didn't want you to have to," he said hollowly. "Only Dunstan and I knew what Caedmon had become. I didn't want you to know, and I didn't want it to become public knowledge, what Caedmon did in Ixbridge. I thought 'twould be better than way."

"Ignorance is never better."

He nodded slowly, his gaze on the sheet of parchment in his hand.

"What is that?" she asked.

He handed it to her. "A letter from Lord Alberic."

The seal was broken. She looked at Orrik.

"You weren't here," he said reticently. "I thought it might be important."

She unfolded the letter. Alberic's clerk always wrote to her in Latin rather than French, assuming, perhaps, that she couldn't understand the vernacular of her new Norman masters.

"It's about de Périgueux," Orrik said. "He turned himself in to Lord Alberic."

"What? When?"

"This morning."

"You see? He *wasn't* afraid of a fair trial!" Faithe scanned the letter as Orrik briefed her on its contents.

"According to Alberic," the bailiff said, "your lord husband showed up at Foxhyrst Castle shortly after dawn, demanding to be taken to London and tried in the *curia Regis*—William's own court. However, Alberic seems to have other plans."

"Oh, no." Faithe swiftly read through the letter. The king's court, Alberic maintained, was overburdened with matters involving King William's barons and knights. Such matters could just as properly be considered the responsibility of the king's commissioners—his sheriffs and itinerant justices—who were authorized to dispense high justice in the king's name. Since Alberic's jurisdiction as sheriff encompassed Hauekleah, he would take it upon himself to pass judgment on the murder of Lord Caedmon. A panel of jurors was being assembled so that the matter could be adjudicated in Alberic's shire court at Foxhyrst Castle beginning tomorrow morning. Lady Faithe was welcome to attend the proceedings, or to send a representative if she preferred.

"Tomorrow morning!" Faithe exclaimed. "So soon?"

" 'Tis best that the matter be dispensed with quickly," Orrik said.

"This is bad," Faithe murmured. "Alberic hates Luke. Did you notice the words he used? 'Crime.' 'Murder.' Luke will never get a fair trial from this man."

Orrik stroked his beard thoughtfully. "A pity."

Faithe shot him a look.

"I mean it," he said, looking hurt. "All I want is justice. I know that must be difficult for you to believe, after everything that's happened. 'Tis my own fault." He looked at the ground. "I . . . reacted rashly when Sir Luke confessed to the killing. My concern was for you, but you're right. I was misguided. I hope someday you can find it in your heart to forgive me."

"It's too late for forgiveness, Orrik," she said quietly. "Too much has happened. And, no matter what you say now, I know you'll never find it in your heart to accept Luke as your master."

"You're assuming he'll return to Hauekleah," Orrik said.

"I intend to see that he does." She refolded Alberic's letter. "Do you know where Nyle is?"

"Why?"

"I can't be in Foxhyrst tomorrow morning. I'll be . . . somewhere else. But I need to get a message to Alberic."

"I'll take it."

"Nay."

"You've truly lost all trust in me, haven't you?" he asked.

" 'Twas your doing, Orrik," she replied sadly. "I'd trust that snake, Baldric, before I'd trust you."

Orrik shifted his gaze and cleared his throat. "Baldric is dead."

"Dead! What happened?"

"We found him hanging by his neck in the storehouse this morning."

"Hanging! Like . . ."

"Like Vance. Aye."

"But . . . why?"

"The only thing I can figure is he must have been consumed by guilt for having let de Périgueux escape. I *told* him not to open the door, not for any reason. Shame can drive a man to such an act."

"My God," she whispered, not because she believed him, but because she didn't. Baldric was incapable of feeling shame. A wily little toad, he would never have taken his own life, for any reason. And, if Baldric didn't hang himself, she knew full well who did. She'd have to decide what to do about this, but right now her overriding concern was Luke; she would take care of Orrik later.

"Nyle is beside himself over his brother's death," Orrik said, "and of course he's got to bury him. No one else can be spared. Except for me, of course."

"I told you—no."

"Faithe . . . I . . ." Orrik shook his head in evident frustration. "I'm sorry. Truly I am. For everything. I was wrong. I reacted angrily, and in haste. But I repent all that now—especially seeing the mistrust in your eyes. It cuts me to the quick, that it does. Give me a chance to prove myself. Let me take your message to Alberic."

"I'll find someone else," she said. "In the meantime, you're to remain at Hauekleah. You're not to leave here until I return. I'll deal with you then. Do you understand?"

Orrik executed one of his impudent little bows. "All too well, my lady."

Chapter 24

Luke tried not to flinch when Ham, the hangman, lifted the red-hot pincers from the brazier and held them in front of his face.

"And this here," Ham said, turning the fiery instrument slowly as he examined it with deep-set rodent eyes, "is what I'm going to use to tear the flesh from your body, bit by bit."

Luke breathed in the smell of superheated iron, felt its stinging heat—but he stood still, unwilling to give the bastard the satisfaction of seeing him cringe. He did shift his wrists reflexively against the manacles that bound his hands behind his back, which made his shoulder wound burn with pain.

Jerking his gaze away from the sinister device, Luke scanned the cavelike cellar of Foxhyrst Castle, refurbished by Lord Alberic into a proper Norman-style torture chamber. Chains hung from the ceiling; an iron chair fitted with restraints stood in a corner, and next to it a set of leg vises; a ladder for dislocating the limbs leaned at an angle against the damp stone wall next to the subterranean cell in which Luke had spent the night—another night with next to no sleep.

"And when I get done with that," Ham said, his breath hot and foul on Luke's face, "I aim to chain you up and flog you till there ain't no skin left on your back."

With his free hand, Ham reached into the pouch on his belt, withdrew some dried leaves—Luke smelled catnip—and tossed them into his mouth. He was a hulking creature with a hairless head that sprouted from his shoulders without the benefit of a neck. The lack of hair was evidently deliberate; Luke could make out a dusting of coppery stubble all over the milk-white scalp.

"Then maybe," Ham said as he chewed, "I'll gouge out one of your eyes, the one that's already swole up, and cut off one of your ears—just one each, so's you can still hear and see what's happenin' to you. Then I'll pour brandy on your hair and set it on fire." Ham swallowed and grinned, displaying a sparse mouthful of yellowing teeth. "So's you'll look like me. That'll begin to pay you back some for killin' my sister."

"I didn't kill your—"

Ham drove a giant fist into Luke's stomach, landing him on his back in the sawdust. He gasped for air as the pain and nausea receded.

"Helig died runnin' away from you." Ham squatted over Luke, holding the pincers over his face. "You killed her just as dead as if you'd stuck a knife in her gut. And I aim to make you suffer for it."

"I haven't even been tried yet, much less found guilty." Luke had come to Foxhyrst Castle yesterday and formally surrendered himself to Alberic, for transport to the king's court, only to be handed over to Ham for incarceration. At dawn the hangman had dragged him out of his dank oubliette and announced that he was to be tried in Alberic's shire court that very day—no doubt so that "justice" could be dispensed before William caught wind of it. Luke had expected to be taken upstairs immediately, but instead Ham had treated him to this little demonstration of the punishments in store for him once he was found guilty—punishments that would conclude with a public hanging.

For the hundredth time since coming here, Luke chastised himself for ignoring Alex's advice and putting himself in Alberic's hands rather than riding directly to London. At first, he couldn't believe the sheriff was actually going to try him, a knight of the realm, in his own shire court. He had to know that William would be furious when he discovered his power being usurped this way. For a fawning little worm like Alberic to risk the king's wrath didn't make any sense. Alberic hated Luke because of the display of cowardice Luke had witnessed at Hastings, but Luke had never made public what he'd seen. He'd thought his discretion would protect him from Alberic's retribution, but clearly he'd been wrong about that. Most likely Alberic greatly feared Luke—or rather, what Luke knew about him and might someday reveal.

"You *will* be found guilty," Ham said, with seemingly complete confidence. "And then you'll be handed over to me. Perhaps I should give you a little taste of what's in store for you tonight." He brought the pincers closer, until their glowing tips were poised a hairsbreadth from Luke's nose.

"Easy, Ham," came a smooth-voiced command from the winding corner stairwell. Luke and the hangman both turned to find Alberic, in fur-trimmed silk, leaning carelessly against the wall, two guards towering over him. "There will be plenty of time for this sort of thing after the trial."

Ham grabbed Luke by his tunic and yanked him to his feet. "I'll *need* plenty of time to do it right."

Alberic chuckled. "Ham displays remarkable enthusiasm for the work, especially for one of his race. The English are a rather uninspired lot when it comes to such matters. When I arrived here, his idea of torture was forcing a prisoner to stay awake all night, or walking him around and around in circles. But he's caught on surprisingly well to our Norman methods . . . surprisingly well."

"I don't doubt it," said Luke as he watched Ham withdraw another dose of catnip from his pouch.

"Bring him upstairs," Alberic instructed the guards. "We're ready to begin."

By midday, any lingering hope for a fair trial that Luke might have entertained was long gone. For hours he'd stood in the center of Foxhyrst Castle's gloomy hall, flanked by the massive guards, his hands still shackled behind him, watching and listening as Alberic went through the motions of "trying" him. Seated at the high table on either side of the sheriff were a dozen soldiers unknown to Luke but owing allegiance to Alberic, his far from impartial jury. Alex, who'd accompanied Luke to Foxhyrst, was nowhere to be seen; presumably he'd been banned from the proceedings. Griswold and his other former mates were likewise absent. And as for Faithe . . . well, he wouldn't have expected her to come, and in a way he was glad she hadn't. Although he was desperate to see her, this travesty would be all the more humiliating if she were here to witness it.

Charges were read, questions asked, "witnesses" trotted forth. The man who'd found Caedmon's body testified that Caedmon had been beaten to death "over the whore." Other Cottwyk citizens upheld his account and described how they'd come across Helig's body after she'd "run for her life" from the murderer. They all glanced uncomfortably toward Luke, as if they couldn't believe he was the man responsible. Alberic's clerk, who sat next to him and apparently understood the Anglo-Saxon tongue, translated their testimony for his lordship and the jury.

At nones, a guard came into the hall, bowed to Alberic, and murmured something. "Indeed," Alberic said. "Show him in."

Luke turned with the others to find Orrik being led forward, a sealed letter in his hand. The bailiff spared a smug glance for Luke as he approached the high table and handed the missive to Alberic. "A message from my lady Faithe of Hauekleah," he said, without bowing.

A message from Faithe? Suddenly alert, Luke watched with interest as Alberic broke the seal and unfolded the parchment, then handed it to the clerk, a diminutive, tonsured fellow in black robes. He read it with an expression of intense concentration, then leaned over to whisper into Alberic's ear.

The sheriff's frown transformed gradually into a sly smile. Luke felt chilly.

"It seems," Alberic began, glancing around the table, "that Sir Luke's lady wife feels compelled to add certain comments to the proceedings." Meeting Luke's gaze, he said, " 'Twould appear that Lady Faithe shares the general consensus regarding her husband's temperament and inclinations. She characterizes him as 'savage,' 'vicious,' and"—he leaned toward the little clerk—"what was that part about being capable of—"

"Capable," the clerk said, reading directly from the letter as he traced the words with a finger, "of acts of the most irredeemable brutality. There is no doubt in my mind that Luke de Périgueux murdered my husband, Caedmon of Hauekleah, with no provocation save his own evil nature. I implore your lordship to find him guilty of the crime of murder, and to punish him as befits such an offense."

Luke shook his head. "Nay . . ."

"I'm afraid so." Alberic snatched the letter from his clerk and held it up. "His own wife condemns him as a murderer. Can we do less?"

The soldiers whispered among themselves.

"Let me see that letter!" Luke said.

Alberic glowered at him. "You are in no position to make demands of this court, Luke de Périgueux."

Luke stepped forward. The guards seized him and yanked him back. "I insist on seeing that letter!"

"Remove him from the hall," Alberic told the guards. "We'll reconvene after dinner."

Luke had no idea what the sheriff and his guests dined on. His midday meal, which he didn't eat, consisted of porridge heavily laced with salt and wine that had long since turned to vinegar.

He contemplated the letter from Faithe. Could she have written such things—denounced him so unconditionally? Forcing himself to view the situation from her perspective, he had to concede that it was possible. He'd admitted to killing Caedmon, and never had a chance to explain the circumstances to her. He'd always admired her strength of will. In all likelihood she was calling on that strength now to put him out of her life for good. It made his soul ache to know that she'd so thoroughly abandoned him.

When the trial resumed in the early afternoon, Luke was asked for his version of the killing, and gave it, after which Alberic described it as "the fabrication of a desperate man." Orrik was called upon to give his predictable account of the Black Dragon's many character flaws—his "infinite capacity for violence." He scoffed at the notion that Caedmon had been mad, or even ill, and insisted that he was incapable of attacking a woman. Other Hauekleah servants were called up, all of whom commended their former master for his agreeable nature and peaceful ways. Through translations by his clerk, Alberic encouraged this praise for Caedmon, which Luke found ironic, considering the sheriff's unreasoning hatred of Saxons. He must be very determined to see Luke hang if he was willing to set that hatred aside, even for a moment.

When all the testimony had been delivered, Alberic asked Luke if he felt any remorse at all for having murdered Caedmon.

"I committed no murder," Luke said.

"That's not a proper answer to my question," Alberic said.

" 'Tis the only answer I can give."

Alberic sighed disgustedly. "Take him back to the cellar so I may consult with the jury in private."

Ham took this opportunity to taunt his prisoner with yet more descriptions of the agonies in store for him. Luke tried to be unmoved, reminding himself that escape was impossible now, that all he had left was his dignity. He'd endured pain before, and he'd long ago gotten used to the idea of death. In truth, it was the knowledge that his fragile bond of love with Faithe had been destroyed that truly tormented him. He would go to his death less than whole for having lost that.

The guards came downstairs. "His lordship says they're ready." They escorted Luke back to the hall, where he was made to stand where he'd stood all day, facing the high table. Alberic half hid his smile behind steepled fingers. Orrik, standing off to the side, wore a look of immense self-satisfaction.

Alberic rose. "It is found by the jurors of the shire court of Foxhyrst," he intoned as the clerk took notes, "that the accused Luke de Périgueux did, wrongfully and with malicious intent, slay one Caedmon of Hauekleah in the village of Cottwyk. It is also determined that he did assail the woman known as Helig, who thereupon fled her home and perished most cruelly by lightning. Therefore the said Luke de Périgueux is condemned to death by hanging at dawn tomorrow, after first suffering such varied punishments as the hangman may see fit, in retribution for his impenitence."

"What cause has he for penitence?" came a woman's breathless cry from behind. *Faithe?* Luke wheeled around to find her standing in the doorway. "He's done nothing wrong!"

"Guards, eject that woman!" Alberic ordered.

A man grabbed for her arm. "Let go of her!" Luke roared; the guard recoiled and held his hands up placatingly.

"You invited me here, Lord Alberic." Faithe withdrew a letter from beneath her mantle. Her face was flushed, her hair wild, her clothes in disarray; she had never looked more beautiful to him. "You told me I could attend my husband's trial."

"Or send a representative," Alberic said. "You sent your bailiff, bearing your letter to the court."

"My bailiff! I sent another man with that letter." She frowned at Orrik. "What did you do to him?"

"He was needed elsewhere," Orrik said.

"It matters not," Alberic said. "Your letter was delivered. If you now have cause to regret it, 'tis too late. The trial is concluded, and your husband has been convicted of murder."

"My husband," Faithe said, "is innocent of murder." She met Luke's gaze with a brief look of reassurance, then motioned to someone outside, who followed her into the hall—a woman, humbly dressed and wearing a hooded cloak that cast her face in shadow. "This woman can prove it. She's the woman from Ixbridge whom I referred to in my letter."

"Your letter made no mention of a woman," Alberic sputtered.

"Of course it did. I wrote of the woman Matfrid, from Ixbridge." Faithe nodded toward her companion, who reached up slowly and lowered her hood. She was young and black-haired, and might have been pretty were it not for a knife scar along one cheek and another across her forehead. They looked like the kind of scars that might all but disappear in time; but for now, they were still angry and disfiguring slashes.

Luke saw Orrik's eyes light with recognition when he got a good look at her face. He grimaced, clearly displeased to see her here.

"Matfrid," Faithe said, guiding the young woman

by her arm into the hall, "is the woman who . . . who Caedmon attacked in Ixbridge while he was awaiting battle. I described the incident in my letter."

Alberic addressed his clerk. "Brother Damian, was there anything in that letter about a woman from—"

"Nay, milord!" The little man produced the letter in question. "I swear it!"

"Aye, 'tis all there," Faithe insisted.

"What Saxon trickery is this?" Alberic muttered.

"Watch your tongue when you speak to my wife," Luke growled. He swore Alberic shrank back, despite the fact that Luke was in manacles and surrounded by guards.

"Matfrid," Faithe said in English, urging the girl forward, "tell his lordship what happened. Go ahead, it's all right."

Matfrid stared into the rushes and spoke—so softly that a great quiet descended over the hall. Every man there strained to hear her halting words, although most of them could understand only the clerk's French translation. " 'Twas last autumn. September, it was. They came to the inn where I worked—the one they called Caedmon, and that one"—she nodded hesitantly toward Orrik—"and three or four others. Lord Caedmon, he"—she twisted her skirt in her hands—"he paid me tuppence to . . . well . . . he had a room upstairs, and . . ."

"Yes, go on," Alberic said shortly.

"Well, we . . . he done what he paid me for."

Some of the soldiers snickered, but fell silent when Alberic glared at them.

Faithe lifted her chin gamely. "Tell him about . . . the knife," she prompted gently.

"He pulled out this knife," Matfrid said. "I didn't expect it. I mean, he'd been actin' . . . well . . . a bit off. Wrong. But I didn't think much of it. Then out comes this knife. I tried to get him to put it away. Then he starts hollerin' at me. And I see his arm goin' back and forth, and these flashes, like . . ." Her hand drifted up to touch her scars. "I didn't even feel it at first. I saw the blood on him, and thought he was cutting himself. Then I realized he was cutting me, and I started screaming."

The hall was filled with the low buzz of conversation.

"They pulled him off me," Matfrid said, "and gave me two shillings, and left. I never seen any of them again." She glanced toward Orrik. "Till now."

"My husband is telling the truth about what happened in Cottwyk," Faithe said. "He was trying to protect that woman from Lord Caedmon—nothing more. Caedmon wasn't evil. He'd been very ill, and his illness affected his mind. I explained all of that in my letter."

Alberic whipped the sheet of parchment from his clerk's hand and held it out to Faithe. "This is the only letter from you that we received today—the one in which you denounce Sir Luke as—"

"Denounce him!" Crossing the hall swiftly, Faithe snatched the letter from Alberic and stared at it in outrage. "I didn't write this. I never would have written this."

She looked toward Orrik; so did Alberic and the soldiers who comprised the jury.

Orrik pressed himself against the stone wall and licked his lips nervously. "I did it for you, Faithe."

"You wrote this and pretended it came from me?"

"I did it for you! For you!"

Faithe shook her head. "Oh, Orrik."

"Am I to understand," Alberic ground out, "that this man"—he pointed to Orrik—"forged that letter and presented it to the court as genuine?"

Orrik needed no translator to comprehend the sheriff's rage. " 'Twas the only way!" he insisted, moving sideways along the wall toward the door. "The only way! I had to protect her! 'Twas up to me!"

"Guards." Alberic pointed to Orrik. His men leapt on the bailiff, pinioning his hands behind him. "I knew you Saxons were a devious lot, but this is outrageous. You've made a fool out of me and a mockery of this court, and I intend to see that you pay with your life."

"Please," Faithe implored the sheriff, "he thought he was helping me. I beg you to be merciful."

"Mercy in this case," Alberic said, "would be a swift execution, with no preliminaries. That is the most generous punishment I feel disposed to mete out."

Faithe looked stricken. "Could you not perhaps . . . imprison him, or—"

"I'd rather hang than putrefy in some Norman prison!" Orrik declared.

Shaking her head slowly, Faithe took a step toward the man who'd been, for most of her life, like a father to her. "Why, Orrik?" she said, her voice quavering with emotion. "Why did you force me to choose between you and my husband? I begged you not to. I loved you. I didn't want this to happen, but you doomed yourself."

" 'Twas these greedy, murdering Norman bastards who doomed me," he spat out. "These whoresons have doomed all of us. They seized our country and ravished it, and that was bad enough, but when they took *you,* my little girl, my wee Faithe, and gave you to that bloodthirsty son of a—"

"That's enough, Saxon!" Alberic interjected. "If you want a quick death, you'll hold your tongue." His attention turned to Luke. For a long moment the two men regarded each other in eloquent silence.

Luke had been vindicated, thanks to Faithe. There was nothing to be done now but release him. The sheriff's dark gaze and clenched fists attested to his displeasure at that prospect, but in the end he simply turned to his guards and muttered, "Remove Sir Luke's restraints. He's free to go."

One of the guards produced a key and unlocked Luke's manacles. "Don't let him go!" Orrik exclaimed as the guards dragged him toward the cellar. "Are you mad?"

Flinging the shackles aside, Luke crossed to Faithe and gathered her in his arms, murmuring her name and kissing her hair.

"I did it for you!" Orrik screamed to Faithe as he was wrestled into the stairwell. "Did you *want* to be bound in marriage to the Black Dragon?"

"The Black Dragon doesn't exist," she replied. "My husband is Luke of Hauekleah, and I'm taking him home now."

Epilogue

May 1068
Hauekleah

"This way," Luke whispered, guiding Faithe by her hand through the darkened woods.

"Why are you whispering?" Faithe asked. "Everyone's gone home by now."

It was almost dawn; the last of the May Day celebrants had long since retired for the night. Luke had insisted on waiting until the woods were empty before bringing Faithe out here. Nevertheless, he'd been surprisingly eager to do so; in fact, it had been his idea.

"This is it." He led her into a small clearing, silvery with moonlight and the faint, luminous promise of daybreak. New grass and spring wildflowers scented the air. Birds chattered raucously all around them.

Luke unpinned his mantle and spread it on the grass, then urged her to lie down with him. Gathering her in his arms, he kissed her deeply; she returned the kiss with joyous passion. He caressed her with unhurried hands, moving her wrapper aside to cup a breast through her shift. She glided her hands beneath his shirt, reveling in his warmth and strength, so familiar to her now, yet still so intoxicating. Had it only been a year since he'd come to Hauekleah—the victorious invader claiming his war prize?

The Black Dragon was gone, along with Caedmon. The past, with all its pain and sorrow, lay dead and buried. The future was curled up in Faithe's belly, waiting to be born.

She gasped and pressed his palm to her stomach, just beginning to swell with their child. Another faint kick thudded against his hand. *He* gasped, and then laughed delightedly, along with her.

Closing a hand around his neck to draw him nearer, she kissed him, then reached down to untie his chausses.

"Are you sure?" he asked. "What of the baby? Now that I've felt him move, I can't help but think we'd be disturbing him if we—"

"The baby," she replied as she pulled him down on top of her, "had better get used to this. Because I have no intention of giving it up. I'll never stop loving you . . . with my body or with my heart."

"Nay," he murmured as they joined together, moving as one to a rhythm as ancient as time itself, "don't ever stop. And neither will I."

Dear Reader,

Unlike most of my books, the story for *Secret Thunder* came to me fully formed, in a burst of inspiration that I couldn't ignore. I was sitting in bed reading, and something started me thinking about dark heroes. Within minutes I'd conjured up Luke de Périgueux, a bloodthirsty Norman knight with a dreadful secret.

Faithe materialized with the same kind of preternatural ease. To me, she personifies the pluck and adaptability of the English people as they survived centuries of invasion and assimilation of foreign peoples. Like her ancestors before her, she will do whatever it takes to preserve her home and way of life—even to the extent of giving herself in marriage to a conquering soldier with a ferocious reputation.

Secret Thunder, a story in which a woman's love redeems a man who's come to view himself as a monster, is very much a Beauty and the Beast tale. While writing it, I was truly swept away into the events of the story. I hope your reading experience was equally absorbing.

I'm hard at work on another medieval romance, as yet untitled, which will be a 1998 release from Topaz. Meanwhile, I would love to hear what you thought of *Secret Thunder.* Please write to me at P.O. Box 26207, Rochester, New York 14626. Or you can e-mail me at p.ryan10@genie.geis.com—I look forward to hearing from you!

Patricia Ryan

A SNEAK PREVIEW
from Patricia Ryan of the continuation of Alex's story Coming from Topaz in the Spring of 1998 . . .

July 1073, Normandy:
William the Conqueror's Rouen palace

One figure, a woman, stood perfectly still amidst the swirls of multicolored silk, the ripple of veils and glint of jewels. Pale and slender, as unreal as a church statue carved of pearly marble, she met Alex's eyes across the crowded courtyard. . . .

Across the years, for she'd looked much the same the first time his gaze had fallen upon her nine long summers ago. Her beauty had a transfixing harmony to it—high, wide cheekbones, sharp little chin, willowy throat. She'd worn white that day, too, although then her hair had flowed in a gleaming flaxen stream down her back; today it was plaited in two braids over which a veil of gossamer sendal silk trembled in the breeze. Then, as now, her sea-green eyes were large and quiet and intent.

"That's her," Faithe said. "The woman in white. The one who was looking at you so oddly."

From the corner of his eye, Alex saw Luke turn toward the woman in question; recognizing her instantly, he shot an apprehensive glance toward Alex.

Faithe noticed this. "You do know each other."

"She's Nicolette de St. Clair." Alex fingered the worst of his scars from that misbegotten summer, a puckered little rivulet that snaked down his forehead, carving a small bare patch through his right eyebrow. "My cousin's wife."

He definitely should have stayed in England.